THE GUMSHOE CHRONICLES
1922

a novel by T-J Viola

T J Viol

This is a work of fiction. The events described herein referring to actual places and/or historical characters are imaginary. All other events and characters described herein are also imaginary and are not intended to refer to specific places or living persons. The opinions expressed in this manuscript are solely the opinions of the author and do not represent the opinions or thoughts of the publisher.

The Gumshoe Chronicles 1922
All Rights Reserved.
Copyright © 2014 TJ Viola
v3.0

This book may not be reproduced, transmitted, or stored in whole or in part by any means, including graphic, electronic, or mechanical without the express written consent of the publisher except in the case of brief quotations embodied in critical articles and reviews.

Outskirts Press, Inc.
http://www.outskirtspress.com

ISBN: 978-1-4787-3893-0

Outskirts Press and the "OP" logo are trademarks belonging to Outskirts Press, Inc.

PRINTED IN THE UNITED STATES OF AMERICA

This book is dedicated to our Grandparents and Great-Grandparents who emigrated from Italy and Ireland in search of new opportunities for themselves and future generations, and in the process helped build one of the greatest cities in the world. They worked along the waterfront of New York City as longshoremen, in law enforcement, and as business owners. Times were difficult for immigrants during the turn of the century and in subsequent years. The rise of crime during Prohibition, the Great Depression and two World Wars didn't deter them from their dreams nor strip them of their values, which we have been privileged to pass on to our children.

Acknowledgements

Special thanks to Teresa R. Funke for her continued encouragement and coaching during our writing journey; Saundie Weiss for copy editing; Kendra Spanjer, graphic designer of The Gumshoe Chronicles unique cover designs; and Don and Bette Sailors for providing a final review.

Also by TJ Viola

The Gumshoe Chronicles – 1920
The Gumshoe Chronicles – 1921

About the Authors

Tom and Judy were both raised on Staten Island, New York. They met in high school and have been married for forty-six years.

Tom retired from Hewlett Packard Company after thirty years and Judy is a retired middle school teacher and registered nurse.

They are founding members of the Soaring Eagle Ecology Center in Red Feather Lakes, Colorado. You can learn about the Ecology Center by visiting www.seec.redfeatherlakes.org

This is their third novel, which completes *The Gumshoe Chronicles* Trilogy. They are currently working on a science fiction novel as their next project.

Chapter 1

In New York City, in the age of Prohibition, everyone knew to hunker down after a gangland shooting. But today was different. Castellano, the local Mafia boss, had been shot.

When the screech of cars careening around the end of our block replaced the sound of bullets, the local street kids went from building to building spreading the bad news. In their wake, a human wave flowed down the brownstone stoops that lined Market Street toward the pizza shop where Castellano held reign.

My uncle Luigi and I shoved our way deep into the throng only to have the surge of bodies separate us and push me toward an alleyway between two rows of buildings. Desperate to get to Castellano, I pulled one of my rods to fire shots in the air to clear a path when I noticed the garbage truck lane behind the buildings was deserted. I grabbed Luigi's arm and pulled him into the alley. It didn't take us long to get to the side entrance of Castellano's office.

Some of those who had shoved their way to the front entrance of the pizza shop noticed us banging on the side door near the back of the building. Carmine, Castellano's son, who was inside, recognized my voice just in time. The massive metal door flew open, hitting Luigi in the shoulder, as an onslaught of bodies rushed toward us. I shoved Luigi inside, slammed the door shut, and turned to face the carnage in the room.

Castellano was down, with his back leaning against the

side of his desk. Despite three bullet wounds to his torso, he was still breathing. Two other bodies were sprawled near each other in a pool of blood next to the door that led to the back of the pizza joint. Carmine stood to the side of the desk rubbing his blood-soaked hands on his trousers, his brow and shirt streaked in red. He had tried unsuccessfully to stop his father's bleeding.

I knelt next to Castellano. "Take off your belts," I shouted.

Carmine and my uncle handed them over and watched as I linked the belts together and used the leather straps to tighten the pressure on a makeshift bandage that Carmine had applied to one of Castellano's chest wounds. Carmine, regaining his wits, ran out of the office into the pizza parlor and returned with four more belts for the other two bandages. Once Castellano's bleeding had slowed, I lowered him to the floor and gently covered him with my overcoat. I then went over to the other two bodies. Both were dead.

Luigi looked away when he recognized them, but I didn't flinch. That's when I knew part of me had indeed died in the war. I'd seen far too many scenes like this one. There were few areas on Mrs. Marino and her grandson that weren't riddled with lead and drained of blood. It was evident from their condition and location in the room that they had been leaving Castellano's office when Big Ben Napoli's men opened up their choppers. Castellano, in his usual gentlemanly fashion, must have let them exit his office first, with his hands on their shoulders. That simple gesture had most likely saved his life, as Mrs. Marino and her grandson inadvertently became human shields.

I glanced back at Castellano and saw my uncle Luigi dab his old friend's lips with a damp cloth and Carmine kneel by his father's side to grip his hand. There was nothing more I could do for Castellano, so I entered the pizza parlor to see if anyone was alive.

Toby Tobias, Castellano's ex-bodyguard who'd recently been hired by Carmine, stood at the front of the joint shouting obscenities and waving a Tommy gun at the crowd as they pushed against the windows and the glass-paneled door.

"Batista," he shouted when he saw me. "This is your damn fault. You convinced Castellano to continue overseeing the neighborhood while Carmine ran the docks. He should never have been here. Now some of my men who were guarding him are dead."

This wasn't the time to clash with Toby yet again, so I ignored him and surveyed the room. In spite of the massacre that lay before me—dead customers littering the floor, their blood intermingled with spilled food and overturned tables—my attention was drawn to shattered pictures of Italy's sunny countryside. The broken frames clung precariously to blood-splattered walls pockmarked with all too familiar bullet holes. Toby's renewed ranting snapped me back to the present, out of the war, out of the memories that more and more frequently burst onto my consciousness.

It looked as though a few folks had made it out alive, but not many. There were eight victims sprawled about the room, but ten coats hanging on the wall hooks. Fortunately, even though the food was exceptional, the joint had not been overly crowded lately. Not after the last massacre. Aside from some of Toby's men, who were always hanging around, there were usually a few fools in the joint who liked to give the impression they had connections to the mob. And then there were the out-of-towners who didn't know the restaurant's reputation.

One of those tourists had tried to protect his wife and

landed on top of her. Neither was moving. I checked the others—all dead. I was headed back to see how Castellano was doing when I heard a low moan. I turned toward the sound and saw the woman's leg twitch. I rolled her husband off her and found she was clutching an infant.

"My baby," she uttered, gasping to catch her breath.

I shrugged out of my jacket and placed it over the child. I then applied pressure to the woman's wound using a cloth napkin. As I removed her husband's belt to hold the cloth in place a commotion erupted outside. The crowd parted to allow an ambulance to back up to the door, but they still blocked four police cars from getting too close. Only the local beat cops would have access until Carmine and the rest of us had left. The onlookers knew that anyone inside would be taken downtown for questioning and booked on violating the Sullivan Act, which required a license to possess a firearm.

Toby ordered the first stretcher crew to the back room and closed the door after the second team entered. I got up and waved one of the medics over.

"She doesn't know her baby is dead," I whispered, pointing to the woman on the floor.

He nodded and knelt over her, purposely shifting her head to the side as another medic removed the child. Once Castellano and the woman were loaded into the ambulance, the crowd turned its attention to the police who had abandoned their cars and were trying to make their way toward the entrance.

As the ambulance drove off, Luigi asked Carmine for a ride to the hospital. Carmine ignored his request and tossed Toby another Tommy gun and grabbed two for himself from his father's arsenal.

"What makes you think I'm goin' to the hospital? My old man is either gonna make it or end up wearin' a wooden kimono."

"Then where are you headin'?" I asked.

"The same place you should be. From what I heard, they also tried to take out you and your family."

"That's exactly what Big Ben expects. He'll be ready for us."

"Then tell me, mister *war hero*, what the hell are we gonna do?"

I grabbed hold of his Tommy guns and yanked. "Put down the artillery and take some time to think."

Toby moved toward me but stopped short when Luigi held a gun to his head. "I suggest we stay out of this," he said.

I put Carmine's weapons on a small bar in Castellano's office, went back into the pizza parlor, and righted a table and two chairs.

"Carmine, take a seat."

Carmine sat across from me, his face contorted in frustration and anger. He looked as if he wanted to rip someone's heart out, and I had a feeling it was mine.

"Let me lay it out for you," I said. "A few days ago you became the boss of the entire East Side waterfront and, at the same time, pissed off one of the more powerful syndicate families. To make matters worse, you inherited an organization that was decimated by Butch, leaving you with only Toby and maybe a handful of other loyal goons."

"None of that makes any difference. This is about honor. Mine and yours," Carmine shouted.

"You're wrong. This is about buying time and staying alive. I'll take care of Big Ben."

"What makes you think you can do a better job than me?"

"Until a few days ago, you were a businessman sitting behind a desk. In the PI business, fighting scum like Napoli is what I do. It's what I did in the war."

"Fine! How much time?"

"A week, maybe two."

"You're bonkers. There'll be nothing left of my organization."

We both knew he was right.

"Hire more muscle and focus on protecting the docks and let me take care of Big Ben."

"Who the hell do you think is gonna work for me after what just happened?"

I gathered up two more chairs and told my uncle to bring Toby over.

"Toby, if you don't want to end up being one of Big Ben's lackeys, I suggest you recruit more of your buddies to keep his men away from our docks."

"More muscle isn't enough to stop this from happening again," my uncle said, glancing at the dead bodies.

"I agree. That's why I need you to organize the neighborhood and block off this street from outside traffic. Set up a barricade and have it manned around the clock. That should keep any of Ben's men away from the folks."

Luigi smiled. "Consider it done."

Carmine pulled his pistol from his shoulder holster and placed it on the table. "I don't like you spitting out orders when my pop is clinging to life. I'm in charge, not you. Remember that."

"Look, Carmine. I know you're in charge. I was there and supported you. Or did you forget?"

"I can't let this go unchallenged."

"You asked for this, so get your shit together and use the one advantage you have over Big Ben—your brain."

Carmine took a deep breath and leaned back in his chair. "Batista, you better be as good as you think you are. I'll try it your way. I'll hire more wiseguys and post some on the rooftops along Market Street to take out any cars that run the barricade Luigi sets up. The rest will guard the piers to make sure cargo keeps flowing."

"Now you're talking like your old man," Luigi said.

Carmine pushed back his chair and stood tall. "I'll give you one week. That's it. Then I go after Big Ben. What happens next, happens," he said, and left the building with Toby in tow.

* * * * *

Luigi and I were about to leave the way we had entered when O'Reilly, a local homicide detective, showed up with his crew. He dispersed the crowd and dismissed the cops who never did make it through the mass of onlookers.

O'Reilly came in first and surveyed the damage. "I take it this is Big Ben's handiwork," he said. "You know my hands are tied. He has the mayor and everyone down the line on his payroll."

"The best you can do for us is stay out of the way," I said.

"Sounds like you're getting involved. Thought you wanted to get untangled from the mob."

"After they finished here, they came after me and my family. I have no choice."

"What about Carmine?" O'Reilly asked.

"He's given me a week. After that, he'll be planning his own funeral."

"Let me know if you need my help," he said, as he went into Castellano's office. Looking down at the bodies, he shook his head. "What the hell was Mrs. Marino doing here?"

"Her grandson came down with polio last year and Castellano has been covering his medical bills. My guess is she brought him by to say thanks."

As O'Reilly's men entered the joint, Luigi and I headed for the back door.

"I take it no one was hurt at your place?" O'Reilly asked.

"Ma was shaken up, but other than that, everyone's fine. And I intend to keep it that way."

Chapter 2

My partner, Jackie, met us on the stoop before we entered Luigi's apartment building.

"Your ma's pretty upset. One of the bullets came damn close. She's also worried about Castellano. Is he alive?"

"Let's just say he's not dead. How's my pop reacting?"

"He's set on vengeance. I think he's cleaned his guns at least twice, including some of yours."

"What about the others?"

"Rosalie, Sadie, and Martha are with your mother," she said, then turned toward my uncle. "Sorry, Luigi, your last two tenants just gave notice and are moving out tomorrow."

Luigi shook his head, patted me on the shoulder, and said, "Your rent just doubled." He then went upstairs to bring down his own arsenal for cleaning.

* * * * *

I waved Martha into the hall outside my parents' apartment.

"I don't have time to explain. Go up to the office and call Fort Hamilton. Ask for Colonel Benton. Set up a meeting for today—no later than tomorrow morning."

"Who's Colonel Benton? You never mentioned him before."

"Can't you for once follow a simple request?"

9

She smiled and headed for the stairs. "Not everything is as easy as you think. I'll never get past his secretary. Someone that high up isn't going to rearrange his schedule for a civilian."

"Tell her it's urgent that 'Mr. Deadman' meet with the Colonel."

Martha grabbed the handrail and took two steps backward. "Mister who?"

"I'll fill you in later," I said and went into the kitchen to give Ma a hug. She pushed me away, saying she was fine, and suggested I join the others at the dining room table.

"When are we leaving?" Pop asked me.

"Soon."

Luigi appeared in the doorway, loaded down with iron. "Vito, help me make sure these are ready for action."

Pop followed Luigi into his shoe repair shop across the hall where they could make good use of the workbench.

Ma joined the rest of us at the table after Pop and Luigi had left. "Is Castellano gonna make it?" she asked me.

"It's hard to tell, but I've seen worse."

"Joey, I know in the past I've pushed you to always protect your family's name, but this is different. This is Big Ben. It'll just make everything worse."

"Sorry, Ma. We have to do something."

Jackie placed another bottle of bootleg whiskey on the table. "Remember what I told you about the Mafia wars in Detroit? Once it starts, everyone dies."

Ma clung to my hand. "She's right, Joey. Big Ben has a huge family. If you kill him, they won't stop until they avenge his death."

"The same will happen if we *don't* take him out," I said.

Jackie put her arms around my neck and brushed the side

of my face with her lips. "I have too much invested in our business to see you throw your life away. Force Big Ben to call a truce without killing anyone close to him."

"That sounds impossible."

"It's not," she said, sitting down. "Send him a clear message that he and his family are vulnerable, and then find ways to shut down his ability to make money."

Luigi came back into the dining room and placed a Tommy gun on the table in front of me. "A present. Make good use of it," he said and returned to the workshop.

I looked over at Rosalie and saw fear in her eyes.

"What's wrong?" I asked.

She pushed aside the gun. "I already lost one family. I don't want to lose another."

I took hold of her hand, remembering the night her old man shot her mother in a drunken rage. "Hey, everything's gonna be fine. Before you know it you'll be finished with your nursing training, and then meet a nice guy and have a place of your own. But until then, you're stuck with us and this neighborhood."

She gripped my hand with both of hers and pulled me forward. "I'll never leave the neighborhood. It's my home. So keep it safe, but don't get yourself killed."

"You don't have to worry. I have no intention of getting whacked. I have too much to live for, but that's not gonna stop me from doing what needs to be done."

Sadie got up and placed a hand on my shoulder, nodding toward the door. I followed her into the hall.

"I have to get back to Frank. He's preparing for an important trial."

"Is he gonna pull his law office out of the building?"

"Not a chance. He says you're good for business. Every

time he uses your services, his cases end up on the front page of the *Daily News*."

"What about you?"

"Me, I'm okay. I'll stand by your side, just as I have since we were kids. But if I were you, I'd take Jackie's advice."

Before I could answer, Martha interrupted us.

"You have a meeting with the Colonel tomorrow morning at seven sharp, and he said for you to be on time, soldier."

My uncle Luigi and Pop emerged from the workshop loaded down with every weapon imaginable.

"Why aren't you ready?" Pop asked.

I looked at Luigi. "Why aren't you organizing the roadblocks on both ends of the street?"

"We're not really gonna hunker down, are we?"

"Until I figure out how to get Big Ben to back off, like Jackie advised, that's the plan."

"What the hell do broads know about dealing with the likes of Napoli?" Pop asked.

"Trust me. This one does."

* * * * *

I had a restless sleep. One of my wartime nightmares had repeated throughout the night, so I got ready early for my meeting with the Colonel. I sat at the kitchen table sipping a cup of joe and fingering the yellow ribbon that always made its way into my dreams. I had removed it from Bernadette's lifeless body in a hotel in a remote village in France. She had been a young member of the resistance, no more than a teenager. As I raised the coffee to my lips, an image of the last time I saw Anita, my first love, flashed through my mind. She had worn a similar yellow ribbon.

When I looked up, both Jackie and Martha were sitting at the table.

Martha couldn't contain herself. "We need to know what the hell is going on. Who is Mr. Deadman? Why are you seeing an army colonel? Are you going up against Big Ben, and what about Ronnie and Debbie? We can't leave her in his clutches forever."

"She's not in immediate danger. At worst Ronnie's forced her back into working in one of his whorehouses in Detroit. As he said, he needs her to build back his business."

As usual, Jackie spoke with more finesse. "Joey, we want to help."

I folded the ribbon, placed it in my shirt pocket and poured them each a cup of coffee.

"There's more. Ronnie has put a contract on me, and our so-called friend Cafiero has taken the job."

Jackie put her cup down so hard coffee spilled out. "Why didn't you tell us?"

"I didn't expect Big Ben to move into the neighborhood so quickly. Cafiero has given me two weeks to take Ronnie down before he acts on the contract. I've already lost two of those days."

Jackie had had enough.

"There's no way you can deal with all of this on your own. I'll go to Detroit, take care of Ronnie, and bring Debbie home," she said, pushing back her chair.

"The hell you will. Ronnie is too deadly and too clever. I know I need help, and that's why I'm meeting with the Colonel. He owes me a favor, and I'm gonna collect."

A plan was forming in my mind for dealing with Ronnie;

13

the only problem was I wasn't confident it would work. But that was the least of my concerns. First, I had to figure out how to follow through on Jackie's suggestion to force Big Ben to back down, and then I could worry about Ronnie and Cafiero.

Time was the problem. As usual, it was running out.

Chapter 3

The moment I stepped into the Colonel's office and saw the war mementos on display and noticed how he had aged, I knew the Colonel had been fighting his own demons. The most prominent display was on the wall behind his desk. A large plaque with gold-plated lettering hung over a circle of ten individual pictures of the men who had died from our special unit. In the center of this *Circle of Honor* was a group picture of those who had survived: myself and two others. We had beaten the odds, impossible odds. No one in the *Death Squad* was expected to come home—something we'd all understood.

As the Colonel came from behind his desk, my thoughts returned to our first meeting.

Soon after completing basic training, my buddies and I had been waiting to board buses headed for the waterfront to be shipped overseas when two of the Colonel's orderlies pulled me out of line and escorted me to his office. The conversation with the Colonel was brief.

"I've been reviewing your file, Batista, and it says here that you're fluent in four languages. How's that possible, soldier?"

"My mother's family lived in northern Italy and traveled all over Switzerland selling their wares. As a young kid, she easily picked up different languages. When I came along, she decided to speak to me in Italian, French, German, and English."

"Amazing! And how do you explain your near-perfect marksmanship?"

"Most weekends my uncle took me to a farm that belonged to his friend on Staten Island. We'd hunt rabbit for dinner. When I became a better shot than him, he set up a target range and introduced me to more advanced weapons. I was ten at the time."

"Was he in the Italian military?"

"He never speaks about his past."

"Equally interesting. Did you know you had the highest score among your unit in every category during training?"

"No sir."

The Colonel leaned back in his chair and stared at me as I stood at attention.

"Batista, a lot of men are going to die in this war. Some will die senselessly because of a poor decision by their commanding officer. Some because it's their time, and others will exhibit unusual bravery that will cost them their lives. You understand what I'm saying, Batista?"

"Yes sir."

"I'm putting together a small group, a special unit that will be trained for nearly impossible missions. Sooner or later everyone in this unit will die because the odds are they'll eventually fail their assignment, and failure will be fatal. Batista, I want you in this unit, and all I can offer you in return for your commitment is death with honor."

"How do I sign up, sir?"

"You don't want time to think this over?"

"No sir."

There was nothing to think about. I had joined the war effort intending *not* to return. The girl I had planned to marry had disappeared shortly after we'd had an argument, and she was assumed dead. The argument had been senseless. I had objected when she said she expected us to run her father's farm after we were married. I couldn't control my anger, thinking only of myself, and left her sitting on the top step of her porch crying. That evening she didn't return home from a solitary walk. I never saw her again. The guilt I felt, even after a year of searching, was more than I could bear, but I was too much of a coward to take my own life. So the army seemed like a good solution, and the Colonel's offer an even better one.

The Colonel's voice brought me back to the present. "I never expected to see *you* again, Batista. Why are you here?"

"I need help—your kind of help."

"I'm surprised to hear that. You're capable of handling yourself."

"A Mafia war is about to erupt that involves my neighborhood. If I don't stop it, I will lose everyone I care about."

"What makes you think I can do anything about that?"

"I want to ask the other two survivors of our unit to join me."

The Colonel got up, paced the room, and stopped in front of the pictures on his wall. He took down the center picture and placed it on the desk facing me.

"That is a difficult request on several levels. Before I released you from active duty, the three of you agreed to never contact each other."

"Sir, one of the lessons you hammered into us was to be flexible, to avoid rigidity. I'm asking you to do the same now."

He pointed to the person standing next to me in the picture. "Hawk is no longer with us."

"What happened?"

"We trained all three of you to be private investigators

in hope you would use the skills you acquired for the benefit of society. Like you, Hawk was successful. That is until recently. He was investigating a murder and disappeared a few weeks ago. Chances are he's dead. A fate I hope you can avoid."

"What about Diamond?"

"He wasn't able to function in a free society, so we had to pull him back into the service."

"Where is he now?"

"Solitary confinement, where he belongs."

I knew the Colonel never deviated from regulations, but I suspected from the pictures on the wall that he had deep regrets.

"So, what will it be, Colonel? A few years ago I handed my life over to you and now I'm asking for it back."

He picked up the picture and put it back in position in the center of his ring of heroes.

"I'll get someone to escort you to Diamond's cell. If after talking to him you still want his help, I'll make it happen. One more thing, Batista. If it looks like anything you do might come back to this office, you will both vanish. Is that understood?"

If I knew the Colonel, there was nothing more to be said.

I turned to leave but instead, removed the ribbon from my shirt pocket.

"Colonel, sir, I have a gift for you and a suggestion."

"What is it, soldier?"

I offered him the ribbon. "I took that from the body of a young girl in France who could have saved her own life, but decided the mission you had sent me on was more important."

"So, what's the point?"

"The men on that wall made a difference and they did it knowing the cost. I suggest you take those pictures down, keep their memories close, as I do, and move on."

He reached for the ribbon. "Have you, soldier? Have you moved on?"

"I'm making progress."

* * * * *

The belowground confinement cells, void of natural light, smelled of dampness and radiated a penetrating chill. The fort had been built in the 1800s, with little, if any, regard for inmates.

Diamond was sound asleep in his bunk, snoring as loudly as ever. That was one of the main things I remembered about him since we had been ordered not to disclose personal information and were constantly pitted against one another during training. Forming friendships was not allowed. We had shared one mission together and met up again in the sanitarium, along with Hawk, at the end of the war. The three of us were placed there because the army didn't know what to do with us. The top brass were convinced that with the skills we'd acquired to execute our clandestine missions, we would turn to crime when released back into society. If I hadn't suggested they train us to become private investigators, Hawk and I would no doubt be occupying a cell next to Diamond.

"Wake up, soldier," I shouted.

Diamond popped up and hit his head on the top bunk, then fell back and rolled over to face the wall.

"Whoever you are, get the hell out of here. I'm in solitary confinement."

"Is that how you treat one of your war buddies?" I asked.

"Go away. I don't have any war buddies. They're all dead."

"Not all."

Diamond turned and shaded his eyes with a hand to block the glare from a bare bulb hanging from the ceiling.

"Deadman, is that you?"

"In the flesh. So far I haven't been able to live up to my code name."

He jumped out of bed and threw his arms around me.

"They told me Hawk took a nose dive and I figured you for a goner a long time ago," he said.

"Let's just say the grim reaper is gaining ground."

"Why are you here?"

"I'm in a bit of a jam."

"The same is true for me," he said, looking around his cell.

"The Colonel said you're a little unstable."

"The Colonel is being generous. I drink too much, I fight too much, and I don't like to work for my money. It's just too easy to blow a hole in a bank safe."

We sat on his bunk.

"Do you remember the first time we met as a unit?" I asked.

"Sure, I have the Colonel's speech memorized.

"Gentleman, you no longer exist. Any record of you entering the army has been wiped clean. This unit doesn't exist. I don't exist. The guys standing next to you don't exist. Since you don't exist, you don't have names. That's a problem. Therefore, you will now give me a code name that will be yours for the duration of the war.

"You were first in line and I'll never forget the Colonel's face when you shouted out your new name—*Deadman, sir.*"

"Soldier, the object of this unit is to stay alive as long as possible, complete your mission, train for another, complete that mission, and continue until you are killed in action. I thought I made that perfectly clear when you signed on to this unit. So let me ask you again. Is that clear to you? To all of you?"

"Yes sir!"

"Good. Now son, give me another name."

"Deadman, sir."

"Very well, Mr. Deadman, but let me offer you something to live for, for all of you to live for. If by some slim chance this war ends before your luck runs out, you will have the skills necessary to deal with the issues you faced in civilian life that drove you to join this unit. And I know what they are. In your case, Mr. Deadman, you will find answers."

"What did he mean by that?" Diamond asked.

"It's a long story, one that I've put behind me. But I will tell you this, the Colonel was right. I think it's time we tell each other our real names."

"Dom, Dom Marchio. You can call me Dom."

"Batista, Joey Batista."

"So, Joey, what do you want from me?"

"Help."

"What do I get in return?"

"A second chance to make it on the outside."

"And if I fail?"

"We both cease to exist, as the Colonel would say, and I'm afraid it would be for the last time."

I filled him in on the details and he didn't hesitate.

"Sounds like you lead an exciting life, Batista. Count me in."

* * * * *

I pulled my car over to the side entrance of the fort and waited for Dom. A few minutes later he threw a small duffle bag in the backseat.

"Where are we headed?" he asked.

I looked behind me. "Is that all you got?"

"When they came for me, I didn't have the option to pack. The cops were closing in."

"What about dough? You got any?"

"Scratch isn't a problem. I have plenty stashed away. Like I said, I was pretty good at pulling bank jobs."

"We need to get you some clothes, then an apartment in my uncle's brownstone. He's desperate for tenants."

I drove past the sentry and out the gate. "What about the cops, Dom? Are you still wanted?"

"Nah, the Colonel took care of everything. I'm free to create mayhem, which is exactly what you need."

"That and a whole lot of luck. Let's hope we didn't use it all up in the war."

Chapter 4

Dom leaned against the side of my car and looked up at the brownstone.

"Damn, Joey, you weren't kidding. You're involved in some serious shit. There's not a window left in this place. This wasn't a warning. They wanted you dead. Anyone killed?"

Before I could answer, a work truck drove up with panels of glass attached to the sides. Luigi wasn't wasting any time repairing the damage.

"No. Most of the tenants had already moved out. My uncle had taken steps to shield my folks' apartment, and, luckily, I realized what was happening when the first shots were fired down the street. I was able to get my girls to safety before the windows were shot out."

"Girls?"

"My secretary and my partner."

"You have a woman partner in the PI business? I gotta see this. She must be one tough, ugly bitch."

I gave him a heavy handed slap on the back. "Don't get too excited. She's tough, but she's far from ugly. So she's not for you."

"Don't *you* start. I got enough crap from the other cretins in the unit. I may not be the best-looking guy in town, but I know how to treat a woman and have a good time."

"I didn't mean anything by it. But if I were you, I wouldn't use foul language around my ma."

"Hey, don't forget I took down every one of you giants in

training, even though you were all nearly twice my size. If I can do that, I can handle your mother."

"I don't know, she's pretty good with a frying pan."

Dom laughed, and then got serious. "Let's get to that apartment. I gotta take a leak."

* * * * *

Luigi was ecstatic to have a new tenant until I explained who Dom was and why I recruited him.

"Don't expect me to give everyone you know a break on the rent. You and your dames are enough."

"Don't worry, he has plenty of dough."

"Good!"

Ma wasn't as easy to please.

"I'm gonna have to get a bigger table if you hire any more people. Maybe I should open a restaurant."

"It's just for a few weeks until life gets back to normal."

"Normal! Look around you. This *is* normal since you returned home from the war."

"Ma, it's not me. It's the way things have always been in this city. It's just gotten worse with Prohibition."

"It's not only Prohibition. Look at how the young girls dress with their legs showing, wearing makeup and other goings on."

"You talkin' about Martha?"

"Don't get me started. The way the three of you carry on, and she's with a different friend every couple of months. And now Jackie is going out more. If you're not careful, you're gonna lose them both."

I gave her a hug. "Don't worry, Castellano's gonna make it. I'll take care of Big Ben, and someday I'll make sense of my life. Until then, we have one more for dinner, and don't forget I'm having a meeting tonight, so expect a crowd."

I kissed her on the cheek and headed up the stairs to my office before she could react.

* * * * *

Dom stunned the women by helping set the table for dinner and impressed both Pop and Luigi with his knowledge of weapons and explosives. Afterwards they went into Pop's workshop and discussed ways to increase the fire power of a Thompson submachine gun. They were shoulder-to-shoulder making sketches when I announced that O'Reilly had arrived and we needed to get down to business.

Dom tried to get on O'Reilly's good side, but took the wrong approach.

"O'Reilly, that's an interesting name. What part of Italy are you from?" he asked with a straight face.

O'Reilly was about to answer when he caught himself mid-sentence. "Northern... That'll be enough of that."

"Sorry, not used to being around a flatfoot."

"Homicide," O'Reilly said.

"That explains your lack of humor. No sense cracking jokes when you're hangin' around stiffs all day. What's the story with you? Why's a cop backing Joey?" Dom asked.

"This is my neighborhood and I intend to keep it that way."

"I don't get it. When the boat landed from Ireland, did your family take a right as everyone else turned left? Why would you live in an all Italian neighborhood?"

O'Reilly shook his head and looked at me. "Where'd you get this guy?"

"Solitary confinement!"

"That figures."

I introduced Jackie to Dom as she came into the room. Dom let out a low whistle and pulled out a chair. "Joey tells me you have a plan," he said to her.

"I have an idea. We still have to come up with a plan."

"I expect Carmine any minute," I said, and asked Ma to break out a few bottles of whiskey.

Dom eyed the bottles. "Luigi also owns a speakeasy," Pop explained.

As a bottle made the rounds, Carmine entered with Toby and Fat Sal, a former dockworker recruited by Toby. Fat Sal was anything but fat now, but the name had stuck from when he was a kid.

"Who's this guy?" Carmine asked me, pointing to Dom.

"He's the buddy of mine from the war I told you about. He's agreed to help us deal with Big Ben."

"What are you talkin' about? He's a runt. I need muscle. He doesn't look like he can take care of himself let alone Big ..."

Dom swirled out of his chair, disarmed Carmine, elbowed him in the chest, kicked Toby in the groin, and held a knife to Fat Sal's throat, all in under five seconds. I was the only one who had reacted to Dom's sudden moves and had my gun aimed at Toby.

"Everybody calm down," O'Reilly said. "Dom, you made your point. Carmine, take a seat."

It was an interesting beginning to our meeting, but the hard part was yet to come. Convincing Carmine to go along with Jackie's approach for avenging the attack on his father would not be easy.

I placed a small mirror on the table in front of Carmine. He picked it up and turned it over.

"What the hell is this for?"

"I want you to look at everyone in the room, including yourself."

"What? My father clings to life and you want to play parlor games?"

"It's not a game," I said. "If we kill Big Ben, everyone in this room, and also Angela, your wife, will be dead in a matter of weeks."

"What are you suggesting? That I run away and let Big Ben take over everything including my self-respect?"

"What I'm suggesting is we get even, but in a way that causes him to back off."

"There isn't a chance in hell that will happen. Big Ben has been waiting for years to take over the entire waterfront, and the only thing that stood in his way was my old man."

"Jackie, tell Carmine your suggestion for dealing with Big Ben."

Carmine looked at Jackie, then back at me. "What the hell are you talking about? This *broad* is gonna tell *me* how to avenge the attack on my father?"

Carmine got up, grabbed his fedora off the coat rack, and placed it firmly on his head, then reached for his overcoat. A knife pinned the coat to the wall, and as Carmine turned, flinging open his jacket to pull his rod, two more knives hit their marks. One sliced through the leather of his shoulder holster, grazing his shirt, and the other took his hat off and nailed it to the wall just above his overcoat.

"What the hell just happened?" Dom yelled.

"Carmine," Jackie said, ready to let two more knives fly.

"This isn't just about you. If you want to get out of here alive, I suggest you sit down. None of us intend to take a bullet for you. And I think that includes your two Neanderthals, since they haven't moved a muscle."

Carmine took a seat.

I leaned over to Dom. "Like I said, you were half right. She is one tough bitch."

Ma had had enough. "You're acting like a pack of children. Get serious. Big Ben is no doubt planning his next move," she said, ordering Pop to collect everyone's weapons.

"Carmine, what would it take for you to back off Big Ben?" Jackie asked.

Carmine jumped out of his chair and pounded the table. "I'd want him on his knees begging for mercy."

"That's a start, but why don't we go for something more reasonable. How about an apology at one of Vigliotti's syndicate meetings?"

"That's not enough. He also needs to recognize Carmine as the boss of the East Side Waterfront," I said.

Carmine stared at me, and then sat down. "I can live with that."

Luigi knew the most about Big Ben since he and Castellano had tangled with him when they first established themselves in the neighborhood, so we asked him to fill us in. Big Ben had moved quickly to consolidate the waterfront under his control, but Luigi and Castellano, along with Ronnie Ligotti and several other rough Sicilians from the old country, had succeeded in limiting his territory.

Jackie asked more questions about Big Ben and his family, and the discussion turned toward how to convince him to capitulate.

"Sounds to me like this Ben guy isn't too worried about

his own hide, but he might feel differently about his kids," Dom said.

"That's right," Luigi said. "And it shouldn't be difficult to round two of them up since they have their father's appetite for women. You can find them in a whorehouse most days of the week."

Jackie cautioned us. "So you rough up his boys. But remember, we don't want to kill anyone, just show Big Ben his family is vulnerable."

"We can't stop there. Like you said, we need to shut off his flow of money and destroy some of his prize possessions. That will get his attention," Luigi added.

"Still not enough," Pop said. "To get him to back off, we need to go after everything at the same time. He needs to feel overwhelmed—unable to act. If we play tit-for-tat, we lose."

That got Carmine's attention. "I like that idea."

"Good, that's what we'll do. Make it clear that we can take him and his family out at any time and cut off his money supply," Jackie said. "Where does he get his dough?"

"His sources are typical for one of Vigliotti's syndicate boys," I said. "In addition to the waterfront, he runs the gamut of illegal moneymaking enterprises. I would think the most vulnerable would be his speakeasies and whorehouses."

"That brings up a potential problem. If we go after one of Vigliotti's bosses, do we need to worry about retaliation from the other families?" Jackie asked.

"That's already been settled," Carmine said. "Vigliotti has agreed this is between our two families, mine and Big Ben's."

O'Reilly finally jumped into the conversation. Until then, he had been satisfied with nursing his whiskey.

"I have a buddy in the Bureau of Investigation who would like nothing better than to make a name for himself. I'll get a few of my stoolies in Big Ben's organization to provide me with his overland liquor supply routes out of Canada and the location of his storage warehouses. My friend will make quick use of that information."

"How quick?" Pop asked.

"He'll have a small army mobilized within hours." O'Reilly pushed back his chair and headed for the door.

"That should dry up his liquor supply and shut down his speakeasies," Pop said.

"Can we do anything about his canhouses?" Jackie asked.

"Nothing will slow down *that* business, short of burning down the joints," Luigi said.

Ma placed a large bowl on the table filled with meatballs and sausages, along with bread fresh from the oven.

"Syphilis," Ma said. "It's tough to get rid of false rumors."

"It'll take too long for rumors like that to be taken seriously," Pop said.

Ma pointed to Rosalie who was wearing her nursing uniform. "Not if she makes the rounds at the hospitals in Big Ben's part of town and slips the right patients enough dough," Ma said.

"Can she adopt me?" Dom asked.

Even Carmine laughed, and it got him thinking.

"I can disrupt the waterways. All the cargo ships that arrive along the waterfront are managed by my shipping company. With scratch placed in the right hands, shipping manifests can become inaccurate. Nothing would move off Big Ben's piers for days, maybe even weeks."

I refilled everyone's glass. "That all sounds good, but we need something dramatic, something that will send a real message for Napoli to back off."

Dom threw back his drink and held his glass up for more. "Dramatic? I can do dramatic," he said.

"Everyone in our unit had a specialty," I explained to the group. "Mine was infiltration into enemy ranks. Dom, tell them about yours."

He grinned. "I love to blow things up. As a kid, the Fourth of July was my idea of heaven."

"What do you have in mind?" Jackie asked.

"Luigi said this Big Ben has a mansion on Long Island that he uses as a family retreat. I say blow it to hell."

"You can do that?" Pop asked.

"Not a problem. Why stop there? Let's take out one of his piers!"

Carmine looked skeptical. "Are you talking about one of his warehouse piers on the Hudson?"

"If that doesn't make him genuflect in front of you, nothing will," Dom said.

"It's a plan then," Ma said. "Now eat."

When everyone had their fill, I broke up the meeting with a simple statement.

"We start tonight."

Chapter 5

Jackie borrowed one of Rosalie's nursing uniforms, and together they ventured into the night. Dressed in white with black capes flowing behind them, they looked like angels of mercy on a mission to visit the infirm—which they intended to do—and hand out C-notes to anyone who would claim they had come down with syphilis after visiting one of Big Ben's establishments.

Martha packed a suitcase and headed for Long Island to get the lowdown on Big Ben's summer home. Carmine headed back to the waterfront with Toby and Fat Sal to hire more men to beef up security.

A few hours after everyone had left, O'Reilly called to say two of Big Ben's warehouses would be raided during the night and his friend from the Bureau would have men positioned to stop several truckloads of booze arriving the following evening. O'Reilly had more helpful information. One of his buddies in homicide on the West Side of town told him two of Big Ben's three sons relied on each other for protection when hitting the night life in their dad's territory. They seldom used bodyguards when they traveled together and tonight was no exception. They had been seen entering their favorite brothel.

Dom, Luigi, and I concocted a quick plan, picked up what we needed from Luigi's joint, and headed to the heart of Big Ben's section of town.

The Gumshoe Chronicles 1922

* * * * *

Two of the Napoli brothers stumbled out of an upscale brownstone a little past midnight and hailed a taxi. I had slipped a cabbie a few C-notes to borrow his hack for the evening and picked up the unsuspecting brothers.

Five minutes into the ride I made a sharp turn.

"Hey, you're taken the wrong road," one of the brothers mumbled, barely able to lift his head off the backseat.

"Relax, there's a roadblock up ahead. A truck loaded with drums of gasoline overturned earlier," I said, keeping my eyes on the road. It was important to get the brothers to a deserted part of town so no one would witness what was about to happen.

When I reached a prearranged spot, I fiddled with the choke. The car backfired several times, and then stalled. I turned toward the passengers, to ease any concerns they might have, but it wasn't necessary—they were out cold. Dom had delivered two bottles of aged Canadian Scotch whiskey to the brothel to be served to the Napoli brothers. It was a "gift from their father." It looked like Dom had been a little too generous when he'd added the knockout drug to the bottles of booze.

Pop pulled up behind me. Luigi jumped out of the car and held a gun on the brothers, just in case they regained consciousness, as Dom disarmed them. Removing them from the hack and loading them into the back of Pop's flivver was more difficult.

Pop took off as soon as Luigi and Dom jumped back into his car. They had gagged the brothers, tied their hands behind them, and put sacks over their heads. In the morning they would wake under the Brooklyn Bridge with one hell of a headache, and most likely without their clothes. No doubt some of the hobos who used the bridge for shelter were going to be walking around tomorrow with some expensive duds.

I returned the cab and pulled into traffic behind the wheel of my own car. It was time to pay Big Ben Napoli a late night visit.

* * * * *

I hadn't gotten far when I felt cold steel jammed against my neck.

"Pull over." Cafiero had a distinctive guttural voice.

"Always check the backseat before getting in. Didn't they teach you that in detective school?"

"I took a mail order course."

"That explains a lot. Why aren't you in Detroit? You're running out of time."

"I'm surprised you haven't noticed that I'm facing a more pressing issue."

"I know what's going on and what you're thinking. You'll worry about me later. Bad decision, Joey."

"You got a better idea?"

He pulled the gun away. "You need my help."

"That didn't occur to me."

"Remember, I came out of retirement and took the contract Ronnie placed on your head as a favor to *you*."

"I'm still having a problem with that logic."

"Better a friend, who gives you a way out than a stranger who walks up to you and blows your brains out. But that's not important right now. Based on your activities tonight, I take it you're on your way to pay Napoli a visit."

"Good guess."

"Are his sons dead?"

"No. We're just sending a warning."

"Then I don't understand what the hell you're up to."

"We're trying to end this without more bloodshed."

Cafiero leaned against the backseat as I reentered the traffic flow.

"Your plan stinks. It'll never work. Castellano's been shot and your neighbors are being buried. Understand this, Joey, only blood pays for blood."

"I'm trying to avoid a war that we can't win."

"Now you're making some sense. You need to show Napoli that he can't control the outcome of what he's set in motion. But that's not enough. Spare Big Ben and his family but take out as many of his men as possible, as quickly as possible. The more wiseguys he loses, the more likely he'll get the message and back off—for now. Eventually he'll have to save face."

"That I understand, which is why I intend to decimate his entire operation in the next few days—to buy more time."

"This I gotta see."

"You will," I said, swerving to avoid a drunk driver. "I'm taking you up on your offer to help."

* * * * *

I reached back over the seat and handed Cafiero the sketch my uncle Luigi had made of Napoli's stronghold.

"Not a bad layout. He walled off the center of the top floor. No windows, easy access to the roof, if he needs it, and a private staircase down to the ground floor with exits on all four sides of the building."

"I guess there's a reason he's held a firm grip on his territory for three decades. He's not stupid," I said.

"You walk into that place, you're gonna be carried out feet first or shoved into a car. My guess is they'll do you in spectacular fashion in or near your neighborhood."

"Let's think positive. Can you set up on the opposite building?" I asked.

"He'll have at least two or three men positioned along that roof, maybe more. Shouldn't be a problem."

I pulled over to let Cafiero out a few blocks away from Napoli's building.

"Let's get this over with," I said.

"If you do come out alive, you're gonna be escorted by several of his goons. How will I know if you're walking out a free man or about to go for a one-way ride?"

"Just before I step off the stoop, I'll throw myself against the guy on my right and boot anyone in front of me down the steps. You worry about the rest. If *I* don't make a move, you don't."

"If I were you, I'd figure out a way to park this heap in front of his building. You're gonna want to get the hell out of this neighborhood once I open fire."

Cafiero got out of the car and stuck his hand in my window. "Hand over your guns," he ordered.

"What the hell for?"

"Why waste the firepower? That's the first thing they'll take. I'll put them to good use."

He shoved the rods into his waistband. "Don't worry about me, I'll do my job. Just make sure you do yours and stay alive. I'm looking forward to seeing how things work out in Detroit," he said, then disappeared into the shadow of an alleyway.

The Gumshoe Chronicles 1922

* * * * *

When I drove up to Napoli's building, I spotted five of his men positioned out front. Two on the stoop of the brownstone, one leaning on a parked car at the foot of the stairs, and two across the street from the entrance. I was sure there were more, but I didn't have time to take a better look. Big Ben's men had a reputation for inhospitality when it came to strangers lurking around.

I stopped in the middle of the street and stepped out, yelling at the henchman leaning against the car.

"Hey, move that heap so I can park my car."

He pushed himself off the fender and walked toward me. He reached inside his coat. "Get movin' before I plug you full of lead."

The others closed ranks. "Hold up," someone shouted and pushed them aside. "What's your business here?"

"I came to see Big Ben," I said, adjusting my fedora, exposing my empty shoulder holsters as my arms moved.

"He expectin' ya?"

"It's a surprise. But he'll see me—I got two of his sons."

"Who the hell are you?"

"Joey Batista." The brute stepped back and turned to his men. "Frisk him, then let him park his car. I'll check with the boss."

It didn't take him long to return.

"The boss said for me to personally search you here and again before you enter his apartment."

"I'm unarmed."

"That's what they all say. Put your hands behind your head and spread your legs. Consider yourself lucky. Some guys have to walk in naked."

*****

The interior of the building was designed with one purpose—to protect Napoli. The route to the top floor was a windowless maze of dead-end staircases, and long and short corridors partitioned by steel doors with manual locking mechanisms. A virtual death trap for anyone with hostile intent.

Two of Big Ben's bodyguards stood on either side of me as we waited for him to come out of his bedroom. The main area served a dual purpose—business and pleasure. A large, intricately carved mahogany desk was the focal point on one side, along with a matching meeting table and leather chairs. The other side of the room had a bar and three round tables sprinkled among traditional sofas. A bearskin rug placed on the wooden floor in front of a huge stone fireplace separated the two halves of the room. The ceiling had a complex wooden beam structure that continued down the walls, trimming false window frames that gave the place, when combined with the fireplace, a rustic feel.

Napoli stepped into the room while tying a sash around his robe.

"Frisk him again," he ordered.

"I'm not armed."

"You should be. What's this nonsense about my sons?"

"Just a warning."

"A warning? You're giving me a warning? What? Am I supposed to cave in to Carmine's demands because of my idiot sons?"

"That was the idea, along with a few other calamities that are about to take place."

Napoli walked over to his desk, lit a cigar, and paced in front of the fireplace.

"You wanna know something, Batista? Your luck has just run out. If you dropped those bastards of mine in the bay, you'd be doing me a favor. The other bosses would rally to my side, and Carmine, his father, and you would all be history."

"Not the reaction I expected."

"I bet not. Those sons-of-bitches told me to retire. Can you imagine that? Me, Big Ben, too old to run the business. If I'd had a gun in my hand, I would have shot those ingrates myself."

He was walking toward me when someone burst into the room and pulled Napoli aside. Red-faced, Napoli turned to me.

"Two of my warehouses were raided tonight by the feds. Is this your game?"

"Like I said, it's just the beginning."

"Get this bum out of here and wake up his neighborhood so they can watch you blow his brains out," Napoli ordered.

He then threw his cigar into the fireplace and went back into his bedroom.

* * * * *

Each goon grabbed hold of one of my arms as they pulled me through the front door and onto the stoop. When we got to the edge of the steps, I dropped down, tugging both of them off balance. I hoped that Cafiero recognized my swift movement as the intended signal. A gunshot echoed off the buildings, and at the same time, my left arm jerked free as the goon at my side fell backwards. I reached up and pulled a gun from my remaining assailant and heaved him headfirst down the concrete stairs. At the same time, screams from a body flying off the roof across the street distracted two of Napoli's men who stood at the foot of the stairs. That second of hesitation cost them their lives, giving me the chance to get off a couple of shots as I came at them.

I stepped over their bodies and crouched next to my car for cover when I noticed a ghostly figure running toward me. I was about to shoot when I saw it was a woman dressed in white wearing a black cape.

"Stay down!" she yelled.

Three more shots rang out and two knives whizzed over my head. Two of Napoli's men, who had rushed out the front door, tumbled down the steps, and another fell out of the shadow of the stoop onto the sidewalk. He had a butcher knife lodged in his neck.

Jackie ran past me and retrieved her knifes.

I didn't know where the hell she had come from, but I was grateful she was there, especially when I rounded the front of the car and saw another one of Jackie's victims lying in the street.

She flung open the passenger door of my car and yelled, "Let's get the hell out of here!"

We could still hear gunfire as we cut across traffic, narrowly missing an oncoming truck.

Cafiero was on his own.

Chapter 6

I barreled out of Big Ben's street, weaved past two cars, and damn near rode up the rear of another. Horns blared in anger so I backed off the gas. Jackie dropped her knives on the floorboard and turned to look out the back window to see if any cars were in pursuit.

Satisfied, she flopped back in her seat and brushed strands of hair from her face. "That was close," she said.

"My driving or the bloodshed?"

"Both! If I didn't know better, I'd say you have a death wish."

"Just tryin' to keep those I care about alive. Now, tell me how you showed up exactly when I needed you."

"You got lucky. On the way to the first hospital to spread the rumor there was a syphilis epidemic in Big Ben's territory, we passed a group of guys hangin' out on a street corner. I nudged Rosalie and asked loudly how many cases were admitted this week. She caught on real fast. You should've seen the men's faces when they overheard our conversation. No doubt our nurse's uniforms gave us instant credibility."

Once again, having a streetwise partner was paying off big time. "How many corners did you hit?"

"Trust me, enough to ensure Big Ben will see a sudden drop in business at his canhouses tonight."

"You still haven't answered my question about how you got here."

"Rosalie and I had come as close to Big Ben's street

as we dared and were waving down a cab to head home when we heard a barrage of gunfire. I didn't know what you were up to tonight, but given that we were in Big Ben's neighborhood, I thought there was a good chance you were involved."

"You took a hell of a risk."

"I didn't think I was in danger, especially in this uniform. I'm sure I just looked like a nurse running toward people who might need help."

"Where is Rosalie?"

"I was about to get in the cab after her, but when I heard the shots, I slammed the cab door shut and told the cabbie to take off. He didn't hesitate."

The sound of sirens pulled my attention back to the road. Several police cars and meat wagons shot past us, weaving between cars that flowed in both directions. It was fortunate that I had blended into traffic when I did. The last thing we needed was to get copped for a traffic violation in the vicinity of such bloodshed.

"We're not out of danger yet," I said, looking for a place to pull over.

Jackie leaned toward me, resting her arm on my shoulder, and watched the chaos as cars swerved to avoid colliding with other panicked drivers.

"Lucky for you the cops took their time responding to the shootings," Jackie said.

"That's typical when gunfire is heavy. The risk is too high that they'll get caught in the middle of a shootout if they arrive early," I said, thinking that the real reason lay in the hope that the wiseguys would wipe each other out.

I took a sharp turn into the parking lot of an all-night diner and swerved into a dark corner away from other cars.

"Hmm. What do you have in mind?" Jackie asked with a slight smile.

"I don't know about you, but I need some grub and time to think."

"I guess danger affects us differently."

I pulled her close and held her in a tight embrace as we kissed.

"Not really," I said. "But we're not finished with Big Ben tonight, and I'm damn hungry."

She pushed away. "You're not going back now, not after what just happened. The place will be swarming with cops."

"Hey, this was your plan. We need to relentlessly hit Big Ben from every side. If we don't, we're all dead. Let's not forget that."

I placed my hand over her mouth. "Don't worry, I'm not going back alone."

* * * * *

When we entered the diner, the waitress took one look at Jackie, grabbed an apron off a wall hook and came running over. Others turned to see what was going on. That's when I noticed blood stains on the front of Jackie's nursing uniform. She had gotten careless with the knives she'd retrieved from her two victims.

"Oh, my poor dear. You must have had a rough night at the hospital, but I can't have you looking like this in front of my customers," the waitress said, as she placed the apron over Jackie's bloody clothes and tied it behind her back. She then directed us to a back booth, filled two coffee cups and placed menus on the table.

"Whatever you want, it's on me," she said. "I don't know what we'd do without dedicated nurses and doctors like you. There's so much violence in this town."

"If she only knew," Jackie said, taking a sip of coffee.

Jackie's eyes sparkled and her red hair flamed under the glare of the overhead lights. Mesmerized by her beauty, I found it difficult to reconcile her tender side with the woman who had walked into the middle of a gunfight and taken out two goons with no show of emotion or regret.

"You saved my life tonight," I said.

"I wasn't the only one. Who was helping you?"

"Cafiero."

"How did he know what you were up to?"

"Let's just say for now he's my guardian angel. But if I don't get to Detroit in the next few days and take out Ronnie, Cafiero will become my executioner."

"As complicated as that sounds, I understand Cafiero's logic. What I don't understand is what happened tonight. I thought we had agreed to limit the bloodshed," Jackie said, with a hint of anger in her emerald-green eyes.

The waitress refilled our cups and asked if we wanted something to eat.

"I'll take a steak with whatever fixin's you got," I said.

"Sautéed onions, mushrooms, a side of mashed potatoes and beans should do ya. What about that steak? How do you want it cooked?"

"Rare."

"That figures. What about you, hon?"

"Maybe later," Jackie said.

"I don't blame you," the waitress said, shaking her head. "But don't worry, I won't make his steak too bloody."

When the waitress was out of earshot, I answered Jackie's question.

"On the way over to Big Ben's, Cafiero got the drop on me and convinced me otherwise. He said if we didn't avenge the shooting of Castellano in blood, it would embolden Big Ben. I agreed, so we focused on his crew. In my gut I knew Cafiero was right, but even with what we did tonight, we still have a huge problem."

Jackie placed her coffee cup on the saucer. "I know."

"I'm not talking about Big Ben. It's his sons I'm worried about now."

"What about them? I did a story about Big Ben and his family when I was working at the *Daily News*. From all accounts, his sons aren't a threat. Two of them only care about drugs, booze, and women, and in that order. The young one is a different story. For some reason he works on the docks and seldom hangs out with his brothers."

I told her how Big Ben reacted when I informed him that we had kidnapped his two oldest boys.

"So, that's your worry," Jackie said. "Since you didn't knock them off, they now have an opportunity to show their old man they have what it takes to run the show."

"There's no doubt when they get the chance, they'll come at us hard, and we can't take them out since they're his family. But we have some time."

"What makes you say that?"

"Luigi and Dom dumped them under the Brooklyn Bridge where there's a hobo camp. When they wake up, they'll be lucky if they've still got as much as their skivvies to walk home in."

"That won't slow them down for long," Jackie said.

"No, but O'Reilly will soon pick them up on vagrancy

charges. He's confident he can bury them in the prison system for a few weeks. To get it done he'll have to use up some favors owed him."

Jackie had changed her mind when my food arrived and ordered the late night special.

"Do us a favor and make that quick," I said to the waitress. "We have to get back to our shift."

"What's the hurry?" Jackie asked.

"I can see only one way out of this mess. Like I said, we have to move fast."

"How fast?"

"Before sunrise," I said. I then went to work on my food in silence. Finished, I drained my cup of joe and slid out of the booth.

Jackie got up to follow.

I grabbed her arm. "Hold on. You have time to eat. I can set what I need in motion with a phone call."

When I returned, Jackie had finished the special and was halfway through a slice of pie smothered in whipped cream.

"You're gonna pack on the pounds if you eat like that."

"If there's a chance I'm gonna hit the dust, I'd rather do it on a full stomach."

"I think you need to take the rest of the night off. Saving my life once in a day is enough."

Jackie picked up her napkin and gently wiped it across her blood-red lips. "Think again. If, as you say, you're following my plan, then I'm in all the way."

I couldn't argue with that, so I ordered a slice of pie for myself.

"You gonna tell me what you have planned?" Jackie asked.

"You'll find out when we get home," I said, diving into my dessert.

*****

It was three in the morning and my parents' apartment was bustling with activity, which is what I expected would happen after I hung up the phone at the diner.

"Will someone tell me what's goin' on?" Jackie asked from the doorway. "This place smells like a chemical factory."

Dom was all smiles, sitting at the kitchen table, mixing some kind of concoction on one of Ma's cutting boards.

"It is, and if I were you, I wouldn't distract me unless you're tired of living," he said without looking up.

"Excuse me," Pop said, brushing past Jackie, holding three empty mason jars.

Dom stopped what he was doing and reached for the jars.

"That's as thin as I dare grind down the bottoms," Pop said. "It took five tries. The others shattered with a gentle tap."

Dom handed one back to Pop. "Light the stove and hold this one over the flame. If it takes longer than ten seconds to crack, you need to go thinner."

I could see that everyone was counting to themselves. I got to eight when the bottom popped.

"Perfect!" Dom said.

Next, it was Ma's turn to get into the action. She opened a can of kerosene and filled a similar-sized jar to within an inch of the brim. Pop panicked and took the can out of her hand.

"Vito, I've canned with these older-style jars for years. I don't need your help sealing this one."

"You've never sealed a jar full of kerosene. That paraffin wax is hot enough to ignite this stuff."

"Men!" Ma said, as she reached for a wax plug she had removed from a jar of preserved jelly.

We watched as she placed the plug on top of the kerosene, removed it, shaved wax off the bottom and placed it back. The wax plug floated to within an eighth of an inch from the top of the jar. She skillfully took a hot metal spatula and gently moved the wax until the edges were sealed. Satisfied, she slowly filled the remaining mouth of the jar with hot wax.

"There," she said in triumph. "The kerosene won't spill, and I didn't burn down the building."

"Not yet," Pop said. "You still have one more to do. Let's hope you're as lucky."

She quickly sealed another. "Luck had nothing to do with it. Now, why don't you go do something useful?"

Pop grunted, picked up his shotgun, shoved a handful of shells in his pocket, and went out to check on the neighborhood.

I took the wax-sealed jars from Ma and placed them on the table, then pulled up a chair next to Jackie, who was intently watching Dom practice his trade. She looked at me, and then back at Dom.

"One of you tell me right now what the hell is goin' on," she said, reaching for some of the stuff Dom was kneading.

"Whoa! Don't touch that," Dom shouted.

"Tell me."

"Okay, just back away from the table."

Jackie did as she was told.

"Big Ben thinks he's safe in his cocoon at the top of his fortified building, but Joey has found a clever way to penetrate his fortress," Dom said, still focused on his task. He gently placed .45 caliber shells in the Mason jars Pop had given him, poured in kerosene, and screwed the zinc caps on tight.

Dom then scooped up the mixture he had made on Ma's cutting board and gingerly packed it into another Mason jar. Beads of sweat dripped from his brow. There was no doubt we were in danger if he did something wrong.

To ease the tension, I picked up where Dom left off. "Big Ben has a huge fireplace in the main room of his apartment. There were still hot embers smoldering when I was escorted into the room a few hours ago. My guess is someone lights it sometime after sunset."

"So, what does the fireplace have to do with all of this?"

"Big Ben's place is on the top floor of his building, but given how the building is designed, it's impossible to reach him without getting blasted by his goons. The chimney is the key to getting to Big Ben."

"That's lunacy. You can't fit down a chimney no matter how large a fireplace he has."

"*I* can't fit, but these jars can," I said. "The ceiling in his apartment is twelve feet high and the chimney, I'm guessing, extends another two feet above the roof. We're going to hang the jars down the chimney caps. Pop ground down the bottoms of two jars, so when the fireplace is lit, the glass will crack, releasing the kerosene and the bullets. A huge fire ball will shoot out of the fireplace and up the chimney. Soon after, the two jars Ma sealed with wax, hanging by string, will fall onto the logs in the fireplace. As the wax seals melt, flaming kerosene will flow out of the fireplace onto the wooden floor in the apartment."

"Right about then the heat should set off the ammunition," Dom said with a smug grin.

"Sounds like you guys are trying to kill Big Ben," Jackie said.

"No, just scare him and his crew enough to get them out of the apartment," I said. "The noise of the exploding ammunition and the flames spreading into the room should have that effect. I know what you're thinking, but the bullets are harmless because the casings will rupture from the heat without firing the actual bullets."

"So, what's the point?" Jackie asked.

"It's all part of your plan—immobilize Big Ben by creating chaos."

Dom sealed his jar and smiled. "This jar, which will be positioned higher up in the chimney, contains my secret mixture, and will explode last from the heat with sufficient force to blow a hole through the brick wall into the apartment," Dom said with pride.

"Why wouldn't all the jars fall into the fire at the same time?" Jackie asked.

"That's the crucial part. Each jar will hang down the chimney at different heights. The last jar that is designed to explode will be secured with electrical wire. It won't drop, but when the material inside reaches a critical temperature, it will explode, as Dom had just explained," I said.

Dom carefully packed each jar into a doctor's bag that Pop had found in Gino's room. Gino was an old family friend who had turned to booze when his family was murdered years ago. Ma and Pop had tried to help him last year by giving him a job, but, as we all learned, it's hard to change someone's destiny.

Jackie and I both looked at each other. I'm sure we shared the same thoughts. Even with everything going on, we hadn't forgotten we only had a few days to get to Detroit to rescue Debbie and avenge Gino's murder before Cafiero acted on his contract.

"We're ready," Dom said. "The jars are labeled, and large fishing hooks are fastened to the end of each cord. The lengths of the cords are already set. I also packed five leather belts in the bag with the jars."

"What are the belts for?" Jackie asked.

"You'd be surprised how handy they are."

"Dom, you didn't answer my question."

"Let me try," I said. "I need a way to fasten the fishhooks securely to the top of the chimney. I can link the leather belts together and wrap them around the top of the chimney, and then fasten the hooks to the leather."

Pop walked back in with his shotgun slung over his shoulder. He had just come from the waterfront where he had checked on Carmine's progress. Jackie took the opportunity to run upstairs to change out of the nursing uniform into something more suitable for night maneuvers.

"She's not comin' with us, is she?" Dom asked.

"Our guns won't do us much good. We fire one shot after what happened earlier and Big Ben's entire neighborhood will be on us. You've seen how Jackie handles knives."

"You never did explain how she got so good."

"Not now," I said and turned to Pop. "Has Carmine recruited any more muscle?"

"Word got around fast that Carmine is paying big bucks for talent. That, combined with what you did to Big Ben's organization tonight, has already gotten some people's attention. Luigi is helping him weed out the undesirables."

That was good to hear. My one worry was that Big Ben would retaliate tonight, but I thought the chances slim. He needed time to lick his wounds and deal with the chaos bringing down his businesses. I expected it would take two days or more for his canhouses to shut down from the rumors Jackie and Rosalie had set into motion. His booze deliveries should dry up soon, but he'd have enough on hand at each speakeasy to last a few days longer. If Jackie's plan had any chance of working, we had to keep the pressure on.

Jackie came back into the apartment dressed from head to toe in black. On the way out, Pop wished us luck.

Jackie was headed down the stairs toward my car when I called her back.

"Hold on. We have to wait for O'Reilly."

Dom overheard me, as he carefully hauled his bundle of destruction through the massive doorway. "Don't tell me you're also bringing a copper along on the job."

"How else do you expect to get anywhere near Big Ben's neighborhood, let alone his building?"

Jackie sat down on the stoop. "What's takin' him so damn long? We don't have much time before sunrise."

"He'll be along shortly. He's taking care of Big Ben's sons."

I'd hardly finished the sentence when his car pulled alongside mine. Dom put the medical bag in the front seat and we crammed into the back.

O'Reilly handed me three sets of handcuffs. "Put those on so you're linked together, and clamp the ends on the metal handle attached to the car's frame."

Dom objected until I told him to clam up and do what he was told. O'Reilly handed me a set of keys and took off for the West Side. Time was running out. We had only two hours before daybreak.

*****

O'Reilly got through the police barricade without incident and waved over a cop he knew.

"McDonald, looks like you have a mess on your hands."

"Nothing we can't handle, O'Reilly. Aren't you a little out of your jurisdiction, or are you lost?"

"If you ask me, we have a Mafia war on our hands. The same thing happened in my neighborhood not long ago so I thought I'd nose around a bit."

"I heard about that. I guess there's no doubt now, but nobody thought Carmine had the moxie or the resources to go up against Big Ben after Castellano was shot."

"How many dead?" O'Reilly asked.

"Still counting. There's at least three on the roof across from Big Ben's place and five in the street. One of them looks like he was thrown off the building."

"Are they all from Big Ben's crew?"

"Hard to tell. The younger wiseguys hire out to the highest bidder lookin' to make a name for themselves. I guess one or two could be Carmine's, but I suspect most, if not all, are Big Ben's."

McDonald looked over the scene. "These poor schmucks didn't know what hit them. Get this, two of them were taken out with a knife. You don't see that too often."

"How many shooters?" O'Reilly asked.

"Who knows? But it looks like one of them took a hit as he tried to get away. There's a trail of blood in an alleyway two buildings over from where we picked up some spent shells, and another dead body."

"Any chance I can get a few minutes alone with Big Ben?" O'Reilly asked.

"The chief took him and a few of his men down to the stationhouse for questioning. More for show—publicity—you know how it works." McDonald looked in the backseat. "What's the story here?"

"Nailed them casing out a bank not far from here. I suspect one of them is a soupman," O'Reilly said, patting the black bag on his front seat.

McDonald backed away from the car. "You're not tellin' me you have nitro in this heap."

"It's possible. The short one back there got the heebie-jeebies when I tossed his sack onto the seat. You mind if I transfer them to one of your guys to take in for interrogation. I'd like to look around."

"In case you haven't noticed, O'Reilly, we're a little busy here. If you're gonna nose around, why don't you park around back, just in case that stuff decides to blow. It doesn't look like your plugs will lam off the way you have them shackled. Besides, the last thing I need are innocent corpses in the street. We have the back alleyway blocked off so it's deserted back there."

O'Reilly flashed his buzzer at the cop who was blocking off the corridor behind the row of brownstones. He let us pass without incident. O'Reilly parked at the end of the alleyway that ran along the side of Big Ben's building. He said he thought it best to have his police car visible from the main street to keep any curious cops from nosing around while we went to work.

Once we freed ourselves, O'Reilly headed down the

alley toward the crime scene to find his friend McDonald. O'Reilly insisted we take no more than fifteen minutes to get our work done. He didn't want anyone to get suspicious that he was somehow involved when all hell broke loose the next night when Big Ben lit his fireplace.

* * * * *

We didn't have any time to waste. Jackie walked the back alleyway to make sure it was deserted. Dom got his bundle from the front seat, and I cased the building for an easy way to the roof. The fire escape would make too much noise. It looked possible to scale the façade, but I decided to shimmy up a six-inch drain pipe attached to the building. I unraveled a rope I had in a sack and told Dom I would pull up his bag of jars once I made it to the roof. I was about six feet above ground when Jackie called out. She was bent over a hobo curled alongside trash boxes. As I watched, she rose suddenly and waved me down.

"It's Cafiero. He's taken a blade to the gut."

I had to think fast. O'Reilly would be back in another ten to twelve minutes. I couldn't afford to abandon the job for Cafiero. He knew the risk when he agreed to back me up earlier in the night.

"Dom, I have some medical supplies in my bag. Do what you can to stop the bleeding, then get him into the car. I'll go it alone."

"What? You goin' off the track in the middle of a job? Who cares if this guy blips off? What's he to you?" Dom said louder than necessary.

"Dom, keep it down. He's a friend and we're not leaving him."

"Since when do we care about those left behind? Tell me. I wanna know. Why didn't we go back for Shooter?" Dom shouted, visibly shaken.

Jackie got my medical supplies and shoved them hard against Dom's gut. She leaned in and said something in his ear, then pushed him toward Cafiero. Dom stumbled, but was able to steady himself. He wiped his arm across his brow to remove the sweat dripping into his eyes, looked at both of us, and then went over to Cafiero.

"You'll need someone to cover your back," Jackie said to me.

"We have to take that chance. I don't have time to pull you up, unless you think you can scale this drain pipe."

Jackie looked at the pipe. "You better get going. I'll stay here."

"Watch out for that last jar, the one with my special mixture. Chances are it's a bit unstable," Dom said.

Once on the roof, I took my time hauling up the medical bag full of jars, making sure it didn't bump against the side of the building. I knew to take Dom's warning seriously. I had seen the damage one of his homemade bombs had done when it had exploded prematurely on the one mission we'd shared during the war.

It didn't take me long to locate Big Ben's chimney stack since it was unusual to have an actual wood-burning fireplace in one of the city's brownstones. All the buildings had central coal-burning furnaces. His chimney had a chimney cap with three large ceramic pipes extending out of the top to prevent a downdraft from the winds that whipped around the harbor. As far as I could tell, the roof was deserted. I linked the leather belts together and lashed them tightly around the rim of the chimney. I had brought along one of Pop's augers to make a hole for the last buckle. Once the belts were in place, I lowered the jars in the order Dom had instructed and looped the fish hooks through the holes in the belts.

I was about to climb over the side when the door to the roof opened. A cop stepped out and lit a cigarette. There wasn't much I could do besides wait until he had finished his smoke and hope he would go back into the building when he finished. He had just thrown down his butt and had taken several steps to look around when someone called out from inside the stairwell. As soon as the cop turned, I flipped over the short wall and clambered down the pipe. O'Reilly was already in the car and had seen Cafiero's condition.

"We need to get this guy to a hospital," he said, and took off.

Dom sat between Jackie and me in the backseat and shook his head. "You gotta tell me why we risked our lives for some bum."

"I'll explain later," I said. "All you need to think about now is how you're gonna blow the hell out of Big Ben's summer home tomorrow."

Dom leaned his head back against the seat and closed his eyes. "Tomorrow can't come soon enough."

Chapter 7

O'Reilly dropped us off at the hospital, and then headed back to headquarters to finish out his night shift. The rest of us stayed together waiting for Cafiero to get out of surgery, but two hours of monotony was all Dom could take. He popped out of his seat and paced the room. First he walked in a circle with his hands behind his back, then shoved them in his pant's pockets, and repeatedly marched from one end of the waiting room to the other. Just as abruptly, he stopped in front of us.

"Tell me *now* why we're wasting so much time for some street bum," he said, slapping the back of his hand into his palm. "We need to get over to Long Island and meet up with Martha."

I knew Dom craved action, just as I did. For some reason it helped block out memories of what we saw and did during the war. So, I wasn't surprised by his sudden outburst.

"He's not a bum. He's a torpedo for the mob and he saved my life tonight. Don't worry about Long Island. Martha will have the information and everything else we need when we get there."

"A hitman? Why are you involved with a hitman?"

"A Detroit mobster put out a contract on my head and he took the job."

"Did I hear that right? He arrives in town to blow you away, and then saves your life. That makes no sense."

"It's complicated," Jackie said.

"Everything about you guys is complicated. I'm still

waiting to hear how you got so damn good at throwing butcher knives."

"Practice."

"Take a seat and I'll explain," I said, just as the surgeon walked into the waiting room.

"Your friend was lucky. The blade missed vital organs. We repaired the damage to his large intestine and cleaned him out as best we could. Only time will tell if he can fight off any infections."

"Is he going to make it?" Jackie asked.

"That's hard to say. He's lost a lot of blood and, unfortunately, we've used up our supply. He has a rare blood type. We're making calls to the other hospitals in the city. Keep your fingers crossed."

"Can we see him?" Jackie asked.

"He's weak from blood loss and still a bit groggy from the anesthesia. Don't stay too long."

The doc led the way through the double doors and had a nurse take us to the recovery room.

* * * * *

Cafiero slowly turned toward us.

"How did I get here?"

"We found you in a trash heap behind Big Ben's building," I answered.

Cafiero smiled. "I knew you'd be back. But it makes no difference. I'm still gonna kill you if you don't settle with Ronnie Ligotti soon."

"Given your condition I think I have a little more time."

"I wouldn't count on it," he said, rolling his head to the side.

The nurse came into the room and opened a space in the curtain surrounding Cafiero's bed. "You'll have to leave soon."

"We just need a few more minutes," Jackie said.

When she left, Jackie nudged Cafiero's shoulder. At first he mumbled nonsense, but then Jackie gave a gentle shake, and he became alert again.

"What happened? How did you end up where we found you wearing a tattered flogger, looking like a hobo?" she asked.

"Once you guys hightailed out of the neighborhood, I made my way across the rooftops and down to an alleyway. In the alley I was surprised by someone and we got into a tussle. I got off two shots, but not before he sliced me open."

"What does that have to do with the overcoat?" I asked.

"There was no way I'd make it out of there alive in my condition. I took the coat off a drunken bum asleep in the alleyway. I limped across the street and fell into the trash pile."

"What made you think I'd be back?"

Cafiero smiled. "You're predictable."

The nurse came in again and insisted we leave. I was behind Jackie on the way out when Cafiero muttered something strange. I turned to ask what he meant, but by then he was out cold.

Back in the waiting room, Jackie wanted to know what Cafiero had said.

I hesitated, still unsure. "Something about an ordinary man; I think he said watch out for an ordinary man."

"What's that supposed to mean?"

"I have no idea, and I'm not gonna worry about it now.

We have a big day ahead of us so let's head home and get some rest."

We found Dom outside the hospital leaning on my car surrounded by half-smoked cigarette butts. He was more than ready to leave.

* * * * *

My family was eating breakfast when we entered the apartment. Ma was the first to notice us and rushed to give Jackie and me a hug. As she backed away, she noticed Dom looking dejected and yanked him into her arms.

"When you didn't return soon after sunrise, we were worried something went wrong," she said, pulling us all together.

"What the hell took so long?" Luigi demanded.

"We found Cafiero lying in the alley behind Big Ben's building among a pile of trash. He had taken a knife to the gut earlier when he was covering me."

"O'Reilly dropped us off at the hospital, and we hung around to see if Cafiero made it through surgery," Jackie added, while pouring the three of us coffee.

"Why the hell would you save his life? He's gonna try to kill you as soon as he gets fit," Pop said in disbelief.

"It's worse than that," Dom said. "Your son was more concerned for this Cafiero guy than his own life. He placed those jars down Big Ben's chimney without any backup. We could've all been killed if he was spotted. Civilian life has made him soft and a danger to our mission."

Dom was getting on my nerves. "We're not in a war zone."

"Then tell me why I'm here if you don't think this is a

war? Did you forget our motto—no prisoners, no emotion, and no retreat!" Dom shouted.

I knew why he was so upset. We had all left others behind to complete our assignments. But the blood, the screams, all of it—especially the guilt—never went away.

Luigi looked at Pop in disbelief. Pop said nothing. He just rolled his eyes. They had seen their share of death in the old county and had found a way to accept it. I hoped that time would do the same for Dom and me.

Ma had a different way of dealing with stress. She lit the stove, scrambled eggs with a vengeance, and slapped a pound of bacon onto a skillet, then came over to the table.

"All I have to say is I'm glad there still is a streak of humanity in my son and I'm proud of him. Now, the three of you sit and eat something," she said, chasing Pop and Luigi out of the kitchen. While we ate, Ma went out to do some food shopping.

"We need to gather up the necessary supplies and get over to Long Island," Dom said, as he finished wiping down his plate with a piece of bread. He shoved it into his mouth.

"That can wait," Jackie said, putting down her napkin. "It's been a long night. We need to get some rest."

I pulled back her chair as she rose from the table. She put her hands around my waist, stood on her toes to give me a gentle kiss, and led me toward the door.

"Hold on, hold on," Dom said. "I want Big Ben's house to explode around the same time as his apartment tonight. We don't have time for what you guys have in mind."

Jackie turned to face Dom. "I disagree. There's always time. Besides, if Big Ben thinks the attack is over, and then we hit him again the next day by blowing up his vacation home, it'll have a bigger impact." she said with a smile.

"But—"

"Dom, get a couple hours of rest. Joey owes me for saving his life last night, and I intend to collect."

* * * * *

Later that day, after we all got together, Jackie reluctantly agreed to stay behind to help protect the home front. She took out her frustration on the sandwiches she pounded together for a late lunch.

Ma handed me the picnic basket they had packed and threw in some dried salami to make up for the mangled sandwiches. I was about to go console Jackie when Carmine showed up carrying an engraved rifle case with a gold handle.

"Hey Joey, I got a present for you. I took it off one of Big Ben's men who tried to sneak into the neighborhood late last night."

Dom mumbled some obscenities, complaining it would be next week before we got to Long Island, and went to have a smoke on the front stoop. Luigi and Pop heard the commotion and came out of the repair shop where they were modifying a Thompson submachine gun based on the drawing Dom had previously sketched.

Carmine handed me the case. It held a top-of-the-line, high-powered sniper rifle. I'd never seen anything like it. I reached for it, but Luigi beat me to it.

"This is custom made," he said, as he felt the balance and tried the action.

"Just what we need, another gun in the house," Ma said.

"How many men did Big Ben send?" I asked Carmine.

"Two! From the looks of the firepower they brought along, they were intent on doing some serious damage."

"I suspect they're good at their trade or Big Ben would have sent in more men," I said.

Carmine agreed. "My guess is he hired these guys after he shot up our neighborhood to take the both of us out. Once that was done, he expected to move in without much resistance. I think Big Ben has learned his lesson and has more respect for our local war hero."

"It's not over yet," I said.

"Where are these guys now?" Jackie asked.

"You'll have to ask Toby. The last time I saw them they were in a small boat wrapped in heavy chains, headed out to the middle of the bay," Carmine said with a straight face.

"Have you heard anything from Vigliotti?" I asked.

"Not a peep, but it looks like he's a man of his word. He's keeping the other Mafia bosses out of our feud and pulling strings in City Hall. I'm sure you noticed that cops have been scarce in the neighborhood and even the DA hasn't come snooping around."

"What's the jabber on the street?" Luigi asked.

"Big Ben's goons are jumping ship faster than he can recruit. Rumors are running rampant about his whorehouses, and most of his booze has been confiscated or is filling up the city's sewage system. I'm also doing my part. By tomorrow morning, his first ship should arrive with the wrong cargo manifest," Carmine said with a sadistic grin. "I had one of my tugboat captains board a cargo ship he was guiding into the harbor and make the switch when no one was looking."

"If I were you, I'd clamp down harder on security tonight. Big Ben and his lieutenants are in for an explosive evening, thanks to Dom," I said, just as Dom returned from having his smoke.

Carmine looked at Dom. "How the hell did you rig one of his pier warehouses so fast?"

"I didn't. We're saving that for our grand finale. Joey added a little twist to our plan. When the commotion died down last night, after Joey took out half of Big Ben's crew, he felt it was a good time to strike again, so we went back and planted a different surprise."

Carmine patted me on the back and said he'd never doubt me again. He was about to leave when Luigi asked about Castellano.

"Hey Carmine, how's your old man? They won't let him have visitors except for family."

"Looks like he's gonna pull through. He's a tough old bird, just like you guys. What the hell did they feed you back in Sicily?"

"Moxie, that's what we ate, and we had it twice a day, every day. Without it you were dead."

"You sure had your share," he said.

Carmine left, but not before he gave us a warning.

"Big Ben is trying to convince Vigliotti that you took out two of his sons, so watch your back. If they don't show up soon, we may find ourselves goin' up against the entire syndicate."

I didn't have time to track down Vigliotti and explain what we had done with Big Ben's boys, so I asked Luigi to make a trip to Little Italy. As he was about to head out, I remembered the warning Cafiero had given me last night. I thought it might be important so I asked everyone to help figure out its meaning. When I told them what he had said, even Ma joined us at the table.

"That's the rambling of a man who had just come out of surgery. There's no reason to fear an 'ordinary man,'" she said.

"Ah, what the hell is this all about? We don't need to solve a riddle ginned up by a drugged hitman," Dom said.

Pop agreed with Dom, but Luigi took it more seriously.

"Didn't Cafiero say there weren't many interested in takin' on the hit due to your reputation?" Luigi asked me.

"That's right. Only two signed on, and Cafiero took the other guy out."

"Why would he do that?" Dom asked.

Jackie answered for me. "Cafiero doesn't like competition."

Luigi poured himself a hefty drink. "I bet Cafiero was trying to tell you that Ronnie had hired three not two. I know Ronnie. He's not a patient man, and he's also cheap. He's not gonna pay for what he doesn't need, but if Joey isn't dead soon, he's gonna release the third."

"And who's that?" Dom asked.

"An ordinary man. Someone you'd never suspect would be a Mafia torpedo."

"And that makes him more dangerous," Pop said.

Ma took Luigi's drink and threw it back in one smooth motion.

* * * * *

Luigi had packed my car with enough dynamite to take down the Statue of Liberty, which made Dom almost giddy. I tried to convince Ma and Pop to shut down their business and take a short vacation until we returned, but they refused. They were set in their ways and weren't about to let a two-bit gangster scare them out of their neighborhood.

Dom and I crossed the Brooklyn Bridge and drove along the north shore of Long Island, then turned inland and met Martha at a small rural hotel. She had booked the last two rooms, and after we agreed to meet in the dining room for dinner, she ushered me into her room, leaving Dom in the hallway. Once inside, Martha wasn't about to waste time. What willpower I had to resist her advances didn't last long as she pushed me backwards onto the four-poster bed. Most guys would say I was lucky, but I wasn't so sure. I felt stuck in no man's land between two beautiful women, one insatiable and the other seductive. But Jackie had made it clear that she could see other men, and she knew I was attracted to Martha. I guess you could say she was justified in being angry about staying behind.

Martha caught me admiring her figure as she dried her hair in front of a full-length mirror. "Don't you wish we could stay young forever," she said, as she wrapped the towel around her waist and came over and sat on my lap. She put her arms around my neck, and as we kissed, I picked her up and walked toward the bed.

"Oh, no you don't," she said. "We're running late, and I have a lot to tell you and Dom. Save your energy for tonight. You're gonna need it."

*****

We were ten minutes late for our dinner reservation and were surprised to find that Dom hadn't arrived yet. I was about to run upstairs to rouse him out of his room when the waiter showed us to our table and mentioned that our friend was on the front porch.

"He made quite the scene," the waiter said.

The porch was littered with cigarette butts where Dom was pacing. As soon as he saw me, he moved in real close and blew smoke in my face.

"This is a *dry* hotel. They actually support the Prohibition Law," he said, throwing his cigarette down and crushing it under foot.

"I'm sure you can go one night without a drink."

"Maybe you can, because you have other things to occupy your time. I don't."

"How long were you in solitary confinement?"

"Too long."

The Colonel had been right. Dom wasn't the most stable guy around. I wished Hawk was with me instead, but I had to deal with what I had.

"In a few more days you'll be a civilian again. Then you'll have the freedom to get at the dough you have stashed and do whatever you want. But for now, you need to stay focused on the mission."

"You're sounding more like the Colonel than a friend."

I couldn't deny his accusation. "Let's join Martha for dinner and get you something to drink. She's always prepared."

Dom went straight to the table and sat next to Martha.

"You got a flask on you?"

She pulled up the side of her skirt discreetly and handed Dom a pint of whiskey. "So that's what all the fuss was about?"

"Lady, let me give you a piece of advice. Don't ever separate a man from his booze. Things can get ugly pretty fast," Dom said, downing half the flask in one gulp.

As we waited for the food to arrive, Martha filled us in on what she'd been up to.

"Luigi had a couple of guys drive the truck you wanted into an abandoned barn not far from here. It's loaded down with plumbing supplies, and there are two sets of workmen coveralls in the front seat."

"What about Big Ben's place? Did you get a chance to check it out?" I asked.

"It's a little ways inland. You might say it's in the 'poorer' section of the island. He only has about twenty acres. The house is a large Victorian, nice but nothing like the mansions you saw along the coast."

"Did you notice any guards or staff around?" Dom asked.

"I would guess he has a gardener taking care of the grounds, but given that its winter and most of the shrubs and stuff are dormant, I don't expect him to show up. I didn't notice any security guards, but cops are all over the shoreline protecting the more exclusive houses."

"What about servants, staff, anyone Big Ben might keep on his payroll when he's not using the place?" I asked.

"Hard to tell. I didn't want to look like I was lingering around the property. I did see a young girl playing with a small dog in front of the house."

I noticed it was getting dark outside and saw a waiter light one of the fireplaces in the dining room. As I watched the kindling ignite the logs, I pictured the series of events taking place in Big Ben's chimney as the mason jars we'd hung inside followed the planned sequence. Big Ben and his lieutenants were no doubt scrambling to get out of the burning apartment.

"We leave at sunrise," I said when we finished our desserts.

I helped Martha up from her chair, and then reached into my inside jacket pocket and handed Dom my flask. "I have everything I need to keep me warm tonight."

Chapter 8

Martha led the way to an old barn where Luigi had stashed the truck full of plumbing supplies. Dom and I changed into the coveralls and moved the dynamite from my car to two work satchels in the back of the truck. Dom backed the truck out of the barn, and I drove my car in to keep it out of sight. Martha turned onto the main highway first, and we followed a few minutes later. We managed to catch up with her before she turned inland. When she gave us a hand signal, we drove onto a gravel road that took us to the entrance of Big Ben's estate. As planned, Martha continued driving. She would eventually turn around and head back to the city. It would have been difficult to explain her presence to the caretaker who watched over the estate during Big Ben's absence.

Dom walked up the front steps and knocked on the door as I dumped some of the piping onto the driveway by the side of the house, making an unholy racket. A stern-looking elderly woman answered the door with a young girl peeking out from behind her skirt.

"What is your business here, young man?" she asked Dom. She scowled at me when I dropped a large pipe on the growing pile. I turned away and pulled my cap down lower.

"I have a work order to replace some of the water lines located in the basement," he said.

"There's nothing wrong with our pipes. You must have the wrong address." She closed the door.

Dom knocked again.

"I told you there's nothing wrong."

"I guess it's possible I have the wrong address. Does a Mr. Napoli own this house?"

"He does."

"Are you Mrs. Napoli?"

"No, I oversee the household staff and make sure everything is in order when Mr. Napoli and his associates visit the estate."

"Mr. Napoli said his builder recommended he change out several pipes as soon as possible because the ones he installed were defective. See, here's the bill that's already been paid by the builder."

The door opened wider and a woman in her late twenties picked up the little girl. "Mother, we don't want to upset Mr. Napoli. Let the men do their job," she said.

"Oh, all right," the older woman said. "You can use the cellar entrance by the side of the house. My daughter-in-law will give you the key."

Dom tipped his hat. "Thank you, madam. I will need to turn off the main water supply until we're finished with the repairs."

The young woman walked Dom to the side cellar entrance. "Please don't mind her. She hates not being informed. Mr. Napoli refuses to put in a phone because he doesn't want to be disturbed when he's here."

"Sounds like he's an important man. I suspect he could use some peace and quiet," Dom said with a friendly grin.

* * * * *

I continued to unload the truck and lug pipes to the side of the house. The little girl, Rebecca, wanted to help and carried some of the small fittings. I noticed that Dom got right to work attaching a series of fuse lines to the top of the doorframe to the cellar entrance. It didn't take him more than half an hour to rig the entire basement. Dom, too excited to wait, was about to light the fuses when I shouted for him to stop.

"Don't worry. We have time to drive away."

I picked up the girl. "It's not us I'm concerned about."

I walked to the front of the house with Rebecca sitting on my shoulders. When I knocked on the front door, I lowered her to the porch and waited for someone to answer. Rebecca's mother stepped onto the porch and closed the door behind her.

"Is Rebecca getting in your way?"

"No, she's been a big help."

"My name's Margie," she said, extending her hand.

"Are you visiting, or do you live here?" I asked.

"We moved in with my mother-in-law after my husband died in the war. I had no other option. Sometimes I think she blames me for not stopping him from joining the army."

"I'm sorry for your loss. A lot of good men sacrificed their lives. I was one of the lucky ones who made it back in one piece."

I needed to find a way to get the three of them out of the house. The only thing I could come up with was to tell the truth.

"Would you mind walking around to where we're working? I have something to show you."

When we got to the bottom of the steps, Rebecca ran over to a swing that hung from an old tree. As we walked toward the swing, I asked Margie if she knew much about Mr. Napoli.

"Just that he's in the import business. My husband never talked about Mr. Napoli, other than to say that he was good to him and his mother."

"Then I'm afraid what I'm about to tell you is going to come as a shock, but I need you to stay calm and listen carefully."

She rushed over to her daughter and snatched her off the swing. Her sudden reaction told me she hadn't been straight with me. She no doubt knew she was living in a mobster's house and sensed trouble.

With Rebecca in her arms, she was about to run toward the house when I grabbed her around the waist and put my hand over her mouth to smother a scream.

"He's a ruthless Mafia boss and I believe you know that's true. He recently killed innocent people in my neighborhood and attempted to kill me and my parents. I need to stop him."

The sudden sadness in her eyes told me I could let her go, and I did.

"I know who he is," she said. "I had nowhere else to live, no one else to ask for help except my husband's mother."

"We mean you no harm, but I must convince Napoli that he needs to end what he's started. The only way I know how to do that is to destroy everything he owns. If that doesn't work, I will kill him."

I walked to the side of the house and stood by the brick steps that led to the basement door. I waved her over. At first she hesitated, but then came and stood at my side.

"We've attached dynamite to all the main support columns. Five minutes after we light the fuses attached to the doorframe, this place will be a pile of rubble."

"My mother-in-law!"

"That's why I'm telling you this. I need your help to get her outside, and we don't have much time."

"I know her. With strangers on the grounds, she won't leave the house unprotected. She has a shotgun by the front door."

"Then we need to give her a good reason. Is that your car parked in front of our truck?"

"Yes, my husband bought it before he left for overseas."

"Give me the keys. Put Rebecca in the backseat and then run into the house screaming that your daughter's hurt. Get your mother-in-law to sit in the back with her. Before she realizes Rebecca's fine, I'll have us down by the entrance away from the house."

She hesitated and put the keys back in her pocket. Dom had had enough delays. He lit the main fuse. As soon as Margie saw the smoke and heard the hissing sound, she ran toward her car with Rebecca. I couldn't take the chance that the old lady wouldn't leave the house, so I headed for the back door. By the time I rounded the side of the building, Dom was already starting up our truck. When I heard Margie screaming for her mother-in-law to help her daughter, I kicked in the back door and ran down a long dark hallway toward the front entrance. The old lady grabbed her shotgun and would've taken me out if Margie hadn't opened the front door and pulled her off balance. The shotgun went off, shattering the hall chandelier. I hit the old biddy hard in full stride and heaved her over my shoulder, ripping the shotgun from her hand. Margie had the car running and hopped into the driver's seat. The old bitch was struggling to get out of my grip, so I ran past the car down the driveway with her bouncing on my shoulder. Dom had the truck parked by the estate's entrance with the engine running. Margie drove past me, kicking up gravel, and swerved off the driveway into some bushes to avoid ramming Dom's truck. I was only halfway to the entrance when I veered off into the foliage. The old lady struggled and screamed the entire time and even tried to bite into my back. Her screeches were drowned out by a horrendous explosion that lifted the house off its foundation. It obliterated the structure. I plopped her against the trunk of a large oak tree and clocked her one. She never got a good look at me, and I wanted to keep it that way.

I went over to Margie to make sure she and her daughter were unharmed. Satisfied, I took the keys out of the ignition so they couldn't get help or follow us. Margie sat behind the wheel crying.

"I'm sorry, I had no choice," I said.

"What are we to do now? I have nowhere to go."

I shook her shoulder to get her attention. "Margie, if you don't cooperate with the cops, I'll find you and get you a job. I promise."

I hopped into the truck with Dom, and we took off. Dom turned onto a dirt road that would take us back to the barn where my car was stashed. Looking back to see if any cop cars had responded to the thunderous explosion and the billowing cloud of smoke, I noticed we were kicking up a small dust storm as we sped away.

"Dom, we need to stop and hoof it or we'll get caught. You can see our dust trail for miles."

He pulled off to the side of the road and drove behind a row of barren trees. He stood on top of the roof of the cab to get his bearings.

"The barn's just beyond this field. Damn, you should see this. The coastal road is swarming with cop cars heading toward the explosion. We need to get the hell out of here," he shouted.

He grabbed several sticks of dynamite out of the satchel in the back of the truck, and tucked some inside his shirt. He took a coil of slow-burning fuse line out, attached one end to a stick of dynamite and dropped the stick back into the satchel. He uncoiled the line as we ran across the field toward the barn, puffing on a cigarette. When the fuse line was uncoiled, he inserted the end near the bottom of the cigarette and placed the cigarette between two rocks to keep it upright to assure it would burn down to the fuse.

"The cops will have a roadblock up before we can get off the main road. When this truck blows, it should give us a diversion to make a run for it if we're in a pinch," he said. Satisfied that the fuse would light, we headed toward the barn.

Dom made his way around the front of the barn and gave the all clear. In no time we were on the road back to the city.

We hadn't gotten very far when we saw Martha coming toward us. She waved us to follow her and pulled off the main road.

"Hop in. The cops are stopping every car and pulling over anyone who looks suspicious."

"We thought you'd be in the city by now," I said, as Dom and I ditched our coveralls.

"I hung around in case something went wrong."

Martha and I got in the backseat of her car. I told Dom to drive, but he sauntered over to my car instead and lit a cigarette. After a few puffs he pulled the last of the dynamite out of his shirt, tossed all but one stick into the back seat. He took a few more drags, fiddled with the fuse and placed the last of the dynamite with the others. He ran over to Martha's car and we took off again.

"What was that all about?" I asked.

"Just a little more insurance. Your car would have led the cops right to your door."

"What's he talking about?" Martha asked.

"It's an old trick kids use to give them a chance to get away when they light off firecrackers in front of a store or someone's apartment door. The cigarette acts as a delayed fuse. My car should go up in flames in a few minutes."

As we drove onto a straightaway, we spotted a police barricade a mile down the road. Dom drove up to the line of cop cars and pulled over to where he was directed.

"Where are you guys headed?" an officer asked.

"Back to the city. We came out for a picnic lunch and to look at some of the mansions along the road."

The cop noticed the basket in the front seat and was about to wave us through when an explosion went off in the distance, followed by another not far from the barricade. Several of the parked cop cars broke ranks and raced toward the smoke.

"You guys better get the hell out of here. Looks like we got a lunatic on the loose."

"Good luck, officer," Dom said and drove away.

I didn't know what was waiting for us back at the neighborhood, but one thing I knew for sure was that Big Ben would either capitulate or go on a rampage.

* * * * *

Once on the Manhattan side of the Queensboro Bridge, Dom drove into Big Ben's neighborhood. He wanted to see the results of his handiwork from the other night. I didn't try to stop him. I too was curious to see if the mason jars we'd hung down Big Ben's chimney had worked the way he had designed. The street was blocked off by wooden barricades, so we parked and went in on foot. A horrific sight confronted us when we turned the corner and looked at what was left of Big Ben's building. The top floor was gone and the remaining building gutted. Dom's jaw dropped when he saw the damage. He turned to a group of young men standing near us.

"What the hell happened?" he asked, pointing to the building.

"Our local boss got his ass kicked, is what happened," one of them said.

"Anyone killed?" Martha asked.

"Nah, my old man was there. A fire broke out, then some shots were fired. Everyone had made it to the main stairwell and was headed down when an explosion tore into the top floor."

"The papers say we got ourselves a Mafia war," another man said, "and by the number of dead bodies from the other night, and now this, I'd say we're losing."

We headed back to our car. This time I drove, and Dom sat in the back with Martha. I didn't want to take any more side trips. I was more anxious than ever to check on our own neighborhood.

Dom looked out the back window at the damage again and mumbled something about getting a patent.

Chapter 9

The two cars barricading the entrance to Market Street separated when Tony the Butcher waved us through. I had just cleared the opening as my uncle Luigi stepped out from behind a parked truck with a chopper slung over his shoulder. I stopped the car in the middle of the street and went to greet him, eager to find out if Big Ben had retaliated for the devastation we had brought to his doorstep.

Luigi grabbed my outstretched hand and yanked me into one of his brutal bear hugs.

"Glad you made it back—what you did these last two days will be remembered for generations."

"Only if we win this feud with Big Ben, and to do that I need to breathe again," I said, squirming to break his grip.

"Sorry, I'm just so glad to see you."

"Same here," I said, stepping back. "Has Big Ben reacted?"

"Not yet. The neighborhood is sealed off and on the lookout for strangers. So far there's been no one other than the two torpedoes Big Ben sent over the other night, but you already know about them."

"What about Carmine?"

"His organization is back to full strength. If you ask me, he's taken on some unsavory characters, though."

"I was afraid that would happen."

"Not much we can do about it now, nor should we. Rumor has it Big Ben's businesses are in chaos and he's flipped the rails. Neither he nor his crews know what the hell to do next. I'm also hearing grumblings that his men are anxious about getting paid."

"Sounds like we have old Ben right where we want him. I gotta believe Vigliotti's gonna step into this mess and put an end to our dispute. He needs the dough Big Ben brings into the coffers."

Luigi agreed, and then he hit me with a bombshell. "So far I've given you the good news, but there's something else. It has to do with O'Reilly. Don't worry, he's not hurt. Check with Jackie. She knows more than I do. I don't want to give you bum information."

Before I could question him, a car pulled in behind Martha's, and the driver got out and pounded on Martha's hood, demanding that Dom move his heap of junk out of the way. Dom popped out of the driver's side and the two went at it.

"You better get to Dom before he kills that drunk," Luigi warned as he moved aside to let me pass.

Martha had gotten behind the wheel and maneuvered her car to the curb. I yanked Dom off the poor sap, who lay sprawled on the street in his own vomit, blood pouring from his busted nose. It wasn't easy to get Dom into the back seat.

"Get us home now," I said to Martha, holding Dom in a firm grip.

"Why? What's up?"

"I don't know yet, but Luigi said Jackie has some bad news about O'Reilly."

Martha hit the gas pedal and narrowly missed sideswiping an oncoming ice truck. You'd think I would have learned by now never to give Martha a direct order. She either throws it back in my face or takes it to the extreme. With Martha, there's no middle ground.

*****

When we got home, Ma had an antipasti salad waiting in the icebox, pasta fagioli soup simmering on the stove, and freshly made bread lying on a carving board in the middle of the table. She, along with Rosalie and Sadie, had anticipated our return from Long Island. Although they were glad to see us, their mood was somber.

"You heard?" Ma asked me.

"Luigi stopped us on the way home. Where's Jackie?"

"She's with Frank in his office. But, Joey, Vigliotti picked up Pop earlier to go visit Castellano and he said he wanted to see you as soon as you returned."

"He'll have to wait," I said. I headed for the stairs.

Dom had pulled up a chair and smothered a slice of bread with butter. As I took the steps two at a time, I heard him bragging about the destruction of Big Ben's house. To use his words—a feat of brilliant engineering. Martha and Sadie followed me to Frank's office, leaving Ma and Rosalie to humor Dom as he exaggerated the complexity of his job.

When we entered the office, Frank was sitting at his desk reading a report, with Jackie leaning over his shoulder. Jackie looked up first and ran to give me a hug, but I held her back.

"What's goin' on?" I asked.

"I can't believe no one told you. O'Reilly got pinched for a murder rap."

All I could imagine was that the DA had found a way to frame O'Reilly. He hated his guts and mine, but I thought for sure he'd come after me first. I'm the one who had shoved a gun in his gut and would have finished him off if Jackie hadn't stopped me.

"We were just going through the homicide report again when you entered," Frank said. "O'Reilly's wife was found dead in bed with another guy. She was shot once. The boyfriend wasn't so lucky. Whoever killed them emptied the rest of his clip into him and pulverized his face with the butt of the gun."

"How bad does it look for O'Reilly?" I asked.

Frank handed me the report, but Martha grabbed it first. "Bad," Frank said. "He was in the apartment shortly after the shots were fired and was taken down by three of his neighbors who had gone to investigate and found him there holding a gun."

"What's O'Reilly's side of the story?"

Jackie moved in closer. "Sorry, Joey. Our time with O'Reilly was limited by the prosecutor's office. All we got out of O'Reilly is that he swears he didn't do it. Frank is working on getting a court order to lift the DA's restrictions."

Frank went back to his desk and picked up a special edition of the paper. "Look, Joey. Jackie and I can handle O'Reilly's case for now. I think you have a more urgent problem. A lot of big shots on Long Island are upset that one of their own was attacked on their precious island. They're calling for someone's head. You better have a good alibi."

I skimmed through the article and gave the paper back to Frank. "Big Ben isn't gonna drop a dime on me or Carmine. He knows better than to break the Mafia's code of silence. It's Dom I'm worried about. The caretaker at Big Ben's house got a good look at his face, and Dom always had trouble keeping his trap shut. He's downstairs bragging about his exploits right now. If the DA discovers he's an explosives expert, we'll end up in the clink."

"Then I suggest you get Dom to move out and to keep his trap shut. As you read, there's a huge reward for any information that leads to an arrest. Those elites want to send a clear message that any threat to their exclusive cocoon will be dealt with severely," Frank said.

I could think of only one solution, and that was to call the Colonel. He agreed to send men over immediately to pick up Dom and hold him for a few weeks until things blew over. The Colonel had a couple of men stationed at a recruiting center in the ferry terminal, so he didn't think it would take them long to arrive.

When I hung up the phone, I turned to Martha. "Tell Luigi that the military will be entering the neighborhood. Have him keep the street open until they leave."

She didn't budge. "This is no way to treat a friend. Without Dom we would've been caught."

"It's for his own good, and ours. He'll calm down when he thinks it through."

"I hope you're right, because I wouldn't want him comin' after me," Martha said, handing Frank back the homicide report.

I knew I should be there when the MPs arrived, but I had to know more about O'Reilly's situation. As soon as Martha left, I turned to Jackie.

"Have you investigated the crime scene?"

"The apartment is guarded around the clock. The homicide cops and the coroner's office are still collecting evidence."

"What about the neighbors? Did they have anything to say that might be helpful?"

Jackie picked up a steno pad from Frank's desk. "I talked to everyone on O'Reilly's floor. No one saw or heard anything unusual until the shots were fired."

"Did O'Reilly's wife have frequent visitors when he was working?"

"Not that anyone would say. A guy on the first floor said he heard the fire escape rattle a few times a month, late at night, but didn't give it any mind. He suspected that some of the young ladies in the building were having company their parents would find objectionable. His attitude was that it wasn't any of his business."

I'd forgotten that Sadie was in the room until she cleared her throat.

"Sadie, have you heard anything?" I asked.

"You know how this neighborhood works. There are no secrets. If the rumors are true, O'Reilly's wife was a bit of a chippy and skated around with more than one sugar daddy behind his back. Sorry, Joey, I know that doesn't help, but the DA will find out."

Before I could say anything, Frank slammed the police report down on his desk. "Great, that changes everything. I was going on the assumption he's innocent."

"You don't know O'Reilly like I do. He would never kill someone in cold blood. Not even his cheating wife."

"Maybe so, but I wouldn't bet on it. I can't say what I would do in a similar situation, especially if I had a gun on me. Besides, didn't you tell me he took out the guy who killed his kid brother?"

"That's different," I said in O'Reilly's defense.

"Different? You think it's different? His job is to arrest people, not be judge and jury. Look, Joey, I know he's your friend, but don't let that blind you to the truth. All

I'm saying is that we need to go where the evidence takes us."

"Then I suggest we gather more information before we jump to conclusions that are based on speculation," I shouted, moving toward Frank's desk.

There was a commotion downstairs.

Jackie stepped in front of me. "Joey, you better go talk to Dom right now. Then get over to the hospital before Vigliotti leaves. Your mom said he seemed overly agitated."

"Frank and I need to finish this conversation."

"Then let's meet for dinner at Maria's tonight at six. We'll try to have more details by then," Jackie said.

* * * * *

When I entered the kitchen, the table was overturned, and Dom was standing against the wall holding off two military police officers with a carving knife.

"Sir, we have orders from Colonel Benton to take you into protective custody. Put down the knife and come along peacefully," one of the officers ordered, his hand hovering near his holster.

I waved the other officer over and asked if I could have a few minutes alone with Dom. I explained that I was the one who had asked the Colonel to pick up Dom. He agreed. They backed out of the room and stepped outside onto the stoop to have a smoke.

"What's goin' on?" Dom shouted at me.

"I'm not gonna talk to you until you put down the knife and help me pick up this table."

Dom looked at me, then over to Ma and Rosalie, who

were backed up against the sink, holding each other. Dom put the knife down and apologized to them both.

We righted the table and sat on opposite ends. "Dom, I'm sorry, but I had no choice."

"What the hell does that mean? I thought we were in the clear."

"There's a huge reward for the capture of those who destroyed Big Ben's vacation home and that caretaker woman got a good look at you. The cops will have your description and possibly a sketch. Trust me, it won't take long for the DA to come nosing around here."

"Why would he do that?"

"Because anyone with a brain knows there's a feud goin' on between Carmine and Big Ben. We destroyed Big Ben's apartment building and blew up his summer home. Where else are they gonna look?"

"Why pick on me? You think the cops don't have a description of *you*? That young woman wasn't blind and the old lady was pretty sharp."

"The caretaker never gave me a second look. I was just a lowly helper. Besides, when I dropped her off my shoulder, I sapped her before she hit the ground."

"What about her daughter-in-law and the kid?"

"Look, Dom. I don't have time to argue with you. You're a demolition expert, and you're living in my uncle's apartment building. I need to get you the hell out of here."

"If you want to get rid of me, why not stash me in a brothel?"

I struggled to hold back a chuckle.

"Two weeks, maybe three, and then you're on your own—out of the military."

"You're sure?"

"I have the Colonel's word. You just need to stay out of trouble."

Dom pushed his chair back and paced by me a few times. "I don't like this one bit, but I'll go along. If I get nabbed, and the Colonel's pulled into this mess, he'll have us both killed. He always follows through on his promises and threats."

I stood and offered Dom my hand. He shook it.

"I don't know how to thank you, Dom. Ma told me the syndicate boss of Little Italy wants to see me. I'm sure he's gonna call for Carmine and Big Ben to come to terms."

"Hey, if he doesn't, there's always that pier warehouse to blow. I was so looking forward to that challenge," Dom said. He walked out of the apartment in the custody of the military police.

I expected a real tongue lashing from Ma, but when she came over, she pulled me into a hug. "I don't understand what you just did to Dom, but I know it was for his own good or you're not the man I raised." She pushed me back. "Now take a shower, you need one, and get over to the hospital and hope that Vigliotti hasn't left."

Chapter 10

I was out the door and headed for the hospital in less than fifteen minutes, showered, clean shaven, and holding Pop's car key in my hand. As soon as I entered Castellano's room, Vigliotti shoved me back into the hall.

"We need to talk," he said.

"I came to see Castellano."

He pushed me into an empty office. "That can wait. Didn't I make it clear that Ben's family was off limits?"

"Tell that to Castellano, and when you're done, tell me why you think Big Ben's sons weren't involved in Castellano's shooting and the death of all those innocent people—including a baby!"

"That was unfortunate," Vigliotti said.

If he wasn't the most powerful underworld figure in New York City, I would have smashed his head against the wall.

"Unfortunate! Those bastards shot up the pizza joint and my uncle's apartment without caring who they murdered. I'm telling you, if my parents had been killed, Big Ben would be dead, and *you* wouldn't be standing here."

Vigliotti shook his head.

"You need to get this through that thick skull of yours. There's a line you don't cross, and you're damn close. I have great respect for your uncle Torrio in Chicago, but our friendship only goes so far. You get what I mean? I don't know how you managed to shut down Big Ben's businesses and destroy just about everything he owns in the last few days, but I'll tell you this, if you killed his sons, you, your family, your friends, your partner—all dead—and your precious neighborhood, burned to the ground. On this you have my word."

It was time to back off. "His sons are alive."

"Good! That's what I wanted to hear, from *your* mouth. Bring them to my meeting tomorrow morning at nine. I'm putting an end to this nonsense. We have enough to deal with without fighting among ourselves. I made it clear to Carmine that my pronouncement during the meeting will be final. If you or he won't accept that, I'll be glad to pay for your funerals."

Vigliotti stormed from the office, leaving me wondering how the hell I was going to locate Big Ben's sons with O'Reilly rotting in a jail cell.

I called Frank's office and caught him on the way out the door for another meeting with O'Reilly. I told him O'Reilly was the only one who knew where Big Ben's sons were stashed in the prison system and that I needed them in my office no later than eight the next morning.

* * * * *

Maria, the proprietress of La Cucina Restaurant, was glad to see us. With Castellano in the hospital, and her other regular customers afraid to go anywhere near one of his haunts, the place was nearly empty. Soon after Frank, Jackie, and I had arrived, Pop and Martha joined us.

"Martha mentioned you guys were meeting to get O'Reilly out of his jam. I wanna help," Pop said.

I didn't argue because I knew O'Reilly's old man had once saved Pop's life. Pop needed to repay that debt.

We gave Maria our food order and got down to business. Jackie spoke up first.

"You remember the night O'Reilly drove us to the hospital to drop off Cafiero? Well, he didn't go back to headquarters as he intended. He was tired and called it an early night."

"So his wife didn't expect him home for an hour or so," I said.

"That's right."

"Did O'Reilly tell you what happened?"

Frank took over the narrative.

"He heard shots when he drove by his apartment building looking for a parking space. He ran up the stairs and entered his apartment to make sure his wife was okay. He didn't know where the shots had come from, but they sounded like they came from his floor or the roof. His apartment was the only one with a light on."

"What happened next?"

"He heard a noise coming from the bedroom, and when he opened the door, he saw a horrific site. His wife and some guy were sprawled on the bed, naked, drenched in blood. The wall behind them, splattered red. He didn't know how long he stood in the doorway before a brisk breeze rushed through an open window and swirled the drapes into the room. He then heard the fire escape rattle as someone scurried down. Rather than chase after the person, he went to his wife. She was choking on her own blood, shot in the neck. The bullet had severed her carotid. There was nothing he could do. She died as he went to her. The guy had been shot multiple times in the back. As I said earlier, his face was caved in by the butt of a gun. The gun was on the bed between the bodies. O'Reilly, still in shock, picked up the weapon because it looked like one of his. About that time, his neighbors got the courage to investigate and found him leaning over the dead guy holding a bloody gun in his hand. It might take the DA's office some time to determine the identity of the stiff. It's kind of hard to identify a corpse with its face beaten to a pulp."

Jackie was almost in tears as she listened to Frank. "O'Reilly confided in me a few weeks ago that he suspected his wife was cheating on him, but he didn't want to believe it," she said.

I thought there must be a reason O'Reilly had been drinking heavily again. "Why the hell didn't he tell me?" I asked, more to myself than either of them.

"Come on, Joey, no guy wants to admit to another that his wife is cheating on him," Frank said.

I knew Frank was right, but it was still frustrating. I felt a need to do something. "I want into that apartment tonight."

"That's impossible," Frank said. "It's still an active crime scene."

Pop poured himself a drink. "I know a way. The building next to his is identical, and the alley windows line up. All you'll need is a twelve-foot ladder to span between the window sills. That should give us about two feet for leverage."

"Pop, can you make the necessary arrangements so we can get in tonight, say around ten? After we finish dinner, the girls and I need to lay out how we're gonna deal with everything else that's happening. Jackie and Martha will be running the office after today. I'm heading for Detroit mid-afternoon if the meeting I have with Vigliotti goes the way I expect."

"And if it doesn't?" Martha asked.

"If it doesn't, O'Reilly's on his own, because we'll be fighting for *our* lives."

"Wait a minute. Who decided you should go to Detroit by yourself?" Jackie asked.

I removed my napkin from the table. "That's why we need to talk."

Two waiters brought over our food, and Maria filled the wine glasses with her best Chianti, compliments of Luigi's speakeasy. One of the advantages of living in the neighborhood that controls the waterfront was that our speakeasies got the best booze smuggled in from other countries. Pop ordered two more bottles. We ate and drank in silence.

* * * * *

When I got to the vacant apartment opposite O'Reilly's, Pop had everything ready. All we had to do was maneuver the ladder into position.

"How did you get in here?"

"The super is a friend of mine, and I guess it helped that I promised him a pair of custom-made shoes."

It was slow going as we inched the ladder out the window toward O'Reilly's apartment across the narrow alleyway. For an old man, Pop was still surprisingly strong after years of tanning leather. Between the two of us we were able to push down on the end of the ladder enough to keep it elevated as we inched it out the window to rest on O'Reilly's windowsill. Once in place, Pop secured the ladder to radiators on either side of the window using two sections of heavy rope.

"Why's that necessary?" I asked.

"Unless you're a hell of a lot stronger than you look, there's no way we can prevent the ladder from falling when we pull it back off the windowsill. The sudden loss of support will rip it out of our hands. Now, tell me how you're gonna get from here to there without goin' over the edge?"

"Not a problem."

I cat-walked across the ladder and was in O'Reilly's apartment in less than two minutes.

The spare bedroom led to the parlor where the door to the apartment was located. Trying to keep quiet, I sat in an armchair to the right of the door, waiting for Jackie and Martha to distract the cop assigned to watch the apartment. I thought about how ironic it would be if he and I were sitting right now with our backs to each other separated only by the apartment wall.

Martha broke the silence when she let out a shrill scream and called for help.

"What's goin' on down there?" the officer yelled.

I heard Martha running up the stairs.

"Some scruffy kid came out of nowhere and ripped my purse away. Please go after him. He can't be far."

"Sorry, madam, but I can't leave my post."

"My rent money. I'll get put out on the street."

"I got him," Jackie yelled from the lobby of the building.

"Wait here, and don't let anyone near this door," the officer said, stomping down the stairs.

"Hurry, he got away from me. He went out the front," Jackie yelled.

I heard the cop's whistle trail off as he ran down the street.

I unlocked the door and Jackie slipped inside.

"Find anything?" Jackie asked.

"Not yet. Who'd you get to help?"

"Little Johnny, he's fast. He'll get away," she said, leaning over an end table to yank the chain on a small lamp.

The door to the bedroom was ajar, and provided us with a glimpse of the horror that had taken place. The room was in stark contrast to the rest of the apartment, which was immaculate. Nothing seemed out of place. No dishes in the sink, not a speck of dust anywhere.

I entered the bedroom ahead of Jackie. The bodies had been removed. The room looked undisturbed except for the bed. Everything was just as Frank had described. If it wasn't for the blood and ruffled bed sheets, you'd never know a double murder had taken place.

"She expected company," Jackie said.

"What makes you say that?"

Jackie pointed to a corner of the room. "What do you see on that chair?"

"A folded set of sheets."

"Need I say more?"

Jackie moved toward the bed, but I held her back.

"Wait a minute. Something doesn't feel right."

I looked around the room again, and that's when I realized what felt out of place. An empty shoulder holster hung on one of the bed's backboard posts. It should've held a gun. Knowing O'Reilly, he would have kept a gun loaded and ready to fire in case someone broke in during the night.

"What's wrong?" Jackie asked.

"Hold on," I said, as I went over to inspect the holster. I only had a moment before Martha banged on the front door to warn us the cop was coming back. But it was long enough.

"We've gotta go," I said.

I took hold of Jackie's hand and led her toward the other bedroom. As I crossed the threshold, she pulled away and ran back to turn off the light. When she entered the room again and saw the ladder stretching across the alleyway, she wasn't happy.

"You expect me to crawl across that thing?"

"It's either that or go to jail. Just do as I do. When you get close, Pop and I will pull you through the window."

"Damn, did I ever tell you I hate heights? Well, I'm telling you now. This is the second time you've made me climb out a window several stories above ground."

"Look at it this way. The more you practice, the better you'll get."

I didn't move out the window fast enough. She gave me one hell of a slap. My only consolation was that Jackie's palm probably stung as much as my butt.

*****

The girls and I headed straight to Frank's office to discuss what Jackie and I had observed in O'Reilly's apartment.

Frank thought it was interesting that O'Reilly's wife was expecting her lover. "The lady was either off her rocker or enjoyed living dangerously. You know how everyone likes to gossip in this town. Tell me, how the hell did she expect to hide what was goin' on from O'Reilly?"

"Maybe she didn't," Martha said.

"That makes no sense," Frank replied.

"Give me a chance to explain before you toss my idea aside as usual," Martha said, clearly still miffed that Frank had fired her as his secretary two years ago.

Frank threw his arms in the air and took a seat behind his desk. "Fine, tell us your theory."

Martha turned to me. "Joey, didn't you once tell Jackie that O'Reilly's wife was putting pressure on him to go on the take, like most of the other cops on the force?"

"That was confidential," I blurted out.

"You didn't mention that," Jackie said.

Martha continued, "That's not important. What's important is she wanted to move up in the world. She wanted a better place to live, fancier clothes, and no doubt a few sparkles here and there."

"Get to the point," Frank said.

"She found herself a real sugar daddy who would give her those things."

"I think you're onto something," Jackie said. "O'Reilly would never give her a divorce."

"Unless she humiliated him in public," I said.

Frank shook his head. "That's all speculation. It's just as possible he caught her unaware and shot her, which is probably what he did."

"Frank, are you gonna defend O'Reilly or send him to the chair?" Jackie yelled.

"Calm down. I'll defend him whether he's innocent or not. All I'm saying is he sure had a hell of a motive, and the jury will see it that way."

It was getting late and I needed to hit the sack. "Frank, we're wasting time. You obviously have doubts. So fire away."

Frank smiled. "I'm glad to see someone in your agency has a level head." Frank quickly raised his hand to stop Martha from jumping out of her seat. "Sorry, it was a bad joke."

Frank sat on the front of his desk and folded his arms across his chest. "It's not a bad theory you have there, Martha, but I don't see some rich guy sneaking around an apartment building in this neighborhood in the middle of the night."

"I was about to make that point when I got interrupted," Martha said. "I agree. It wasn't her sugar daddy in bed with her that night. She was using another sucker to embarrass O'Reilly."

"So you're sayin' she was sleeping with two guys, maybe more. Okay, I'll buy that, given what Sadie told us earlier," Frank said. "Now, Joey, you mentioned that the apartment was immaculate. Everything was in its place. I want you to think back. Other than in the bedroom, was there anything that didn't fit or that would give us a clue as to what happened that night?"

"I'm tellin' you, Frank, the place looked like it wasn't lived in. The ashtrays were spotless; the kitchen looked like it had never been used. A coat was hanging on the coat rack. Nothing was out of place."

"That's it!" Jackie blurted out. "The coat."

"What about it?" Frank asked.

"There was a coat on the rack," Jackie said. "Given the condition of the apartment, if it was O'Reilly's coat, his wife would have hung it in the closet and not left it on the rack. There's no way that O'Reilly took the time to remove his coat when he barged into the apartment after hearing gun fire. The coat must have belonged to the guy who was shot."

"Or the guy who did the shooting," I said.

That got Frank's attention. "So, if the coat didn't belong to the dead guy, we might have some evidence to back up Martha's theory that the wife was messin' around with more than one guy. A second lover showed up unexpectedly, hung up his coat, opened the bedroom door, and found her in bed with another guy?"

"It's possible," I said. "And since everyone locks their doors at night, he must have had a key."

Frank turned to Sadie. "Are you getting all this down?"

"Every word."

"Okay, now tell me again about the empty gun holster hanging on the bed post," Frank said to me.

"I didn't get a good look, but I did notice that it was smeared with blood."

"So you're suggesting that the real killer shot them with his own piece, removed the gun from the bedpost, smeared it with blood and tossed it on the bed to make it look like O'Reilly did the killings?"

"It's a possible explanation," I said.

Frank pushed off the desk and shoved his hands into his pockets. "No jury would buy that," he said, pacing in front of us. "O'Reilly had at least two rods on him, so why would he grab the gun in the holster? And how would he have made it to the bed post to take the gun without having a tussle with the guy who died? And then there's the fact that ballistics will show that the gun isn't the murder weapon."

"How about this?" Jackie said. "The guy in bed with O'Reilly's wife hears someone in the parlor and reaches for the gun. Before he can get a shot off, he's full of lead. The killer grabs the gun and beats his face in, and for good measure shoots him again. O'Reilly kicks in the front door, the murderer panics, tosses the gun on the bed, and hightails it out the window."

"Now that's a plausible explanation," Frank said. "The problem is we could come up with a dozen more scenarios, and I'm sure the prosecutor will as well."

It was late and I had a big day ahead. Vigliotti had made it clear he wasn't going to accept any crap from anyone when we all meet in the morning. I suggested to Frank that he get a court order to allow him and Jackie access to the crime scene to do a more thorough search. He agreed.

Satisfied, I got up to leave. That's when we heard Ma screech Pop's name. As my hand touched the knob of Frank's door, a shotgun blast boomed in the hallway.

Ma, still holding her gun, was flat on her backside up against the wall that faced my open office door, shaking uncontrollably. Jackie and Martha rushed to her side as I ripped the shotgun out of her grip, tossed it aside, and entered my office crouching low to the ground with my rod drawn.

Pop was sprawled on the floor with a stranger face down on top of his legs. Both were covered in blood. The guy, still clutching a gun, had taken the full force of Ma's blast and was literally spineless in the lower part of his back. I yanked him aside and examined Pop. Except for a bruise on his forehead and a few pellet wounds to his legs, he looked unharmed. The blood that had soaked the back of his shirt was from the stranger.

Sadie entered behind me. Seeing that Pop was unharmed, she went into the bathroom and returned with a damp cloth. As she knelt beside him to wipe his face, Pop slapped her hand aside and let loose a torrent of obscenities.

"Pop, calm down! Ma's fine and you've had worse. Just tell us what happened."

"You wanna know what happened? *You* happened. Why didn't you become a butcher or a tailor? Better yet, how about a shoemaker?"

Ma, supported by Martha and Jackie, stepped forward and pointed to the stiff on the floor.

"Joey, there's the 'ordinary man' Cafiero warned you about. If Pop hadn't shouted into the apartment that he was taking some fella upstairs to see you, we might all be dead."

"How did you know for sure?" I asked.

"There was something in Pop's voice, and when was the last time your pop walked someone up to your office? I got curious and saw the gun he held against Pop's back as they climbed the stairs."

It still didn't make sense. "Pop, why would you open the door to a stranger in the middle of the night?"

Pop sat in a chair, wiping his face. "He wasn't a stranger. He moved into the neighborhood over a week ago and had me repair a pair of shoes for him. He seemed like a nice guy, so when he said it was urgent that he speak with you, I opened the door. I told him you were busy and couldn't take on new clients and suggested he come back in a month or so. That's when he pulled a rod on me. What was I supposed to do?"

"Nothing, Pop. He was gonna get in one way or another."

The girls took my folks back to their apartment and left me with a mess on my hands. I figured Carmine owed me a favor so I called. He agreed to send a crew over to dispose of the body and clean up the place.

I had a few minutes alone with the stiff before they arrived. I had underestimated Ronnie. He had hired three hit men and set them loose at the same time. He had predicted that I would rush to the clinic when I had heard about Gino and Debbie and had two ready to take me out. If they failed, he knew we would be on the lookout for other professional hit men—so he sent an "ordinary man."

Now that all three had failed, Ronnie would be waiting for me to come to him.

I left Carmine's men to clean up the mess in my office and headed downstairs to check on my folks. Satisfied they were safe, I went back upstairs to make sure Carmine's men were doing a thorough job, and then went to my place to hit the hay.

An hour later, Jackie and Martha knocked on my door, waking me out of a deep sleep.

"We've been talking, and we think you need our help in Detroit," Jackie said, as they stepped into the apartment.

I took them both by the arms and led them back into the hallway, slammed the door shut, bolted it, and went back to bed.

I knew there would be hell to pay in the morning, but that was then and this was now. I needed some rest.

Chapter 11

I got up extra early to see how Ma was doing, only to find that everyone else had had the same idea. In fact, I was the last to arrive for breakfast. All the women, except for Ma, were either cooking or setting the table. Pop and Luigi were sitting on either side of Ma trying to comfort her. Luigi had his arm around her back, and Pop was holding her hand.

She glanced up when I entered. "Joey, I've never killed anyone before."

I leaned over and gave her a kiss on the cheek. "I'm sorry this happened to you and Pop, but remember this guy killed for a living. Think of all the lives you saved, and I'm not just talking about ours."

"Joey's right," Pop said.

There was a knock on the door, and Luigi rose to answer it. Carmine entered the room ahead of him. "You can smell the bacon a block away. Hope I'm not too late."

"I didn't expect you this early," I said.

"Thought we should talk before the meeting with Vigliotti. I also wanted to make sure you'd have Big Ben's sons in tow. I don't know about you, but I'm not goin' anywhere near that meeting without them looking healthy."

"They should arrive any minute," Frank said. "I got the information from O'Reilly and made the arrangements."

"That's good," Carmine answered. "Hey Luigi, that

was quite the mess you made last night. I didn't take you for a back shooter. Who was the guy?"

"Ronnie sent another shooter to take out Joey. The bloke had a gun in Vito's back, so he left me no choice."

We had all agreed the night before to keep Ma out of the picture, so when I had called Carmine to send over a clean-up crew, I told him Luigi had taken out a torpedo.

"Damn, Joey, you've been home only two years, and you've angered just about every major crime boss from here to Chicago. You're not gonna be around long if you don't settle down," Carmine said, taking a bite of his bacon sandwich.

"I'm hopin' once we get Big Ben off your back, and I settle with Ronnie, things will calm down, and Jackie and I can get back to runnin' our detective agency."

I expected Jackie and Martha to say something, but they kept their heads down and focused on eating. It was clear they were pretty damn upset with me, since I was the only one without a plate of food and they had gone out of their way not to sit next to me. Ma noticed and roused herself to fix me a plate. I had just taken my first mouthful of scrambled eggs when Lieutenant Sullivan and one of his officers showed up with Big Ben's boys wearing prison garb and shackles.

"Joey, where do you want your new guests?"

"They can sit in the parlor for now. Everyone, this is Lieutenant Sullivan from Staten Island. He's a close friend of O'Reilly's," I said, as I introduced him to those he didn't know.

"Lieutenant, would you like something to eat?" Ma asked.

"The way O'Reilly talks about your home cookin', the

sergeant and I will have some even though we already had breakfast earlier."

"What about your prisoners?"

"Thank you, but they have their bellies full of our renowned institutional grub."

Sullivan had the good sense not to ask about O'Reilly or the feud between Big Ben and Carmine, so as soon as we finished eating, I asked him to join Carmine and me in my office. Pop and Luigi went into the parlor to entertain our guests while the ladies cleared the table and converged on the kitchen.

We were just reaching the top stairs on the second floor when we heard Jackie yelling from the parlor.

"Tell me, damn it, or I'll cut your hand off."

"Easy lady, it's only a tattoo."

"Then tell me!"

By the time we got back to the parlor, the officer was pulling Jackie back by her arms, and Luigi was holding one of her knives to the neck of Big Ben's oldest son. Martha had a gun pointed at the other brother.

"What the hell is goin' on?" I shouted.

"Look at the back of his hand," Jackie yelled. "He could be one of the bastards who killed Gino's family."

The tattoo on the back of his hand was the same as the picture Gino had drawn the day he recalled the murder of his wife and child. I was about to confront them myself when I realized they were both too young. The guys who had killed Gino's family would be in their late forties or older by now.

"Relax, all of you. This guy was just a kid when Gino lost his family. But I bet he knows something that will set us on the right path to the real killers."

I took the knife from Luigi and moved him aside. "What's your name?" I asked Ben's oldest boy.

"Bobby."

"Is that Little Bobby, Big Bobby, or what?"

"Just Bobby."

"Okay, just Bobby. I realize you don't know what's been happening to your old man, so listen closely. He's been tryin' to take over our neighborhood, and he's having some difficulty. In fact, his big, beautiful home on Long Island is no more. The same is true of his apartment building. His businesses are all collapsing, and Carmine and I are about to take you to see him and Vigliotti. You can greet your old man with one hand or two. Which will it be?"

"It's a gang symbol."

"Good. How come your brother doesn't have the same tattoo?"

"The gang broke up years ago. I was only twelve when it happened."

"Why? Why did it break up?"

"Some of the older guys left town suddenly, and there was no one left in charge. That's all I know."

I wanted to probe deeper, but Carmine interrupted.

"Joey, we gotta go. It's gettin' late."

"I know. Martha, give Luigi back his gun. Lieutenant, would you mind loading these guys into your car and following us to our meeting?"

"Not a problem, but any chance of discreetly getting them into the building will be blown when I show up."

"That's my intent. The angrier Big Ben gets, the better Carmine will look."

"You don't kid around do you, Batista."

"I learned the hard way, Lieutenant. If you're gonna play tough, you gotta take advantage of every opportunity," I said shaking his hand. "Look, I'm sure you want to know what's happening with O'Reilly's case, so why don't you come back after handing these guys over to me at Vigliotti's meeting and talk with Frank. He has the latest on where we stand in our investigation."

Before he could answer, I turned to Carmine. "I need a few minutes with the girls."

"Make it quick."

I ushered Jackie and Martha into Pop's repair shop and closed the door behind me. "Look, I'm sorry about last night. I wasn't in the mood to argue and I needed some rest. I know you're worried, but I can handle Ronnie."

"Who decided that you should make all the decisions?" Jackie demanded.

"I know we're partners, but we have other issues facing us. O'Reilly needs our help, and we just got a break in finding out who killed Gino's family. We can all go to Detroit or get back into the PI business. I need you both to stay here and take care of things."

Carmine stuck his head in the room. "We gotta go now!"

I looked back at the girls on the way out. "We can talk more when I get back from the meeting. I still need to pack."

As Carmine and I left the building, I told him that he'd have to drive, since I was minus a car at the moment.

"I heard about your great escape from Long Island," he said, tossing me a car key. "This beauty has all the latest enhancements available on the open market. It's yours. It's the least I can do."

"So, you admit I saved your life by talking you out of roaring into Big Ben's neighborhood with guns blazing."

"It would have been a hell of a way to go," Carmine said with a grin.

The Gumshoe Chronicles 1922

* * * * *

Big Ben flipped off the tracks when he saw his sons paraded into the meeting room shackled and in prison garb. But Vigliotti, who had been standing by a window, had a hard time suppressing a smile.

"Big Ben, I suggest you control yourself. You accused Batista of killing your sons without any proof. If we had acted on that reckless charge, our organization would be in shambles. Several of our families have ties to his uncle Torrio's enterprises in Chicago."

"This is an outrage and an insult to my family," Big Ben yelled.

"I wouldn't care if they were standing here naked. The only outrage is the fact that Carmine has taken down your entire organization in a matter of days."

"Carmine couldn't take down an old lady. It was Batista! If any of you had any brains, you would recognize the threat he represents."

Vigliotti pounded his fist on the table. "The only threat to this organization is you. You're an embarrassment. You're inability to protect your interests made us all look weak. If anyone is gonna leave this room feet first, it might be you."

Big Ben sat back down when he sensed the other bosses agreeing with Vigliotti.

"Carmine, take your father's seat at the table," Vigliotti said. Then he ordered two of his bodyguards to remove Big Ben's sons from the room. As they were leaving, Vigliotti gave me an order.

"Batista, give them the key to the shackles and then take a seat. I want you to hear what I have to say."

Vigliotti picked up some papers and looked around the table.

"Let me give you all some facts: dough flowing into our coffers is down by twenty percent in the last week, and rival gangs are moving into our territories eating into our drug and gambling profits. They are getting more aggressive every day, and we need to take swift action. But the first order of business is to stop this feud within our own ranks."

He paused for effect and looked at each person. "I'll take comments now from anyone except Carmine and Big Ben."

The boss of Staten Island stood. "What Mr. Vigliotti speaks of I have seen. Fear is what we need. I say we all weed out this corruption in our territories without mercy. There will be headlines for a few days, and then things will return to normal. To Carmine, I want to say this—you have shown great constraint and wisdom. If my father was shot down like a dog, I would have reacted differently and caused great harm to our organization."

The rest of the bosses stood and raised their glasses to Carmine. With that gesture of support, Vigliotti ended all further discussion.

"It is settled. We will unleash our men this week in a coordinated fashion and regain control over all our enterprises. Big Ben, you will focus your energy on rebuilding your organization. Carmine, you committed to exceed Big Ben's contribution to this organization within two years. I'm holding you to that commitment. If you don't meet it, then Big Ben will control the entire waterfront."

Big Ben stood and objected, but he was shouted down by the other bosses.

"As for you, Big Ben. If you, your sons, or anyone associated with you interferes with Carmine, you will be eliminated, and Carmine will be given control over the waterfront. Does anyone, aside from Big Ben, object?"

The question was met with silence.

"What about Batista?" Big Ben shouted.

Vigliotti didn't take his eyes off of Big Ben. "Batista, if you, your family, or any of your associates are attacked in any way, you have permission to retaliate with deadly force."

"I have a case that will take me into Big Ben's territory. Twenty-five years ago a family was murdered by two members of a local gang. I intend to find them," I said.

"You have a right to run your business. If your cases ever impact my organization, though, you will bring the matter to this council."

I agreed.

Vigliotti ended the meeting.

Big Ben pulled me aside as everyone else exited the meeting room.

"You set so much as a toe in my neighborhood, and I'll have it cut off."

"You should know something, Ben. I was just getting started when Vigliotti called this meeting. So if you want to tangle with me again, I'm ready, and this time there are no constraints placed on me by Vigliotti. As far as my investigation, I'll go wherever the hell it takes me, so I suggest you turn the other cheek."

Chapter 12

I had intended to take the train to Detroit but opted to drive now that I had a car again. I didn't know what was waiting for me when I hit Detroit, but I was confident Ronnie would have taken steps to protect himself in the event that his hitmen botched their assignment. I was walking into a trap, and I knew it. Driving would allow me to bring more gear and get the hell out of town fast—if I survived.

The girls had capitulated and agreed to stay and help Frank with O'Reilly's case, as well as look into the disbanded street gang that Ben's son had called "The Anchor Boys." Having said my goodbyes, I headed out of town loaded down with hardware that I hoped I wouldn't need.

I hadn't gotten far when I decided to take a short detour to visit Castellano in the hospital. When I arrived, Castellano was sitting up in bed talking with Angela, Carmine's wife.

"Joey, I was hoping you'd stop by. I heard you're heading out to confront Ronnie," Castellano said.

"I guess its tough keeping secrets in this town."

"Don't kid yourself. You can be sure Ronnie knows you're coming, and he won't wait until you arrive to stop you."

"I can deal with whatever he has planned, but just in case, I came by to see you. I wanted to express my appreciation for all you've done for our neighborhood over the years."

"To be honest, Joey, life in America didn't turn out the

way any of us expected, but it's still better than in the old country. I have a lot of regrets, but in my defense, all I can say is I was often confronted with choosing between two evils."

I thought back to the conversation we had months ago when he explained how his organization made money for the syndicate. I couldn't say if given the same choices he'd had that I would have done anything differently. At least he had shielded us from most of the corruption that infected other neighborhoods.

"Mr. Castellano, you have nothing to be ashamed of. Compared to the rest of the city, we are an oasis in a moral cesspool."

"A cesspool I helped create. But all that's behind me. Just call me Castellano from now on. My son just informed me that he's now Mr. Castellano and expects everyone to show him that sign of respect."

"Frankly, I don't give a damn what Carmine expects. To me, you will always be Mr. Castellano."

"I appreciate that. Let me give you some advice about Ronnie. When you think you have him cornered, you don't. Expect the unexpected. He's devious and will lead you in the direction that he wants."

"I'll keep that in mind."

"One more thing," Castellano said. "That Cafiero guy, the hitman Ronnie hired, walked out of the hospital a few hours ago. Thought you should know."

"Thanks, but how do you know about him?"

"I may not be the boss anymore, but that doesn't mean I don't have connections or give a damn about what happens to my friends."

Angela joined me in the hallway.

"How's he doing?" I asked.

"He intends to return to his home on Staten Island next week when he's discharged. He asked me to continue living with him to help out."

"It's gonna feel strange without him watching over the neighborhood."

"His feelings for his friends run deep. He'll stay informed, and no doubt step in if he has to," Angela said.

"What about Carmine? It'll be tough for him to run things from the Island."

"He'll be staying in the city. Since little Antonio was killed by Butch, Carmine hasn't even spoken to me. I don't think he would care if I disappeared. In fact, I think he would prefer that I did."

I gently pulled her close, and she responded by kissing my cheek. As we separated, I saw moisture in her eyes.

"Thanks, Joey. I needed to know someone cared."

"Hey, you never forget your first love, even if we were only six."

It was good to see her smile.

* * * * *

I had a plan for dealing with Ronnie. To pull it off I needed to hit Detroit close to sunrise on the day of my arrival; so my late start didn't concern me. I took the time to veer down back roads once I was out of the city, to assure that I wasn't being followed. I did have to stop every now and then to ask for directions back to the main road, but the overall delay was worth the peace of mind knowing that I wouldn't be driving into an ambush.

Rather than spend the first night in a roadside inn,

I took a chance that I would find a place to bed down off the beaten path. I was having no luck finding signs of life along a deserted, rutted road when I noticed a light off in the distance down a two-track dirt path. Up to that point it had looked like I'd be spending the night in the car as the sun was setting behind a densely forested hillside. The two-track led to a small farm house with a crusty-looking old man rocking in a chair on a dimly lit porch, smoking a corn pipe. A bloodhound stood beside him making a hell of a ruckus. As I came to a stop in front of the porch, the image of the old man reminded me of a cover you might find on *The People's Home Journal*, one of Ma's favorite magazines.

I got out of the car, walked slowly around the front, and leaned against the passenger door.

"I'm lookin' for a place to bed down for the night."

The old man stopped rocking. "You're either lost or one of those rum runners. Which is it?"

"I'm headin' to Detroit on business and thought I'd get a feel for the backcountry."

He spit over the side railing. "That's too bad. My supply of hooch is runnin' low."

Before I left, I noticed that one of the modifications Carmine had made to the car was two concealed compartments under the backseat. Luigi had stored away a few bottles of Canadian scotch among the hardware he had loaded into the car.

"It so happens I never travel without a few bottles of the finest, just for occasions like this. I'll trade you a couple of bottles for a blanket and a night in that barn," I said, pointing to an old building in disrepair.

"That depends. Pull up a rocker and let me see ya up close."

I rummaged through the car to find the booze, moving some of the hardware to the top of the back seat. The modifications Pop and my uncle had made to a Tommy gun were impressive. Two drums were attached to a slide bar that doubled the capacity. The slide bar also made it easier to change out the drums and reload. The disadvantage was that it was now bulky and damn heavy.

"You gonna take all day?" the old coot yelled.

"Just tryin' to find the hooch," I said, as I closed the compartments, leaving the Tommy gun and an extra set of drums on the back seat.

I handed him the bottles and sat down in a rocker that needed a coat of paint. The old man grinned and called out to someone in the house.

"Peggy, we have company. Set another plate." He smiled again and laughed. "I bet a city boy like you ain't never ate no rabbit stew."

"I haven't had it in many years, but it's one of my favorite dishes. Growing up I had a friend who was a hell of a shot and did all the fixings herself."

"Country girl, no doubt."

"Yes, she was," I said, looking away.

Peggy came onto the porch and introduced herself. I was surprised to see a young girl, no more than nineteen, living in the middle of nowhere with an old man.

"I'm Joey Batista, nice to meet you. I appreciate your hospitality," I said.

The old man must have noticed my hesitation as I shook her hand.

"Peggy came to live with me and the missus when she was ten. She'd come to visit us the day before her parents, my son and his wife, died in a fire, and she's never left. Her grandmother, my missus, passed away a few years back."

"Here, Pops, let me help you up. There's no sense in thinking about those things. We have each other and that's what counts," Peggy said as she walked her grandfather into the house.

"Young man, don't forget my booze. I'll need a sip tonight. Helps me sleep. But don't you try any shenanigans with my Peggy. I have a shotgun by my bed and I know how to use it." He reached down and patted his dog who sat next to his feet. "Old Grumpy here will tell me if you're movin' about."

"I'm sure he will," I said, glancing at Peggy, who had covered her face with her hands to hide the blush that blossomed on her cheeks.

"Don't mind him. I'm old enough to take care of myself," she said with a smile.

Peggy dished out the stew, sat down, took hold of my hand and her grandfather's, and said grace.

The old man insisted that I call him Pops, as we shared two rounds of drinks on the porch. After he went to bed, Peggy and I chatted for a few hours. She wanted to know all about New York. She was fascinated with how Prohibition had changed people's behavior and she'd read stories about the Mafia. Once she discovered that I had been in the war and was now a private investigator, she asked even more questions. I finally suggested that it was time for me to bed down because I wanted to get an early start.

Peggy walked me to the barn with a lantern and helped spread out some hay. The barn was big enough for my car, so I drove it in to keep it out of sight, just in case I'd been followed. Peggy jumped in the car to get a good look at the inside. Her grandfather's car looked old enough to be one of the first Fords built. I forgot that I had the Tommy gun in the backseat until she noticed it.

"What in the world is that thing? It looks like a gun I saw in a magazine, but it's different."

I took the Tommy gun from the car. "I never know what I'm gonna run into in my line of work," I said, loading a set of drums.

I was so focused on demonstrating how the gun worked that I hadn't noticed that Peggy had moved away.

"Is there anything else you need?" she asked.

"No, I'm good."

"Well, I better get back to the house. Good night, Mr. Batista."

"Good night, Peggy, and thanks for a delicious meal."

The light from the lantern she held faded as she closed the barn door.

* * * * *

I should have had an easy time falling asleep on a bed of hay listening to the natural sounds of the countryside, but Castellano's warnings kept swirling in my mind. I couldn't stop thinking through my plan for dealing with Ronnie, over and over. I was finally feeling that foggy haze that engulfs you just before you doze off when the barn door creaked on its rusty hinges. Peggy slipped in and gently closed the door. She held her lantern high and hung it on a nail behind me. Without saying a word, she sat down beside me, pulled her legs up to her chest, and rested her cheek on her knees. I sat up and leaned against a bale of hay.

"Is everything okay?" I asked.

"I was wondering, on your way back from Detroit, if you would take me to visit New York City."

My first instinct was to send her back to the house before her grandfather realized she was in the barn with me. He might be old, but I was sure he knew how to use his shotgun.

"You better get back to bed. We can talk about this in the morning with your grandfather."

She leaned forward to get up, but instead she straddled my lap and kissed me on the neck.

"Peggy, you don't want to do this. I'm a stranger passing by; you'll never see me again."

"Maybe that's best," she said, brushing her lips along my cheek. "In a small town, everyone gossips. Besides, no one ever comes to visit. Pops gets his checks in the mail, and we keep to ourselves."

She moved in close again and laid her cheek against mine. "I've never been to the city, just to the general store down the road. You won't regret taking me. I'll make a good companion."

I heaved her off my lap and plopped her down alongside me. "Are you saying you've never traveled outside this area? What about school?"

Peggy took a deep breath and pouted, grabbing hold of her knees again. "My grandmother taught me my lessons. Pops worked the farm, but now he just sits in his rocking chair and rents out the land."

I found the thought of her sitting on that porch alone someday depressing.

I was about to ask her if she had any other relatives when Grumpy, her bloodhound, let out a howl like a banshee.

"Oh no! Pops will find us," she said.

That was the least of my fears. The dog was making too much of a racket. Something was up. As I slipped on my shoulder holsters, I heard several cars screech to an abrupt stop. I peered out of the crack separating the barn doors and saw three cars parked in a haphazard circle and three men checking things out with guns ready. Castellano had been right. I should have anticipated the unexpected. I had been looking over my shoulder for one car trailing me, not three different ones. They had probably followed me the entire way out of the city and waited for night to make their move. But I couldn't figure out how the hell they knew I was here? I would have noticed if one of them had followed me on the back roads.

Peggy stood by my side. "What's goin' on?"

"I don't have time to explain. Get to the back of the barn and hide behind something that can stop a bullet."

She clutched my arm with incredible strength and turned me around. "What have you done? Why have you brought these people here?"

I grabbed her by the back of the head and kissed her on the forehead. "You need to trust me. I won't let anything happen to you or Pops. Now find a place to hide."

She ran past my car and hid behind several bales of hay stacked three layers deep. Satisfied she was safe, I slowly backed away from the barn doors with both guns ready and blew out the lantern. Suddenly a faint light streamed through the slit where the barn doors met. The house porch light had come on. I had to move fast to draw the gunmen's attention away from the old man.

I holstered my rods and pulled my uncle's modified Tommy gun out of the car, kicked open the barn door, and hit the ground firing. The guy coming toward me got off a few rounds before he was filled with lead. One of his bullets struck the metal base of the lantern. A spark from the bullet ignited the kerosene as it poured onto the hay where Peggy and I had been sitting. Flames surged up to the loft and flared out the small hayloft doors above me.

I was about to run through the flames to get Peggy when I heard glass shatter and the old man yelling like a madman.

"Get the hell off my land, you no good sons of bitches."

One of the remaining two goons shot at the window as he ran up the porch toward the door. I was about to take him out when two bullets whizzed past my head. Without thinking, I dove alongside a water trough for cover. With my face planted in mud, I heard the front door to the house being kicked in and then two shotgun blasts. I took a chance that the old man had nailed the guy who had busted in his door and started firing nonstop, hoping to draw the attention of the last guy, who was shielded by the parked cars. He got off two more erratic shots before ducking down. I knew that the Tommy gun was lousy for accuracy, but I was still amazed that I hadn't even winged him. Sensing that he had me in a vulnerable position, he let loose a hellish volley of bullets, some piercing the wood trough just above my outstretched body.

Peggy was trapped in the barn and running out of time. I could hear her screams as the fire came closer. I had to do something fast. I tossed aside the Tommy gun, yanked my automatic pistols from my shoulder holsters, and sprinted toward the car where I last saw the shooter. Three feet away I leaped off the ground onto the hood and catapulted off, firing as I twisted in the air. I caught him crouched down low, trying to reload. If I had waited another few seconds to act, he would have had me cold.

I ran back to the barn, stripped the jacket off the guy who lay in a pool of his own blood and placed it over my head as I picked up the Tommy gun and rushed through the flames. The hay in the loft was raining down, spreading the flames further into the barn. I found Peggy behind an empty stall in one of the corners. She clung to me as I placed her in the front seat of my car near the rear of the barn. I then riddled the back wall with the remaining bullets in the Tommy gun, reloaded and emptied two more drums. If that hadn't weakened the wall enough to drive through it, we were doomed.

I started the car, grateful for the automatic ignition in the newer Fords, and hit the gas pedal. As we broke through the wall into an empty field, the fire burst through the opening behind us, torching the entire structure as the surge of fresh air fueled the flames. We were safe, but I didn't know about Peggy's grandfather.

* * * * *

The old man lay motionless, stretched out on the floor with his shotgun by his side, his face covered in blood. Peggy let out a wail and pounded on my back in fury as I felt for a pulse.

"Relax. He's alive," I said. "Get me a wet cloth. I think it's just a flesh wound to his scalp. He's gonna be okay, I promise. Now, get me that cloth."

She knelt by my side. I was about to revive the old man, but stopped.

"Why don't you go upstairs and get out of your nightgown. He probably looked for you when he heard the cars stop out front. I sure as hell don't want him turning his shotgun on me when he wakes up."

She returned before her grandfather fully regained consciousness. Cleaned up, with a small bandage, and holding a shot of whiskey, he looked ready to take on another hoodlum. We helped him to the couch and assured him that Peggy was unharmed.

"Joey, who were those men?" Peggy asked.

"The guy I'm after in Detroit knows I'm coming. He sent them. But if I'd thought I was being followed, I never would have stopped here for the night, believe me."

"I smell smoke," Pops said, trying to stand.

Peggy gave him a hand. "The barn is burning down, but the house is safe. The fields are wet from the heavy rains we had over the last few days, so the fire won't spread," she said with confidence.

Smoke was rising high into the sky. The place would soon be swarming with people trying to help. If the cops arrived before I left, I would never get to Detroit.

"I hate to say this, but I have to leave. My chances of survival diminish the longer I stay here. I'll pay for the damages once I get back to the city."

"You can't leave looking like that. At least wash your face and hair in the kitchen sink. You're full of mud," Peggy said.

"Young fella, I'd say the sooner you leave the better. I paid a hell of a price for those bottles of hooch," Pops said.

I did a fast scrub in the sink as Peggy washed the mud from my hair. I figured I'd change my clothes once I was clear of the area.

Peggy walked me out to the car. When we got there, I told her to wait as I went to check the goons' wallets and cars for information that might be useful. They were all from New York City and each had five C-notes. I recognized one of the men. He was one of the longshoremen that worked for Toby Tobias before Toby signed on with Carmine. Someone had paid these guys to go after me, and that someone was in cahoots with Ronnie. In my mind there were only a few possibilities, Toby, Carmine, or both.

When I returned to my car, Peggy asked how she was going to explain the carnage to the police.

"Tell the authorities these cars chased another vehicle down your road and all hell broke loose when they hit your front yard and couldn't drive any further. Tell them you don't know why the men were fighting; you just got caught in the middle."

Peggy nodded and brushed my hair back. "You still look a mess. There's a seldom-used two track path behind the house that will take you back to the main road. It's a little bumpy, but I make the trip all the time in our old heap."

Grumpy started howling again.

"You better go," she said.

I handed her the money I got off the bodies. "Take this for now. I'll stop by on my way back from Detroit. If I get lucky, maybe I'll have the rest of the money you need to fix up this place."

"Pay attention on the way out," she said. "We're not easy to find. All these dirt roads lead to the main road, and it's hard to tell them apart."

As I drove away, I figured out how Ronnie's hired men had found me. They had pulled what I called a bracket. The lead cars would hide on the side roads ahead of me. Then, when I drove by one of them, he pulled out, and soon passed me so I wouldn't get suspicious. When the next driver saw his buddy go by, he would know I wasn't far behind. This continued until I didn't show up. They then backtracked until they found the road I'd taken. Fortunately for them, and unfortunately for us, Pops' house was the only one in the area. They had waited until past midnight to make their move.

They didn't expect to come up against an old man and his dog.

Chapter 13

The rest of the trip to Detroit was uneventful. I stayed in motels off the main road, got an early start on the last morning, and arrived by eight at the diner where Jackie and I had first met the local police chief.

The chief recognized me the instant I walked in and pulled his revolver before I said a word. I approached his booth with my hands held away from my sides, one carrying a large envelope.

"Mind if I take a seat?"

"Where's that crazy dame of yours?"

"I came alone. You and I have some unfinished business."

"We do?"

"Your nephew."

"What about him?"

"I know who killed him."

"Take a seat, and keep your mitts where I can see them," the chief said. He continued to eat his breakfast.

"I have a proposition."

"I'm listening."

"I show you who killed your nephew, and you do what comes naturally."

"Naturally, my first tendency would be to kill the bastard, but it depends on who the person is and if they're connected."

"Ronnie Ligotti."

The chief put his fork down and took a gulp of coffee.

"Let me get this straight. A while back you bribed me to let Ronnie rebuild his organization, and now you want me to nail him. Do I understand or am I confused?"

"You got it right."

"So what's happened between you two? Lover's quarrel?"

"I was under a family obligation to help Ronnie, but since then he killed a friend, kidnapped a girl I promised to protect, and sent six hitmen after me."

The chief let out a low whistle. "Why are you still alive?"

"Five of them are dead and one ended up in the hospital."

The chief finished eating and waved the waitress over.

"How about a refill, doll, and bring a cup of joe for my new friend."

We sat in silence waiting for the waitress to return. The chief never took his eyes off me, probably thinking of his options. When the waitress left, he was ready.

"I like to know who I'm dealing with, so give it to me straight, what's your real name?"

"Joey Batista."

"Joey Batista. I've heard of you. You took out the Twins, and if rumor has it right, you're responsible for the chaos that shutdown part of New York harbor for half a day when a bomb destroyed a building. You know, you're quite the fella. You rescue skirts in distress, take down mob bosses, kill some of the best hitmen in the county, and blow up buildings. Why the hell do you need me to deal with Ronnie?"

"You got a name?" I asked the chief.

"Chief will do just fine."

"Well, Chief, don't you think we should have this discussion outside or in your car?"

He squeezed out of the booth, threw a couple of bucks on the table, and walked out of the diner. I followed.

"So, answer my question. Why do you need me?" he asked again when we were sitting in his car.

"If Ronnie is out of the way, there's less chance of innocent people getting hurt when I go in and get the girl."

"I still don't get it. Just kill the bastard."

"He's expecting me. I'd have to kill a significant number of his men to even get close enough. That would put you and me at risk."

"Me? Why would I give a damn?"

"That kind of bloodshed isn't good for the city's reputation. I imagine the mayor might think he'll need a new police chief."

The chief lit up a cigar and took a few puffs.

"Come to think of it, I did almost lose my job the last time you were in town. You left me with a mob boss and his crew slaughtered and half a city block burned to the ground."

"The way I see it," I said. "You can react in one of three ways: arrest Ronnie based on the evidence I'll provide and enjoy seeing him fry, take him out yourself, or tell me to go to hell because you don't give a damn about your nephew's death. In which case, I'll do it my way."

"Tell me, who's the dame that's causing all this trouble?"

"Her name's Debbie. She was the top earner in Ronnie's canhouse that burned down. She wanted out of the business so I took her back with me to New York. She refused to return to Detroit with Ronnie when the murder charges against him were dropped, so he snatched her."

"Why do you give a damn what happens to her?"

"It's a long story. The short version is that I'm the one who got her hooked up with Ronnie in the first place."

"Turns out I know Debbie. It's hard to believe she would leave the business. She really enjoys her work. But none of that matters now because he sold her."

"What do you mean he *sold her*?"

"He needed some quick dough, and one of her clients made him an offer."

"Who?"

"The mayor, and that makes your life more difficult, since I work for him."

The chief was right. I had to talk fast before he thought of a reason to arrest *me*. He knew I would go after Debbie no matter what.

"We should keep this simple. One way or the other I need to get Ronnie off my back. He's gonna keep hiring goons to take me out. So, what's your answer? Either you take him down or I will."

"Not so fast. First, I want the pictures you took from Bandini's safe. The ones that you used to force me to look the other way as Ronnie rebuilt his organization."

I tapped the envelope that sat on my lap. "They're right here. I have no further use for them."

"Good. Now show me the evidence you have that proves Ronnie killed my nephew."

I removed a picture from the envelope. It had captured the chief's nephew lying on the ground with Ronnie holding him down with a foot on his back and a gun to his head. The picture had caught the action as the bullet and gray matter erupted from the side of his nephew's skull.

The chief's face turned red, and then he held his stomach.

He groped for the handle to open his car door and heaved up his breakfast.

"That son of a bitch. Shooting the bastard is too damn quick. I'm gonna throw the bum in jail and let him stew, waiting to fry. And I'll make sure they botch his execution so he suffers plenty. You got any more evidence?"

I was about to reach into my coat pocket, but thought it wise to let the chief know first.

"I have your nephew's pearl-handle gun that's been missing. It's in my coat pocket."

"Take it out with two fingers."

I did as directed and handed it to him. "I took the gun from Ronnie when he pulled it during a scuffle. I'm sure you can find a way to get his prints on it again. It could be as easy as handing it to him. Unloaded, of course."

"I'll get an arrest warrant tonight and serve it tomorrow morning. You wanna be there?" the chief asked.

"I'll meet you here at eight."

The chief agreed. I got out of his car, slammed the door shut, and handed him the envelope through the open window. Tomorrow morning couldn't come soon enough.

* * * * *

I followed behind the chief in a procession of about ten police cars. At first, I thought the chief had made a mistake when he pulled up to the entrance gate of Nick Bandini's old estate. But it did make sense. The syndicate believed Ronnie had taken down Bandini and his organization when he was on the run from the law. An impressive feat if it had been true. O'Reilly had said Ronnie was moving up fast, and he wasn't kidding.

I had one of my rods on the passenger seat, expecting a bloody confrontation. It never came. The chief removed Ronnie's man at the gate and assigned two of his own to stand guard. As we entered the compound, patrol cars fanned out, surrounding the house, rolling over shrubs and tearing up flower beds. The chief pulled his car up to the front steps, waited for me to join him on the porch, and ordered his men to remain outside.

A butler opened the door, unfazed by the commotion, and asked if he could be of assistance.

"Out of my way, bozo," the chief said, pushing the butler aside.

The chief headed for two large oak-paneled doors to the right of the entrance. The place had been redecorated since my last visit. Back then the doors were French, but they had been shattered when Jackie unleashed her Tommy gun in the foyer.

Ronnie sat on the edge of a large mahogany desk that was positioned in front of an impressive display of antique and current-day firearms. Floor to ceiling windows on the remaining two walls brightened the room with natural sunlight.

"Chief, Joey, nice of you to drop in with such dramatic flair. All work and no play can get monotonous at times," Ronnie said, gesturing for us to take a seat.

"This is not a social visit. I'm here to arrest you for the murder of my nephew," the chief said, pulling out his revolver and tossing the picture I had given him onto Ronnie's desk.

Ronnie glanced at the picture. "Chief, you're not serious. This was years ago, and it doesn't prove a thing. You know that Bandini had us constantly posing for pictures. You even did it yourself back when you worked for him."

"Take a closer look. There's no doubt that you blew his brains out."

What Ronnie said next caught me totally by surprise.

"I guess you got me there, Chief. But you already knew that, so I can assume you got the pictures from Joey showing you doing the same to others."

I reached for my gun, but I wasn't fast enough. The chief had turned his rod on me.

"Batista, I wouldn't do that if I were you," the chief said.

I should have known that I was being double crossed by the chief. The only way he could have known about what I did to Big Ben just a few days ago was through Ronnie. And Ronnie would have had to get that information from Carmine.

Ronnie removed my guns and shoved one hard against my gut. "I don't know how the hell you survived the last few weeks, but lucky for me I never underestimate an opponent."

"How did you know I'd get the chief to help me out?"

"It was easy. The first thing I did when I returned to town was make sure the chief wouldn't interfere with my business. We had a long talk, and he told me about the compromising pictures you found, forcing him to cooperate with me. A clever move, but it was obvious, now that you and I are no longer on friendly terms, that you would give him the pictures in return for his help. I also took other precautions, in case you chose a more direct approach," he said, pointing to one of the windows.

I noticed a sparkle of reflected sunlight in a grove of trees across from an open meadow. He had a sniper, maybe more than one, ready to take me out.

"Quit the bullshit, and get my dough," the chief said to Ronnie.

Ronnie walked back to his desk, pulled out a satchel from the bottom drawer, and dropped it on the floor by the chief's feet.

"I told you, Joey, that the chief could be bribed. In fact, the chief considers dough thicker than blood. A little detail I forgot to mention."

The chief holstered his gun and reached for the satchel.

Ronnie pointed one of my guns at him. "Not so fast, Chief."

"You son of a bitch," the chief yelled.

"I agree, my mother was a real bitch," Ronnie said. "Now, slowly remove your gun using your left hand, place it on the desk, and then back up toward the window. You too, Joey."

"You won't get away with this," the chief shouted.

"Oh, I think I will. I'm going to shoot you with Joey's gun and him with yours," Ronnie said, admiring the chief's revolver. "You have similar taste as your nephew in fancy hardware."

The chief's face contorted in anger and he lunged at Ronnie, who shot him twice in the gut with the revolver. The shots triggered a barrage of gunfire outside the house as the cops and Ronnie's men opened up on each other.

I moved to the edge of the window and raised my arms in the air as Ronnie pointed the revolver at me. Ronnie looked stunned as a bullet pinged through the glass and slammed into his chest.

"I took a few precautions of my own," I said, as a second bullet pierced his heart.

I retrieved my pistols, grabbed the sack full of money off the floor, and kicked open the doors to the foyer. One of

Ronnie's men stood at the top of the stairs firing at a wounded cop pinned behind an ornate hutch. I drew his fire, and the cop took the guy down with one shot. I did what I could to stop the cop's bleeding and helped him to his feet.

I half-lifted, half-dragged him to the front door. "I gotta get you to a hospital."

"Leave me, you'll never make it to a car."

"Don't worry; I have a couple of guardian angels looking after me. We'll head for the chief's car. He was in the lead, so we'll have a clear shot down the driveway to the main road."

In the car, the cop held tight to the tourniquet I had tied around his leg. "What happened to the chief?" he asked.

"Ronnie killed him with his own gun. Those were the first shots you heard."

Halfway down the drive, a goon stepped out from behind a tree, trying to support a chopper with a wounded arm. His head exploded before he had the gun level enough to shoot. The same happened to another guy who took a couple of shots at our car.

I made it through the gate and headed for the hospital. The cop had fainted, so I grabbed the tourniquet with one hand and twisted as hard as I could, while driving with the other hand.

I didn't hang around to see if he made it. He was in good hands, and there wasn't anything more I could do for the guy. I left the chief's car at the hospital and hoofed it back to my hotel. I needed the time to think about how to get Debbie away from the mayor.

* * * * *

Luigi and Cafiero were sitting on the veranda of my hotel when I arrived.

"What happened after I bolted out of the compound?" I asked.

"We took out five or six of Ronnie's men, so the rest threw down their weapons. No one knew where the shots were coming from, but it was obvious that they were the targets," Luigi said.

"How are you feeling?" I asked Cafiero.

"I was getting sick of being laid up, so when your uncle came to me in the hospital and asked if I would help take out Ronnie, I was ready. Besides, I figured I owed you one for saving my life."

"I'm glad you believe in paying your debts. How did you guys know which room was Ronnie's office? That house is huge?"

"We got lucky," Luigi said. "It was easy to follow the police chief. When we saw you entering the grounds, we parked our cars down the street a ways, scaled the wall by some bushes, and landed in a wooded area in Ronnie's compound. Cafiero noticed some movement and went to investigate. Ronnie had someone targeting the house so we figured he had set a trap for you."

A waiter came over and asked if we wanted some refreshments. We all declined and moved into the hotel lobby. Cafiero continued where my uncle had left off.

"The guy didn't expect any trouble so it was easy to take him down. Your uncle and I set up in the same spot and waited. When you raised your arms in the air, we knew it was time to act."

"What are you gonna do now? If it gets out that you

double-crossed your employer, you'll be out of business," I said to Cafiero.

"It's rare that anyone gets to retire in my line of work, so I think it's time I hang up old Betsy and head out West to live near my kids."

"So not everything you told Jackie was a lie. You do have children."

"The best way to lie is to sprinkle in some truth. You sound more believable that way."

Luigi asked about Debbie.

"As far as I know she's with the mayor. He bought her from Ronnie."

"He what?"

"I had the same reaction," I said. "Why don't we go to my room and have this conversation in private? We don't need anyone overhearing us and causing trouble."

Luigi and Cafiero both offered to help get Debbie, but I didn't think the mayor would make much trouble. All I had to do was threaten to go to the newspapers and expose his dealings with Ronnie. My uncle didn't like the idea of leaving me on my own, and he liked my plan even less when I asked if I could borrow his car, since mine was probably impounded by the police. But in the end, he agreed to leave for New York with Cafiero. On the way out of my room, he couldn't resist one last jab.

"At the rate you're losing cars, Ford should give you a volume discount. I expect to see you in a few days. If not, I'm bringing the dames to drag your ass out of trouble."

I didn't bother to respond and walked them to Cafiero's car. I watched as they drove off, and then sat on the veranda for a few hours listening to the banter that went on around me.

The place was abuzz with details about the shootout between a Mafia boss and the local police chief, who gave his life in the line of duty. The way people were talking you'd never know he was a corrupt bastard.

Chapter 14

The mayor's office was jammed with reporters and city officials clamoring for more information on the death of their police chief. The mayor's secretary took control of the chaos by telling us to back off and wait our turn. The commotion in the waiting room calmed down under her hard stare. It was obvious that she had considerable influence over who got to see the mayor, and she was not looking with favor on me, a stranger. I decided to take a more direct approach.

I pinched a pencil and paper from the secretary's desk, scribbled a brief note, and handed it to her.

"If I were you, I'd get off my duff and give this to the mayor right now, or I'm going to tell these reporters something that will embarrass your boss. If you don't believe me, read the note."

"Mister, I've heard every excuse imaginable to get past me, and few have succeeded," she said, unfolding the note. A blush flashed across her face. "What is this nonsense?"

"I suggest you read the note again. No one knows the mayor better than you. If you still think I'm bluffing, give it back." I held out my hand.

She gave me the once over and then parted her way through the crowd to his office. When she came out, she waved me over. I squeezed by her, as she blocked others from entering.

The mayor was young—younger than I'd expected—a

sharp dresser and a man of expensive taste. The décor of his office reflected that taste. Looking around at the opulent furnishings, I was reminded of what my dad had said when I attended my first ward meeting as a kid, "There's only two ways to make it in politics: kiss ass and buy votes. Those who do both, win."

"This is absurd," the mayor said, crumbling my note and tossing it into a wastebasket.

"Like it says, you're holding a whore against her will, and I'm here to take her back to New York."

"And who exactly are you?"

"Nobody you need to care about as long as you turn Debbie over to me. Don't make the same mistake Ronnie did."

"So, you're the one Chief Brown warned me about the night before last."

"That's right."

"I wasn't worried then, and I'm not worried now. Debbie's a member of my household staff. She can leave anytime she wants."

"Prove it."

"I don't have time for this nonsense. I have a police chief and two of his men dead, three in the hospital, and a slew of wiseguys in the morgue, and nobody can give me a straight story on what happened. Just get the hell out of my office."

"If I walk out of here without access to Debbie, I'll announce to that crazed pack of reporters that you're involved in human trafficking. Not a great headline in an election year. It's your choice."

The mayor jotted something on a scrap of paper.

"That would be difficult to prove, but nevertheless embarrassing. As I said, Debbie is free to do as she pleases.

The only one who would've stopped her from leaving town was Ronnie."

"And why would he have done that?"

"As Ronnie had tactlessly put it, he wanted his *merchandise* returned when I grew bored," the mayor said, handing over the piece of paper. "That's my home address. I'll let security know you're coming. I didn't catch your name."

"Joey Batista."

"I'll remember that. Now get out. I don't have time to hassle over a two-bit whore."

If he'd wanted to provoke me, he'd come damn close. I took two cigars from a jeweled box on his desk and placed them in my shirt pocket, making sure he saw the roscoes holstered underneath my jacket.

"I hope for your sake we don't meet again," I said, throwing open his office door and announcing that the mayor would speak to the press now.

* * * * *

The mayor lived on the outskirts of town in a posh neighborhood. I knew from the chief and Ronnie that the mayor had his hand in the city coffers, but I suspected he also came from money. Otherwise, his lifestyle would've raised suspicion, especially in a run-up to an election.

I made it through the security check at the gated entrance without incident and was about to use the knocker on the front door when it flew open, and Debbie launched herself at me. Clutching her, I teetered on the top step, then lost my footing, landing hard against one of the columns that supported the veranda. The back of my head smacked against the post. With Debbie still clinging to me, I reached around to check the damage. When I brought my hand down, blood dripped through my fingers.

"Oh, Joey, I'm so sorry," Debbie said, leading me inside to the kitchen. She handed me a cloth to apply pressure to the wound and then ran upstairs to get antiseptic and bandages. It took a little over five minutes to stop the bleeding.

"Go pack some clothes and let's get out of here," I said, securing the final bandage around my head.

"Why?" Debbie asked.

That wasn't a question I had expected.

"I'm taking you back to New York."

"I don't understand. Why would I leave?"

"I thought that's what you wanted?"

"I found what I want. I have a job and someone who loves me. I'm sure he's going to ask me to marry him."

"I hope you're not talking about the mayor."

"I am. He got me away from Ronnie and offered me a job. Don't you see?" she said, twirling around.

Having been knocked nearly unconscious, I hadn't noticed that she wore a maid's outfit that accented her best features.

"Debbie, I hate to tell you this, but the mayor bought you from Ronnie. It's no different from when he paid to see you at Ronnie's brothel. Except now, you're his personal whore."

"No, no, that's not true. He loves me. He said so."

"Debbie, the mayor's using you. You're fooling yourself."

"Who gave you the right to decide what's good for me?"

"Your sister."

"My sister's dead! A lot of good that clinic did for her. I'm not going back."

"What about Dr. Schwartz? He's been calling our office every day to see if we've made progress finding you."

"All I am to him is a difficult case, no more. I have a home right here," she said, with a sweeping gesture. "I have a man who loves me and a chance to have a family someday. Why would you take that away from me?"

"You're living in a fantasy. The mayor doesn't love you, he doesn't want to marry you, and when he tires of you, you'll be out on the street. He told me so himself."

"Get out of here. I don't ever want to see you again," she yelled, pushing me out of the chair forcing me backward. "Get out, just get out."

She slammed the door shut, and as I turned to leave, I heard her sobbing, banging the door with her fists.

* * * * *

I hesitated by my car wondering if I should go back and try again, but Debbie wasn't thinking rationally. Depressed and disgusted with Debbie's stupidity, I headed for the nearest speakeasy.

To say the joint was swanky would be an understatement. The dance floor was flooded with beautiful dames—dressed to the nines—looking for their sugar daddies, and there were plenty to choose from, all flashing their wealth.

I ignored the skirts as I made my way to a small table in a secluded corner. I ordered a bottle of whiskey, set on getting canned. The more I drank, the quieter the room got and the better I felt. I was halfway to oblivion when an old man with an impressive mane of white hair and a sparkling gold front tooth sat down and poured himself a drink.

"I thought I'd help you out of a jam," he said.

"By drinking my whiskey?"

"Sure, you're gonna end up in the clink if you empty that bottle on your own. After what we did yesterday, that's the one place you want to avoid."

I tried to break free of the stupor that had gripped my mind. The voice sounded like Cafiero's, but it didn't look like him. As the fog lifted from my sight, I saw through his disguise.

"What are you doing here? I thought you and Luigi left yesterday."

"Your uncle likes to have a good time and convinced me we should take advantage of the night life. I think the fact that no one knows him in Detroit gave him a sense of freedom."

"That sounds like my uncle. Why the disguise?"

"I did a few jobs in this area of Detroit, so drawing attention to myself isn't in my best interest."

Cafiero called over a waitress and ordered two cups of black coffee, both for me.

"You gonna tell me what went wrong today?" he asked after the waitress left.

"Who said anything went wrong?"

"Let's not play games. If you had Debbie, you'd be on your way to New York rather than sitting here alone getting smoked. Just want to know if you need help."

"Help, sure I can use some. What do you know about dames?"

"I can sum up what I know in three words: unpredictable, unreliable, and unrealistic."

"Sounds like you haven't had a lot of luck with women."

"You're wrong about that. You just need to have the right expectations and take charge when you have to."

Somehow what he said didn't fit my experience, but then again, it did apply to Debbie. I didn't know if I would ever see Cafiero again, so I asked him something that had been dragging me down, making my sleepless nights even longer.

"I'm sure Luigi told you what's been goin' on along the waterfront. What do you think will happen to my neighborhood?"

Cafiero poured himself another drink and moved the second cup of coffee closer to me.

"The Mafia runs this town, and every other big city, especially New York. You can't fight it, no one can, because it changes; it adapts and spreads like a disease. You might think you're making progress, but you're not. Time isn't on your side."

"You wanna make that a little clearer. I'm not thinking straight yet," I said, sipping my coffee.

"Your neighborhood's gonna change. It might happen this year or two years from now, but it will change. I suggest you accept that fact and become part of the solution and not the problem."

"You sayin' I should join the Mafia?"

"No, you want to stay just far enough away so you can influence the change a bit, and then get the hell out of town and lead a normal life. Something you haven't done since joining the military."

"What do you consider a normal life?"

Cafiero got up and took the bottle off the table. "That you're gonna have to figure out on your own. It's been nice knowing you kid, I'm glad you weren't my last kill."

Chapter 15

The mayor came in a side door and was surprised to see me waiting in his office, smoking one of his cigars.

"How the hell did you get past my secretary?"

"Well, it's not because she's taken a liking to me. It might have something to do with the fact that she knows I can sink your career."

He went to call her into his office but stopped short of the door.

"I'll talk to her later. She obviously needs an adjustment in judgment or a new job."

"I wouldn't be too hard on her. I did come bearing gifts," I said, pointing to a new box of Cuban cigars on a side table.

He lit up and flipped through some papers on his desk. "What do you want, Batista? You got your answer from Debbie."

"Now it's time for us to talk. How much did you pay Ronnie for Debbie?"

He looked at me and smiled.

"Two large, but I can tell you, I'm getting my money's worth."

"I'll double it. Four grand."

"Not enough. I figure, with her reputation, I can get at least six grand from any of the bosses in this town. If you try to bargain, the price goes to ten."

"I'll send the dough when I get back to New York."

He came over to where I was sitting and planted his cigar in an ashtray near my elbow. He had turned his head as he bent over so our faces were real close.

"You take me for a fool, Batista? We'll deal when you have the dough. Now get the hell out!"

I had the cash I'd snatched from Ronnie's office, but I needed that scratch to pay a debt. The mayor left me with only one option—to take Debbie by force.

I walked past the secretary and was heading toward the stairs when I got a crazy idea. I wrote some numbers down and asked her to make a phone call.

"Ask for Johnny Torrio," I said.

The mayor hadn't closed the door all the way and stepped back into the waiting room.

"Is that Torrio, the Chicago mob boss?" he asked.

"That's right."

"What does he have to do with what we talked about?"

"He's my uncle. I figured you'd take an IOU from him."

The mayor put his arm around my shoulder and walked me back into his office. When the call came through, I explained to my uncle the situation. He agreed to send the money and then asked to speak to the mayor.

The mayor's hand shook as he reached for the receiver.

"Not a problem, Mr. Torrio. Your word is good enough for me. In fact, since he's your nephew, I'll give him what he wants. No need to send the dough."

The conversation lasted another two minutes. When he hung up, the mayor was all smiles.

"Bring Debbie here, discreetly, and I'll set her straight," he said, lighting up another cigar.

"Why the sudden change?"

"You're joking. Having Johnny Torrio indebted to me is worth a hell of a lot more than a few grand."

I didn't hang around to find out what kind of favor he had in mind. That was between him and my uncle. I had one objective, and that was to get Debbie back to the clinic where she'd worked before Ronnie had snatched her. There she had a shot at the kind of life she dreamed she had with the mayor.

* * * * *

Debbie refused to come out of her bedroom and insisted I leave her alone. I'd had enough of her idiotic outbursts and kicked in the door. She leaped off her bed and backed up against a wall, looking like a scared kid. I didn't give her a chance to resist, just tossed her over my shoulder and grabbed her coat off the rack on the way out the door.

"Where are you taking me?" she yelled, pounding my back.

"You won't believe me; maybe you'll believe your beloved mayor."

"I hope he puts you in jail for kidnapping."

"Just shut up and get in the car. You're more damn trouble than you're worth. You don't even give a damn that Gino gave his life trying to save you from Ronnie."

"Gino's dead?" she mumbled, collapsing back against the car seat.

I turned around to face her. "If you want to stay in Detroit after talking with the mayor, that's fine with me. But understand this, if you do, you're on your own. You're out of my life and everyone else's back home."

We didn't speak until we got to the mayor's office.

* * * * *

The mayor greeted Debbie with outstretched arms. She rushed to him and gave him a long, passionate kiss. She then turned her fury on me.

Pointing her finger, she yelled, "I want him arrested. He broke into my room and forced me to come here."

The mayor backed away, "Sorry, babe, I can't do that. He owns you now."

"What are you talking about? No one owns me."

"Try to understand. I can't be seen entering brothels during an election year, so I paid Ronnie two grand to take you home."

"You offered me a job. I thought you forced Ronnie to let me go."

"The job was just a cover so you could live in my house without causing rumors."

Debbie shook her head. "I don't believe you. Joey's forcing you to say all this. You said you loved me and that someday we'd get married."

The mayor walked over to the large window behind his desk that overlooked a busy street.

"I want to show you something," he said to Debbie.

It was sad to see how she rushed to his side, even after what he had told her.

"You see that church?" he asked. "When I want to get married, I'm going to attend that church to meet a nice, wholesome young lady. Someone I can trust to raise my kids properly and who will always be home waiting for me."

The mayor stared out the window with his hands behind his back, ignoring Debbie. She backed away and turned toward me. With tears streaming down her face she removed her coat—letting it fall to the floor—and then stripped naked.

"What the hell?" the mayor shouted, when he turned around and saw what she had done.

He tried to reach for her, but I stepped between them. "Keep your grubby hands off her," I said, pushing him back against the window.

Debbie threw her clothes at his face. "I quit, and you know what you can do with your maid uniform."

The mayor rushed toward Debbie again as she headed for the door to the reception area. That's when I decked him. He watched helplessly as flash bulbs fired repeatedly as Debbie posed naked with one hand on her hip and the other on the door frame.

The new police chief and reporters were in the reception area waiting for a meeting with the mayor. Instead, Debbie gave them quite a show.

"I'm the mayor's personal whore. He paid two grand for me, and I'm worth every penny," she announced and then headed toward the stairs to the main lobby.

I picked up Debbie's coat and ran after her, leaving the mayor to deal with the onslaught of reporters. All I could do to shield Debbie from the growing crowd of onlookers was to wrap the coat around her and hold her close as we walked to my car.

Chapter 16

The enormity of her little show at the mayor's office didn't hit Debbie until we were in the confines of my car.

"I'll be on the front cover of every paper in the country," Debbie said, sobbing.

"I wouldn't worry about that," I said, warming up the engine. "No one will remember your face."

Clutching her coat around her, she giggled, wiping away fresh tears. Seeing the reporters running toward us, I hit the gas pedal and swerved into traffic, cutting over into the center lane to avoid a crash.

Debbie glanced back. "I wonder what took them so long to come after us."

"You got lucky. The reporters needed to get pictures of the mayor before he could slip out the back of the building. They knew they had a front page special edition if they caught him in his office right after you came roaring out in all your glory."

Near the edge of town, I made a sharp right and parked the car alongside a three-story building. The sudden maneuver caught Debbie by surprise.

She slumped down in the seat. "Why are we stopping?"

"Don't worry, no one followed us. You need some clothes," I said pointing to the building. "And this is just the place. Tell me your sizes and I'll grab a few things."

She peeked over the doorframe and saw that I had stopped

alongside a clothing store. Her excitement overcame any fear of reporters sneaking up on her as she shoved open the car door.

I grabbed her arm. "Hold on, you can't go in there wearing just a coat."

"Why not? They'll never know, and besides, it's time for me to pick out my own clothes."

"What are you saying?"

"When you work in a brothel, the madam provides you with all your needs, and when it comes to clothing, there isn't much," she said with a slight blush.

The first item she selected was a suitcase, a very large suitcase.

* * * * *

We made one more stop to fill the gas tank and stock up on snacks, and then we hit the road for New York. Debbie slept for the first few hours and avoided any meaningful discussion by yapping about the most trivial things that had happened in her life. I kept my trap shut and focused on driving.

I had risked everything so she'd have the opportunity to start over, to take her life in a different direction, but listening to her blabber, I doubted she would ever change.

A little past sunset I pulled into the parking lot of a roadside inn and sat there until it dawned on her that we had stopped.

"What are we doing?" she asked.

"I'm waiting for you to face reality."

"It's too painful."

"Then I'll do it for you. Gino gave his life, and I almost

lost mine, for you. You should give that some serious thought."

"Why are you doing this?"

"For your own good. Not many people get a chance to go back and start over. I didn't."

We sat in silence for a few minutes, and then she got out of the car. I let her struggle with the bags before I joined her, giving her time to reflect on what I had said. She lifted her suitcase with two hands and handed it to me without a word. Then she picked up my smaller bag. I put my arm around her shoulder, and we walked toward the inn.

During dinner, she talked about how her sister, Shirley, had taken care of her when they were kids, and about the guilt she felt when she discovered the manner in which Shirley had been earning money. She went on to talk about things for which I was ill prepared to give advice. So once again, I kept my trap shut and listened. The difference now was that she was digging up and facing her demons.

The next morning we had a hardy breakfast and hit the road early. As I drove, I told Debbie what had happened on the way to Detroit and that I had to stop back at the farmhouse to see how Peggy and her grandfather were doing.

A little past noon I thought I saw the dirt turnoff that would lead to Peggy's, but I wasn't sure. It didn't take long to realize I was on the right track when I hit two familiar rough patches that tossed us around. It did strike me as odd that so many cars were coming from the other direction. A few more passed us as we got closer to the house, and one pulled out just as we entered the front yard. A single car remained parked over by the remains of the barn, which told me the barnyard had been packed and all the cars we had passed had come from Peggy's.

I didn't want to intrude on Peggy and the old man when they had company, so I walked Debbie through the shootout that had taken place. I was in the middle of the best part when we heard yelling coming from the farmhouse. It didn't take more than a few seconds for me to burst through the front door.

A middle-aged man stood over Peggy, insisting she sign a document. I was on him as he turned to face me and shoved him across the room. He stumbled over a chair and landed on his backside. As he struggled to get up, Peggy wrapped her arms around my waist and sobbed into my shirt. Debbie gently led Peggy back to the table and sat with her as I dealt with the brute.

I pulled my rod and aimed it at the guy. "If I were you, I'd stay down until I figure out what the hell is goin' on."

"I'm a lawyer, and you have no—"

"I have every right to beat the crap out of you for harassing Peggy."

"I—"

"That's enough. Just stay there. Peggy, what is this about? Where's Pops?"

Peggy asked me to put the gun away and invited Mr. Johnston, the lawyer, to join us at the table. I was reluctant to let the guy up, but she insisted.

"Joey, Pops is dead. He was buried out back today," she said, wiping away a few tears. "Mr. Johnston wants me to sign some papers, but I don't understand them."

My hand quivered as I holstered my gun. There was no doubt in my mind that I had hastened the old man's demise.

"Joey, it's not your fault," Peggy said. "Pops was very

ill and knew he didn't have long to live. He knocked off the whiskey you had given him and passed on with a smile. Up to the last minute, he talked about how you flew up into the air and took out that last gunman. 'It was a sight to behold.' Those were his words."

I reached for her hand and said I was sorry. I then focused on Mr. Johnston.

"What are these documents about?"

"I have a buyer for the farm. It's a good price. She can't live out here alone."

"That's for her to decide. Is this how you usually do business? You can't wait until the dirt has settled on the grave before badgering people?"

"My client is investigating other properties. If we're going to close this deal, we need to move quickly. Another offer might not come along for quite a while."

Peggy shoved the contract across the table. "Mr. Johnston, I've lived here essentially on my own these last few years taking care of my grandfather. I'm in no more danger living here now than I was with him. I can shoot his shotgun better than he could, and that's all anyone needs to know."

I showed him the door. "We'll be in touch, Mr. Johnston."

* * * * *

I was amazed how a few days had made a dramatic difference in Peggy's appearance. Her face looked drawn, and the youthful vitality I had found so attractive was gone, replaced by a heaviness that permeated the whole house.

Rather than expecting Peggy to fix dinner for the three of us, I suggested we eat out at a local restaurant.

Once the waitress delivered our food, I delved deeper into what had taken place after I had left Peggy to deal with the authorities and the three corpses that littered her front yard.

"Sorry I left you and Pops with such a mess, but I was concerned about Debbie's safety, which is why I couldn't afford a delay," I said to Peggy.

"To be honest, I was scared. I'd never had to deal with cops in all the years I lived with my grandparents."

"Did they buy your version of what had happened?"

"I didn't have to say much of anything. They said it wasn't unusual for gang violence to occur along the booze routes down from Canada. They assumed that's what happened."

Debbie gave me a nasty look. "I can't believe you left this poor child in such a predicament."

I didn't appreciate her comment. "At the time I didn't know you were living the good life in the mayor's mansion."

Debbie's eyes moistened as she glanced away.

"Look, I'm sorry. I'm sorry for everything that's happened. I just want to make things right," I said to Peggy.

Peggy looked more depressed than when we first entered the restaurant. "Mr. Johnston was right. I can't live alone, but if I sell the farm, I have nowhere to go. I just don't know what to do."

"If your grandfather knew he was dying, why didn't the two of you discuss your future?"

Peggy hesitated.

"You didn't tell me the truth, did you?"

"I didn't want you to feel guilty. Pops had a weak heart, and the excitement of the attack on the farmhouse was more than he could take."

Debbie and I both knew I couldn't walk away. Peggy

was a young, inexperienced girl now on her own because of me.

When Peggy went to the john, Debbie came up with a suggestion.

"I would like to stay with Peggy for awhile," she said.

"This is my problem, not yours."

"It's both of ours. You would never have met her if it wasn't for me, and the old man would still be alive. As you pointed out, I have a lot to think about, and I need time to do that. If I go back now, even to the clinic, nothing will change."

She had a point, and I had a gut feeling that helping Peggy make sense of her life would do the same for Debbie.

When Peggy came back to the table, Debbie made her pitch. To my surprise, Peggy said she was willing to consider the offer but wanted some time to think it over. When we got back to the farmhouse, I stayed on the porch, lit up one of the cigars I had taken from the mayor's office, and sat in the old man's rocking chair. A little before sunset Peggy joined me and asked to go for a walk.

"You know, Joey, I have a sense Debbie is holding something back from me. Even after a few hours of talking, I feel I know more about you than I do about her, and to be honest, I don't know much about you."

"I'm not sure I can sum up who I am in a few words."

"You don't have to. Like I said I don't know much, but I know enough. You're a private detective, you didn't take advantage of me when I was being childish, and you risked your life to save mine. I'm asking about Debbie. Who is she and why did you have to rush off to rescue her?"

I didn't hold anything back, but I also let her know that I respected Debbie. She'd had a hard life in the city, yet proved she had the strength of character to kick a drug habit, and she had shown real compassion for others when she'd helped the girls at the clinic. The clincher for Peggy was when I explained how the mayor had deceived Debbie and her reaction when she discovered the truth.

"That took gumption. I need someone who can teach me to stand up for myself," Peggy said. She turned back toward the farmhouse.

The next morning I left for home feeling like a heel. I had told them I'd check back in a few weeks, but knew I wouldn't. Not with O'Reilly rotting in a jail cell. I also had to contend with Carmine and the doubts I had about his loyalty, not just to me, but to the neighborhood. I didn't want to believe it, but it looked like he had sent those men to take me out before I reached Detroit.

I couldn't help but wonder if it was easier to stay alive in the war than surviving in my own New York neighborhood and staying one step ahead of the Mafia.

One thing's for certain, life hasn't been dull.

Chapter 17

I didn't know it at the time, but I had passed the first sign of trouble as I drove along the waterfront on the way home from Detroit. The remains of the union offices across from Pier 17 had been demolished, and a wrecking crew was removing the rubble. It was Pop who later told me that Carmine intended to build a brothel to "ease the tensions" along the waterfront, something Castellano had refused to do. All such activities in our neighborhood were confined to the backrooms of speakeasies, out of public sight. Cafiero's prediction that change was inevitable was proving to be true. Under normal circumstances I would've tracked down Carmine to find out what the hell was going on, but that would have to wait. O'Reilly was in jail and I was eager to get an update from Jackie and Martha on their progress in proving his innocence.

I expected a warm reception when I opened the office door but instead was greeted with cold accusations.

"You were supposed to save Debbie, but instead you pranced her naked around Detroit, exposing her to national ridicule," Jackie said, shoving a copy of the *Daily News* at me.

"It's not what it looks like."

"Is that not you in the background holding Debbie's coat?" Martha asked. "By the way, where is she?"

I put my arms around both of them and led them into the inner office. "It's complicated."

The phone rang, giving me a chance to pull Jackie into a tighter embrace as Martha went to her desk to take the call. Jackie backed away.

"You have some explaining to do," she said.

Martha stuck her head into the office and said the Colonel was on the line. The girls stood next to me with arms folded, listening in on the conversation. It was brief and one sided. I didn't get off a single complete sentence before he disconnected.

I hung up slowly.

"I have to leave. The Colonel gave me no choice in the matter. He has a lead on Hawk's whereabouts."

"Who the hell is Hawk? And why is he more important than O'Reilly or anyone else?" Martha demanded.

Jackie answered for me. "He's the only other survivor of Joey's unit besides Dom."

Martha looked at me in disbelief. "At some point, Joey, you need to put the war behind you. Why jump to attention when he calls?"

"I owe the Colonel a favor, but it's not just that. Hawk would do the same for me."

"So tell us, you were a sniper, a spy, and who knows what else. Dom was an explosives expert. What was Hawk's specialty?" Jackie asked.

"Everything," I said, heading for the door.

Jackie stopped me with a few words. It wasn't what she said; it was how she said it. Her voice was muted and lacked her usual spark. She sounded sad. "We do need to talk," she said.

The three of us agreed to meet at La Cucina's for dinner in two hours to go over all that had happened since I left for Detroit. As I drove to the Colonel's, I had an uneasy feeling.

I realized Jackie was saying she and *I* needed to talk. My guess was that she was more upset about Debbie than she'd let on.

* * * * *

I wasn't the least bit surprised to find Dom leaning back in the Colonel's chair with his feet resting on his desk.

"Pull up a chair, partner," Dom said with a grin, and an offer of the Colonel's finest whiskey.

"Should I be worried that the Colonel is stuffed in one of those closets?"

"Now, Joey, why would you say a thing like that? You know I'm not a violent person. The Colonel's in a meeting and told me to make you feel at home."

"Do you know what's goin' on?"

"All he said was he had new information about Hawk, and then he left. I hope this doesn't delay my release from the service. I have a ton of dough waiting now that the cops no longer suspect me of pulling a series of bank jobs—thanks to the Colonel. He's actually a good guy once you get to know him."

"Then why the hell is the Colonel still keeping tabs on us? And while you're at it, tell me how he pulled you back into the service? I know you're not dumb enough to have signed up again. You'd think the army would have closed their books on us by now."

"I'm afraid that's never gonna happen, buddy. The three of us are joined at the hip, and the Colonel too. It's his neck on the line if we mess up in civilian life. Don't forget, he's the one who got us released from that sanitarium. That's why he reeled me back and tossed my ass in solitary confinement."

"I can see why the cops nabbing you for a string of bank jobs would have looked bad to the upper brass. You could've exposed the details of our unit. The Colonel's outfit was, at best, clandestine and, at worse, a violation of international law."

"There's your answer, Joey. The Colonel's so-called 'Death Squad' was an unofficial unit. They didn't expect any of us to survive. The military owns us, and in a way, we own them. The difference is we can be swatted away without anyone taking notice."

* * * * *

The Colonel wasted no time taking control as he walked into his office.

"Dom, get the hell out of my chair, and if I find you drinking my booze again, I'll send you back to your eight-by-eight cell. Is that clear enough for you?"

"Yes, sir."

"Good. Joey, thanks for coming on short notice."

"You didn't give me a choice."

"The army doesn't give choices. If it did, we would never win a war."

"I'm not in the army, sir."

The Colonel smirked. "You obviously didn't read the fine print when you signed up for my unit or when you put your John Hancock to your discharge papers from the sanitarium. You should always read the fine print. That goes for you too, Dom, as well as Hawk."

I felt beads of sweat form on my forehead. "Sir, I've been a civilian for the past three years."

"No, son, you've been on indefinite, unpaid leave. You

made a long-term commitment to serve your county, and *we* are grateful. That commitment and my assurances to the powers above are the only things that have kept you alive these past few years."

Dom shot out of his chair, shoving it back against the wall. "Damn you, Colonel. You gave your word that I'd be out of here in another week."

Two MPs burst into the room, grabbed Dom, and dragged him toward the door. The Colonel scurried from behind his desk.

"At ease, men. We were having a heated discussion on… religion. Nothing serious. Go back to your post."

I took hold of Dom as he tried to go after one of the MPs and pulled him over to his chair.

"Fine mess you got me into, Batista. I could've disappeared if it wasn't for you. I saved your ass from that Big Ben fella, and what do I get in return? You have the Colonel drag me back into his web."

"That's enough, soldier," the Colonel said.

The Colonel sat back down and lit a cigar. He took a few puffs and then smashed it out in an oversized, overused ashtray—swearing under his breath at his doctors.

"Now that we understand each other, let's get down to business. Hawk has been missing for some time. We assumed he was dead, but yesterday he was spotted at a secret Communist Party meeting."

"Hold on, Colonel," I said. "There's no way in hell Hawk would become a Communist."

"Easy soldier. I wasn't saying that. As far as I know, he's still working for me."

"Doing what? The war is over, and as I recall, Russia

was on our side until they pulled out after they got their butts kicked by the German army."

"War is never over. An ally today is tomorrow's potential enemy. You should know that from history. War smolders in the underbrush of society. It's one of mankind's fatal flaws."

"Look, Colonel, I didn't come here to get a lesson in psychology. Why is the army concerned about the Communist Party?"

"If you spent more time reading the newspaper and less time dodging bullets, you'd know why."

The Colonel put his hand up to stop me from objecting.

"Okay, let's both stop the bullshit. I've been assigned to work with the Justice Department to infiltrate the Party. After all, who better than me—who better than us—to do it? Infiltrating the German High Command was a good training experience, wouldn't you say?"

"How much of a threat does the Communist Party represent?" I asked. "From what I've read, the Party has split into several factions and has been driven underground."

"That's the problem. Now that it's underground, it's hard to keep track of the tentacles weaving their way through our counties and cities. There's even a youth group emerging that's part of Communist International."

None of this made any sense to me. Why would the Justice Department turn to the army for help?

"Colonel, you're not leveling with us. What's really goin' on?"

"I would think you could answer that question better than me. Didn't you ask yourself who was backing Jack Donnelly as he fought to set up a labor union in your own backyard?"

"How do you know about him?"

"I just told you, it's my job to know," the Colonel said, standing. "If the Communist Party takes over the labor unions, the industrial heart of this country, our republic will go up in flames. You're so damn worried about your neighborhood—what about your country?"

"Whoa! What's Jack Donnelly got to do with any of this, and why drag me into your nightmare?"

The Colonel poured out three drinks. "Take a seat, Joey. Let's start over, and this time I'll be straight with you."

Dom emptied his glass before the Colonel topped mine off. Then he sat back and continued to listen.

"Everything I told you about Hawk is true. He was missing. What I said about the Justice Department was a half-truth. They didn't come to me, I went to them with a crazy scheme. Given what I...we... accomplished in the war, they gave me the green light."

"So, you got Hawk imbedded into a branch of the Communist Party," I stated.

"Better than that, he got elected as a delegate to one of their conventions. Soon after that, we lost contact. It's been two months, but now that he's resurfaced, we expected him to use one of our normal methods to reconnect, but he hasn't."

"I can see why you're concerned, but why involve us, and what does the mess Jack Donnelly created on my waterfront have to do with any of this?"

The Colonel finished his drink and leaned forward.

"When I saw how brutally the Mafia—your Mafia—destroyed the Party's efforts to unionize the waterfront, I convinced the Justice Department the only way to stop the Communist movement, which appeals strongly to the working class, is to have another underground organization take over its main source of recruitment, the unions. That's where you and your contacts with the Mafia come into the picture."

I couldn't believe what I was hearing. "Are you telling me you actually proposed that the U.S. government use the Mafia to stop the Communist Party from gaining a foothold in our country?"

"Don't kid yourself, Joey. We need all the help we can get. We live in a republic, a democratic society, and the basic concepts of socialism appeal to the masses, especially those who want something for nothing."

"My parents didn't come here for a handout. They came for the freedom to succeed or fail and try again if necessary."

"I agree, and ninety percent of the immigrants coming through Ellis Island feel the same way. But movements like Communism start small and fester. They grow in our subculture, integrate into our institutions. Then someday, your kids or grandkids will wake up in a suppressive society and won't even realize what the hell they've lost."

"That will never happen in this country," I said.

"It's already started. The various communist factions held a unity convention in Woodstock, New York, on May 15th of last year, and preached armed insurrection by the working class."

"And you actually believe that the solution is for the Mafia to take control of the unions that are forming?"

"Do you have a better idea? Without the unions, the Communist movement will shrivel up and disappear."

"So, we trade one evil for another."

"In a situation like this, you choose the lesser of the two. A decision, no doubt, you've had to make many times or you wouldn't be alive today. The Mafia has no interest in overthrowing the government. All they want is money, as much as they can get their hands on. That is something the government can deal with down the road."

I had the feeling we could spend the whole day arguing and I would still end up involved in his crazy scheme whether I wanted to or not.

"Just tell us what you want, so we can get on with our lives."

"I want to know where Hawk has been, what he knows, and if he's in danger. He's never been gone this long without finding a way to get in touch."

"Don't you have people who can do that? It sounds easy enough," Dom said.

"Nothing is easy in this business. I can't take the chance that I'll blow Hawk's cover or expose another agent if he has turned. What's more natural than a couple of war buddies excited to reunite after a couple of years?"

"Does Hawk know about your plan to involve the Mafia?" I asked.

"He does, and he also knows that his relationship to you and your contacts will be key for him to convince the higher ups to get in bed with the Mafia."

"You're telling me that Hawk's assignment is to convince the Communist Party that if they partner with the Mafia, they'd be more successful in forming unions and growing membership. And my assignment is to convince the Mafia that it's in their best interest to partner with the Communists for now, and then to eventually take over the unions."

"You've got it!"

"Colonel, you're a son of a bitch. You intended to drag

me into this mess long before I contacted you to help me find Dom and Hawk."

"Don't you love it when things just fall into place?" The Colonel handed me an envelope. "This contains Hawk's address in Hoboken, the name of the speakeasy he frequents, and two cards you'll need to get in the joint."

I knew at that moment I had to find a way to wrestle control away from the Colonel. If I didn't, I would never know when the army would swoop in and disrupt my life again, or end it.

"Colonel, we'll agree to this not because of your threats, but because Hawk might need our help. But from what you told us, it doesn't appear that he's in immediate danger. I suspect your real problem is that you've never told your superiors that you've lost contact with Hawk."

"That's right, soldier. If I lose track of one of you, my deal with the upper brass is over, and that means trouble for all of us. If they find out, you and your buddy here will never see the light of day. Do you understand?"

"What I understand is that none of this would have been an issue if you'd had the guts to tell your superiors to cut us loose long ago."

"That's the Joey I've been looking for," he said, reaching into a drawer. "I have your *official* discharge papers right here. All you have to do is make contact with Hawk, find out what the hell is goin' on, and give him the help he needs."

I turned my attention to Dom and handed him the paper with Hawk's current address. "Rent a place not far from where Hawk's living, so it won't be suspicious that we happen to end up in the same speakeasy. I'll join you in a week or so after I take care of some business." I headed for the door.

"Wait a minute," the Colonel shouted. "I need you to get on this now, not two weeks from now."

"With all due respect, Colonel, I suggest *you* wait a minute. You deceived us and now are trying to regain control of our lives. It ends here. I'll make contact with Hawk as soon as I can. In the meantime, I'll take my discharge papers, and so will Dom."

"You have roots. I know you'll follow through," he said, handing me my papers.

"What about mine?" Dom asked.

The Colonel looked over at Dom. "You'll get yours when the job's done."

Chapter 18

Having just returned from a disturbing meeting with the Colonel, I was in no mood for another confrontation with Jackie and Martha about Debbie, especially over dinner. I didn't know if it was my demeanor as I approached their table or if they felt compassion for all that I'd been through, but their attitudes had tempered a bit from earlier in the day.

"We were about to order," Martha said.

"Sorry, the Colonel and I had a disagreement. The meeting lasted longer than I expected."

"Anything serious?" Martha asked.

"It's too early to tell, but I can say this—he surprised the hell out of me."

"What's the story on Hawk?" Jackie asked, without looking up from her menu.

"Do either of you know much about the Communist Labor Party?"

"What does that have to do with this Hawk fella?" Martha asked.

"Hawk infiltrated the Party, disappeared for a couple of months, and resurfaced a few days ago. The Colonel wants Dom and me to make contact with Hawk as soon as possible."

That got Jackie's attention. "Don't we have enough problems with the Mafia? Do we now have to worry about Communist thugs and federal agents too?"

"Why would we have to fear the government?" Martha asked.

As Jackie explained, she had accumulated a wealth of knowledge about the Communist Party during her days as an assistant editor of the *Daily News*. She shared some of that with us. Martha and I hadn't known, for example, that the Communist Labor Party, one of many fractions of the Communist movement, had relocated their headquarters from Cleveland to New York in 1919. More shocking, Jackie said, was how fast the Party had grown. On the evening of November 8, 1919, seventy-one enclaves of the Communist Party of America were simultaneously raided throughout New York City by the local cops under the direction of the Feds. Jackie also knew about several major underground conventions held in the city since the raid.

"We don't need this," Jackie went on to say. "Sedition is a serious charge, and many arrested are still awaiting trial."

"So, you think the threat to our government is real?" I asked.

"Real and growing. Even though there's friction within the movement, everything is directly orchestrated from a Comintern in Moscow."

"A what?" Martha blurted out.

"A Comintern is a committee in Moscow with legislative power to spread Communism internationally. And believe me when I say, they have an enforcement arm."

That's all I needed to hear. One meeting with Hawk, and then the Colonel could go to hell. I wasn't going to let him entangle us in international politics.

"Look, based on what the Colonel said, I don't think Hawk's in any real danger. I told the Colonel that Dom and I would contact Hawk in a few weeks, and all we have to do is get some information. Right now we have more pressing issues facing us, like O'Reilly's murder trial."

"Not so fast," Martha said. "What about that photo of Debbie traipsing around naked?"

I gave the girls a detailed account of Ronnie's demise and Debbie's saga.

"I guess it'll be a long time before the mayor of Detroit wins another political race," Martha said. "Where is Debbie?"

That was the question I hoped they wouldn't ask.

"She's with Peggy."

They both looked at each other and asked in unison, "Who's Peggy?"

Neither one touched their food as I explained why Debbie hadn't returned. Martha couldn't take her eyes off me as I told about the gun fight. In contrast, Jackie waited till I'd finished before she turned her gaze on me.

"Do you have any other obligations to women we don't know about?" Jackie asked with a dose of sarcasm.

"What's that supposed to mean?"

"I'm getting fed up with all the women who just happen to pop into your life. It seems you can't go anywhere without finding a damsel in distress these days."

Jackie grabbed her purse from the table.

"I hope when I return from the powder room, we can discuss something important, like O'Reilly's case. You remember him? Your best friend."

I reached for her hand, but she yanked it away and headed to the back of the restaurant.

I turned to Martha. "What's bothering her?"

"I probably shouldn't tell you this, but she's seeing that guy from last year again, the one who took over as editor of the newspaper where she worked. He's putting a lot of pressure on her."

"Why didn't she say something? I could take care of him."

"Not that kind of pressure. He's asked her to marry him."

"That's ridiculous. They went out a few times, and it ended."

"You're wrong about that," Martha said. "Ask Jackie." Martha discreetly inched up her skirt and removed a flask she had strapped to her thigh. "It's gin," she said. "Keep it. You'll need it more than I do."

I took two swigs and shoved the flask into my coat pocket. Martha's news was so preposterous I didn't know what to say.

Jackie returned. "Are we ready to talk about O'Reilly?" she asked.

"Sure," I stammered, wanting to confront her now, but sensing I should wait until we were alone.

"Good, because if we don't come up with a miracle, he's gonna fry."

That got me out of my daze.

"Fry? What the hell changed in the few days I was gone? It sounds like you believe he's guilty now."

"It turns out the dead guy in bed with O'Reilly's wife, Bridget, was a neighbor from two doors down and a friend of O'Reilly's. Did I forget to mention he was also a cop?"

"What does that prove?"

"The DA is pushing the idea that O'Reilly was so outraged when he discovered his friend in bed with his wife, he went berserk and pummeled the guy's face—in an uncontrollable rage—after he shot him to death."

"That's just speculation," I said.

Jackie knocked off her drink and called for another. "Well, Frank thinks the jury will buy it. Then, there's the fact that the bullets were fired from O'Reilly's gun. The ballistic tests were a perfect match."

"That makes no sense. O'Reilly had two rods on him. If he was in such a rage, he would've pulled one of those and not reached for a gun hanging on the bedpost several feet away. Besides, as we discussed in the past, if he had, there would have been a struggle. The guy was shot in the back multiple times and never got a chance to get off Bridget."

"That's one of many things we've got to figure out... You know, Joey, maybe we could have gotten further if you hadn't been gallivanting around the country with wayward women."

"That's uncalled for."

"You think so? Tell that to O'Reilly. I gotta go. I've lost my appetite."

She grabbed her coat and purse and headed for the door.

Martha and I pushed past our bewildered waiter as we left the restaurant to catch up with Jackie.

* * * * *

I was surprised by how far ahead Jackie had walked. I took hold of Martha's hand and tried to move her along, but Martha resisted. She prodded me against the side of one of the brownstone porches that lined our street.

"I think it best to give Jackie a chance to gather her thoughts."

I watched Jackie climb the stairs and enter our building.

"How can she even consider such a proposal?"

"I don't know if you realize it, but we are no longer important in your life—we're just a small part."

"How can you say that?"

"Given our relationship, it doesn't bother me that you don't care that I'm seeing Rivisi. But Jackie's a different story. Did you ever tell her how you felt about her dating someone else?"

"No. I was jealous, but I can't control your lives. You understand that. I thought Jackie did too."

"I'm afraid it's too late for such a simple explanation. As I said, her friend has made a commitment and proposed."

My insides were churning. I had to do something, but what? Right now I didn't want to get tied down, but I couldn't lose Jackie.

"Look. Jackie said she wasn't ready to sit at home changing diapers, so I figured that was the end of any serious conversation."

"Never listen to what a woman *says*, because she'll say what she thinks you want to hear. Instead, listen to *how* she says it." Martha grabbed hold of my arm as we walked toward home.

"What about you?" I asked.

"Me? I'm the exception. I always say what I mean. Maybe that's why I'll never get married."

* * * * *

Ma was waiting for us as we entered the building. "Joey, what happened to Jackie? She came in crying and ran upstairs."

Martha gave me a peck on the cheek and headed toward the stairs.

"Good night, Mrs. Batista. I hope you can talk some sense into your son. Joey, if I were you, I'd get an update on O'Reilly's case from Frank. I've got a feeling Jackie's not gonna be much help for a few days."

"What's goin' on?" Ma asked, in a tone she hadn't used since I was a kid.

"The guy Jackie's been seeing proposed."

"And what did you do about it?"

"Nothing yet. I just found out from Martha."

"You have a lot to learn about women. Come inside, we need to talk."

Ma placed a bottle of whiskey on the table and filled two glasses.

"Now tell me, do you love Jackie?"

I didn't hesitate. "I do. I'm just not ready to get married."

"Who said anything about marriage? Look, Joey, a woman has two basic fears and they're related: getting too old to have kids and ending up a spinster. I don't think Jackie wants to get married now, but she's been asked to make a decision, and from the way she ran upstairs, I think she doesn't understand where your relationship's going."

I felt as confused as ever. "If she loves this guy, maybe it's best for everyone if she accepts his proposal."

Ma shook her head and rubbed her face with both hands.

"Joey, I'm gonna say something that's gonna hurt, but it needs to be said. Do you regret walking away from Anita?"

I had to look down. "Every day of my life. She would be alive today if I'd stayed and told her how I felt. I know we could've found a way to make things work."

Ma squeezed my hand and then went into her bedroom.

She came back with a small velvet box. It contained a ring with a sparkling green stone.

"This belonged to your grandmother. It's not worth much, but in a way, it's priceless. I want you to have it. Just remember, getting engaged doesn't mean you need to get married tomorrow. It's a commitment, and I think that's all Jackie needs. I could be wrong, but it's worth a try. At least it will tell her how you feel."

* * * * *

I stood in front of Jackie's apartment door and then walked away, only to return. If I didn't act, chances were that Jackie would be out of my life forever. Even though I didn't want that to happen, I still hesitated, wondering if Ma was right.

Right or not, I had to do something. I couldn't make the same mistake again. I knocked.

Chapter 19

Jackie blocked me from entering her apartment with her body when she saw it was me.

"I don't want to see you tonight," she said, wiping tears from her cheeks.

I pushed her back and closed the door behind me. "You don't have a choice. You said it yourself—we need to talk."

"There's nothing to talk about."

"How can you say that? Have the last couple of years meant nothing to you?"

A slap in the face I might have expected, but not a right punch to the jaw. Since I didn't see it coming, it hurt like hell. She sure knew how to throw a right cross.

"You ask me that when it's you who can't keep your hands off Martha, who seduced Gloria with the sorry excuse that it was the only way to make sure she wouldn't talk to the DA. I'm not a fool, Joey."

"We covered all of this before. How many times do we have to agree that neither of us is ready to settle down?"

"As many times as it takes for you to stop hearing only what you want to hear."

I pulled her in close, not knowing how she would react. She held on tight.

"This is too important for us to be yelling at each other. Let's start over," I said.

We separated.

"I need a few moments alone," Jackie said and walked into her bedroom.

I went into the kitchen and put on a pot of coffee. I stood there, deep in my own thoughts, as the coffee percolated, pinging against the small glass dome over and over, taking on a darker color.

Jackie inched me aside, looking refreshed, and turned off the flame.

"If it gets much stronger, we'll be up all night," she said, placing two cups on the opposite ends of her table.

I spilled some, as the first sip burned my lips. Jackie let out a small chuckle.

"Serves you right," she said, holding her cup and gently blowing across the surface of the coffee.

"Martha tells me someone has asked you to marry him. How long have you been seeing him?"

Jackie put down her cup. "I thought you'd never ask."

"It's not that I wasn't interested. I didn't want to know the details—I was jealous."

"He worked for my husband, and actually, he took over his position after his death. I worked closely with him in the past. We went out a few times last year, and then I broke things off, until recently. He called while you were in Detroit."

I tried the coffee again, this time with success. I needed time to think.

"When I first met you, it appeared you had everything a woman could want—money, prestige, a loving husband—yet something seemed lacking in your life."

"I was bored. My world was artificial, devoid of the unexpected."

"But if you marry this guy, wouldn't you be returning to the same life? Is that what you want now?"

"No, I don't want to go backwards. What I want, and have always wanted, is to go forward with you. But I need to know that's possible; that we can have a normal life without fearing death every waking moment. That much excitement I can do without."

I moved my chair closer and took hold of her hands.

"Jackie, I want you to know this, and I hope you already do—I love you, and I want the same as you. But I can't desert my family or my neighbors when they need me the most."

Tears filled Jackie's eyes as she gripped my hands tighter.

"I'm not asking you to turn your back on your neighborhood, and neither would I. What I'm asking for is some assurance that we will have a life together, a fairly normal one."

I reached into my pocket and took out the velvet ring box Ma had given me.

"This ring belonged to my grandmother. I'd like you to take it as an engagement ring or simply as a sign of my love for you. In either case, I'm committing myself to you."

Jackie first held the ring in the palm of her hand, and then she put it on her ring finger. Her next move surprised me. She flew out of her chair onto my lap and landed so hard that we tumbled onto the floor. We rolled around until she ended up on top and pinned me down.

"Promise me one thing. When O'Reilly and Hawk are safe and the neighborhood is stable, with or without the Mafia, we will try to build a real business. One that doesn't have us constantly looking over our shoulders and tripping over dead bodies."

"Does this mean we're engaged?" I asked, smiling.

"It does. So, no more women, and that includes Martha."

I put on a serious face. "That's gonna create a big void in my life."

Jackie pulled me up from the floor. "Then I suggest we start filling that void right now."

Chapter 20

The next morning, Jackie and I walked into the office together. As the door opened, Martha turned away from a filing cabinet and came toward us.

"Well, are we still a team?" she asked.

Jackie showed her the ring and received a big hug. Martha turned to me but then looked back at Jackie.

"One last time?"

Jackie nodded, and Martha planted a kiss on me that sent us both reeling backward. I raised my hands, trying not to respond. Jackie cracked up.

As Martha slowly backed away, she whispered in my ear. "You're gonna miss me." She then gave me a gentle kiss on the cheek.

"So, when's the big day?" Martha asked Jackie.

"We're not in any hurry. We have a real detective agency to build first, and that's where you can help."

"I'm all for that," Martha said, pointing to a file drawer of cases she had turned away in the past.

Just then, Ma flung open the door. "I'm not waiting any longer. Are you two getting married or did you give my son the bum's rush?" she asked, looking straight at Jackie.

Jackie held out her hand and was yanked into a crushing embrace. "I'm gonna be a grandmother. We gotta have a big party. I'll take care of everything, don't you worry," Ma said. She ran to tell Pop the news.

All we could do was laugh. Jackie wanted to stop Ma

before she planned a block party, but I thought it could wait until dinner when everyone was together. It was more important to hear what Frank had to say about the mounting evidence against O'Reilly.

* * * * *

When the three of us entered Frank's office, Sadie said a polite hello and took a seat in a corner, ready to take notes. It hadn't taken Frank long to mold her into the secretary he wanted—a sharp contrast to Martha's style.

Frank's report was no laughing matter.

"The DA has expedited a court hearing. We don't have much time to mount a defense."

"Did you guys get the chance to go through the apartment after I left for Detroit?"

"Once the DA and his men trashed the place, we were allowed to look around. Jackie did notice a few differences from when you two had entered illegally before the investigators finished with the crime scene," Frank said. He asked Jackie to give me the details.

"The holster hanging on the bedpost was gone, and the coat we saw on the rack in the parlor was replaced with a more common, inexpensive overcoat. Everything else looked the same except for the mess the cops left behind. They emptied closets and tossed the bureau contents on the floor."

"I suspect the DA was looking for evidence that O'Reilly was on the take," Frank said.

I didn't think that was as important as what Jackie had said about the coat. "Why aren't you guys more excited about the coat? It's a significant piece of evidence."

"Joey, what do you expect me to say during the trial? 'Gentlemen of the jury, my investigative team broke into the crime scene before the authorities arrived and noticed an expensive Chesterfield sable-lined overcoat, which has since disappeared from the scene, thus proving without a doubt that someone besides the dead flatfoot and Officer O'Reilly were in the room on that fatal night.'"

"It might lead us to the killer," I said.

"I hope it does, but without corroborating evidence, it's inadmissible."

Begrudgingly I admitted that Frank was right. I had hoped for a break, but it didn't sound like they had made any real progress. "What information have you gathered on the guy who got knocked off, aside from the fact that he was a flatfoot?"

Jackie poured herself a glass of water. "There's not much. He was a sergeant, single, who seldom had company."

"That's it? None of O'Reilly's neighbors heard or saw anything?"

"Not that they would say to us," Jackie said.

"You interviewed everyone?"

"We have a lot more to go," Martha said.

"I know we don't have much more to go on, but let's see if we can add to our original theory of what took place on the night of the murders. I'll start." I said.

"Bridget wanted a better life, and O'Reilly wasn't providing it. She probably found herself a sugar daddy, but knew O'Reilly would never agree to a divorce. That left her with only two choices: have him bumped off or make his life so unbearable that he would seek a divorce."

"She seduced this poor sap, who was on the force and a friend of O'Reilly's, hoping she'd get caught in the act," Jackie added.

Martha picked up the narrative. "But instead of O'Reilly, mister money bags shows up unexpectedly."

"That's where I have a problem," Frank said. "Like I said before, this is all supposition. How do you know someone else entered the apartment before O'Reilly, and that he was rich?"

"The overcoat," Jackie and I said in unison. I nodded for her to explain.

"You said it yourself, Frank. It was an expensive coat. So who did the coat belong to? Certainly not O'Reilly or the dead cop."

Frank threw up his hands. "Okay, we have some rich guy who enters the apartment. What happens next?"

"He's outraged," I said. "Sees the gun in a holster hanging on the bedpost and shoots them both. He's halfway down the fire escape when O'Reilly arrives."

Frank shook his head. "We still have the issue of how he grabbed the gun without a struggle. Let's not forget the guy in bed was shot multiple times in the back. It's more likely that O'Reilly had the gun—normally hanging by the bedside—on him and killed them both. Why he had that gun on him that night, I don't know. But it would explain the evidence."

"Frank, we don't have all the facts. You should know that, and if you don't start believing in O'Reilly, I'm gonna tell him to hire a different lawyer."

Frank was about to respond when Jackie spoke up.

"Boys, let's calm down. None of this is helping O'Reilly."

Jackie turned to Martha. "You've been unusually quiet. What do you think?"

"Right now, I'm like the rest of you with more questions

than answers. But, I don't think it's a good time to ask them."

"Do you think O'Reilly is guilty?"

"No, so I don't have a problem with where we're headed with the investigation as long as we go where the evidence takes us."

Martha had made a good point. We needed to put our emotional feelings aside and be professional.

"I realize we can sit here all day shooting holes in our theory," I said. "But we're going with it because it fits with the evidence we've gathered so far and the little we know about O'Reilly's wife, Bridget. It also assumes that O'Reilly is innocent, which is where we need to start our investigation."

"It's great to have a theory," Frank said. "But how do we find this guy and prove he did the killings?

"The key assumption here is that the killer is wealthy, so we should ask the waiters at the most expensive restaurants in the city if they recognize Bridget's picture," Jackie said.

"If her sugar daddy wanted to avoid a scandal, we should start with the restaurants furthest away," Martha suggested.

I explained to Frank that I had another pressing case and Carmine to deal with, so he agreed to hire a couple of low-rent gumshoes to hit the high-class joints around town with a picture of O'Reilly's wife. It was a long shot, but worth a try. Frank also agreed to set up a visit with O'Reilly so I could get his side of the story firsthand. We shook and ended on good terms.

Jackie and I were headed back to our office when images of the murder scene flashed through my mind. Jackie didn't notice that I had stopped walking.

"Jackie, I just thought of something important," I said, heading back to Frank's office and throwing the door open.

"Sorry, Frank, but we've overlooked a key piece of evidence. Jackie, do you remember seeing any shell casings the day we broke into O'Reilly's apartment?"

She thought for a moment.

"No, but couldn't they have been removed by the detectives?"

"It was still an active crime scene, and the lab guys hadn't arrived. With so many shots fired, shell casings should have littered the floor and some could have landed on the bed."

"What are you getting at?" Frank asked.

"If O'Reilly was in such a rage, why would he gather up the shell casings? Did he have them on him when they picked him up? And if not, where did they go? You said his neighbors were on him within minutes after the shots were fired. The only logical answer is that the guy O'Reilly heard climbing down the fire escape took them with him."

"I haven't been given access to all the evidence the DA has gathered, but so far, there's been no mention of shell casings or of an overcoat," Frank said.

"Until we figure out the significance of the missing casings, I suggest you keep this quiet. It might be something you can spring on the jury during the trial."

As Jackie and I walked back to our office, I made a bold confession to her. "I have to admit there was a part of me that wondered if O'Reilly did do it. Who could blame him?"

Chapter 21

While the others moved ahead with O'Reilly's case, it was time to confront Carmine.

At first I was surprised to hear Carmine had moved into Castellano's old office behind the pizza shop, but then again, it had been the center of the neighborhood since he was a kid. Even more surprising was the fact that—given the recent violence there—the joint was jammed, and people were waiting behind us to get in.

I spotted Carmine sitting with Toby and a couple of his men at Castellano's private booth. Carmine glanced at us as we entered but paid no mind as Jackie and I approached his table.

Toby reacted first. "I see you brought your bodyguard. Should I be afraid of getting my throat slit, because I can think of better ways I'd rather die in her gorgeous hands."

He and his two men laughed.

"Cut the crap, you guys," Carmine said, looking up from his plate of pasta. "Batista, this is not a good time."

"Then I suggest we move into your office. Your pal, Ronnie Ligotti, is dead, along with the trash you sent to take me out on the way to Detroit."

Carmine glanced over at Toby as he wiped his napkin across his lips. "Take your boys and find another table. I have some private business to discuss with Batista."

Toby was about to object, then thought better of it. He shoved several customers out of their nearby chairs and sat within earshot. Carmine ignored Toby's defiance.

Jackie had positioned herself at a table not far from Carmine's so she could keep an eye on us and Toby. I'd never thought of Jackie as my bodyguard, but right now, there was no one I'd rather have watching my back.

I took a seat next to Carmine and poured myself a drink.

"We'll talk here for a few minutes and then head to the office," Carmine said. "Let's start with Ronnie. I'm sure he got what he deserved, but from your tone it sounds like you think I tried to stop you. Why would you think—after all we've been through together—that I would side with him?"

"Carmine, cut the bullshit. If I hadn't gotten Big Ben off your back, you'd be holed up in an abandoned basement in Canada by now. You talk tough, but scare easy, always have."

"You're forgetting who you're talking to. That might not be wise."

"What's the matter, does the truth hurt? You and I both know that you need to form alliances to keep Big Ben at bay. After all, Big Ben's been around a long time. It would be easy for him to get others to interfere with your operations. Who better for you to start an alliance with than Ronnie?"

"That thought never crossed my mind."

"I'm surprised. Then there's the fact that the goons who ambushed me were all from around here."

"Why are you surprised? Everyone knew what your intent was when you left for Detroit. Don't forget Ronnie has been idolized in the neighborhood since we were kids for killing that hitman Big Ben had sent to take out Luigi and my pop. Besides, even if those three goons were my men, I can't control everything they do."

"I didn't mention there were three."

Carmine rolled up a fork full of spaghetti. "That's how many men I'm missing," he said with a grin, then shoved the food into his mouth.

I reached for a half-eaten plate of antipasti and stuck a toothpick in a marinated olive. "Well, at least you know Toby isn't hiring cowards. They died the way they lived. If you're not careful, that could happen to you."

Carmine raised his voice above the din of the crowd. "You're threatening me?"

"Take it any way you want, but I saw what you're building down along the waterfront. If you screw up my neighborhood, you'll know for certain what I mean."

"*Your* neighborhood!" Carmine yelled. "I'm the boss, not you. Don't you forget that."

Toby reached for one of his rods as he came toward me. Jackie had a shiv against the side of his neck before the gun was out of its holster. She removed his guns and tossed them on the floor.

"I suggest you tell your men to put their iron away and join me for a slice of pizza," she said, leading him to her table.

Seeing that the place was emptying out, Carmine threw down his napkin and headed for his office. I followed.

* * * * *

"Are you out of your mind? You know I can't tolerate that kind of disrespect," Carmine shouted.

"You're right, I can't prove that you or Toby sent those men after me so I'll ignore what happened on my way to Detroit, but I won't let you turn this neighborhood into a dung heap like the rest of the city."

"Whorehouses are as common as restaurants. What's the harm in making a little extra cash and keeping it in the neighborhood? It's gonna get spent anyway."

"That's not how your father looked at things."

"My father isn't the saint you take him for. You know damn well what goes on in the backrooms of all his speakeasies. Ask your uncle why he has so many waitresses working in his joint?"

"It's not blatant, though, and the girls aren't owned by some overpriced madam."

"Oh, so that makes it acceptable? You have a strange sense of decency. Tell me something, mister righteousness, were you and I at the same meeting with Vigliotti? I have two years to contribute more to the syndicate coffers than Big Ben or lose everything—including my life. Unless you have a different idea, I'm gonna have several houses up and running within six months."

I knew where this was heading and I had to stop it.

"Carmine, don't take this path. It will lead to trouble, more than you can imagine."

Carmine shoved me back. "What's the alternative? You want Big Ben to run things around here… I didn't think so."

"There's gotta be a better way."

"When you find one, let me know. But for now, there's prostitution, drugs, protection, and gambling. And they're all coming to town. Get used to it."

Carmine opened the door.

I stopped at the threshold. "You know what this means," I said, locking eyes with him.

"I do, so watch your back because the next time someone comes after you, it will be on my orders. Your friendship isn't worth dying for— it never has been."

When Carmine slammed the door behind me, Toby turned. The place had completely emptied except for Jackie, Toby, and the new owner, who was also the chef.

I pulled up a chair and picked up the butcher knife Jackie had placed on the table near her right hand.

"I'm surprised you didn't make a move while Jackie ate," I said to Toby, sitting down next to Jackie.

"I'm not an idiot. I've heard of her reputation."

"Apparently, so have your men." I cut a slice from a loaf of bread. "Toby, I'm gonna give you some good advice—get the hell out of town. There's only one way things are gonna end for you in the long run, and it's not good."

"Funny, I was thinking the same about you two," he said, ripping off a chunk of bread. "I'm gonna enjoy slicing you up for fish bait, but first, I'm gonna have some fun with your whore."

I heaved my side of the table on edge and shoved it against his chest sending him over backwards and trapping him in his chair. As he struggled to get out from under the table, I shoved my gun against his temple.

"Get out of town, because the next time you provoke me—you're dead."

On the way out, Jackie picked up the rods from the floor and tossed them over the counter, away from the chef. She then took hold of my arm as we left the pizza parlor.

"It's good to see that our engagement improved your temperament," she said.

I knew better than to respond. The normal life she had talked about when she accepted my proposal wasn't looking possible in this neighborhood or any other part of the city.

Chapter 22

As we entered the apartment building, the aroma of fresh basil filled the hallway, along with the sound of Ma singing in Italian. Rather than interrupt the making of a culinary masterpiece, Jackie and I glanced into Pop's shoe repair shop to say hello. He had a line of customers backed up, so he gave us a quick wave and refocused on a pair of shoes with a broken strap.

We stopped in on Frank to see if he had arranged a visitation with O'Reilly at the prison.

"We have an eight o'clock meeting tomorrow morning. The DA objected, but he didn't have a choice. O'Reilly hired your detective agency. Here's the contract he signed."

"How much time do we have?" Jackie asked.

"Not much, an hour, so have your questions ready."

"How's he doing?" I asked.

"He was more worried about you. He knew you were going after Ronnie," Frank said, heading for the door. "I'm expecting a client. I'll pick you guys up outside at seven-thirty."

No sooner did the door shut when Martha stuck her head into the hallway.

"Angela is on the phone and she's on the verge of hysterics—something about Carmine wanting to kill the both of you."

* * * * *

Carmine hadn't spoken directly to his wife, Angela, but she had overheard Castellano arguing with Carmine on the phone.

"Angela, you don't need to worry," I said. "Carmine and I aren't going to clash anytime soon. My hope is he'll come to his senses and not destroy what his father spent most of his life protecting."

I actually believed what I was saying until Angela mentioned that Carmine had also threatened Castellano if he tried to interfere with how he planned on running his territory.

Castellano then grabbed the phone from Angela and insisted Luigi and I come to his place to discuss how to deal with his son. I tried to push back, but he hung up on me mid-sentence.

"That didn't sound like it went well," Jackie said.

"I'm afraid I'm gonna have to round up Luigi and head over to Staten Island."

"What about O'Reilly?" Martha asked. "Jackie said you have a meeting with him in the morning and you need to prepare. This might be your only chance to speak with him before the preliminary hearing."

She had a point, but from the urgency in Castellano's voice, there was a good chance I had underestimated the danger Carmine posed, and not just to me.

"In truth, the two of you would have to spend half the night bringing me up to speed. Jackie can drive the conversation tomorrow. I'll ask follow-up questions as they come to me."

Martha looked over to Jackie. "Do I sense a new level of trust?"

Jackie smiled and held up her ring finger. "It is amazing what a man will do to keep his woman happy."

* * * * *

With everything that had happened since I'd been back in town, I'd never asked if Luigi had returned from Detroit. I didn't think it critical that he come along to Castellano's, so if he wasn't at his speakeasy, I intended to leave without him.

I was a step away from opening the door to the front of the building when Ma stepped into the hallway and called out.

"Hey Joey, what's a matter with you? You don't say hello to your mother anymore? What am I, just someone who cooks around here?"

"Sorry Ma, I've got a lot on my mind."

"Don't we all? You comin' to dinner tonight? I'm makin' something extra special."

"What's the occasion?"

"How do I know? I'm just the cook. Luigi said he has a surprise for us and I should make a feast."

I went over and hugged her. "What are you always tellin' me about Italian food?"

"The best-tasting food in the world."

"I agree, but don't forget it tastes even better on the second day."

She put her hands on her hips and gave me one of those looks that said, don't you dare tell me you're not coming to dinner.

I gave her a peck on the cheek and ran for the exit. "Sorry Ma, Luigi doesn't know it yet, but Castellano wants to see us both right now. Not sure we'll be back in time."

She had cussed in every language she knew by the time the door closed.

The Gumshoe Chronicles 1922

* * * * *

Luigi's joint was as busy as usual, and I found myself counting the number of waitresses Luigi had working. Carmine was right. My uncle had way more than he needed. I even noticed a couple of new faces. One woman was fixing drinks behind the bar, which had to be a first in this town.

Luigi usually liked to work the crowd, so when I didn't spot him making the rounds, I entered his office. He was sitting behind his desk staring at a blank wall with a drink in his hand and two bottles by his elbow—one already three-fourths empty and the other opened, ready to go.

I took the glass from his hand, poured the whiskey down the sink and capped both bottles. I wanted to dunk his head in the john but, instead, opted for a wet cloth. He looked up at me with glazed eyes.

"Uncle, you're lucky you don't buy that cheap rot gut that most other joints stock. If you did, I'd be calling the funeral hall right now."

"Nothin' but the best for my customers," Luigi slurred, then slumped back in his chair.

"Don't move. I'm goin' to get some coffee."

I waved over the broad behind the bar.

"I need a pot of joe for Luigi, and make it fast."

She grabbed the coffee, rounded the corner of the bar, and headed straight for the office. "Is somethin' wrong with my sweetie?" she asked.

She poured Luigi a cup of coffee and put it in his hand. "I don't know what I got myself into. He's been like this since we left Detroit."

"You're from Detroit?"

Luigi looked up. "Joey, meet Gracie. Gracie, meet your new nephew, Joey."

Gracie clapped both hands upside my head and planted one hell of a kiss on my lips. When she let go, I stammered out some unintelligible words.

"Joey, Gracie's my, er, my wife."

Gracie put her arm through mine and yanked me close. "Oh, it was all so romantic. He picked me out of all those younger girls, and once he told me he owned a speakeasy and an apartment building in New York City, I knew he was the man for me. Would you believe there was a preacher in the next room? It was just meant to be."

My first thought was to ask Frank if he knew a good divorce lawyer, but that would have to wait until I got back from Castellano's.

"I need to get him sober enough to travel to Staten Island for a meeting. How about giving me a hand?"

"Don't you worry, honey, I have a lot of experience with this sort of thing. I'll have him throwing up that rot gut in no time. Then after a cold shower and a few more cups of coffee, he'll be as sober as me."

I wasn't sure how sober that was, but I helped get Luigi to a room they had reserved for themselves and left him in her questionable hands.

* * * * *

An hour and a half later, Luigi was leaning over the back railing of a ferryboat—halfway between Manhattan and Staten Island—heaving up his guts. Some color returned to his face as I helped him over to the side railing where a short wooden bench was positioned outside the interior cabin. The fresh air was having a sobering effect as he stood and spit over the side.

"You gonna tell me what this is all about?" he asked. "Forget that. Get me something to wash out my mouth, and then you can tell me what the hell is goin' on."

I returned with a cup of water from the refreshment stand and waited until he settled back down.

"You go first," I said. "I've never seen you so smashed. Is it because of her? All you have to do is get a divorce. It doesn't sound like you were married in a church."

"Hell, why would I want a divorce? Gracie is one hell of a woman. She's not bad lookin', knows how to have a good time, she's great in bed, and to top it off, she has a head for business. What more could I ask?"

"So, what's the problem? Why did I find you wallowing in a bucket of booze?"

"Your folks are the problem. How am I gonna explain to them that I married a used-up whore?"

"You're right. You do have a problem."

Thanks, you're a big help. Now it's your turn. Why the rush to see Castellano?"

"Carmine and I had a run-in today. I guess I'm gonna end up tellin' Castellano that sooner or later I'll have to kill his son."

Luigi finished the last of the water and crushed the paper cup.

"You know somethin', Joey? I don't think that will come as a shock to him."

"What do you mean?"

"Did you ever wonder why Castellano asked you to take over as the neighborhood boss rather than Carmine?"

"He basically told me he didn't trust Carmine, but when I turned him down, he asked me to help his son."

"I guess in the end, a parent always hopes for the best. When you were kids, though, did you ever see Castellano spend time with Carmine?"

"I assumed he was too busy."

"Think about it. The boss can do whatever he wants. He chose not to be with his son because he hated the boy's mother and resented having him."

"I thought she died during childbirth."

"She did, and he was grateful. He never wanted to marry her, but she got him drunk, got pregnant, and back home in those days there were no excuses. You had to do the right thing."

"What was she like?"

"She was a nomad, a Gypsy, a beautiful woman, and evil to the core. She had used Castellano to get a better life. After she died, she was buried at sea. It was your mother who took care of Carmine on board ship, and for a little more than a year. When Castellano got established, he hired a live-in nanny."

The ferry slid into the slip, jolting us against each other.

"We better get in the car so we don't hold up the other drivers," I said, offering to help. He pushed my hand away, looking more sober than I had expected.

We sat in silence as I inched the car off the ferry and exited the terminal. Luigi was absorbed in his own thoughts, and I needed the time to reflect on what my uncle had revealed. If there wasn't a strong bond between Castellano and his son, how far would Castellano go to keep Carmine from corrupting the neighborhood? What would happen if I had to defend myself against Carmine?

Given Castellano's earlier tone on the phone, I was about to find out.

Chapter 23

As we entered Castellano's driveway, I noticed Angela leaning against a support column on the front porch, clutching a long sweater around herself. She waved as we came closer.

I dropped Luigi off by the front step and was about to go park the car when he popped his head through the open window.

"Take a walk with Angela and give me fifteen minutes alone with Castellano. That way I'll have a chance to find out what the hell is on his mind."

Angela had walked over to the car and took hold of my arm as I got out.

"Luigi said we should take a short stroll."

"How have you been?" I asked.

"I'm doing as well as can be expected."

"Carmine hasn't changed his attitude about your abduction?"

"No, but I'm not surprised. I was never an important part of his life. I knew he had other women. I was just a storefront that helped legitimize his business, someone to prove that he was a family man, a person who could be trusted. In his eyes, I'm no longer useful to his career."

"Sounds like you got caught up in a marriage of convenience. He got what he wanted, a beautiful woman, and you became a member of the Boss's family?"

"I was young and impressionable. Your mother once

told me not to marry for the wrong reasons—I wish I had listened."

I put my arm around her shoulder, and she rested her head against me as we continued along a cobblestone path that wove through flower beds.

"What happened today between Carmine and Castellano?"

She stopped at a bench and gestured for me to join her.

"Carmine called and said you were interfering with how he wanted to run things. The more they talked, the angrier Castellano became. He reminded Carmine that he and others had made a sacred oath to protect and help each other when they arrived from Sicily, and that you and your family were included in that pledge."

"I'm sure Carmine didn't give a damn about a pledge made twenty-five years ago."

"To be honest, Joey, it wouldn't make a difference if the pledge was made yesterday. We better head back. Castellano is anxious to talk with you."

"How is he recovering from his wounds?"

"He has numbness in his left arm. Other than that, he's back to his old self."

"What about his grandson? Has Castellano come to grips with what actually happened?"

"A local priest has been spending time with him. I think it's helping."

"What about you?" I asked, taking hold of her hand.

She smiled. "We haven't held hands since we were little kids."

"Sometimes we all need a hand to hold."

"I miss Antonio. He was my strength. Now I have his grandfather, but soon he will no longer need me."

"Don't worry about Castellano, he'll never abandon you."

We returned to the house in silence.

* * * * *

Angela snatched the whiskey bottle my uncle and Castellano were sharing from the table.

"Getting smoked has never solved a problem. It'll just give you a headache and a rotten disposition."

"What did I tell you?" Castellano said to Luigi. "I'm stuck with the daughter-in-law from hell."

"I heard that," Angela said, placing a pot of coffee on the table, along with three mugs. "All I can say is you deserve me. I'll leave the three of you alone so you can solve your issues in private. If you need something, I'll be upstairs in my room."

When she was gone, Castellano got right to the heart of the matter.

"Joey, if you kill my son, no matter what the provocation, you, and possibly those around you, will be slaughtered within the week."

I looked over to my uncle. I didn't expect a threat from Castellano, especially after what Luigi had just told me on the ferry about Castellano's relationship with Carmine.

"He's talking about the syndicate," Luigi said. "Big Ben has been trying to convince the other bosses that you're a danger to the entire organization. Kill Carmine and you'll make his point."

"What the hell am I supposed to do? Just sit by and let him destroy the neighborhood?"

Castellano took a sip of coffee. "You need to understand something. It's not your neighborhood. It's mine, and Carmine is running it. The sooner you realize that, the longer you'll live."

"Are you saying my only option is to leave the streets where I was raised?"

"No, of course not. You have the right to protect yourself and those you care about. Just don't kill my son."

"No matter what he does?"

"You got it."

There wasn't much more to be said. I rose to leave.

"Remember, Joey, I gave you the chance to run things. You turned me down."

I'd admired Castellano since I was a kid. Now I had my doubts.

"If you gave a damn about the neighborhood, you'd never have put Carmine in your position. You knew what he would do, but you didn't care then and you don't care now. I'll back off, but if he harms anyone close to me, I'll destroy his organization, and if it comes down to him or me, I think you know how that's gonna end."

Luigi got up and tried to usher me to the front door, but I wasn't done. I had more to say.

"You're the only one who can stop Carmine. Even though he threatened you, you just sit here day after day wallowing in self-pity. When are you gonna realize that you didn't kill your grandson? Butch did. Angela understands that, and it's about time you did too. There was no reason for you to abdicate your position as Boss."

"Batista, as long as I'm alive and rational, I'm still the Boss, and if my son can't handle his new responsibilities, I'll deal with him—not you or anyone else. You better get that through your thick skull."

Luigi shoved me out the door.

As I drove out of Castellano's estate, Luigi lit up a smoke.

"You sure know how to sober up a guy. I never heard anyone speak to Castellano that way."

"It needed to be said."

"I've known him all my life, and if I were you, I wouldn't assume he's not a threat. If he's pushed to the edge, I promise, you won't recognize the man."

"I'm not the one pushing him, Carmine is! Tell me why the hell did he order us to come to his place? He could've told me to back off over the phone."

"While you were with Angela, Castellano and I agreed on how to help Carmine understand how best to run things in the neighborhood."

"How's that?"

"Leave that to us. You're too young to understand the old ways, and, given how Carmine's acting, neither does he."

I knew pressing Luigi further would be fruitless. Besides, I'd had enough of Castellano and Carmine for one day. Let them solve their own problems. I had other concerns.

* * * * *

The ferry ride back to Manhattan was better than our earlier ride to Staten Island. Luigi, now sober, wanted to know about O'Reilly and if I thought he was guilty. He then probed, as he often did when we were alone, into the type of missions I went on during the war, which I gave vague answers to, as usual.

"Sorry, kid. I guess there are some things we all need to keep to ourselves. I certainly have mine. But that's not gonna stop me from asking."

"Maybe someday we'll swap stories, but not now. It's too soon. The memories too vivid."

Luigi lit up a stogie. "War stinks."

Several passengers moved away. "And so does your cigar," I said.

Luigi noticed we were standing alone and laughed.

Chapter 24

Luigi had me drop him off at his speakeasy and gave me the task of asking Ma to set an extra place at the dinner table for the next night.

"Why do I have to tell her about Gracie?" I asked. "She's gonna drill me for details that I know nothing about."

"Good, the less you know the better. Besides, you owe me."

"How do you figure that?"

"Isn't this my car you've been driving around?"

"So? You haven't missed it. My guess is you and Gracie haven't left the speakeasy since you arrived back in town. You've got everything you need right here: booze, a woman, your business, and a place to bed down."

"Don't be such a wise guy. When am I getting my jalopy back?"

"In two days. That's when my new car arrives."

Luigi put his hand out. "Okay, so gimme my key."

He knew I couldn't do that. I needed a car. "All right, I'll tell Ma, but first, I'm coming up for a few drinks. I'm gonna need them. With any luck, she'll be in bed before I get home."

* * * * *

Gracie popped out from behind the bar, gave Luigi a kiss on the cheek, and led us to a booth.

"What can I get you, nephew? I know what he needs, more coffee. He's still looking peaked."

"I'll have a couple of beers, and keep 'em comin'," I said.

Luigi stood and announced he was going to bed. He'd had enough coffee and wanted to sleep off his headache.

Gracie came back, placed a tray of beers on the table, and sat opposite me. "Here's to tomorrow night, dinner with the family," she said and knocked off half a glass before I got mine to my lips.

"So Joey, what do you want to know?"

"Did you marry my uncle for his money?"

"Of course I did."

It was my turn to gulp down a beer. "Do you love him?"

She scrunched up her face and weaved ever so slightly from side-to-side. "I like him, he's fun to be with, but love? That's a strong word. It'll come with time."

"Why did you leave the business?"

"Age. I was the oldest girl, and the customers were few and far between. At most, I had a year left before I was tossed out of the house."

She took hold of my hand. "Joey, I'm not going to hurt him. You may not think this, but he's a lonely man. We need each other."

She got up to leave. I asked her to sit back down.

"What did you do before getting in the business?"

"I was a hoofer, or thought I was. I always liked dancing, but I wasn't good enough to make a living. I even tried singing, but a canary I'm not."

"So how did you get started in the business?"

"I met this guy. We went out a few times, and one morning I found money on my dresser. That night a friend of his came over. I knew what he wanted and I was desperate. The rest is, as they say, old history."

I was sure half the women working the houses had similar stories.

"Can you cook?"

"You mean like bacon and eggs?"

I had to chuckle.

"Let me give you some advice. Tomorrow night, when you come over to meet the family, don't try to hide who you are. If they don't figure it out, Luigi will probably tell them after a few drinks."

"Then what?"

"Relax. Ask my ma if she will teach you some of Luigi's favorite dishes. Be honest like you have been with me, and show them you care for Luigi. You do that and no one will judge you by your past."

Gracie's eyes filled with tears. "I hope you're right, but at this point in my life, it's hard to believe such people exist."

* * * * *

By the time I finished talking with Gracie and got home, my folks were getting ready for bed. I first thought it best to break the news about Gracie in the morning, but changed my mind as I walked up the stairs to my apartment. It occurred to me that it might be better if they slept on the news.

I answered their questions as candidly as I could. Pop didn't have much to say. He only wanted to know if she was good looking. It was harder to tell how Ma really felt, but her reaction was as pragmatic as ever. "It's about time he found a woman. Maybe now he won't be so grumpy. We don't have to worry about Luigi. If she's only after his dough, she won't last long. He's the biggest tightwad I've ever met."

I laughed and kissed her good night. I had done my part. The rest was up to Luigi and Gracie.

Chapter 25

If there was one honest cop in the city, it was O'Reilly. I never thought I'd see him in prison garb.

We shook hands and embraced. "It looks like prison food agrees with you," I said. "You're looking pretty fit."

"They have me in solitary confinement—cops don't last long in the slammer when mixed in the general population. To kill time I've been doing sit-ups and push-ups."

"And it hasn't hurt you've had to lay off the booze," Frank said.

"Oh, I wouldn't be so sure I've done that," O'Reilly said with a broad smile. "I have a few friends on the force."

Jackie sat down at the head of the only table in the room and spread out her papers.

"We have only an hour so I suggest we use it wisely."

I sat on one side of Jackie, and O'Reilly took the seat opposite me. Frank, though, stood in a corner with his arms folded. He knew if he asked questions during this meeting, it would influence our investigation. He had said he wanted an independent perspective, free of his own preconceived biases.

"Mike, Jackie's going to ask the majority of the questions, and I'll limit mine to points of clarification."

O'Reilly shifted his chair to face Jackie.

"One of the things that concerns us is we haven't found anyone who saw or heard you enter the building or run up the stairs. The prosecution will argue that's because you were already in your apartment before the shots were fired. It's important we know how many minutes passed from the time you heard the shots to the time you entered the bedroom."

O'Reilly took a deep breath. "It felt like forever. I was driving by my apartment building looking for a parking space when I heard several gunshots. They sounded like they came from the top of the building."

"How did you hear the shots so clearly? Weren't you still in your car?" I asked.

"I had the window down, and the street was deserted."

"What happened next?" Jackie asked.

"I slammed on the brakes, left the car in the street, and ran up the stoop. We live in a secure building, so the front door was locked. I had my gun in one hand and keys in the other. The keys dropped as I tried to open the door, and then I had trouble locating the correct one in the dark. It took two or three tries to get the door unlocked."

Frank stepped away from the wall. "Is any of this in the statement you made before you called me?"

"No. I knew not to say much."

"Good. Let's keep the bit about the keys to ourselves for now."

"Was there anyone in the halls or stairwells as you ran to your apartment?" Jackie continued, looking up from her notes.

"Everyone in the city knows better than to hang around or stick his head out the door when shots are fired."

"What made you suspect that the shots came from your apartment and not someone else's or from the rooftop?"

"When I got out of my patrol car, I noticed the only light in the front of the building came from one of my rooms."

"So, you didn't hesitate once you got into the building. You went up four flights of stairs and right to your door," I said.

"That's right."

"When you got there, was the door unlocked?" Jackie asked.

"No."

"Why didn't you kick in the door?"

"I had a key."

I could hear Frank shift his position. He knew the prosecutor would hone in on that one. The jury would believe that most men in O'Reilly's position wouldn't waste time fiddling with a key. Especially a cop.

Jackie continued her questioning. "What did you see when you entered?"

"The apartment was dark, except for a dim light coming from our bedroom. The wall behind the bed was streaked red."

"How long were you in the apartment before the neighbors pinned you down and called the cops?"

"I don't know."

"You said in your statement to the police that you heard someone on the fire escape. Why didn't you make chase?"

"Bridget was bleeding to death."

"Why did you touch the gun on the bed? You knew better than that."

"It was laying on her, on my wife."

Jackie looked away. I took the questioning in a different direction.

"Tell us about the gun and holster you had hanging on the bed post. Was it always there? Did you ever use it for work?"

"It belonged to my dad. It's the one he had on him the night he was shot and killed. I never used it but felt safe with it close just in case someone broke in during the night."

"So, you kept it chambered?"

"That's right. It also reminded me every morning to carry at least two guns. If my dad had, he'd be alive today."

"Why do you say that?" Jackie asked.

"He was shot in the hand. The bullet grazed his gun and shattered the joint of his thumb. The gun went flying, leaving him defenseless. He was shot five times in the chest and twice in the head."

Jackie cleared her throat. "Sorry to make you relive that."

"It's ironic that he gave me two of the same guns when he bought his. If only he had taken his own advice and purchased an extra Colt .45 for himself."

I was about to ask about the shell casings, but Jackie beat me to it.

"Now that you mention it," O'Reilly said. "I don't remember seeing any casings."

"When the cops searched you, they didn't find any on you?"

"I said I didn't see any casings."

"Would that be documented in the police report?" I asked.

"Not that specifically, but everything I had in my possession should be in the report."

A jailer stuck his head into the room and said we had ten minutes left.

It was time for O'Reilly to ask his questions.

"The face of the guy in bed with my wife was so badly

beaten that I didn't recognize him. I'm told he was my neighbor."

"That's right," Frank said.

O'Reilly stood and leaned back against the wall, keeping all of us in his view. "You know that makes no sense. My wife would go after money. This guy was a beat cop and broke most of the time."

"We have a theory about that, but we're not ready to discuss it until we have some proof," Frank said.

It was clear as O'Reilly moved toward Frank that his answer didn't sit well with O'Reilly. He wanted to know now.

"Take it easy," Frank said, backing away. "We think she wanted you to catch her with this guy. She needed a divorce so she could marry someone else."

"Who?"

"Someone with money."

The guard came in and led O'Reilly back to his cell. Another moment and Frank would have spilled his guts even more—if that was possible.

* * * * *

Jackie gathered up her papers, I put the chairs back in position and Frank just looked chagrined.

"What do we know that we didn't when we came in?" he asked.

Jackie responded. "We can establish a timeline of events tied to when O'Reilly arrived on the scene, and we know that he didn't pick up the spent shells."

I wasn't satisfied and I doubt Frank was either. I had the sense that we had overlooked something, something important. The meeting had also left me depressed. For a brief moment, I had seen the world through O'Reilly's eyes. His dad and brother had both died violent deaths and now his wife. It didn't make any difference that he and his wife had a lousy relationship. As far as I knew, he had no living relatives. He was now all alone.

As we left the interrogation room, Jackie shoved the last of her notes into her handbag.

"I never got to ask my last set of questions," she mused.

"What were they?" Frank asked.

"We know next to nothing about Bridget."

I put my arm around Jackie's shoulder. "My guess is Luigi can fill in some gaps. He knows just about everyone in the neighborhood, including their family history."

"Now's as good a time as any," Jackie said.

* * * * *

"Why are you asking me about Bridget?" Luigi asked.

"How long have you been friends with O'Reilly?"

"Several years. More so since I've returned from the war."

"In all that time did he ever talk about his wife?"

"Not much," I said.

"Then you know more than I do. Your pop and I didn't have much to do with him until you guys became friends."

"I guess that means you can't help us?"

"I didn't say that. There's a diner along the waterfront halfway between here and the ferry terminal. Ask for Molly Ferguson and tell her I sent you. I suspect she can tell you about Bridget."

Once he mentioned Molly's name, I recalled meeting

her the day Butch beat Bobby Stefano to death. She had mentioned she used to babysit O'Reilly and that they had stayed in contact over the years. Maybe Luigi was on to something.

* * * * *

Jackie assumed we would head straight for the diner, but I had other plans.

"I need to check first with Martha to see if Dom called. He should have enough information by now for us to make contact with Hawk in Brooklyn. Dom knows we can only put the Colonel off for so long."

I opened the car door for Jackie, but she didn't enter. "You just said a meeting with us. Are you saying you want me along?"

"You and Martha. Dom's gonna need a date to make our reunion with Hawk look unplanned."

Jackie looked up as I closed the door. "What about O'Reilly?"

"We have time, and Molly Ferguson isn't going anywhere."

"I sure hope you know what you're getting us into."

"Yeah, me too."

* * * * *

Martha was more perturbed than Jackie about joining my clandestine meeting with Hawk, and not for the reason I expected.

"I don't need or want you arranging dates for me, especially with Dom. If anyone has a few screws loose, he does. I wouldn't doubt that he sleeps with explosives under his pillow."

"It's just for one night," Jackie said.

"Joey better tell him that I'm tagging along as part of my job. I don't want Dom pestering me."

"Don't worry. When he calls, I'll make it clear we need you along to help maintain Hawk's cover," I said.

"Dom already called. He's made arrangements. He said it would be best for you to meet him at his new apartment tonight, and then you guys will head over to the speakeasy where Hawk hangs out."

Martha picked up a scrap of paper from her desk and handed it over.

"You'll have to call him back. We can't do this tonight, both Ma and Luigi will kill me if we don't join them for dinner when Gracie meets the family."

"I already thought of that and told Dom he'd have to wait till tomorrow night. I didn't know at the time I was involved. Now I'll have to break a date I have for tomorrow night."

Before I could get myself deeper in trouble, Jackie came to my rescue.

"Did you ever get the chance to search the *Daily News* archives to pull together some facts about the Communist movement?" she asked Martha.

"I did and it's damn complicated. If you ask me, it's not something we want to get dragged into."

"Joey and I need to compare notes on our meeting with O'Reilly. Why don't you give us a few minutes, and then join us to go over what you've uncovered."

It was uncanny to see how quickly Martha's demeanor changed. Her facial expression switched from one of irritation to enthusiasm as she went to her desk and gathered up note papers she had scattered on the surface.

"I'll be in as soon as I can jot down a decent summary," Martha said, and then she went to work. When she finished, she joined us.

The details Martha had gathered weren't much different from what the Colonel and Jackie had said, but it was important that Martha discover for herself that Hawk was doing important work at great risk to his own safety. It was the only way to get her truly on board.

When she was finished, I asked Martha a simple question and her answer strengthened my resolve to do whatever it took to help stop the growth of the Communist Party.

"In a few sentences tell us what you've learned from your research."

Martha set her notes aside. "The articles I read don't tell the whole story. I tracked down some of the writers and it's what they didn't print that concerns me the most.

"In spite of the fact that the Party is in total disarray with four or five splinter groups—the numbers of people joining are growing rapidly. Our government is running scared. The whole concept of Communism is counter to the foundation of our core principles of economic and personal freedom. Yet to the masses, listening to a dynamic speaker, the message can be one of hope, equality, and an easy way out of poverty.

"Since the Sedition Act was repealed in 1920, the strategy, orchestrated out of Russia, is to penetrate existing unions and to create new ones based on socialist principles."

When Martha finished, we sat in silence, considering what she had said.

"I guess given all this, I don't mind going on a date with

Dom tomorrow night if it helps," Martha said, walking back to her desk.

*****

All conversation around the table that night stopped when Luigi and Gracie entered the apartment. Luigi stood awkwardly in the doorway blocking our view of Gracie. Pop hugged his brother and welcomed Gracie. He then brought her into the room and made introductions. Gracie's eyes glistened as everyone greeted her and congratulated Luigi.

Gracie was a big hit with the crowd, with the possible exception of Ma. This was not something Gracie would notice, but I did. Ma wasn't her usual welcoming self.

Gracie didn't pretend to be anyone other than who she was, an outgoing, assertive woman, looking for a man to take care of her. No one else had a problem with that, especially Martha.

"I would give anything to find a man as good as Luigi," she said.

Everyone stopped to stare at her.

"Of course, he would have to be younger, much younger. And taller, thinner, gentler, more considerate, and—"

"That's enough," Luigi shouted, snatching a bottle of wine from the table. "Some of us have more important things to discuss," he said, heading into the sitting area.

Pop followed. Frank made a quick exit, and I grabbed Jackie's hand and brought her into the room with me. The remaining ladies cleared the table.

Pop waved us over to a couch. "I hear you two had a run-in with Carmine yesterday."

"Carmine intends to rule like any other Mafia boss in the

city and use every means possible to rake in as much dough as he can."

"What are you gonna do about it?" Pop asked.

"Stop him."

"Why?"

Luigi spoke up before I could answer.

"Look, Joey, Castellano took a lot of heat from the syndicate over the years for not contributing more money to the coffers. We can't expect Carmine to do the same."

"Why not?"

"Two good reasons: Big Ben and the fact that he's not half the man his father is."

"That's not good enough for me."

Pop sided with Luigi. "You know, Joey, we need to face the fact that it takes resources to protect the neighborhood. Why shouldn't the businesses chip in a little? Whore houses, that's nothing new. I say we focus our efforts on keeping drugs out of the hands of our kids and help our neighbors not get indebted to Carmine."

Jackie squeezed my hand and spoke up.

"You and most of the merchants around here have lived under Castellano's umbrella since arriving from Italy. You have no idea what Carmine has in mind for your neighborhood. I was raised in Chicago, so I do. I'm telling you—you're not gonna like how things are about to change."

Pop surprised me. "If things get out of hand, we'll deal with Carmine as a community. And let's not forget that Little Italy functions just fine under the thumb of the Mafia. So will we."

What Pop and Luigi said was difficult to hear, but they were handing me an opportunity to pull myself back from the neighborhood. I took Jackie's hand and turned toward the kitchen to say goodnight to the rest of the folks. But there was one more thing I felt compelled to say to Pop and my uncle.

"Watch out for Toby. I know his kind. He's gonna do things on his own, and I doubt Carmine will realize the danger Toby represents until it's too late."

"I discussed that possibility with Castellano when you were out walking with Angela," Luigi said.

"Don't forget, Joey," Pop said. "We've all dealt with problems in the neighborhood long before you came home from the war."

I didn't like it, but Pop was right.

* * * * *

I walked Jackie to her door and kissed her good night. As I turned to leave, she touched my arm.

"Did you do that for me? Back down, I mean."

"I did it for both of us. You were right; I can't protect the neighborhood forever."

Jackie let go of my arm and was about to enter her apartment when she glanced back.

"It's getting late," I said.

"I don't want to wake up alone tomorrow morning. You don't mind, do you?"

That wasn't a question that needed an answer.

Chapter 26

The next morning, I walked into Pop's shop and flipped over the open sign. I then shook the chimes hanging on the door to make him think he had a customer.

"Hey Pop, let's take a walk and visit the newlyweds."

"You can't let it go, can you? I knew you wouldn't be able to."

"There was a lot of booze flowing last night, and you both were light on details."

Pop shook a shoe at me that he was polishing in the back of the shop. "We told you we'd deal with Carmine if it comes down to that."

"I want to know how."

Pop turned the sign back over. "I have a business to run."

"Come on, Pop. Humor me."

Pop used his own key to enter the speakeasy in case Gracie and Luigi were still sleeping off the celebration from the previous night. As it turned out, they were both up and getting ready for a new business day. Gracie stood behind the bar restocking the revolving shelves with a shipment of booze, and Luigi sat on a barstool counting the take for the week.

"Damn, you almost gave me a heart attack walking in like that. What are you guys up to this early in the morning?" Luigi grumbled.

"My son wants to jaw about Carmine again," Pop said,

walking over to Gracie, who was pouring us both a cup of joe.

"There's nothing more to discuss," Luigi said. "We pay him for protection and mind our own business. What he does along the waterfront is of no concern to us."

Pop took the two cups of coffee over to a table and pulled out four chairs. "Let's sit together. You too, Gracie."

"Now look what you've done," Luigi said to me. "He's gonna give us a lecture."

Pop ignored my uncle's wisecrack. "Joey, in the last two years both Luigi and I have been shot, our businesses have been destroyed and rebuilt, and Luigi's apartment building was bombed. Now tell me, are things gonna get worse or better if we interfere with Carmine?"

Gracie squeezed my hand. "There comes a point where you have to stop fighting and make the best you can out of a bad situation."

"I'm not here to argue. You're all telling me to back off, and that's fine. Believe me when I say I want to."

"So, what's the problem?" Luigi asked.

"I need to know your plan. What are you gonna do when Carmine's men start roughing up some of the shop owners?"

Luigi looked at Pop. "We hope that won't happen. We're gonna call a meeting with all the merchants and explain how we see things now that Castellano is retired."

"We'll ask everyone to pay for protection and chip into a fund to help those who run short of cash so they won't have to go to Carmine for a loan," Pop added.

"You think that's not going to anger Carmine?"

"We all have to give in a little. If Carmine has half a brain, he'll understand and meet us halfway," Luigi said.

"And if he doesn't?"

"Then we go to Castellano and ask him to educate his son," Luigi added.

I wasn't sure who they were trying to kid. Any influence Castellano had over Carmine had vanished when he didn't react to his son's threat. I knew that, and so did they.

"Have it your way. I've got a murder case to solve and a war buddy that needs my help."

Luigi got the pot of coffee and topped off our cups. "Are you done worrying or do we have to hold your hand some more?"

I had to laugh. My uncle—always the wise guy.

"I'm done, at least for now."

Chapter 27

Late morning we left for Brooklyn, just in case we had difficulty finding the apartment Dom had rented. I also wanted an excuse to treat the girls to lunch at an upscale restaurant.

The location of Dom's apartment surprised me. I doubted that Hawk would be living in a ritzy neighborhood as a delegate for the Communist Party.

The doorman knew Dom expected company and held open the door once we identified ourselves. Dom greeted us on the second floor outside his apartment. He was pleased but confused to see Jackie and Martha.

"Aren't we making contact with Hawk tonight?" he asked after the girls entered.

"We are. I thought the skirts would make our running into him more believable. I didn't think you'd mind."

Dom threw back his shoulders and went straight for Martha, twirling her around.

"Hey doll, can I get you a drink?"

Martha took a step back and gave me a nasty look. "What did you tell him?"

I couldn't resist having some fun at Martha's expense, even though I knew I would pay a steep price for what I was about to say.

"Just that you were looking forward to a good time."

Martha took a deep breath and didn't hesitate to put Dom in his place.

"Look Dom," she said. "You're a nice guy, but not my

type. So get this through your skull—I'm not your doll. I'm working and getting paid by the hour—double my normal amount."

Dom wasn't fazed. "I've got just what you need, a stiff drink and a comfortable couch."

Martha gave up and joined Jackie on the sofa. I helped Dom mix the drinks.

"I thought I told you to get an apartment near Hawk."

"Not my kind of place. You never know when you might have a dame to entertain," he said, looking over at Martha with a smile. "Besides, the Colonel is paying the rent."

"How are we gonna explain bumping into Hawk in some dive?"

"Slumming. Rich folk do it all the time."

* * * * *

Dom had been tailing Hawk for several days and had made a point of entering the joint Hawk frequented when Hawk wasn't around. By this time he was friends with the door keeper, so we got in without incident. As we passed through a set of curtains, I stood off to the side to get my bearings. There was a long bar to my right, a small dance floor in front of me with tables on three sides and booths along the side and back walls. I walked to my left, along a path between the booths and tables, and selected a table in the back row that gave us a clear view of the entrance, but was dark enough that we wouldn't be visible to anyone entering. We ordered drinks and waited, but not for long.

Hawk showed up with two blonde brutes who contrasted sharply with Hawk's slender build and black hair. His companions needed to duck as they passed through the doorframe, and one had to turn slightly to avoid hitting his shoulder in the narrow entryway. It was easy to tell they were Russian—from head to toe.

They went straight to the bar and ordered drinks. With Hawk sitting between them, it was difficult to determine if they were his bodyguards or jailors.

It didn't take Dom long to come up with a plan to get Hawk's attention—start a brawl, which is what he did. He dragged Martha onto the dance floor and, after some wild dance moves, bumped into some poor sap. When the guy turned, Dom popped him one in the face, then cursed him and his ancestry for generations back. The dance floor cleared except for three guys who stood their ground. Two others rushed at Dom from a side table. Dom had picked on the wrong guy; he had a lot of friends.

Jackie gave me a shove. "Aren't you gonna help?"

"Not until Hawk takes notice."

Dom loved to fight. He could take a punch and deliver two in return. He was a born street fighter who had mastered every dirty move ever used. With Dom there were no rules. A kick to the groin, then a knee to the face was his view of a friendly skirmish. But six to one was more than he could handle. When Hawk turned to watch, I rushed into the melee, heaving one brute off Dom and smashing him onto a table. Two came at me with their heads down low and arms outstretched. They lifted me off my feet and ran through two rows of tables, then tossed me into the air against the back of one of the Russians. He swatted me away and was about to squash one of my attackers when I got to the guy first and knocked out two of his front teeth. The Russian grinned with approval, showing the gap in his smile. The other guy ran for the exit. I was headed back to help Dom when Hawk grabbed me by the collar

"Deadman, is that you?" he shouted.

I turned and looked surprised. "In the flesh. Don't just sit there, give us a hand," I said, shoving aside tables to get back into the fight.

Hawk whizzed past me and decimated Dom's attackers in less than five minutes. He was our squadron's martial arts instructor and now lived up to his reputation. I stood off to the side watching as he anticipated every move against him and countered with devastating precision. During training we had called him Four Eyes, not because he wore glasses, but because we were sure he had eyes in the back of his head.

He stepped over the bodies on the floor and went to give Dom a hug.

"What the hell are you guys doing here?"

"We're with a couple of broads who wanted to see how the other half lived," I said, pointing to where the girls were sitting.

"Give me a minute and I'll join you. I have a few friends I need to get rid of," he said, nodding toward the bar.

Dom grinned. "Guess that got him to notice us, huh?"

I turned Dom in the direction of the bathroom and gave him a shove. "Go clean up. I don't think Martha wants to be splattered with blood."

I watched as he wobbled, weak-kneed, toward the john, then I rejoined the girls at the table.

Jackie wiped blood from my lip and Martha did the same to my knuckles.

"Next time," Jackie said. "You should let us come up with a less violent solution to your problems. A woman's charm can be more effective than a fist."

"I'll remember that," I said, as a commotion broke out at the bar.

Hawk was arguing with his two Neanderthal friends, who evidently wanted him to stay with them. The argument ended when Hawk waved over the bartender and asked for a wooden cutting board. What happened next had me in stitches. I'd seen Hawk pull the same stunt on leave during our training. Hawk held the board firmly with a hand on each side and at arm's length in front of him. One of the Russians let loose a wicked swing and smashed his fist against the board, buckling his wrist. The other Russian laughed at his comrade until Hawk offered him the same opportunity, which he refused. Hawk then handed him the board and broke it in half with one blow. He then placed both pieces together, doubling the thickness. This time the boards didn't break, but the force sent the Russian backwards into two bystanders, all of whom ended up on the floor. The Russians got the message and left the speakeasy, one cradling a broken wrist.

Hawk swiped the two bottles they were drinking from the bar and joined us.

"Damn, Deadman, it's good to see you. But before you tell me what the hell you're doing hanging around with Diamond, introduce me to these two gorgeous dames."

"Jackie is my business partner and fiancée. Martha's our office manager. Like you, we're in the PI business."

"I take it our meeting isn't a coincidence. I can't blame the Colonel for getting the jitters. With those two statues by my side, making contact was out of the question. Sorry he dragged you guys into this mess, but it was inevitable that he'd get you involved."

"He admitted as much."

"Did he tell you that the success of my mission depends on your connections with the Mafia?"

"He did, but first, he wants to know what the hell you've been doing these past few months—those are his words not mine. Once we know you're still on our side, I'm supposed to help."

"I see the Colonel hasn't changed. He was always checking that we were still committed to his unit before training us for our next mission."

Dom returned from the john, looking more human as he straddled a chair at the table, then punched Hawk's shoulder.

"Thanks for coming to my rescue. My buddy here wasn't of much help," he said, pointing to me while pouring a stiff drink.

"Hey, not fair. My job was to pull Hawk into the fray and I did."

"I can see you two haven't changed," Hawk said. "Why don't we go to my place? It's not wise to talk here. Everyone in this dive is trying to get dirt on someone else so they can move up the ranks of the Party."

As we got up to leave, Dom stayed put and finished his drink.

"Sorry, Hawk. I've seen where you live. Besides, if this joint is being watched, so is your apartment."

Dom filled his glass again, threw it back in one gulp, and put it down with a thud. "We're goin' to my place."

He led the way out using the shoulders of a few seated customers to steady himself.

Chapter 28

Dom insisted on driving. As I attempted to pull him out of the driver's seat, a couple of beat cops noticed us.

"Let him drive," Hawk said, looking over his shoulder. "We don't need coppers poking into our business. You never can tell what Dom will say when he's smashed."

Grudgingly, I backed off. Once on the road, it didn't take long to notice Hawk's Russian friends were tagging along a few cars behind.

"Why the tail?" I asked Hawk.

"After what happened to Jack Donnelly, their assignment is to protect me at all costs, and, given the price of failure, I'm confident they will."

"Who's this Jack Donnelly I keep hearing about?" Dom slurred.

Hawk slapped Dom on the back of the head. "Diamond, why don't you keep your eyes on the road? You can ask questions when we get to your place, assuming we get there."

"I have a suggestion," Jackie said. "Joey told me the Colonel didn't allow anyone to use their given names, but since the war is over, why don't you guys drop the code names? But first Dom, pull the hell over before you kill us all."

Dom did as Jackie ordered. He and I traded places, but before reentering traffic, I reached back and extended my hand to Hawk.

"Hawk, I'm Joey Batista, and the drunk next to me is Dominic. He prefers to be called Dom."

Dom had closed his eyes, so I gave him a shake. "Hey Dom, what's your last name? I forgot."

"My last name? I know the answer to that question. Dominic, Dominic's my name."

I shook him again. "Your last name. What's your last name?"

"Marchio. Dominic Marchio. Now how about a drink?"

"Is he always like this?" Hawk asked.

"No, he's celebrating early. Once we give the Colonel a report, Dom's a free man again with a whole lot of dough."

"That tells me he used his skills for nefarious means," Hawk said with a chuckle.

"Let's just say he left behind a few empty bank vaults around town," I said, parking in front of Dom's apartment building.

* * * * *

When Hawk and I returned from putting Dom to bed, it was Hawk's turn to open up.

"Some of this is classified," he said, looking at the girls.

"We have no secrets from each other. Both Jackie and Martha know all about the Colonel's latest interest."

"Hawk, you never did tell us your real name?" Jackie said.

"It's Hawk."

I didn't believe him. "I doubt the Colonel would let you use your actual name."

"Why not? Can you think of a better code name? I'm half Cherokee. That's how I got the name. And I'm half

Japanese. My father was placed in a temple at an early age and mastered several forms of martial arts. When he decided a monk's life wasn't for him, he came to America."

"Were you sent on the same type of missions as Joey and Dom?" Martha asked.

Hawk downed a drink. "I guess after all these years I can tell the truth. You might say I was a scout and a shadow when I wasn't training these guys."

"A shadow? What does that mean?" Jackie asked.

Hawk turned to me. "Joey, didn't you ever notice you were incredibly lucky on your more difficult assignments, especially the ones that required you using the emergency escape routes?"

He didn't give me a chance to answer.

"It was my job to plan those routes and to provide you with cover."

"Some of my missions took weeks. Are you telling me you stayed in hiding not knowing if or when you'd need to go into action?"

"That's right. There were two of us, and we monitored activity on the routes around the clock."

I thought back to some of my more treacherous escapes. "So that rock slide in the Alps that blocked the road after I had passed wasn't luck?"

"That was easy. The one that I'm particularly proud of is when I had to take an impossible shot to save your life."

I didn't know what he was talking about and shrugged my shoulders.

"You'll remember this. You were about to have your car filled with bullets when the car chasing you went out of control, flying over a cliff. If my aim had been a little off and I'd missed that front tire, we wouldn't be having this conversation."

The girls found his exploits fascinating and, honestly, so did I, but reliving old times was not why we had come together.

It was time to focus on the present.

*****

"Let's get to the Colonel's concerns," I said. "What have you been up to these last few months?"

"Indoctrination and training in Russia."

"Russia."

"My proposal to team up with the Mafia was radical enough that the higher-ups wanted to question me in person."

"Are their training methods effective?"

"I'm a fast learner. But if you're asking if I'm a Communist, not a chance."

"How'd you become a delegate?"

"I had an influential sponsor. That's all I can say. If you want to know more, ask the Colonel."

"Do you think using the Mafia to blunt the Communist Party is the best way to stop their ideology from spreading?"

"If you come up with a better idea, tell the Colonel."

"What about the Russians?"

"They're on board."

"You must be a hell of a salesman."

"Like it or not pal, you have connections with the two largest crime organizations in the country—New York City and Chicago—and I have a legitimate tie to you."

"It's hard to believe the Russians actually bought all this."

"As a delegate, my assignment is to get you to help

me unionize the waterfront for the Communist Party. Jack Donnelly failed because he was opposed by the Mafia."

"And how are you supposed to convert me?"

"Money. The Russians believe Americans will do anything to acquire wealth. After all, isn't greed the core of capitalism?"

"You're sounding like a convert," Jackie said to Hawk.

"That's good, because if I don't, I won't last long. Not with those two brutes following me around."

Martha hadn't said anything, but the more Hawk explained, the angrier she looked. It finally got to the point where she couldn't contain herself.

"Do you realize what you've done? You and the Colonel have dragged Joey into a Communist conspiracy, without his knowledge, and by doing so, you've put his life and ours at risk."

Hawk got up to leave. "He was willing to sacrifice his life during the war, and if you ask me, communism is a bigger threat to our freedom."

"Don't go just yet," I said. "I need more details for the Colonel."

"There's nothing more to say. Just tell him what I told you. I was successful, and now it's up to you and me to make his plan work. Get in touch when you have a meeting set up with your Mafia pals. I shouldn't keep my ride waiting too long."

"Oh, by the way, tell the Colonel he created a problem," Hawk said. "How the hell am I going to convince my comrades that you just happened to run into me?"

"I don't think Dom will mind living here for a few months to maintain our cover. We'll visit from time-to-time and hit some less reputable speakeasies. That should make it all seem legit."

Martha rolled her eyes, but Jackie was quick to mention that dating Dom should, indeed, come with hazard pay. I could hardly disagree.

None of us spoke on the way back to the city until Jackie summed up my thoughts.

"Our lives just got a lot more complicated."

"Who'd have thought that was possible?" Martha said from the back seat.

Chapter 29

No matter how tired you are, remaining in bed after a sleepless night isn't an option. If your bladder doesn't get you up, the backache will. If you still try to resist, as I did, then your head will start to throb. I threw in the towel and got up to take a shower and wait for sunrise.

Jackie and I had talked till two in the morning about Hawk's revelations and concluded we had to cooperate with Hawk. As far as the Colonel and the Russians were concerned, we were already in the game. But we agreed to some terms of our own: first, O'Reilly's case was our top priority, and second, we would pull out as soon as we could and get on with our lives. I expected we'd spend the rest of the night together when we finished talking, but Jackie shoved me out the door.

"You need time to think about how you're gonna get Carmine to cooperate on unionizing the dock workers, especially after our last run-in with him and Toby."

As usual, she was right, and that's what had caused the sleepless night. While staring at the ceiling, however, I did come up with a plan.

*****

Banging on Luigi's apartment door only succeeded in rousing a few new tenants and my folks. Pop was a bit more understanding than most.

"Joey, what the hell are you doing? Regular folk need their sleep."

"Sorry Pop, sorry everyone. It won't happen again," I shouted, taking two steps at a time down to Pop.

"I need Luigi's advice, yours too. Where is he this early in the morning?"

"He and Gracie haven't used the apartment since they arrived in town. They're still living at the speakeasy and eating at La Cucina's."

Ma came into the hallway, knotting her robe. "What kind of trouble are you in now?"

"Nothing, Ma. Pop, do me a favor and get dressed. By the time we get to the speakeasy, they should be up."

"But I haven't had breakfast."

"Gracie can throw something together."

"You'll be lucky if she can brew a cup of coffee."

"That she can do, but not much else," I said.

Pop went to get dressed, and I followed Ma into the kitchen. "Why don't you invite Gracie and Luigi over for dinner a few times a week and get her in the kitchen?"

"Oh, now I have to be teacher and chef, not to mention a gun-slinging moll? Your uncle messed up his bed, let him fix it."

I ignored her comment. "While you're at it, why not include Rosalie?"

"What for? She's been watching me cook for years."

"But she's never cooked a meal. She'll be graduating from nursing school soon and moving out. She'll never find a man if she can't cook."

"You don't need to worry about Rosalie. She has a new boyfriend."

"Who?"

"All she'll say is that he's from another neighborhood. If Gracie can snag a man, Rosalie shouldn't have a problem, even if she can't cook—which I don't believe. She's helped me enough."

Pop came out of the bedroom. We downed our coffee and headed for the door, against Ma's protest.

* * * * *

"Another early morning visit? What's goin' on here? Are you two trying to ruin my honeymoon?" Luigi grumbled.

"You're not getting off that cheap," Gracie said, moving him aside. "You got six months to plan a real honeymoon or we're sleeping in separate bedrooms."

"I see you discovered how to motivate my uncle," I said.

"Men are all the same. All you guys care about is money, sex, food and booze. Money comes first because you need it to buy the other three."

"You forgot the most important one," Pop said.

Gracie stopped making coffee. "And what's that?"

"Honor," Pop said. "You can't buy that with money."

I knew what Pop was getting at and so did Gracie. She placed four cups on our table and sat next to Luigi.

"Okay, I'll give you one chance to get out of this marriage. Do you want a divorce?"

Luigi picked up his empty cup. "Where's the coffee?"

"Didn't you hear what I asked?"

"No, I don't want a divorce. What about you?"

"I'm happy."

"Good, now get the coffee. If I know these guys, we have important stuff to discuss."

Gracie filled our cups and sat down. Luigi suggested she leave so we could talk. She pushed back without hesitation. "Don't tell me to leave. I married into this family, and I want to know what I got myself into."

I agreed, but wanted her to know the stakes involved. "What I'm about to say has to stay among us. People will die if this information gets into the wrong hands."

I held nothing back. I told them everything. When I was done, I asked Pop and Luigi for their thoughts. They both knew of the growing communist threat and thought using the Mafia was a creative solution.

"Your Colonel is one devious SOB. How did you survive under his command?" Pop asked

"I wasn't supposed to."

"It just might work, but I can tell you one damn thing, and that's not to trust Carmine. We need to hook your friend up with Vigliotti and your uncle Torrio," Luigi said. "I'll make the arrangements and get back to you."

Gracie looked startled. "Your uncle is Johnny Torrio? The Mafia boss out of Chicago?"

"That's right. He's Ma's brother."

"Do you know him?" Luigi asked, looking a little worried.

"No, not personally, but I've heard of him."

"Can we stop the chitchat? I came here on a serious matter and need advice," I said.

"Listen to Luigi," Pop said. "Carmine's over his head, and you may have been right about Toby Tobias."

"What's happened to make you say that?"

"Did you know that old man Spiro's in the hospital? The rumor is a crate fell off a tall stack and fractured his leg. But make no mistake, Joey, it's no coincidence that Spiro had an accident. He was the first in the neighborhood to refuse to pay protection money."

Luigi agreed.

"Keep me informed if any more accidents happen, and let me know if you want my help," I said.

"We will."

With that, Pop and I headed home. On the way, Pop asked how things were going with O'Reilly's case. I thought it best not to reveal too much.

"We just need a break."

"I hope it comes soon. Did you talk to Frank yesterday?"

"Never got the chance."

"The preliminary hearing didn't go well. First degree murder and no bail."

* * * * *

When I got back to the office, I found Sadie, Martha, and Jackie sitting on the floor rifling through a cardboard box.

I slammed the door behind me. "Why didn't Frank tell us the hearing was moved up?"

Sadie came to Frank's defense. "The DA pulled a fast one. We were given an hour's notice."

"How much time do we have?"

"The trial is in six weeks. This is one of the evidence boxes the DA's office turned over to Frank after the judge decided to go forward with the trial," Sadie said. She went back to inspecting two pictures she held in her hand.

Jackie got up and waved me into the inner office.

"What's wrong?" I asked.

"We have a problem. There's an affidavit from a neighbor

who lives across the street from O'Reilly. He swears he saw O'Reilly enter the building before shots were fired."

"Anything else?"

"Not yet. We just got started."

"How many boxes?"

"Two. Mostly pictures of the crime scene and interviews with neighbors, friends, and a few relatives."

"Whose relatives?"

"Bridget's."

"Don't trust him."

"Who?"

"The DA," I said. "Assume he's holding back evidence. If he's interviewing Bridget's relatives, make sure you have a statement from everyone."

"Joey, we don't have that kind of manpower."

"Use Sadie, use the detectives Frank hired to track down our mythical sugar daddy. Have they had any luck?"

"No."

There was a knock on the door. Sadie stuck her head inside.

"Can I come in?"

"Did you find something?" I asked.

"I'm not sure. Didn't you tell Frank that there was an overcoat with a fur collar on the coat rack in the parlor?" she asked, handing me a picture.

I held the photograph up so Jackie could see.

"That's not the coat Joey and I saw when we broke into the crime scene," she said, snatching the picture from my hand.

"If you take a closer look, you'll notice that it's hanging over another coat. There's a second hem at the bottom," Sadie said.

This was the break I was hoping we'd find. I pulled Sadie into a tight embrace.

"You just narrowed our suspect list from thousands to a handful."

"How?" she asked.

"All of the crime scene photos were taken within hours of the murders, and only certain personnel were allowed into that apartment. Only someone with access could have tampered with the coats. I don't know why I didn't think of this earlier when Jackie mentioned that the original coat had disappeared."

"If we stick to our original theory that Bridget's lover had more money than O'Reilly, that leaves only a few possibilities," Jackie said.

I called Martha into the room and explained the implications of the picture Sadie had handed me. Within minutes we had a list of suspects: the Police Commissioner, the Homicide Captain, the DA or his assistant, the coroner, and the mayor.

"Why would the mayor show up at a homicide?" Martha challenged.

Since I was the one who threw his name out, I responded. "O'Reilly was recently promoted to Lieutenant and is now accused of killing another cop. The mayor would come to the crime scene seeking answers to give to a relentless press, and, don't forget, he's wealthy."

Martha read the list I'd made and shook her head.

"There's only one problem with all this. How could the killer get cleaned up fast enough to get back to the apartment before these pictures were taken?"

"That's a good question," I said. "And why did the killer leave his coat behind? We still have plenty of questions to answer, but we have our first break, so I suggest we follow up."

"I'll try to track down where all these people were on the night of the murders," Martha said. "What about you two?"

"We're gonna go back in time to see if any of them are somehow connected to Bridget," I said.

As Sadie and Martha left our office, I took hold of Martha's arm.

"Do me a favor. Find out who Rosalie's dating and get what you can on him."

"That's a strange request. What's your concern?"

"Ma said she's dating someone from outside the neighborhood. With everything going on, I just want to make sure she's safe."

"I'll see what I can do."

When we were alone, Jackie asked what I meant when I said we were going back in time.

"Remember that Luigi had suggested we talk with a waitress named Molly Ferguson."

"He never did say who she is and why she would know Bridget."

"She's a scarlet woman who knows about everyone in our neighborhood and their secrets—including O'Reilly's. I've been to the diner where she works."

"So you know her?"

"Not really. I ran into her the day Butch and Stefano had their fight to the death on Pier 17. I'm sure you remember that day."

"I do, but—"

"Jackie, we have a lot of work to do. How about saving your questions for when we meet her."

She went to her desk and didn't speak to me for the next hour. Women! I was starting to think Cafiero had the right attitude about how to deal with them.

Chapter 30

Molly had just locked the front door to the diner when I called out. Startled, she nearly lost her footing on the top step. She grabbed the metal railing to steady herself. "Damn, you scared the bejesus out of me. We're closed."

"It's Joey Batista."

"I was wondering when you would get around to me," she said, coming down the steps. She brushed past me and offered her hand to Jackie. "You must be Jackie. I'm Molly Ferguson. Nice to meet ya."

"How do you know me?"

"I heard Joey got engaged to his partner, and since most men don't cheat that quickly on their fiancée', I assumed you were her. I hope I didn't misjudge Joey."

"Not that I know of."

Molly stepped back and took a good look at Jackie.

"Batista, you have good taste, but I'm not sure I can say the same for your fiancée. From what I hear, you're a dangerous man, but then again if the rumors are true, Jackie's no pushover."

"You're well-informed, which is why we're here."

"O'Reilly?"

"We have a theory and some suspects, but the evidence is piling up against him."

"If you believe the papers, he's headed for the chair. I was gonna pay you a call if you didn't come by soon. I didn't want to step back into your neighborhood business unless it was necessary."

"Is there someplace we can talk?"

"I need to take a load off these dogs, so let's go to my place. It's around the block."

* * * * *

Molly lived in a low-rent tenement building that should've been demolished years ago. Wash hung from makeshift clotheslines above an alleyway littered with trash and overfed rats that didn't bother to scurry off as we passed. Wooden banisters leading up to the stoop had long ago rotted through and now lay off to the side of the steps. The inside hallways reeked of mold clinging to patches of blistered plaster that lined the walls and ceilings. I'm sure the stairs creaked as we made our way to the third floor, but it was hard to hear over the din of screaming babies and domestic arguments echoing up the stairwell.

Molly wasn't the least bit embarrassed by her surroundings, but she did joke that she could move up in the world if only her customers weren't so tight with their tips. When she flipped on the lights and closed the door, it felt like we had entered a different part of town. Her place was immaculate. The linoleum floors sparkled, as did the glassware in an antique breakfront. Her furniture was old, but well cared for, and everything was in its place. The lady had class.

She noticed my surprise as she opened her kitchen cabinet, which was stocked with a large variety of booze.

"When we first met I told you that your uncle Luigi and I go way back. He enjoys his drink and made sure I had his favorites on hand—which is just about everything."

"If you don't mind, coffee would do just fine," I said.

She fired up a pot of joe and rejoined us in the sitting room.

"Were you as surprised as I was that he got married?" she asked.

"Surprised is an understatement."

"If I had known he was that lonely, I would've accepted his proposal."

We were both jolted by that revelation.

"Why didn't you?" Jackie asked.

"I'd already lost one husband to the Mafia, and I wasn't about to go through that again."

"Luigi's not in the Mafia, never has been," I said.

"He popped the question around the time Castellano got shot last year, and I thought he was a natural replacement. After all, he and Castellano had established the neighborhood, with help from Ronnie Ligotti. But you know the neighborhood history, at least you should.

"So tell me, what can I do to help O'Reilly beat his murder rap?"

Jackie interrupted. "I'm sorry, Molly, but Joey hasn't explained to me how you're connected to O'Reilly and how you know so much about an area where you don't live."

Molly reached over and squeezed my hand. "I think he was trying to protect me. Isn't that right, Joey? But I'm not ashamed of my past. We all make mistakes. When I was young, I lived in Joey's neighborhood and earned money by taking care of children while their parents worked. In those days I was an attractive woman and I got involved with more than one of the husbands. It didn't take long before I was forced to leave. O'Reilly was one of the children I watched, and we stayed in contact all through the years."

Jackie seemed satisfied, so I moved on.

"We'd like to know more about Bridget. I've known for a few years that they were having problems, but O'Reilly is not one to open up."

"I can tell you that Bridget has been a troublemaker since the day she arrived in town."

"What makes you say that?"

"The boys that O'Reilly hung out with were the best of friends until she came along. She was a bit of a chippy—I should know—and used sex to get whatever and whoever she wanted. You know what they say, 'Old habits are hard to break.'"

"How did she end up with O'Reilly?" Jackie asked.

"Joey, you didn't really get friendly with O'Reilly until after his brother, Shawn, died in a street fight, but you might recall that the O'Reilly family was better off than most. His old man was a cop, and a damn good one, but he could be bribed."

"How does that explain why she married O'Reilly?" I asked.

"He had his heart set on being a cop, while the other guys in the group had no ambition. We all thought they'd spend most of their lives hanging out on the same street corner."

"Did they?" Jackie asked.

"Most, and as a result, they ended up dead, thanks to the brutal rampage Butch went on before Joey killed him—they worked for Castellano."

"You said most. What happened to the others?" I asked.

"Fate, as it sometimes does, intervened, and two of them made something of themselves. Let me see your list of suspects."

I handed her the names. She smirked and shook her head ever so slightly. She laid the paper on an end table and went into the kitchen to remove the coffee pot from the burner. Jackie and I said nothing. When she returned, we nursed our coffee and waited.

"One of the boys never did fit in and showed no interest in the shenanigans that the others pulled in the neighborhood. He kept his head stuck in a book and went on to go to college. The other left town and went to live with his wealthy aunt after his parents were murdered—they witnessed a mob hit and were silenced. I never did understand why he would want to come back and serve the community that took his parents away."

"Are either of their names on that piece of paper?" Jackie asked.

"They both are, and based on what I know—one of them *is* your killer."

Chapter 31

Jackie and I sat in my car outside Molly's apartment building trying to make sense of everything she had told us. I knew when we had put that list of prominent suspects together that O'Reilly's defense wouldn't be easy. If any one of them were the killer, the jury wouldn't buy it unless we had irrefutable evidence, and even with that, there was no guarantee that O'Reilly would get off. There was too much corruption in this town, and fear and money often held sway over some jurors—especially fear of reprisal on loved ones.

Molly had narrowed the list down to one name, and I had no reason to doubt the truthfulness of what she had said. Jackie wasn't as convinced.

"If Molly is such a good friend of O'Reilly's, why didn't she tell him his wife was two-timing him?"

"That's not something O'Reilly would ask, and she's not the type that would betray a confidence. Molly did say she and Bridget became friends long before Bridget married O'Reilly."

"How did she get to know Bridget so well? She's years older than her, and the diner isn't a kids' hangout, probably never has been."

"My guess is O'Reilly introduced her to Molly. Why are you so skeptical?"

"If we follow her lead, we're betting O'Reilly's life on her word."

"We really don't have a choice. The trial date is closing

in, and we have nothing on the other suspects. Besides, O'Reilly would bet his life on her word. That's good enough for me."

"Where are we goin' now?" Jackie asked, as I rolled into traffic.

"Frank's, to see if he or the girls have any new information that might corroborate Molly's accusation."

* * * * *

We ran into Frank coming out of Pop's repair shop when we entered the building.

He held up a pair of shoes. "You'd think your old man would give his friends a break. Instead, he's raising his prices."

"Just hope Luigi doesn't do the same," I said, as we all climbed the stairs.

Jackie continued on with Frank to his office, while I stepped into ours to grab Martha. She was with Sadie and had just finished an inventory of the evidence boxes. They gathered up some of the documents they thought most interesting, and we joined Frank and Jackie.

Frank waited until Sadie was ready to take notes. "It looks as though we all have something to say. Joey, why don't you and Jackie start?"

"We paid a visit to Molly Ferguson, a longtime friend of O'Reilly and—as it turned out—a confidant of Bridget's. Presented with the names of suspects we had put together, she didn't hesitate to select one as the likely killer."

Jackie was about to say something until I touched her arm.

Frank noticed and wasn't pleased.

"We're not playing games here, Joey. O'Reilly's life is on the line. Are you gonna tell us who this Ferguson dame named or not?"

Frank was under a lot of pressure, so I let his comment pass. "I think it best we hear what everyone else has to say before we spill who she pinned the murders on."

"Fair enough," Frank said. "I showed O'Reilly the names and explained our theory."

"What did he think?"

"He immediately found a handful of flaws in our reasoning."

"Like what?" Martha asked.

Frank took out a note pad and read off a litany of questions: "Why would such a high-profile person risk coming to the apartment? Did he have a key? If not, how did he get in without Bridget and her lover hearing him? If he had murder on his mind, why did he take off his coat? Why did he pick up the shell casings if he used the gun hanging on the bedpost? And then the question we've all been curious about, how did he get to the gun without a struggle?"

Sadie looked up from her steno pad. "Maybe we should be asking who had a motive to kill the guy in bed with Bridget. He was shot multiple times."

Jackie took a seat next to Martha and Sadie. "Given what was goin' on in that room, it's not surprising the victim took most of the bullets in the back. From all we've dug up, he had a nothing life. I say we stick with our theory and keep digging until we find answers to O'Reilly's questions."

I agreed with Jackie and pushed Frank for more details.

"Putting all those questions aside, what did O'Reilly have to say about the people we suspect?"

"He dismissed everyone except the mayor and the

DA. He's not aware of any contact the others had with his wife."

"How well did Bridget know them?" Martha asked Frank.

"They grew up together in the neighborhood. At one point they were all good friends."

It was time to drop Molly's bombshell. "According to Molly Ferguson, Bridget and the DA have been having an affair for over two years."

Frank let out a low whistle. "That would explain why the DA has been so hostile to O'Reilly."

"Two years, and O'Reilly never knew the DA was coming to his apartment? I find that hard to believe," Sadie said.

Martha smiled at Frank and patted Sadie on the back as he gave Sadie a nasty look. "Don't mind him. Frank doesn't like his secretaries to think."

Jackie answered Sadie. "They never met at the apartment. They would use small, remote motels. O'Reilly rotated shifts, so it was easy for them to meet as often as they wanted without raising suspicion."

Frank got out from behind his desk and paced as he lit his pipe. "What then would cause the DA to come to the apartment that night?" he asked, after taking a few puffs.

"That's another lengthy discussion," I said. "I don't know about you guys, but we're famished. Let's take a break for dinner. You know my mother; she's probably waiting for us before she serves the others."

"I'd prefer to keep going," Frank said. "I'm sure she won't mind if we grabbed some grub and brought it back to the office."

Jackie walked toward the door. "I have a better idea.

Since I was with Joey, he can fill you in on the rest of what Molly had to say, and I'll get food for everyone."

We agreed.

"Did Molly give you a possible motive? An affair is one thing, but it doesn't necessarily follow that the DA is our man." Frank asked as Jackie left.

"Bridget was upset because the *Daily News* had reported that the DA was dating a socialite."

"Did she confront him?"

"Of course."

"What happened?"

"The DA told Bridget that O'Reilly would never divorce her, and she should know that, but they could continue their relationship in quiet even if he did get married."

Martha shook her head in disgust. "Nice guy. How did she react to that suggestion?"

"Here's the clincher. Bridget told the DA how she planned to get O'Reilly to file for divorce."

"I'll be damned," Martha said. "There's your motive, Frank. Bridget had no intention of playing second fiddle, and he was beginning to see just how far she'd go to get what she wants. If her relationship with the DA ever went public, it would have blown the DA's chances to marry into some serious dough."

Jackie and I had come to the same conclusion after talking to Molly, but thought it best if Frank and the others reached their own conclusion. Frank looked pleased and repacked his pipe with fresh tobacco.

The aroma of fresh basil permeated the office before Jackie, Ma, and Pop entered the room, each carrying a tray full of food.

"Tell me this," Sadie asked, through a mouthful of cake

she had snatched as Ma walked past her. "Molly knew you were investigating the murders. Why didn't she come to you with all this information?"

"She didn't think anyone would believe her, not without proof. But when she saw the DA's name on our list of suspects, she opened up," Jackie answered.

Ma stopped serving. "Are you talking about Molly Ferguson? Don't believe a word that woman says."

"Now Ma," Pop said as they left the room. "People do change."

"That's easy for you to say. You're a man."

Ma emphasized her point by slamming the office door behind her.

I wanted to keep the conversation moving and not have to explain Molly's past to Martha and Sadie. "Martha, earlier when I walked in on you and Sadie, you both seemed keyed up about something. What was it?"

Martha slid her plate aside. "Believe me when I say it's hard to get excited when you spend the whole day reading witness statements. But you're right. We did find an interesting clue. It's only right that Sadie share what we uncovered in one of the evidence boxes. She brought it to my attention."

Sadie placed several pictures on the front of Frank's desk and tapped two of them.

"Here we have pictures of the same scene taken at different times," Sadie said.

Jackie picked up the pictures. "How do you know?"

"Look at the blood splatter on the wall behind the bed. The streaks of blood are different lengths, and in this one, the horizontal streaks have some smaller offshoots that aren't in the other photo."

Jackie handed me both pictures. Once I knew what to

look for, it was easy to tell which had been taken first, but I didn't get the significance until Martha told me to focus on the photo paper.

"The quality of the photo paper is different," I said. "These pictures were taken by two different photographers."

Martha smiled. "Either that or developed by two different people, which I doubt. No self-respecting crime scene photographer would let someone else develop his shots."

Jackie took the pictures back. "How can you be so sure?"

"You can feel the difference in thickness and the texture on the back of the pictures. I agree with Martha. There must have been two photographers on scene at different times."

"So where does that lead us?" Frank asked me.

"If you were a crime scene investigator and a close friend of O'Reilly's, would you wait to see if you're assigned to the case or would you hightail it over to the crime scene?"

"Most likely, but I don't see how that possibility helps us clear O'Reilly."

"It a potential lead, and we don't have many. It's worth following up. There might be more pictures that the DA is holding back," I said.

"That's a good point. I'll ask O'Reilly if he knows of someone who might have taken matters into his own hands and arrived on the scene without authorization," Frank said. "But before I see him again, I need answers to his concerns about our theory. No doubt he'll bring them up again."

I felt that we were jumping around too much and not getting closure on anything. "Hold on. Are we all agreed to focus on the DA as our killer?"

No one objected, so Frank took out his notes again. "Let's go through O'Reilly's questions with the DA in mind."

"Why would a high-profile person risk coming to the apartment?"

"My guess is the DA took the risk because he figured out a way to get rid of Bridget—to keep her from exposing their relationship—and, at the same time, frame O'Reilly for her murder," Jackie said.

"Let's go with that for now," Frank looked down at his notes. *"Did he have a key?"*

Martha didn't hesitate. "Of course he did. I'd give him one. Didn't Molly say they'd been meeting for a few years?"

I pushed back on Martha's assertion. "If they never met at her apartment, why would he need a key?"

Jackie came up with a plausible explanation.

"Maybe she didn't. If he had planned to kill Bridget a week or so in advance, he could have easily gotten his hands on her key and had a copy made. She would never know if he had taken a wax imprint of her apartment key and then had a locksmith make a duplicate."

"If he had murder on his mind, why did he take off his coat?"

I threw out a possibility. "It was late at night, he couldn't take the chance that Bridget would wake and not recognize him. She might scream."

"Or maybe he took it off because he heard voices and realized she was with another man, and he was anticipating a struggle," Sadie suggested.

"That gets us to the final two questions. *Why did he pick up the shell casings and how did he reach the gun without a struggle?"*

"When we figure that out, we'll be closer to getting O'Reilly out of the slammer," I said.

"So what do we do next?" Martha asked.

"Get the gumshoes we hired to now show pictures of Bridget and the DA to the clerks at every cheap motel they can find."

"That's easy enough."

"Then I suggest you and Sadie go through the evidence boxes the DA turned over a few more times. Check to see if there are any gaps, people he should have interviewed, but didn't. Look for stories that changed. Things like that."

"What about you guys?" Frank asked.

"We'll question the neighbors and follow up on leads the rest of you provide."

I was about to close the door, when I stuck my head back into Frank's office.

"Martha, keep your evenings open."

"What for?"

"We're gonna hit the town with Dom a few more times."

Martha glanced around for something to throw. Luckily, Frank grabbed his mug from his desk before she could reach it.

"Batista, you don't pay me enough."

Chapter 32

Three days of climbing stairs, and nothing to show for it except more damning evidence against O'Reilly. Not a single person in his building saw or heard O'Reilly enter his apartment or run up the stairs. Frustrated and exhausted, I rested my head against the car seat and closed my eyes.

It didn't take long for me to feel Jackie's stare.

"What are we doing? It's late, and I would like to get some sleep rather than sit outside O'Reilly's apartment building."

"I suggest you get some shut-eye. We'll take two-hour shifts. I'll wake you when it's your turn."

"My turn for what?"

"We're going to make a sketch of the buildings across the street and track when the lights in each apartment go out or turn back on. By morning we'll know who to pressure into telling us what they saw and heard on the night of the murders."

"I gotta say, that's brilliant," Jackie said. "I'm gonna stretch out in the backseat."

"Maybe I should join you."

"You're impossible. You come up with a good idea, then you're the first to lose focus. Do your job." She gave me a peck on the cheek as she got out and climbed into the back. As she made herself comfortable, I began to sketch the building.

By morning we had four possibilities. One was the guy who the DA got to sign an affidavit stating he had seen O'Reilly arrive before the murders took place. Since we believed in O'Reilly's innocence, the guy had to be lying.

Frank already had Martha digging into his background and had told us to keep our distance from Mr. Quinlan. That left three for us to interrogate.

We hadn't gotten much sleep so we decided to approach them after they returned home from work and when we were more alert. Our plan was simple. Grab some morning grub at Molly's diner, hit the sack, have dinner, and then get to know O'Reilly's three neighbors that tend to wake early in the morning.

As usual, Molly didn't mince her words.

"You guys look like you slept in an alleyway," she said, filling two cups with coffee.

"Thanks for the compliment. I didn't think we looked that good," I said, reaching for a mug. It was so hot I spilled the coffee when I took a sip.

Jackie held her cup with both hands, gently blowing across the surface.

"In some ways you're brilliant, but in others, you're hopeless," she said with a smile.

"Typical male, always in a rush," Molly said as she wiped up the mess and topped off my cup. "Dare I ask if you're making progress?"

Jackie answered her. "As you suggested, we've agreed to focus on the DA."

"Glad I could help."

"Bridget didn't happen to mention the names of any of the motels they used?"

"I never asked and she never spoke about such details."

"Joey and I spent the last few days talking to everyone in O'Reilly's building. The neighbors who caught him sitting on his bed holding the murder weapon are convinced he did it."

"What makes them so sure?"

"They swear that only a few minutes passed between the last shot and when they entered the bedroom and seized O'Reilly."

Molly slipped into the booth and sat next to Jackie. "I know Frank Galvano is O'Reilly's lawyer. You tell him I said to drill into the first person that entered the hallway and got the others to join him—and to do it on the witness stand."

That got my attention. "Why not before the trial?" I asked her.

"Because they honestly believe they're telling the truth, but they're not. We all want to think we're capable of heroic acts, so we make up a reality that fits that image. Frank needs to hit him hard and fast with tough questions, before he has time to think."

"How can you be so sure?"

"Joey, you've seen where I live. I often see the truth and hear lies. You learn a lot about human nature living in a cesspool."

Molly took our order, and then she got swamped with customers. I made a note to pass on her suggestion to Frank.

* * * * *

When we got home, we found Gracie putting the final ingredients into a large pot of spaghetti sauce under Ma's watchful eye. If Ma was giving away her family recipe, it was a good sign that she was warming up to Gracie, though it was still hard to tell as she stood next to Gracie with her arms tightly folded against her chest. I was about to give them a hand—hoping to lighten things up—when Luigi came in from the hallway and took hold of my arm.

"Your pop and I want to have a talk with you in the

shop. But first, you should know that I arranged a meeting with Torrio, Vigliotti, and Castellano. Make sure you bring your Commie friend to Castellano's a week from today at five."

"Hawk's not a communist."

"Whatever. Just make sure he shows up."

As soon as the last customer left, Luigi flipped over the open sign and pulled down the door shade.

"Two more merchants are in the hospital," Pop said from behind the counter.

"What happened?"

Luigi lit a stogie. "One was found unconscious in the alleyway behind his business with a shiv in his back, and the other was hit by a car. Both had refused to pay for protection."

"Are they gonna make it?"

"The docs aren't sure. We'll know in a few days," Pop said. "You were right Joey. Carmine needs to be dealt with and soon."

Luigi smashed the cigar out in his palm. "That may not be wise. Castellano made it clear that if necessary he'd take care of his son."

I was furious. "He told me not to kill him. He didn't say I couldn't break his leg or beat the crap out of him."

Pop came from behind the counter. "If anyone should be taught a lesson, it's Toby. He's the one doing the damage. Let's continue this after dinner. We shouldn't leave Gracie alone with Ma for too long."

"Is she ever gonna accept Gracie?" Luigi asked.

"Give her time. She's just worried about you."

Luigi stopped walking and stood within inches of Pop. "What do you mean by that?"

"Just that we're all concerned. It's not like any of us really know Gracie. To be honest, not even you."

"Do we really know anyone?" Luigi asked.

He didn't hang around for an answer but went to join the others at the dining table. Pop shook his head and followed. I heard Martha talking to one of the tenants as she came down the stairs, so I waited.

Martha slipped her arm around mine. "I hate to give you bad news before dinner, but Jackie said you guys are going back to O'Reilly's neighborhood when we're done eating."

I hoped she wasn't going to tell me the DA had a solid alibi for the night of the murders. I wasn't even close.

"I did as you asked and hired someone to follow Rosalie. I tried to talk to her, but she won't listen."

Ma waved for us to sit down. "You guys need to get in here so we can say grace. The food's gonna get cold."

"Give us a minute," I shouted back.

"I'm sorry, Joey. But Rosalie's seeing Big Ben's youngest son."

Chapter 33

I don't ever remember having a more unpleasant meal. Everyone kept their heads down, focusing only on their food, not conversation.

I stood.

"There's something I want to say. No, that's not right. There's something I need to say because I don't want to lose my uncle."

Ma looked back down at her plate.

"Gracie, it's obvious this family is having difficulty embracing you. It, no doubt, has to do with the belief that you took advantage of my uncle. We all know Luigi is known for making snap decisions when he's had a few drinks, but we also know he has a reason for everything he does. He's too wise, and as my ma pointed out, too much of a skinflint to blindly throw himself into a marriage."

Ma's neck and face flushed. "That's enough, Joey."

It was too late to stop. "I think everyone should know that you offered Luigi a divorce, and he said no, without hesitation. That's good enough for me. I hope it's good enough for everyone else."

I paused and looked at each person around the table.

Ma hesitated at first but then reached over and squeezed Gracie's hand. She turned to Luigi. "Luigi, I'm sorry to the both of you for the way I've behaved. It's only because I love you. But, as Joey said, we need to respect your decision."

Pop went back to eating. "Who knew my son was so wise?"

* * * * *

Before we left to interview O'Reilly's neighbors, I told Jackie about Rosalie's new boyfriend and that I needed to have a talk with her.

"Whatever you do," Jackie advised, "don't forbid her to date this guy. That will drive her closer to him."

"Then what am I supposed to do?"

"Tell her why you're concerned."

"She knows."

"Then find out why she's willing to put herself in such a dangerous situation."

"It's not just her. She's placing all of us in peril."

"She's not thinking about anyone but herself. You need to help her see the bigger picture."

"And how am I supposed to do that?"

"It might help if you face the fact that she's in love with you—I know that's hard for you to accept or even understand, but if she's ever going to listen, you have to acknowledge it."

"How?"

"I can't help you there."

Jackie took a step to the side and looked past me. "Rosalie just went into her room. I'll wait in the office. Good luck."

"I'll need more than luck," I said. I headed down the outside hall to my old bedroom.

* * * * *

When Rosalie didn't respond to my knock, I gradually opened the door. She was sitting on her bed with her arms wrapped around her knees.

I took a chance and sat next to her.

"I know why you're here," she said, turning her head away.

"We haven't talked in some time."

"We've both been busy."

"Why is it we sometimes ignore the things that mean the most to us?"

She wiped away a tear. "I guess it's too easy to take people for granted."

That hurt, but it was true.

"If that's what I did, I'm sorry."

"Why didn't you tell me you were going to ask Jackie to marry you?"

It appeared Jackie was right. "I would have, but it happened so quickly. Another man had asked her to marry him. That made me realize I didn't want to live without her."

"What about me?"

"We'll always be in each other's lives. We're family," I said, putting my arm around her shoulder.

She started to cry.

"I expected more," she said, facing me. "I know it was childish."

I brushed her tears away. "No, it wasn't. But I hope you see why I viewed our relationship differently. When we were young, I was sorry you had so much tragedy in your life, but at the same time, I was excited to have a sister. Can you understand that I never intended to hurt you?"

Rosalie nodded. She kissed me on the cheek and went into the bathroom. She returned more composed.

"Why don't we talk about why you really came to see me?" she said, sitting back on the bed.

"Do you know who your boyfriend is?"

"I didn't at first."

"How did you meet?"

"We had a small car accident. He was nice."

"Did you cause the accident?"

"No."

"Rosalie, I'm not going to tell you what you can and can't do with your life. I have no right to do that. But you're dating one of Big Ben's sons. You have to ask yourself, how did that happen? Was it planned?"

"He's not like his father."

"Can I tell you what I believe is true? And then, it's up to you."

Rosalie moved away ever so slightly.

"You know that Big Ben shot up our neighborhood and went after Castellano as well as our family. Soon after, I came close to taking down his organization. He swore revenge but was told by Vigliotti not to interfere in our neighborhood or our lives for the next two years. Why Vigliotti gave that order isn't important.

"What is important is that you understand that Sam, Big Ben's youngest, and his other sons are active in the Mafia. They drink heavily and routinely visit the brothels under their father's control. Is that the kind of man you want? Is that the life you want?"

Rosalie walked over to her window and kept her back to me. "He's not like that, but what if he were? Aren't all men more or less the same?"

"I'm not, you know Pop isn't, and neither is Luigi."

Rosalie raised her eyebrows.

"Okay, so Luigi likes his drink, and he did meet Gracie at a brothel, but he's not a wiseguy. He's a good man," I said in Luigi's defense.

"If you're finished, I'd like you to leave. I want to be alone."

I had an uneasy feeling.

"Rosalie, look at me. If you're wrong about Sam, you're putting yourself and our family at risk. Let me make it clear that if I have to go up against Big Ben again, I won't leave anyone behind to take revenge."

"That's what you're good at, isn't it? Killing people."

"It's a useful skill to have in this city, and one I don't hesitate to use when I have to."

"Are you done now?"

Her stupidity was getting to me. If I didn't leave soon, I knew I'd put a further rift in our relationship. But I wasn't done.

"My parents love you, and so do I. They sacrificed a lot to give you a better life, so please don't make the same mistake as your mother—and don't think that car accident was a really an accident. You're being used. To what end, I don't know. But it can't be good."

Rosalie came up close and jabbed her finger in my chest, backing me up against the door with each point she made.

"You don't know that. You don't know Sam, and after all these years you don't know me. If I thought Sam was anything like his family, I'd have nothing to do with him.

"Maybe it's you who needs to open your eyes and see what's really happening around you. You're the one being used—by this neighborhood."

I wrapped my arms around her and held her tight, and then I left without saying a word.

Chapter 34

I had just grabbed the knob on the office door to enter when Jackie gave it a yank from inside. I stumbled into her and she backed into Martha. The three of us ended up sprawled on the floor in a tangled mess. I lay on my back with both girls sprawled across me.

"Now this has potential," Martha said.

The girls became hysterical as we tried to stand. Once we were upright again, I went back out into the hall.

"Where are you going?" Jackie asked, still laughing.

"To try again."

I opened the door just a crack and yelled, "Is it safe to come in?"

"Yes, you may enter," Martha responded.

Both girls stood well back from the door.

"Much better. Are you ladies ready to do some witness interviews?"

Martha looked surprised. "You want me to come along?"

"Of course. You have a knack for picking up fine details. And when we're finished talking to O'Reilly's three neighbors, we can drop in on Dom, just to make sure he hasn't planned another bank job while waiting for us to get back to him."

"As long as it's not another date," Martha said emphatically.

"I need to send Hawk a message, so we'll go out for a few drinks. It won't take long, I promise."

Jackie blocked the office door. "First, tell us how it went with Rosalie?"

"I'll fill you in on the way over to O'Reilly's street. That'll give you both plenty of time to tell me where I messed up."

We were about to step onto the stoop when Pop called out.

"Hey, Joey, we need you for a few minutes."

I asked the girls to wait in the car and then followed Pop into his repair shop. I was surprised to see several other business owners standing with Luigi.

"What's goin' on?"

"We had told you if Carmine needed a lesson on how to run the neighborhood, we would do the teaching," Pop said.

"Tomorrow morning we start school," Luigi said. "We'd like you and Jackie to be there, just in case things get out of hand."

"What do ya have in mind?"

"We're gonna negotiate—old country style," Pop said, walking me out into the hall.

"What does that mean?"

"You'll find out in the morning. See you at seven." Pop gave me a pat on the back. "Make sure you get plenty of rest tonight. You never know what might happen."

* * * * *

Mrs. Flanagan was first on our list to interview. I was surprised she invited us in without hesitation. She walked me into her apartment, holding onto my arm.

"A private detective with two beautiful dames, oh how Mr. Flanagan would have envied you. Come in, come in, all of you and have a seat. I'll brew up some tea, or would you prefer coffee?"

"Tea would be nice," Jackie replied.

Jackie and Martha went into the kitchen with Mrs. Flanagan, giving me a chance to look around the parlor. One wall was plastered with Mr. Flanagan's pictures and accomplishments as an officer of the law. A framed newspaper article noted that his life had ended in 1919, when he was killed attempting to stop a bank robbery. A vase of fresh flowers sat on a small table beneath the pictures.

Two comfortable sofa chairs were positioned catty-cornered, on either side of a window overlooking the main street. Between the chairs, binoculars sat on a coffee table, leaving no doubt that Mrs. Flanagan was a busybody.

Having tasted our tea and sampled some of Mrs. Flanagan's homemade crumb cake, Jackie asked a question that was also on my mind.

"Mrs. Flanagan, why would you let strangers into your home so easily?"

"Oh dear, Mr. Batista is no stranger. I read the papers, and Mike O'Reilly talked about him several times."

"How do you know Officer O'Reilly?" I asked.

"His father and my husband worked together over the years. I've known Mike since he was a tyke. Besides, I have protection," she said, pulling a revolver out from under her unbuttoned sweater.

"Do you mind if I put that on the table?" Martha asked.

"There's no need, dear, you're not in any danger," she said, putting the gun back into her shoulder holster.

We glanced at each other in silent amusement.

"We noticed you wake early in the morning, and I see that

you keep a close eye on the neighborhood," I said, pointing to the window.

"Yes, living alone I like to know what's happening around me."

"Did you hear the shots that were fired on the night Bridget was murdered?"

"I surely did! Scared me half to death. I was sitting right there in my window chair."

"Did you see O'Reilly enter the building?"

"I did. How anyone can suspect him is beyond me. He was still in his car when the mayhem erupted."

"Did anyone from the DA's office or Homicide take your statement?" Jackie asked.

"Yes, of course. I told them what I just told you. O'Reilly is innocent."

"Did they have you sign an affidavit to that effect?" Martha asked.

"Yes, and I offered to testify at his trial. But I haven't heard from anyone."

I looked over to Martha, and she shrugged her shoulders. Evidently, no such affidavit was in the evidence boxes.

"Did you happen to see who did the shooting?" Jackie asked.

"No, I can't say that I did. The drapes were pulled closed. I called the operator to report a shooting right after I saw Mike get out of his car. But I don't think they took me seriously—I do tend to call them a lot."

We finished our tea and thanked Mrs. Flanagan for her cooperation.

The next person on our list wasn't as cordial.

* * * * *

A voice boomed through the door. "You're nuts if you think I'm letting strangers into my place."

"We're investigating the murders that occurred across the street," I said.

"I don't give a damn what you're doing. Unless you're with the police and have a search warrant, you're not setting foot in here."

"Did you see anything on the night your neighbors were killed?" Jackie asked.

"Is that a dame? What the hell is the world coming to? Skirts on the police force? What's next?"

"We're private investigators," I said, tempted to kick in the door.

"I didn't see or hear anything, and if I did, I wouldn't say so to you or anyone else. Stop pestering me and move on."

We were wasting our time. The last tenant we wished to speak with was a Josephine Covina.

* * * * *

"Slip your ticket under the door," a young woman's voice demanded.

Jackie shoved her PI license in after mine. The door opened two inches, before it was stopped by three chain locks evenly positioned along the frame.

"Who's the other one?"

"She's our secretary," I said. "We'd like to talk to you about the murders that took place."

"Which ones?"

"Did you know Officer O'Reilly and his wife?" Jackie asked.

The door closed abruptly but then opened once the chains were released.

"You can come in. I take it you already know my name."

"This will only take a few minutes of your time, Miss Covina," I said.

"Let's not be so formal, Josie's fine."

She took a closer look at our tickets and handed them back.

"Joey Batista, I've read about you. You stopped some nut who was killing young women. Jackie Forsythe, you're the dame that killed her husband. I was at your trial. You sure as hell can handle a shiv."

Josie looked at Martha. "What's your claim to fame?"

"Don't have one. I'm just Martha—the secretary."

"I take it that means you do all the work, and they get all the credit."

Martha tried unsuccessfully to hold back a smile. "How do you know so much about us?"

"I'm a reporter for the *Daily News*."

Josie picked up her coat and went over to Jackie. "You and I joined the paper close to the same time, but I don't have your looks. Even to this day, none of the top brass know I exist. Not that I'm sayin' it was just your looks that got you noticed."

I thought Jackie was going to deck her, but instead she got down to business.

"Good reporters are observant. If you can help us, I'll see what I can do to move your career along."

Josie threw her coat over the back of a chair and gestured for us to take a seat.

"I don't have much time. I shouldn't leave one of my

snitches waiting too long. It's hard enough to gain their confidence."

"Just tell us in your own words what you know and we'll move on," I said.

"I was getting ready to go to work when I heard the first shot. A noise that loud echoed between buildings. It sounded like the gun went off in my parlor. I went straight to the window."

"What did you see?" Jackie asked.

"Nothing. I heard a woman's scream, then more shots were fired."

Martha looked up from her notes. "What happened next?"

"Lights popped on all over the building. I was surprised how fast the cops had arrived, but then realized it was O'Reilly."

"Did he show up after the first shot or before?" I asked.

"During. He stopped his car in the middle of the road and ran up the steps. I climbed out my window onto the fire escape to get a better look. A few minutes later a guy runs out of the alleyway and down the street."

"Can you describe him?"

"It was too dark."

"Did you see where he went?"

"He turned the corner. My guess is he hailed a cab."

Jackie inched forward. "Why would you say that?"

"It was a cold night. He had on a hat, but no coat, and I saw him raise his arm just before turning the corner."

"Anything else?" Jackie asked.

"That's it. Soon after, all hell broke loose."

I walked over to her window and parted the curtain.

"Did you give a statement to the police or anyone in the prosecutor's office?"

"Both, I doubt the prosecution will call me as a witness, though. There's no way O'Reilly's guilty."

* * * * *

I pulled into the parking lot of a diner near Dom's apartment. I wanted to get the girls' take on what they thought of Josephine Corvina and what she had said, before we hit the speakeasies with Dom to look for Hawk.

"So, what are your thoughts?" I asked, after we settled into a booth.

Martha was pouring sugar into her coffee. "I'd always wondered why there was a coat in the apartment, but no hat."

In her musing, she poured way too much sugar.

"Oops, I better get another cup of joe."

I shoved mine across the table.

"Can you think of a plausible explanation why the DA would take his hat and not his coat?"

Martha pushed the sugar jar away. "He ran out of time. For whatever reason he gathered up the spent shells, went into the parlor, put on his hat, and was then startled by someone trying to get into the apartment before he could grab his coat. He ran back into the bedroom and scurried out the window and down the fire escape."

"Most guys put their coat on first, and then carry their hat outside before putting it on."

"Maybe the hat was closer. He'd tossed it on a chair rather than placing it on the coat rack. I don't know. There could be any number of reasons."

"I'll buy that. What about you, Jackie? What struck you today?"

"Every reporter has a camera. Even though taking pictures is not part of her job, I'd bet anything that Josephine grabbed her camera and ran out of her building that night to get a scoop. If you ask me, she's our mystery photographer."

"Now that you mention it, I think the afternoon edition of the *Daily News* on the day of the murders had a front page picture of O'Reilly being held down by his neighbors." I stated. "I think you're on to something. If she took that news picture, then she was inside O'Reilly's apartment even before the cops."

Martha took out her notepad. "I'll check back tomorrow evening and see if she'll give me the negatives. If you ask me, someone from the DA's office confiscated her prints, but only some of them ended up in the evidence box."

I ordered another cup of coffee. "While you're there, try to get a signed statement from her and the old lady. It looks like the DA has a compulsion for suppressing evidence, and Frank might make good use of that fact during the trial."

"Can't say I blame the DA," Martha said. "If I was guilty, I'd do the same damn thing."

I couldn't disagree.

* * * * *

Dom wasn't thrilled to see us.

"Why didn't you call?"

"Gee, sweetie, I thought you'd be glad to see me," Martha said, giving him a gentle tap on the cheek.

Jackie rolled her eyes reminding me that Martha can be a real tease. I knew from experience.

Stunned, Dom stood holding the door open long after we had entered his apartment. When we approached his table, he snapped to and slammed the door shut. He brushed us aside to gather up penciled drawings.

"What are those?" Martha asked, moving to look over his shoulder.

"Never you mind."

"What did you do before you enlisted?" she asked.

"I was an architect. The skill comes in handy when you're assigned to blow up a bridge."

"Or just about anything else," I said, holding up one of the sketches. "You're not still planning on taking down one of Big Ben's piers, are you?"

"I'm just killing time, that's all. By the way, you haven't told me why you're here."

"I need to get a message to Hawk. A meeting with the Mafia has been arranged."

"That was quick. Make yourselves at home. I'll be ready in no time."

I stopped Dom after the girls were in the hallway.

"Is it possible to collapse a whole pier at once?"

"Not a problem, but that's not the right question. You should ask if it can be done without collateral damage."

"Well, can it?"

"That's the real challenge. Day or night, there's a lot of activity on or around the piers."

"Keep working on it. I might need something dramatic to make a point to Vigliotti and his cohorts."

275

Chapter 35

Luigi, Pop, and three other merchants entered the pizza shop together. Jackie and I stood off to the side of the entrance. The place was empty except for Toby and the owner, who was busy mixing a large batch of dough.

Toby stood when he saw us enter and blocked the door to Carmine's office.

"What the hell do you guys want?"

"To negotiate with Carmine," Luigi said in a respectful tone.

"Mr. Castellano is busy, and he doesn't negotiate with peasants."

Jackie held me back. "This is their show."

I put my arm around her waist and gently moved her toward the group. I could feel her knife harness. She was ready for action.

Toby saw us approaching and reached inside his jacket.

"What the hell do you want, Batista?"

"Just here to make sure nothing happens to my pop. He's an old man."

A low grumble came from the group, when suddenly Carmine opened the door to his office.

"What's goin' on out here?"

"They say they're here to negotiate. I told them to get the hell out."

Carmine extended his hand to Luigi. "It's about time you

came to your senses. There's no need for any more people to have unfortunate accidents."

He invited everyone into his office for a drink. Pop and Luigi stood in front of Carmine's desk as he took his seat. Toby positioned himself off to the side, slightly behind Pop. I moved to stand next to Toby, but one of the three merchants discreetly pulled me back.

"What can I do for you?" Carmine asked with a benevolent look, no doubt sensing he was in control.

Luigi took off his hat and held it with both hands in a submissive stance. Something was going on. I put my arm around Jackie and slid out one of her knives.

"Just a minute," Pop said. He then turned toward Toby and smashed his face with a fierce blow.

Toby staggered back into a portable bar. Stunned, he brought his bloody hands down from his nose. He reached for one of his rods, but before he could pull it all the way out, Pop hit him again, but this time low in the gut. Toby doubled over. Pop followed up with an anvil-like fist to his chin, throwing Toby's head back and exposing the front of his neck to a brutal chop.

Carmine gripped the side arms of his chair, staring down the barrel of a .45.

"What the hell are you doing?" Carmine yelled.

"Negotiating," Luigi said. "Relax, it's not painful at all—not for you, not yet. Why don't you place your piece on the desk, like a good boy?"

Pop had spun Toby around and was pounding his kidneys. The cracking of ribs could be heard with each blow. Toby collapsed. His head hit the surface of the bar and his knees landed on the brass foot railing near the floor. Pop let out a grunt and brought his heavy work boot down on the back of

Toby's leg, above the heel. The sound of his ankle snapping and Toby's screams were gut-wrenching.

"That's for my friends," Pop said, wiping his brow with a handkerchief.

Pop waved the other merchants over. Two of them grabbed Toby's limp arms and dragged him toward the side door. The third merchant opened the door and closed it behind them as soon as they'd hauled Toby outside.

Carmine ran to follow. "What are you doing? Where are they taking him?"

Pop sat next to Luigi and said, "He's gonna have one of your unfortunate accidents."

Within seconds, the sound of a truck slamming on its brakes and colliding with the side of a building filled the room.

Carmine didn't look so good as he returned from the alleyway and sat back in his chair.

Luigi handed me Carmine's gun and put his away. "I think we're now ready to negotiate," he said to Carmine.

* * * * *

Carmine listened, struggling to control his breathing. Knowing Carmine, there would be a price to pay for his humiliation. I had no doubt that my uncle and Pop understood the risk.

Pop had done his talking using the muscles he'd developed over years of hard work. It was my uncle's turn to talk in his own way.

"Carmine, no one blames you. Your pop threw you in this position, without any warning or advice, and left you with no crew to speak of."

"I don't need his advice."

"Is that so? How's everything working out so far?"

Carmine bit his lip.

"From the very beginning you made a fundamental mistake. You let Toby pick your crew. But their loyalty should be to you, not to him. They need to know whose giving the orders and paying them. You understand what I'm saying?"

"I'm listening."

"That's a good sign. Now, you should have hired just Sicilians. They will be the most loyal, hopefully you know why. Sicilians are the only ones who can move up into the higher ranks of the Mafia. You wanna be called Mr. Castellano? You gotta earn that respect, and you don't do that by hurting your own people. That was your second and most serious mistake."

"I didn't have a choice. I needed more money for the syndicate. They wouldn't pay up."

"Carmine, you had a choice. All you had to do was come to me. We all wanna help. What you have to understand is some merchants are wealthier than others, and people need time to make arrangements. Payments will begin next week."

"How much?"

"Some will pay five percent of their profit, others ten. I'll provide you with a list tomorrow."

Pop and Luigi pushed back their chairs at the same time and headed for the door. At the threshold, Luigi turned to face Carmine.

"Carmine, if you take any action over what happened here today, you will pay with your life. That's your third lesson—don't mess with me—I'm not as forgiving as your old man."

Jackie went out next, and I closed the door behind us. I hadn't gotten far when I heard Carmine curse and flip over his desk.

On the walk home, Jackie made an interesting comment.

"It seems that violence runs in your family."

"I always wondered how Castellano was able to carve out an Italian neighborhood away from Little Italy. When you think about it, we're surrounded by other ethnic groups. Guess we now know. As my uncle basically said, don't mess with first generation Sicilians."

Jackie tightened her grip of my arm. "I don't think we've heard the last from Carmine."

"That's his decision, and it's evident it could be one of his last."

"Why did Luigi advise him how to organize? Why are they helping him?"

"Out of respect for Castellano."

"I don't think Carmine understood that."

"We'll just have to wait and see what happens next. In the meantime, we have O'Reilly to worry about and the Communist Party to deal with."

"Is that all?" Jackie said. "Life is calming down at last."

We both had a good laugh.

Chapter 36

The big question swirling around the neighborhood was whether Vigliotti would take Toby's death as an assault to his authority or a test of Carmine's ability to control his territory. Either way, there was no doubt there would be consequences. In spite of the uncertainty, the inner workings of the neighborhood moved on as if nothing had happened. Luigi kept his word and collected the first allotment of protection money from the local businesses to hand over to Carmine. Construction of the brothel went undeterred, and the hustle and bustle common to the waterfront never missed a beat.

The tension that existed was evident in more subtle ways: foot traffic was down at the end of the work day, curtains were drawn earlier than usual, shutters remained closed longer and the local gossip moved from the stoops in front of the buildings to behind closed doors.

Most unnerving was that Carmine had disappeared. Not even Castellano knew what his son was up to. This led to speculation that Big Ben might seize the opportunity and once again attempt to take over the waterfront. But no matter how much fear permeated the streets, if the very survival of the neighborhood was threatened, we would all come together. That I was sure of, and so was my uncle. Nevertheless, Luigi wasn't about to take any chances and immediately took control. He employed the local street gangs to watch for strangers or unusual activity along the waterfront that might indicate trouble, and he worked with other business leaders to plan for the worst. Never again would an attack in our streets go unchallenged.

For our part, Jackie and I stayed close to the office, reviewing material for O'Reilly's trial, strategizing with Frank and directing Martha and Sadie as they continued to gather information. I kept in touch with Hawk and Dom by phone and occasionally had Martha join Dom at his local speakeasies to keep the impression alive that our reunion with Hawk was coincidental. Surprisingly, it was becoming easier to get her cooperation.

O'Reilly's trial was rapidly approaching, but not before it was time to deal with the Communist Party and implement the Colonel's plan, crazy as it seemed.

*****

My uncle Torrio descended upon Castellano's estate with an entourage of henchmen loaded down with impressive hardware. Al Capone, his right-hand man, posted men around the periphery of the property and stationed a pair with Tommy guns on the veranda. Vigliotti had already arrived with two bodyguards, who joined him in the house. As a counter measure, Al pulled two of his own men inside.

I had first met Capone when I contacted my uncle Torrio in Chicago to help locate someone whom I suspected had killed Anita, my fiancée. When I questioned my parents as to why they'd never mentioned this uncle before, they had said they didn't want Torrio to have any influence on my life as I grew up. Once Ma told me the details of how her brother had risen in the ranks of the Mafia, I had agreed with their decision.

My uncle had immigrated to America years before my folks and became active in the Five Points Gang that terrorized parts of the city in the late 1800s. It was during that time that Torrio first met Al Capone. Achieving a reputation as a deadly enforcer and acute businessman, my uncle eventually went to work for "Big Jim" Colsimo, out of Chicago, to deal with extortion threats from a rival criminal organization. Eventually, he murdered Colsimo and took over his organization. My uncle then moved quickly into the bootleg business with the help of Al Capone, whom he had previously recruited out of New York. Together they built an impressive Mafia organization that today controls most of the illegal activities in Chicago's downtown and South Side areas.

I asked Capone why he thought it necessary to have such a show of force. He explained several attempts had been made on my uncle's life in the past few months, as they tried to expand their bootlegging businesses into Dion O'Banion's territory on the North Side of Chicago.

I understood the concern, but given the purpose of our meeting, I didn't think it prudent to have bodyguards in the room when Hawk arrived. I had asked Hawk to come a half-hour late so Luigi and I would have a chance to answer any questions Vigliotti and Torrio might have without him present. But we couldn't have that conversation with others in the house.

"What we're about to discuss is sensitive and must stay within a tight group," I said.

Capone was quick to react. "The only way my men are leaving is if I have the only weapons in the room."

Vigliotti and Castellano agreed. I place my rods and two throwing knives onto a nearby table. Luigi was the last to disarm, and as he walked back to his seat, Torrio stopped him.

"Luigi, Al won't hesitate to splatter your brains all over the wall if he notices your ankle holster."

Luigi bent down to pull out a snub-nosed revolver, when Capone drew his piece and ordered him to stop.

"Leave the rod where it is and unstrap the holster. Then hand it over. I don't want to see your hand anywhere near the butt of that gun."

Luigi did as told and returned to his seat. At that point, Al directed his men to search everyone.

"That won't be necessary," Torrio said. "We're among friends and family." Torrio dismissed all four bodyguards.

Satisfied we were alone, I refocused everyone's attention. "We have a few minutes before my contact from the government arrives. This is your chance to ask questions without him present."

Vigliotti was the first to speak. "I have opposed unions and don't see any reason to change my position. They'll limit our influence and control we have over city hall."

"I'm sure Luigi explained that the government is concerned with the rapid growth of the Communist Party, which is being fueled by their ability to organize labor. If this continues, the Party will ultimately have more power over the politicians than you have today. The textile industry has unionized, and the railroad workers' union is expanding and defying federal orders," I said.

Torrio spoke up. "That's not our problem. None of our businesses are threatened."

I'd never had the chance to talk with Castellano in detail about what Hawk would propose, so his comment impressed me.

"When we fought the unionization of the waterfront, I wondered if we were missing an opportunity by choosing to see the unions as a threat."

"What else could they be?" Vigliotti asked Castellano.

"A source of income. Think about it. If we control the unions, we control who joins, and we can charge fees for membership. Let's not forget about the monthly dues. Wouldn't it be better for that money to come to us than the Communist Party?"

"That's not enough reason to get in bed with the government," Vigliotti responded.

Castellano didn't back down. "I'm sure there are more financial benefits that we can't think of right now."

"Getting involved would be a diversion from our main business," Torrio said. "We're having enough trouble keeping up with demand for booze and fighting off rival gangs as they encroach on our territory. We don't need to take on the Russians."

A commotion outside drew our attention. Hawk had arrived. His two Russian bodyguards were insisting on attending the meeting and reached for their weapons, only to be confronted by several more of Capone's men, who emerged from the foliage. Capone didn't like what he saw as he peered out the front window.

"Who the hell are those clowns?"

"They're assigned to protect Hawk, my government contact. Obviously they don't suspect him of being a double agent."

"Your man is playing a dangerous game," Capone said. "Don't kid yourself, Joey, he's really a triple agent."

"What makes you think that?"

"As soon as the government sees an advantage, they'll

turn against us. So your friend is playing all three of us against each other, the Mafia, the Feds, and the Communist Party."

"I suppose that's possible. But as Castellano said, we need to consider all angles. If we end up agreeing with the government's proposal, at some point, we'll need to bring Hawk's bodyguards into the discussion to convince them of that."

"Only if they come in naked," Capone said, seriously.

"Al, be reasonable," Torrio said. "Your men are capable of making sure they're not a threat."

I stepped onto the porch and waved for Hawk to come over. The Russians walked on either side of him as he approached.

"I hope you buffoons realize you have no choice but to hand over your weapons," I said with my hands outstretched.

"We have our orders."

"I don't give a damn about your orders. I've arranged for Hawk to meet with the two biggest mob bosses on the East Coast. Now, hand over your weapons or I'll call off the meeting. Then you'll get to go back and explain that to your comrades."

Hawk took them off to the side where they had an animated exchange. He returned with their weapons and handed them over to Capone's men guarding the front door, along with his own.

"Pat them all down just to make sure," I said to the guards.

The Russians each had an additional gun and two shivs. I still didn't trust them. There was no telling what they were thinking, so I threw them a bone to calm their nerves.

"I need to take Hawk in alone first then you can both join us to hear the details of any agreement so you can report firsthand information back to your superiors. Now grab a seat on the porch and try to relax. I'm sure Hawk told you he's not in any danger."

With that I walked Hawk into the house, but not before he warned Capone's men. "Keep them away from their car. They have enough heat in there to start a small revolution."

* * * * *

Hawk wasn't inside for more than a few seconds when Capone put a cocked gun against the back of his head.

"Frisk him again," he ordered me.

Hawk raised his arms in the air. "Don't worry, Mr. Capone, I'm not dumb enough to come to this meeting armed."

"I've seen people do dumber things," Capone said, as I patted Hawk down.

"How do you know who I am?" Capone asked.

"I've read about all of you," Hawk said, looking around the room. "The government has a dossier on every Mafia boss in the country."

"Then we can dispense with the introductions," Torrio said to Hawk. "We understand your little game, but don't see how it benefits us."

"In a communist country, the government runs everything. You'll be put out of business if the political structure changes."

"All governments are corrupt, and the more corrupt, the more they need people like us to stay in power," Vigliotti said.

"That's not a point I'm going to argue. So here it is. You're being offered access to the unionization of this country. The benefits are money, potentially a lot of money, and influence at the highest levels of government."

Vigliotti wasn't convinced. "We already have both." He turned to the rest of us. "I agree with what Torrio said earlier. Why should we take on the Russians? Let the Feds do their own job."

Torrio nodded to Capone. "Al, how do you see this?"

"A few years ago, we were all scrambling for a sawbuck—pushing gambling, drugs, prostitution, and whatever else we could get our fingers into. We didn't make serious dough until the government handed us a gift."

"What gift?" Castellano asked.

"The Eighteenth Amendment—Prohibition. Until then, we were all small-time hoods. What we have now won't last forever. Given the appetite people have for booze, Prohibition will someday be repealed, and then what?"

The room fell silent.

"What exactly do you expect from us?" Vigliotti asked Hawk.

"Cooperate with the Russians and push for unionization of our core industrial companies. Give the Russians the impression they're in control, and then over time, shove them out."

"And how are we supposed to accomplish that feat?" Capone asked.

Hawk smiled. "Do what you do best."

Castellano leaned forward in his chair. "Let me get this straight. You're saying the government will stay out of our way while all this is going on."

"Until the Communist Party is no longer a threat," Hawk said.

"Then what?"

"Then you're on your own, just like today."

With that, the conversation turned from whether to cooperate with the government to how to outwit the Russians as they worked together to organize unions in the businesses where the Mafia had the most influence. Hawk and I backed out of the conversation and just listened.

Luigi had wisely stayed out of the discussion until there was some agreement to go along with Hawk's proposal.

"The simplest way to gain the Russians' trust is to unionize the waterfront," he said. "The ground work has already been laid, and there's still interest among the workers. Castellano, if you take the lead, I have no doubts you could have a union up and running in a few months."

"What about Carmine?" Vigliotti asked. "He's not gonna like his old man coming back into the picture."

"He'll just have to deal with it," Castellano said. "Besides, I'm not sure I made the right choice turning things over to him, not after the way he's treated some of the business owners."

"I took your advice the last time we met and gave your son a few pointers," Luigi said to Castellano. "As you know, Toby is no longer with us and many of his men have scattered. I suspect Carmine's out looking for a new crew."

"He is," Torrio said. "Carmine just left Chicago with two of my best men. He's headed for Detroit next. I put out the word to help him rebuild his organization. I thought I was doing you guys a favor. Sounds like I should've checked."

"Of the two men Carmine snagged, I'd worry the most about the guy named George," Capone said.

"Why's that?" Luigi asked.

"He's deadly, ambitious, and unpredictable. A worrisome

combination in some circumstances. On the other hand, he's loyal. If you ask me, Carmine has learned his lesson and is pulling together one hell of an organization."

"I'll say it again. Carmine's gonna view your efforts to unionize the dock workers as a direct threat to his authority," Vigliotti said to Castellano.

"Not if it benefits him," Castellano responded. "It would help if you agreed to count fifty percent of the dough that flows into the organization from all future union activities as part of his contribution. That would eliminate any possibility of Big Ben winning council approval to ever take over his territory."

"I'll see what I can do, but don't expect more than twenty-five."

"That should be enough to get Carmine to refocus his efforts on the waterfront and stop milking the neighborhood," I said.

Torrio wasn't interested in our internal issues and got us back on topic.

"To get things rolling on my end, I'll need to get connected with the Communist Party in Chicago," he said to Hawk.

"That's not a problem. I already have men assigned to me for just that purpose. As a delegate to the Communist Party, I'll stay involved with all of you as you interact with Party leaders."

We shook hands and arranged to meet four times a year to assess how things were progressing and set strategies going forward.

It was time to put on a show for Hawk's bodyguards. Everyone understood that his goons had to walk away with the impression that Hawk was fighting hard for the Communist cause. So we agreed that Hawk would prevail on several key points as the final details of an agreement were hashed out in front of the Russians. The most important of those items were structural control of the unions and revenue sharing.

Given that we had agreed to do everything possible to maintain Hawk's credibility with the Communist Party, the Russians were no longer of concern to me. How Carmine would react to his father returning to organize a union became the bigger unknown.

Chapter 37

Even though he was slowly regaining the use of his arm, Castellano still couldn't drive. That didn't stop him from visiting the neighborhood the day after our meeting with Hawk. He had Angela drive him around and kept her by his side as he dropped in on each business owner to apologize for his son's behavior. He then visited those in the hospital, arranged to pay their medical expenses, and committed to cover all business losses sustained due to their injuries.

The few men still loyal to Carmine didn't know what to make of the rumor that Castellano was back in control. So they wisely stayed in the shadows, keeping their options open.

To assure Carmine wouldn't take his presence in the neighborhood as a direct threat to his authority, Castellano moved quickly to set things straight. He notified the dock foremen that he had come back to form a union and reaffirmed Carmine's position as Boss. He still held out hope he could avoid a conflict with his son and that the death of Toby had taught him an important lesson—gaining the support of neighborhood leaders legitimizes a mob boss' authority.

Luigi did his part to demonstrate Castellano's intentions by converting a vacant storefront into an office with a huge union sign posted above the entrance. Hawk followed through on his end and had two Communist Party delegates assigned to work with Castellano. Castellano appointed one as the union representative and the other as union boss. It was now their job to grow membership.

By the end of the week, Castellano's leadership and Vigliotti's silence sent the clear signal that the Mafia now supported the unionization of the waterfront.

The Colonel's plan was set in motion. Time would tell if the government would allow the Mafia to stay in the shadows and have free reign over the unions.

* * * * *

Each day Angela dropped Castellano off at the union office, and then she'd spend her day with Ma and Gracie in the kitchen preparing meals and learning some of the subtleties of old country cooking. In the late afternoon, she picked Castellano up at his headquarters, and they both returned to join us for dinner. The trip back to the Island and Castellano's home took two to three hours depending on the time of day, so they typically didn't linger long after eating.

Normally, on a Friday night, everyone stayed to socialize after the meal and share a few drinks. But not tonight, not with O'Reilly in jail and with the uncertainty Carmine had created. After supper, we all went about our business. Jackie helped clean up the dishes, and I continued reviewing what little material we had for O'Reilly's defense. The only way O'Reilly was going to beat this rap was for us to prove the DA did the killings. At this point, that looked like an impossible legal feat.

I'd just tossed aside a report from Martha when Jackie came into the office with Angela. I was surprised Angela hadn't left yet for the Island.

They sat in the two leather chairs directly in front of my desk, as though they were clients. That told me something was up.

"Angela and I were talking," Jackie said. "She's afraid of Carmine and concerned for Castellano's safety—"

Never one to let others speak for her, Angela interrupted.

"Joey, Carmine hasn't been rational since Butch killed our son. The only attention I get from Carmine is when he beats me. He has also threatened his father more than once. And that was before Castellano started up the union. Carmine's gonna go crazy when he gets back in town and sees what's going on. It sounds like he could arrive in town from Detroit at any time."

"Why didn't you tell me he was mistreating you?"

"You can't solve everyone's problems, but I'm asking for help now."

"Angela, I don't think you need to worry. Everyone knows what really happened to Toby. The first thing Carmine will do to cement his authority is to go after me, Pop, and Luigi for what we did to humiliate him. We'll handle Carmine at that time."

"Maybe. If he hasn't heard about what his father's been doing, but I doubt that. My fear is if Carmine arrives tonight or over the weekend, he might come straight to the house and then deal with you and yours after Castellano's out of the picture."

"You're saying he would kill his own father?"

"I'm telling you, Joey, he's unstable."

"What would you like us to do?"

"Could you and Jackie stay at the house with us until Monday morning?"

I glanced at Jackie.

"I agree with Angela but don't think it's wise for both of us to leave. We just don't know where he'll show up first," she said. "There's also O'Reilly's trial. It's next week, and we still don't have enough to get him off."

I asked Angela to give us a minute. She left the room.

Jackie waited until we heard the outer office door close. "Like I said, she has a valid concern."

"But you're right, we can't both go."

"I think it's best if I stay with your folks. Luigi can take care of himself."

"You don't mind if I go alone?"

"Why should I? Can't I trust you with a beautiful woman?"

"I'm surrounded by beautiful women, but none more than you."

Jackie hesitated at the door. "You never answered my question. Can I trust you in that big house with Angela?"

"I'll tell you Monday morning."

Jackie shook her head and left the office to tell Angela what we had decided. I overheard her tell Martha that men were such idiots.

Martha was quick to agree.

* * * * *

Castellano objected to my staying for the weekend, until Angela confided that Carmine had roughed her up a few times while he was in the hospital recovering from his gunshot wounds.

By the time we got to his estate, a full moon was high in the sky, casting eerie shadows as weeping willow vines swayed in a stiff breeze. The grounds looked deserted, but to be safe, I entered the house first and checked all the rooms.

Angela prepared the guest quarters on the first floor, near the entrance and across from the parlor, and then went to her upstairs bedroom. Castellano and I sat up for a few hours sharing a bottle of his finest bootleg whiskey. We talked about how things were going with his return to the neighborhood.

"I hope you realize your efforts to make amends for what Carmine did are appreciated."

"It's my fault. I didn't prepare Carmine for the job. I had hoped you would step in when the time came."

"I think you know now it's not the type of life I want."

"I understand. It's a nasty business."

"I've got a feeling that running a union isn't gonna be much better. How'd your first days go?"

"Other than having to tell those two Communist zealots that Hawk sent me to tone things down—I'm pleased with the progress."

"Any pushback from the other bosses?"

"Vigliotti did away with any objections by personally launching the unionization of the city's construction workers."

"Have you thought about how you're gonna limit the Communist influence as your union grows?"

"I already took care of that."

"How?"

"Easy. I sat down with five dock foremen I trust and told them to get active in the union. They got the message that they would gain influence over time and be handsomely rewarded."

"I hope you didn't tell them too much."

"Didn't need to. What I said was enough to get their

cooperation. They knew something was going on—the guys I put in charge of the union aren't Italian."

The more I got to know Castellano, the more I admired his organizational and business skills. When you couple that with the brutality I knew he was capable of, I had no doubts that Castellano would ultimately push the Communist Party out of his union.

* * * * *

I had just stepped out of the shower and was putting on my pants when I heard shouting coming from the main part of the house. Recognizing Carmine's voice, I strapped on my holsters without bothering with a shirt and threw open the bedroom door. The scene was chaotic. Carmine had grabbed Castellano's walking cane and had knocked him to the ground. He was about to strike him again when Angela rushed out of the kitchen screeching like a banshee, wielding a cast iron skillet.

Carmine knocked aside the skillet and hit Angela with a backhand that sent her tumbling over an end table.

"Stay out of this, you whore. I always suspected you were cheating on me," he yelled, looking toward me.

I was about to step forward, when I sensed a presence to my left. A gun was pressed against my side before I could react.

"Next time, park your car out of sight," a deep voice said. "Toss your rods on the sofa."

When Castellano attempted to get up. Carmine struck him again, and then pointed the cane at me.

"Joey, you haven't met George. He comes highly recommended by your uncle Torrio. He's gonna take you outside and put a hole in your head. But don't worry. You'll get a prime spot in my pet cemetery, right next to the neighbor's dog that I sliced open when I was a kid just to see what was inside."

"You don't need to do this, Carmine. Your father has no intention of taking the neighborhood away from you."

"Well, the way I see it, there's only one way to make sure of that," he said, looking down at his father. "Besides, your pop and Luigi made it clear that I needed to worry about more than just my old man. Right about now my new men are taking out your folks and that crazy uncle of yours. Then when I'm finished here, the neighborhood will be truly back in my hands."

Castellano grabbed Carmine's leg as Angela came at him again. Carmine swatted her aside and hit Castellano with a wicked blow that opened a bloody gash in the side of his head.

As all this was happening George was shoving me toward the front door. Feeling the gun move from the small of my back to my side, I pivoted and landed an elbow in George's neck. The gun fired. George was dazed long enough for me to grab his wrist, spin him around and slam his face into the back of the door. The gun fell and was kicked aside as we struggled.

I buckled when George landed a blow to my side. The pain was excruciating. That's when I realized the bullet had ripped through my flesh. George, sensing an advantage, held my head down and repeatedly jammed his knee into my chest. I deflected most of his blows with my forearm, and when the shock of the initial pain passed, I slipped my free arm under his thigh. I was about to heave him off his feet when we both froze. The sound of rapid gunfire reverberated throughout the house.

Carmine staggered, looked down at his blood-soaked shirt in disbelief, and collapsed to the floor. Angela then turned the gun on George. He raised his arms and took a step back. I hobbled away from George, knelt next to Angela, and grabbed the gun from her shaking hands.

Angela looked as if she was about to pass out.

"Get a hold of yourself," I shouted.

She jerked her head up and took a deep breath.

"How bad am I hit?" I asked.

"Looks like a flesh wound," she said, handing me a doily from the armrest of the couch we leaned against. "Put pressure on the wound with this until I can get something better."

Seeing that Castellano was out cold, Angela went into the kitchen to get a wet cloth. When she returned, she tossed me a dish cloth and then attended to Castellano. I sat on the couch, holding the towel against my bloody side with one hand and keeping a steady aim on George with the other.

Castellano regained consciousness, and when he saw his son, he stood and kicked him in the head. He then turned to George.

"Who do you work for?" he asked.

George looked confused, glancing from me to Castellano. He pointed to Carmine's body.

"Castellano."

"Capone told us you have a sense of loyalty, and since I'm the only Castellano alive in this room—I'd say you now work for me."

George nodded.

"Joey, put the gun down. George, help my daughter-in-law, Angela, patch us up."

I went to go to the wall phone.

"That won't do you any good," George said. "Carmine cut the phone lines. Besides, whatever happened to your family is over by now. Let me stop the bleeding, and then I'll get you back to the city."

"How many men did Carmine send?"

"Four."

"Are they any good?"

"Some of the best."

"They don't stand a chance," I said solemnly.

"I know," George replied.

"I wasn't referring to my family."

Chapter 38

Angela insisted that we go to the local hospital for stitches, but Castellano and I knew better. Once a gunshot wound was reported, the cops would get involved. Castellano made a phone call and in a few minutes a doctor arrived at the house and worked on the both of us. He urged me to go to his office where he could do a better job cauterizing my wound, but I needed to get back to the city.

It was bad enough that I couldn't call to find out what had happened to my family. Now I had to wait for the croaker to finish his work and for George to dig a shallow grave.

I didn't know much about George, but I did appreciate his sense of humor. When the last patch of dirt was patted down, George went to put the shovel back into the work shed and returned minutes later with a crudely painted wooden plank that he tossed onto the mound—*Gone to the Dogs.*

On the way to the ferry terminal, George pulled over at a roadside gas station so I could get in touch with my folks. The phone operator couldn't get through. She thought the lines were down. I had her try Tony the Butcher's number.

"Tony, this is Joey. Are my folks okay? What about Jackie and the others? ... How bad? ... Anyone else hurt?"... I'm on the Island. Tell them I'll head straight for the hospital."

Tony's next few responses were vague. He knew that an operator might be listening to our conversation.

"What's that?" I asked. "You're doing what for Pop? Did you say you're cleaning up a mess? … Listen, call Vigliotti and tell him what's goin' on. He'll send some guys over to take care of everything … Tony, listen to me. You're not to come to the Island and dump the garbage. Let Vigliotti's crew take care of it. They'll know what to do."

George overheard the conversation.

"That didn't sound good," he said, as we got back in the car.

"It's not, but it could have been a lot worse. I'll tell you this—your pals are all dead, and two of them are being turned into chum for the morning deep sea fishing boats."

"Damn, you have one tough family."

"Neighborhood, we have one tough neighborhood. Let me give you some sound advice, don't ever cross Castellano."

* * * * *

Jackie was waiting outside the hospital. She ran over when she saw I was slow getting out of the car.

She helped me to a nearby bench. "How badly are you hurt?"

"Looks worse than it is."

"What about Angela and Castellano?"

"She's fine. Castellano needed a dozen or so stitches. I heard from Tony that Gracie might not make it?"

I hadn't seen Jackie tear up too often. "She took a couple in the chest. They don't give her much of a chance."

"How's Luigi taking it?"

"He's pretty broken up. She saved his life."

Just then Pop came out of the building to light up a stogie. He noticed us and yelled.

"Luigi's been asking for you. I'll tell him you'll be right up."

"Wait a minute, Pop," I said. As I approached he saw blood seeping through my shirt.

"Is it serious?"

"No, but I better not go in there until I get patched up by one of the neighborhood docs."

"I understand. We have enough cops asking questions. Go to the back entrance. I'll have a friend of mine take a look. He'll do a good job."

"First tell me what happened."

"They hit us in the morning. Outside the speakeasy, they slit the throats of two men Luigi had hired for protection. Then they made their way in. Luigi was in his office sitting in his chair behind the desk. He leaned over to pick up a piece of paper when the office wall exploded in a hail of bullets. Gracie got off both barrels of a shotgun she kept behind the bar, but she was hit with two slugs as the shooters went down. Luigi finished them off.

"I'll tell you this. If it wasn't for Jackie, Ma and I would be dead."

I squeezed Jackie's hand as Pop told me the details.

"Jackie was about to leave the apartment building when she noticed there were two guys standing in the street on either side of the stoop. She'd seen enough in her lifetime to know what that meant."

"Your ma was safe," Jackie said. "I had just left her in the kitchen. I ran into the repair shop and dove behind the counter taking your pop down to the floor as the windows shattered."

"You won't believe what she did next. She racked my shotgun, handed it over, and told me to slouch down to the left of the door after the bullets stopped flying. I did as she said."

Pop took a long drag on his stogie.

"Then what happened?" I asked, impatient with the game he was playing—stringing me along.

"Jackie stood opposite the doorway by the back wall. As the first gunman entered and glanced at her, she pretended to be scared. Thinking she wasn't a threat, he continued down the hallway, signaling for the guy behind him to deal with her."

I turned to Jackie. "Why the hell didn't you take out the first guy?"

"If I had, that would have warned the other one. We all would have been killed, including your mom. Don't forget, they both had Tommy guns."

"She has nerves of steel," Pop said. "The second jerk stepped into the shop and smiled as he raised his gun at Jackie. He said he'd never had the pleasure of killing a redhead before."

"When he fell back into the hallway with one of my butcher knives through his throat, his buddy turned around, and that's when your pop blew a hole in his gut."

"This broad of yours and I make one hell of a team," Pop said, heading back inside the hospital. "I'll tell Luigi you'll come up after my friend gets you patched up. Your ma's fine. She's been with Gracie all day. She won't let go of her hand."

I flung open the hospital door and yelled down the hall.

"Be sure to tell Luigi he doesn't have to worry about Carmine. He'll not threaten us again."

"I'm not sure that's gonna help him feel better. He was

looking forward to ripping Carmine's heart out with his bare hands. But I'll let him know."

* * * * *

While the doctor was cleaning my wound, Jackie came into his office. Gracie didn't make it.

Chapter 39

The whole neighborhood attended Gracie's wake to show their respect and support to Luigi, but there wasn't much anyone could say to console him. After the funeral, Pop advised us to give Luigi a chance to grieve in his own way, which we did.

The doctor had ordered me to stay off my feet to give my side a chance to properly heal. I was reluctant to comply given that O'Reilly's trial was scheduled to begin in a few days. But the reality was that we lacked hard evidence that proved the DA was the killer and we were out of ideas. So there wasn't much for me to do.

I confined myself mostly to the office and focused on developing arguments Frank could use in O'Reilly's defense. The worst part about restricting my movements was dealing with Frank, who was becoming more impatient with each passing hour. Normally I was the one who dropped in on him, but now, he was making the trek to my office at least twice a day. Today, on his fourth visit, he didn't bother to knock. He just barged in and plopped down in his favorite chair. During his earlier sojourn we had hit several dead ends, so there wasn't much to talk about. His frustration was evident as he slumped deeper into the leather chair.

Frank noticed my guns disassembled on a mat on my desk. "What are you doing?" he asked.

"Trying to clear my head by focusing on something

mundane. Making sure the tools of my trade will work when I need them. Don't you ever clean and oil your guns?"

"There is something called the Sullivan Act. Lawyers aren't given an exception to carry guns."

"What about a shiv?"

"I don't believe in violence."

"That's nice, but you know that other people do," I said, reaching into my desk drawer for another Colt .45.

"Since when do you carry three guns? Those things are pretty heavy. Where do you put the third one?"

"This was Carmine's. I took it as a reminder that you can't trust anyone. It also has a nice custom grip."

"I have to admit, compared to his, your wooden ones look pretty cheap."

"Mine are the original grips, and they're just fine."

Frank stared at me as if I had said something strange. "How'd you do that?" he asked.

"Do what?"

"You disassembled that gun in a matter of seconds while looking at me and talking."

"I guess if you do something enough, it becomes second nature. These babies kept me alive during the war, and the conditions weren't always ideal when they needed cleaning. There were times I had to take them apart in the dark after a heavy day of fighting."

Frank watched as I finished oiling the key pieces and then reassembled the three guns.

When I was done, he got up and inspected each of them.

"Do you realize what you just did?"

"What are you talking about now?"

"Parts were scattered on the desk and you randomly selected the pieces for each gun. How's that possible?"

"That's one of the beauties of the Colt design. The parts are interchangeable from gun to gun."

"Joey, I've got it! The DA used his own gun, and then swapped the barrel assembly with the one found at the scene. That's why the ballistics matched."

I felt like an idiot. How could I have missed that?

"Frank, you just answered one of the biggest questions we've had. How did the DA reach O'Reilly's father's gun, hanging on the bedpost, without getting into a struggle with the guy in bed?"

"How fast can you change those pieces out?"

"Just the barrel assemblies? Less than a minute, if you're experienced. But this doesn't explain why the DA took the shell casings. The firing pin is part of the barrel housing, so the strike mark on the casings would back up the ballistics test results."

"Fingerprints," Frank said. "The shell casings would have one or more of his fingerprints. The DA's plan all along was to use the gun hanging on the bedpost to kill Bridget and frame O'Reilly. But when he entered Bridget's bedroom and saw what was goin' on, he improvised. He used his own weapon instead."

Martha and Jackie burst into the room.

"We just got a break in O'Reilly's case," Martha shouted.

* * * * *

"Hold off until I get Sadie to take notes," Frank said, rushing past the girls.

"What's goin' on?" I asked.

"You remember Josephine Covina, the reporter who lives

across the street from O'Reilly?" Martha said. "It turns out she's an artist. She has her own developing lab in one of the bedrooms of her apartment. She takes pictures all over the city and sells them at an art gallery."

"Please tell me she get a shot of the DA and Bridget together."

"We wish," Jackie said."

Frank came in with Sadie.

"I thought I asked you guys to wait. Now you have to start over. Sadie, make sure you get every word."

When they got to the point where they had left off, Frank and I asked the same question.

"How does that help us?"

"Sorry," Jackie said. "We're excited. Let's start over. You recall that Josephine heard the shots, climbed out onto her fire escape, and saw someone dashing out of the alley by O'Reilly's building."

Frank and I both nodded.

"Okay, let's pick it up from there. She grabbed her camera equipment and arrived in the building just as O'Reilly's neighbors were getting the courage to investigate."

Martha took over the narrative. "She shot pictures until the cops booted her out of the apartment. But that didn't stop her. She got plenty of camera shots not only of the murder scene but also from the hallway as the investigators arrived, and then from outside the building as the crowd grew."

Jackie interrupted. "Since she developed the film in her own lab at home, she only brought a few of the pictures into the office for her editor to choose from for the morning edition. When the DA's detectives confiscated the crime scene photos and their negatives from the editor's office, they didn't think to go to the reporter's apartment. The DA hasn't seen all the photos."

Martha put her hand over Jackie's mouth, giddy with excitement. "Let me, let me tell them."

She took two pictures out of a folder and placed them side by side on my desk.

"We have the DA arriving and leaving the scene wearing different overcoats."

"I'll be damned," Frank said.

* * * * *

The next two days were intense as we all worked to get Frank ready for the trial. In the end, he wasn't satisfied. He felt that even with the evidence we had gathered and even if everything went his way on cross examination, there was still a good chance O'Reilly would get convicted.

The DA had witnesses who would state they had caught O'Reilly in the room holding the murder weapon. There was no way around that fact, and all we had was a theory and some photos that put the DA at the scene after the murders. Not enough to convince anyone that he was the real killer. Frank stated the DA could simply say he picked up the wrong coat since he owned one of each type.

* * * * *

There wasn't much more we could do for Frank, so on the evening before the trial, I asked Jackie to help me take care of some unfinished business. My uncle hadn't been seen since Gracie's funeral, and I had a good idea where he might be holed up, no doubt drinking himself into oblivion. It was also time I confronted Rosalie's new boyfriend. It was too much of a coincidence that he just happened to be one of Big Ben's sons.

"Where we going?" she asked.

"To find my uncle and then visit Big Ben's neighborhood. Make sure you wear your knife harness."

"Just the two of us?"

"Don't worry, we'll have the element of surprise."

"Sure, because no one would think we're that stupid."

"That's what I'm counting on."

* * * * *

Molly was wiping down a table when we walked into her diner. She looked up and smiled.

"I was wondering when that detective nose of yours would bring you around."

"How's he doing?" I asked.

"Better than I expected."

"Is he smashed?"

"Hasn't touched the stuff. He just sits around staring off—thinking."

"About what?"

"He hasn't said. Life, I imagine. That's what I did when I lost my Charlie."

"Did you find any answers?" Jackie asked.

Molly sat in a booth and we joined her.

"Can't say I did. We're born, we cry, we live, we cry, and we die. Seems meaningless, doesn't it?"

"If I know my uncle, he's concentrating on the 'we live' part, wondering what the hell he's accomplished with his life."

Molly took hold of my hand and placed the key to her apartment into my palm.

"I suggest you slap him around a bit because that's a bad place to let your mind dwell for too long. It can lead to self-pity and dangerous thoughts."

I couldn't agree more. That's exactly where I was when I lost Anita. I got up and gave Jackie a hand as she slipped out of the booth.

"I'll leave the key under your doormat," I said, as we left the diner.

When we got in the car, Jackie asked what I was gonna say to Luigi.

"Hell if I know. But if you ask me, he needs a drinking partner. Then we'll see where it takes us."

"Why do men think drinking will solve their problems?" Jackie asked, no doubt thinking back to her father who had abandoned her.

"I don't know. It never does, but right now, it's the only thing I can think of to drag Luigi back to a better place."

"That doesn't sound logical."

"I guess not, but it's that or sit around discussing the meaning of life, and I don't think that will help. Not with my uncle."

* * * * *

We used the key Molly had given us to her apartment and found Luigi sitting by a window beside a full bottle of whiskey and an empty glass.

"What are you guys doing here?" he asked without looking to see who had entered.

Jackie nodded toward a mirror where he could see our reflection.

"I need my uncle back in my life."

"What the hell for?"

"If you don't know, my telling you isn't gonna do any good."

"Great answer."

"So, what are you gonna do? Stop living, be bitter, angry? Give up and drown yourself in that bottle?"

"You got a better idea?"

"Those are all rotten choices, and Gracie wouldn't want you to choose any of them. Gracie had lost her dignity, her self-respect, and you gave them back to her. She repaid you with her life. That's how much it meant to her. How much *you* meant to her."

"You're not making matters any better," Luigi said, pouring himself a drink.

I was being too nice. Molly was right. What he needed was a kick in the backside.

"Uncle, get off your ass and open the speakeasy, finish setting up the loan program for our neighbors who've fallen on hard times, and then help the neighborhood get back to normal. That's what Gracie would want, and that's what we all need."

Luigi put his drink down and held his face in his hands. Clearly my approach hadn't worked, so I went into the kitchen to get two more glasses.

Jackie walked over and put her arm around him. He leaned into her.

"I miss her," he said.

"I know, you'll always miss her and you should. But like Joey said, others need you, just as much as you need them."

"Jackie's right. The answer to what you've been thinking about is people. That's what matters. Taking care of the ones you love. Gracie did that for you. Now you need to do that for the rest of us, just like you always have."

We waited while Luigi composed himself. He stood and wrapped his arms around my waist, lifting me off the floor like he did when I was a kid. He then embraced Jackie.

"Uncle, why don't you make yourself more presentable? Return this key to your good friend at the diner, and while you're there, get something to eat—you've lost weight."

"You guys gonna join me?"

"We have some unfinished business to take care of tonight."

We were leaving when Luigi grabbed my arm.

"How are Castellano and Angela?"

I smiled. He was no longer thinking of himself. "Castellano will be fine. Angela, that's a different story. Her scars aren't physical."

"She needs a job. Something to take her mind off things. I can help her with that."

"Now you're talking."

Jackie took hold of my hand as we walked to the car.

"Joey, you surprise me."

"Why do you say that?"

"I didn't give you a chance in hell to get Luigi out of his funk."

"Neither did I. Let's hope our luck holds up for the rest of the night."

* * * * *

Jackie drove in silence until I directed her to turn a corner into Big Ben's neighborhood.

"How about telling me where we're going? I'm not familiar with these streets, and I'm not getting a good feeling here."

"Two blocks down take a right."

"Tell me again, why we're taking this risk?"

"To have a chat with Rosalie's new beau, Sam."

"Big Ben's son! Are you batty?"

"I don't think Rosalie's gonna bring him over for dinner, so I've had someone tailing him. Stop here. There's a speakeasy in the basement of that building, and that's where we'll find Sam."

"It's probably a private club. How are we supposed to get into that joint?"

"I have two passes—a beautiful dame and this," I said, waving a C-note in front of her face.

*****

I'd been given a good description of Sam, so it didn't take me long to spot him leaning against the bar with a couple of his buddies. Jackie and I sat at a table and ordered two beers.

"Now that we're here, what's your plan?"

"I thought you might go up to Sam and say a friend of his father's would like to speak with him, and then bring him to our table."

"That's it? What happens if he recognizes you? You do realize you're not in fighting shape."

"We've never met. At least not that I know of."

It didn't take long before Sam was sitting opposite me.

"So, you're a friend of my father's?"

"You might say we're more acquaintances than friends," I said, taking a sip of my beer.

Sam looked at Jackie, then back at me. "I didn't catch your names."

"This is Jackie and I'm Joey. Joey Batista."

Sam pushed his chair away from the table, giving him more space to react if needed.

"This is about Rosalie, isn't it?"

"That's right."

"How'd you know where to find me? I've got bodyguards, you know?"

"Not tonight, you don't. I know all about you. I've been having you followed."

"You gotta be nuts. If anyone recognizes you, you'll never get out of here alive."

"Let's put it this way, Sammy. If there's any trouble, you'll be the first one to croak. That I guarantee. Now, why don't we get serious? Rosalie said you're not like your father, and it turns out she's right. You work the docks to earn dough when you don't need to, you seldom raise hell, and you don't hang out with your brothers much."

"If you know so much, why this little chat?"

"I wanted to look in your eyes when you tell me you're not using Rosalie to get revenge for the damage I caused to your father's reputation."

"They think Rosalie's just another broad. They don't even know she's connected to you. My father tends not to pay much attention to what I do. You probably know that, but to set you straight, I don't agree with everything my father does and I wouldn't be a part of such a scheme—using a dame. Now, I suggest you and your woman get the hell out of here."

When Jackie and I got up to leave, Sam noticed my limp.

"I gotta say you have a lot of guts coming here in your condition."

"So do you," I said. "Romeo and Juliet stories don't normally end well. If you care for Rosalie, you'll keep that in mind."

* * * * *

"What did that accomplish?" Jackie asked, as she pulled into traffic.

"Peace of mind, so I can concentrate on O'Reilly's trial. Luigi's back and I don't think Rosalie's in imminent danger. If she was, we would have had to fight our way out of that place."

"How convinced were you that fighting wouldn't be necessary?"

"Pretty sure, but you never know."

Jackie smiled. "So all we have to do now is show the world that the DA is a murderer. I would think that should be easy for someone who's a PI, assassin, spy, and now a double agent mixed up with the Communist Party, Mafia, and the Feds."

"The Colonel would say you should expect nothing less from a Death Squad survivor."

We headed back to the safety of our neighborhood, both wondering what was in store for O'Reilly.

Chapter 40

When O'Reilly entered the courtroom shackled and unkempt, escorted by two armed officers, Frank shot up with such fury that his chair crashed into the wooden banister behind his table.

"I object!" he shouted. "My client is innocent until this court finds differently. The DA is blatantly trying to influence the jury."

The courtroom erupted into chaos as reporters raced down the aisle to get clear shots of O'Reilly, blinding the judge and jury with their flash bulbs.

O'Reilly shuffled toward Frank, holding his head high. With each step, the chains from his shackles clanged on the tiled floor. He greeted Frank with manacled hands.

The judge rapped his gavel repeatedly.

"I will have order in this court. If there's another such outburst, I will ban all reporters from the room for the duration of this trial," he said, pounding the gavel again.

He then ordered a fifteen minute recess and told Frank and the DA to meet him in his chambers. When they returned, the judge postponed the trial until the next morning. He didn't bother to provide the jury with an explanation nor did he answer any questions shouted out by reporters as he left the bench.

Security quickly removed O'Reilly from the courtroom but not before O'Reilly whispered a few words to Frank and nodded to me and Jackie.

When the door closed behind O'Reilly, we joined Frank at his table, as Sadie gathered up his court papers.

"What happened in there?" I asked.

"The judge was more outraged than I was. He ordered the DA to treat O'Reilly with the respect a decorated officer of the law deserves."

"How did the DA react?" Jackie asked.

"He argued that O'Reilly was a dangerous murderer trained in police tactics who could easily disarm someone in the courtroom."

"Except for calling O'Reilly a murderer, the DA had a valid point," I said.

"Well, the judge didn't buy it. He reminded the DA everyone authorized to carry a gun had checked their weapons before entering the courtroom, and he said unless the DA doubted the competence of his security team, his argument was moot.

"What happens next?" I asked.

"That's up to the DA, but I'm confident we'll see a different O'Reilly tomorrow."

"Why take the whole day, though? The DA could get O'Reilly looking more presentable in less time than that," Martha said to Frank.

"He didn't come out and say it, but I got the impression the judge is having some personal problems and could use the time. Whatever the reason, we just got an extra day, so let's put it to good use. How about we grab some grub at the diner and have a little chat with Molly. She's been mulling over a request I made."

Sadie declined the offer and headed back to Frank's office to catch up on some work. Martha, on the other hand, never turned down a free meal.

"I assume you're paying," she said to Frank, leading the way out of the courthouse.

* * * * *

Molly was all smiles until Frank stepped out from behind me as we entered the diner. She turned and walked to the back of the counter where she picked up an armful of plates.

Frank motioned us toward a booth and informed us that he and Molly weren't on speaking terms. Martha sat opposite Frank and grabbed the menu from his hand.

"Explain."

"I've asked Molly to take the witness stand, but so far she has refused."

"Can you blame her? The DA would tear into her past and discredit anything she said."

Jackie agreed. "Let's not forget what the DA is capable of doing. Molly wouldn't last two days on the streets after testifying he had an affair with Bridget."

"That's not why I want her on the stand. Let's not discuss the case in public."

"If you didn't want to discuss it here, why did we come? There are closer places to eat," I said.

"I told Molly I'd give her a few days to think about my request. I thought it might help if she saw us all together. She knows the trial started this morning."

A waitress came over to take our order, but Molly told her she'd take care of us.

"Shouldn't you be at O'Reilly's trial?" Molly asked, reaching into her apron pocket for an order book.

Frank answered her. "The judge postponed the start until tomorrow."

"Why?"

"I objected to how the DA brought O'Reilly into the courtroom. He looked a mess and had his hands and ankles shackled."

"What a son of a bitch."

"That's only the beginning. I'm sure the DA has plenty of other surprises planned."

"I know you, Frank. You're trying to badger me into testifying. No need, I already made up my mind. O'Reilly's a good man and a friend. I don't care what the DA does to me. I'll take the stand. Now give me your order."

Frank smiled, but he knew better than to make too much of her decision to cooperate. He simply told her what he wanted for breakfast. "Eggs, bacon, and a side of toast."

"For a lawyer, you're not very specific. How do you want your eggs cooked? You want your bacon light, medium, or well done? What type of toast?"

"Scrambled, medium, and wheat."

"Much better," Molly said. When she'd finished taking our orders and was about to leave, Jackie touched her arm.

"Are you sure you want to testify? You could be putting yourself in danger."

"I've thought about that. O'Reilly means a lot to me. Believe it or not, so do the folks in your neighborhood. Maybe this is my opportunity to let them know that I regret what I did when I was young. I betrayed a trust, and I've been paying the price ever since. More importantly, it's time for me to forgive myself."

Molly left without saying another word. It was Martha who expressed what I believe we were all thinking.

"I like that woman. She has moxie."

* * * * *

When we got back to our apartment building, Ma stopped me on the stairs.

"There's a fella named George waiting in the dining room. He says he works for Castellano and needs to speak with you."

"Do you mind telling him to come up to the office?"

"He said it's confidential. I'm going shopping, so you can stay in the apartment. Pop's in the shop."

I told Frank and the girls I'd be up as soon as I finished with George.

When I entered the apartment, I found George sitting at the dining room table digging into a piece of chocolate cake.

"How's the side?" he asked, wiping frosting from his mouth.

"I'll survive. How's the cake?"

"Your ma is one hell of a cook."

"You should join Castellano sometime when he comes over for dinner. What's on your mind?"

"I want to know what's goin' on."

"What do you mean?"

"Castellano. He's not your typical Mafia boss."

"How so?"

"Just look around. There are no brothels. Everything illegal that comes off the piers leaves the neighborhood. No drug pushers, no enforcers—this place is like an oasis in the middle of chaos."

"Don't worry, we have our share of problems, but I take it you're concerned about your future."

"That's right. In Chicago I was working for Capone.

Now he's goin' places. I only joined Carmine because he had big plans and I was gonna be top dog."

It was obvious where this conversation was headed. George wasn't going to hang around long, but Castellano would need a guy like George when he made his move to boot the Russians out of his union. Guys like George could be hard to control, but that would be true of anyone Castellano hired. Right now he was our best bet.

"You thinking of going back to Capone?"

"Maybe. I hear you're Torrio's nephew. I thought you could put a good word in for me so I could move up in the pecking order. Capone listens to Torrio—you know there wasn't anything personal about that little scuffle we had, right?"

"Don't worry about it—comes with the territory. But if I wanted to make a name for myself, I'd stick it out here and help Castellano be successful with this union business."

"Why?"

"It has potential. Capone said it best. Prohibition is gonna get repealed someday, and when it does, the dough will dry up fast. Control of the unions is the future."

"Sounds like a long shot."

"You should consider the fact that both Torrio and Vigliotti agreed with Capone and are moving aggressively."

"Even more reason for me to head back to Chicago and be a part of things there."

"My bet is that Castellano is gonna retire when things are stable. As you well know, he has no one to take over."

"And you think that could be me?"

"Why not?"

"What about you?"

"I'm not interested, and I've made that clear."

"You would trust me, a stranger, with your neighborhood?"

"I don't trust anyone, but change is coming, not only to the waterfront, but also how the Mafia operates. In my opinion, whoever runs the union is gonna realize it's not worth the trouble to squeeze out a few extra bucks by corrupting our neighborhood."

"It still sounds like a bit of a gamble to me."

"Then consider this. Vigliotti is taking a personal interest in the whole concept of unions and how to make it pay. Someday he's gonna need someone to coordinate across industries. That could be you."

George shoved the last piece of cake in his mouth, finished his milk, and got up to leave. "I'll think about it."

"Do me a favor," I said. "Let me know what you decide."

"Why's that?"

"So I have time to ask my uncle to send someone out to replace you."

George paused at the doorway.

"Hold off on that. I think I'll see what this union business is all about."

* * * * *

By the time I got to Frank's office, he and Martha were having a heated exchange.

"Why the hell should we give up on proving the DA is a murderer? He killed two people in cold blood, and don't forget about the street kids that were slaughtered when he had Jackie kidnapped," Martha argued, standing toe-to-toe with Frank.

"I'm not saying he's not a bad guy, but it's not our job to

convict the DA. What we want is for the jury to find O'Reilly innocent."

Martha threw up her hands in disgust and walked away from Frank.

He turned to me. "Maybe you can talk some sense into her."

"First, I need to know what the hell is going on."

"I think we're making a mistake spending valuable time trying to gather enough evidence to prove that the DA did the murders."

Now I was concerned. "Frank, tell me, how are you going to get O'Reilly off without proving someone else is responsible?"

"All we have to do is convince the jury that it's *possible* someone else did the murders. We don't have to solve the crime."

To my surprise, Jackie agreed with Frank. "Let's face reality. We don't have the evidence against the DA. But to get a hung jury, we only need one juror to believe that O'Reilly's innocent."

"So, what do we do differently?" Martha asked, coming back at Frank.

Frank took a step away from her. "We try a different track. Take the cabdriver, for example. We've mostly ignored his testimony, but maybe it can be effective in raising doubts in the juror's minds. Even though he didn't recognize the person he picked up near the crime scene on the night of the murder, he can testify that he dropped the guy off at a vacant lot, which is suspicious. It creates questions. Who was this person? What was he doing there? Where did he come from, and where was he going? Are you all with me?"

"I get it," Jackie said. "The cabbie will testify that on a cold night he picked up a passenger who was not wearing an overcoat, near the crime scene, close to the time that O'Reilly was nabbed by his neighbors."

Frank nodded. "Why did he have a fedora on and no coat? Why would he get out of the cab in the middle of the night near a vacant lot?"

Martha chimed in next. "We then show the two different coats. Who did they belong to? How did they get switched?"

"Wait a minute," I said. "We all know the DA did this. He's a danger not just to our neighborhood but to the entire community. If we have the goods, I say we use it."

"Joey, I understand your frustration, but it's not credible evidence. Whether you like it or not the DA is good at his job. He's clever, and if he catches on that we know it was him, he'll be ready to defend himself."

Jackie stood alongside Frank. "Joey, if we attack the DA and don't convince the jury, O'Reilly is the one who suffers."

Frank could see I was still unconvinced. "Okay, imagine this. You're sitting in the jury box thinking this was an open and shut case. But then we raise questions in your mind. Lots of questions. And it starts to seem that the only answer is that someone else committed the murders. And then you realize that the man who's being charged is a decorated officer, whose father, by the way, was killed in the line of duty."

"What's that got to do with the case?" Martha asked.

"Nothing," Frank said. "I've learned that sympathy helps, but you see where I'm going? All I have to do is raise enough doubts in the minds of the jurors and O'Reilly will walk. Now, everybody out. I have to prepare for tomorrow morning. Not you, Sadie. I can't get much done without you."

I had never seen Sadie blush before.

Chapter 41

With a packed gallery and security in place, the judge ordered the defendant brought into the courtroom. The door to the right of the bench opened, and after a short delay, O'Reilly appeared unshackled and unattended. He had on his Sunday best and was clean shaven with his hair slicked back. He joined Frank at his table.

O'Reilly entered a plea of not guilty, and the trial began with opening statements. As lead prosecutor, the DA took the floor.

"Gentlemen of the jury, you have taken on the responsibility to sit through a gruesome trial and to pass judgment on a man who has sworn to uphold the law and protect the innocent. To protect you and yours.

"A man who has the right to carry a gun and the right to use it to take anyone's life in the course of performing his sworn duty. Unfortunately, this police officer used that gun—the gun that was given to him to protect you and me—to slaughter his wife and her lover.

"Did he plan to commit murder that night? Evidence will show that he knew his wife had a lover and not just any lover. He was a neighbor, a fellow police officer and a friend. Would you have done the same if you walked in on such a scene with your wife being unfaithful in your own apartment, in your own bed? Maybe so, but that doesn't make it right. Murder is murder, no matter what the circumstances.

"If you believe that Officer O'Reilly, upon entering his bedroom, emptied his handgun into two defenseless people and watched his wife bleed to death from a neck wound, you must find him guilty of murder.

"We will show that Officer O'Reilly was apprehended by his neighbors, just moments after the shots were fired, sitting on that bloody bed with the murder weapon in his hand. *In his hand!*

"His hand, his gun, his bed, his wife, and her lover in a room splattered with fresh blood dripping from the walls.

"He is guilty. We will prove he's guilty. And it is your duty to bring him to justice."

* * * * *

The courtroom was silent with all eyes on Frank as he walked toward the jury box. That lingering image of the murder scene the DA had painted was shattered when Frank slapped the railing with an open palm and shouted at the jury.

"His hand, his gun, his bed, his wife and her lover. Guilty, guilty, guilty—why have a trial? I say let's lynch him."

He pointed at several jurors.

"You, get a rope, you a horse, and you—find a suitable tree."

He paused, looking from juror to juror.

"That's how it was done fifty years ago out west. It was called justice. But today we have trials where evidence has to be presented. Where there can be not a shadow of a doubt. My client, Lieutenant Michael O'Reilly, is innocent until it is proven—proven—that he is guilty."

Frank paced in front of the jury box, stopping now and then to pound the railing with his fist.

"The prosecutor will have you believe that during a moment of passion, Lieutenant O'Reilly *didn't*—let me say it again—did not use either of the guns he carried. No, he went instead to the side of the bed and grabbed his father's weapon that hung on the bedpost in a shoulder holster. The very gun that was shot out of his father's hand as he was protecting you and me as an officer of the law, an officer who died in the line of duty.

"Why didn't my client use his own gun? Why go out of his way to reach for a gun across the room? And how did he get to the supposed murder weapon without a struggle with his wife's lover, who, after all, was also a trained officer of the law.

"These are just a few of the questions I will ask you to think about. You will hear many more.

"If the prosecutor isn't able to provide you with answers, then you must find Lieutenant O'Reilly innocent. There cannot be a reasonable doubt in your mind. Not a one.

"If you are going to find my client guilty, everything must be logical, every bit of evidence must point to the same conclusion, every question must be answered.

"No doubts, no unanswered questions, no other alternatives. Justice demands that a person is innocent until proven otherwise. It is your responsibility to see that justice is done."

The judge ordered a brief recess.

* * * * *

The DA called his first witness, a fellow officer and close friend of O'Reilly's.

"Sergeant Mallory, please explain to the court your relationship to Officer O'Reilly."

"Lieutenant O'Reilly and I joined the police department at the same time and have worked together on several investigations over the years."

"Would you say you're good friends?"

"I would."

"Did Officer O'Reilly ever confide in you that he and his wife were having difficulty?"

"Don't we all?"

That solicited a brief chuckle, mostly from the men in the courtroom. Once the laughter settled down, the DA dug deeper.

"What was his main complaint?"

"That she was constantly harping about not having enough dough."

"Did he suspect that she was having an affair?"

"You'll have to ask him that question. That's not a topic one man would discuss with another."

"When the topic of his wife's complaints came up, how did he deal with his frustration?"

"He ordered another drink."

"My understanding is that Officer O'Reilly drinks quite a bit."

"Not that I've noticed."

"Yes, of course," the DA said, looking at the jury. "You're both Irish—that's all."

The judge used his gavel to quell the laughter.

The DA gestured toward Frank. "He's all yours."

Frank was brief, but effective.

"Sergeant Mallory, in the ten or more years you've known

Lieutenant O'Reilly, how many times has he mentioned his wife?"

"Two, maybe three."

"And how did the subject usually come up?"

"It would start with me. I'd be bitching. I mean complaining about my old lady."

"Did you ever hear Lieutenant O'Reilly threaten his wife?"

"No."

"Anyone else?"

"Not outside the line of duty."

"Did he drink while on duty?"

"Not that I've ever seen."

"Did he ever come to work drunk?"

"Not that I know of."

"Thank you, Sergeant. That will be all."

* * * * *

The DA next called the duty officer who'd been working on the night of the murders.

"I asked you before the trial to review five years of records and determine how many times Officer O'Reilly left in the middle of his shift due to illness or any other excuse. Do you have the results?"

"Yes. The answer is once."

The DA faced the jury. "So, you're telling us the only time Officer O'Reilly left his shift early—in the last five years—is on the night of his wife's murder."

"That's what the records show."

"Your witness, Counselor."

Frank took his time as he approached the witness.

"What happens when an officer calls in sick?"

"Most of the time we have to find a replacement."

"I would imagine that requires you to pull an officer in on his day off or have someone start his shift early and work overtime."

"That's correct."

"Is it fair to say that it is rare for someone to leave before their shift is over?"

"That's true."

"But if they leave, do you always replace them?"

"Not if it's late in the shift."

"Was it late in the shift on the night in question?"

"Yes, I didn't call in a replacement."

"Is that common?"

"I would say ninety percent of the requests occur late in the shift."

"Why is that, aside from the fact that it would not impact another officer?"

"If someone has had a difficult shift, they might decide to call it a night, knowing that another officer will not be called to replace them."

"So what Lieutenant O'Reilly did isn't that unusual."

"When you put it that way, I would agree."

The judge was about to dismiss the witness when the DA asked to cross-examine the witness.

"Did Officer O'Reilly say he was leaving early due to a rough night?" he asked.

"There's no record of unusual activity on his shift."

"Thank you, that's all I needed."

Frank declined any further line of questioning.

The DA was about to call his next witness when a clerk entered the courtroom and approached the bench. The judge crumbled the note he was handed and disappeared into his chambers without comment, leaving the clerk to cancel the proceedings until the next day.

* * * * *

"That was a bit of bad luck," Frank said on the way to his car.

"Why's that?" Jackie asked.

"Every juror will be asking themselves all night about the odds of O'Reilly taking off early, for the first time in years, on the night of his wife's murder."

Frank looked like he needed a drink, so I hurried the girls along to where my car was parked.

I yelled back to Frank. "My folks have a table full of food waiting for us. I'm sure Luigi is doing his part and providing refreshments. We'll meet you there."

On the ride home, Martha made an interesting comment. "I think we're underestimating the DA."

"He didn't get to be DA on his good looks alone," Jackie said. "We need to keep on digging into every detail of that night. Frank has it right. He can't imply that the DA was involved with O'Reilly's wife unless he has solid evidence, but it's starting to look like that might be our only way to get O'Reilly off. The testimony of the duty officer supports the DA's opening claim that O'Reilly knew or suspected his wife was cheating on him."

"We still have people checking the motels around town to see if anyone remembers seeing the DA with O'Reilly's wife," Martha said. "Maybe we'll get lucky."

I wasn't feeling very lucky, but then again, it was O'Reilly who needed the luck. Hopefully, it hadn't run out.

* * * * *

When we got to my parents' apartment, it was jammed with neighbors who were at the trial, and most everyone was bombarding Frank with questions—including Castellano.

"Why did O'Reilly leave work early?"

"If there was a guy on the fire escape, why didn't he go after him?"

"How do you explain the fact that he picked up the gun?"

Frank put an end to all the commotion with a simple question of his own.

"Does anyone here think he killed his wife?"

No one said a word. Most looked down at their drinks.

"What can I say? People make mistakes. O'Reilly's innocent, but it's gonna be damn hard to prove."

Castellano got out of his chair and poured himself another shot of whiskey. "If you're going to raise questions, you better do it now, and not wait until you present your defense."

With that comment hanging in the air, I announced that Frank had to prepare for tomorrow morning and led him into the hallway. The girls loaded up on food and followed us upstairs to Frank's office.

* * * * *

Frank let out his frustration as soon as he sat behind his desk.

"What the hell do they expect? An acquittal a few hours into the trial?"

"Just like us, they're worried about O'Reilly," I said.

"But don't let your anger cause you to ignore the importance of Castellano's comment."

Frank stood and looked out his window. "I know, I know. I set expectations in my opening statement about questions I wanted to raise, and now the DA is taking advantage."

Martha handed Frank a sandwich. "I agree with Joey. Take Castellano's advice. Raise doubts in the jurors' minds during your cross-examination of the DA's witnesses."

"You make it sound easy," Frank said.

Sadie flipped through her steno pad until she got to the page she wanted.

"I called Josephine Covina yesterday, the reporter who lives across from O'Reilly, and she confirmed that the DA also intends to call her as a witness. Maybe you can bring out her testimony for your defense on cross-examination."

Martha placed a sandwich and a big slice of Ma's homemade apple pie on Sadie's desk and then looked at Frank. "I hope you appreciate the fact that I trained her."

Frank ignored Martha's comment and followed up with Sadie.

"Did she tell you anything about his line of questioning?"

"No. The DA warned her not to discuss the details of his interview with anyone not connected to his office."

"Did the DA ask about her testimony for the defense?"

"She refused to cooperate. She did say he doesn't seem to know about the extra pictures or the cab driver."

Frank smiled and picked up the plate of pie, but Martha took it out of his hand.

"That's for Sadie. You'll get yours when O'Reilly walks."

I took the last slice before Frank could get to it. "I'm

concerned about the testimony O'Reilly's neighbor will give. The one who let the others into the apartment after the shots were fired. He's been hailed as a hero in the papers, so he's not gonna change his story," I said. "Not even if you poke holes in it."

It was Jackie who came up with a proposed strategy to deal with him.

"If I were you, Frank," she said, "I'd get him to double down on his statement, and then I'd call his wife to the stand during your defense. She won't be as prepared, and you'll probably be able to trick her into telling the truth about how much time passed between the shots being fired and when her husband actually entered the apartment."

"Maybe I should let the girls defend O'Reilly," Frank said, looking at me.

"Frank, we have confidence in you," I said. "You've just got to outwit the DA and his minions. That's all."

"Easy for you to say. Your work is done. Now I have to match wits with the DA using what little you've given me."

That hurt, but it was the truth. The DA had powerful evidence to work with and we didn't.

Chapter 42

True to Frank's concerns, the DA started the day by trying to beat Frank at his own game—raising questions about O'Reilly's integrity and dedication to his wife.

His first witness of the morning was Miss Betty O'Brien, a waitress at the Slippery Eel, a restaurant along the waterfront that O'Reilly liked to frequent.

"Miss O'Brien, how often does Officer O'Reilly visit your place of work?"

"Two to three times a week when he's on the evening shift."

"Is that when you work?"

"Yes, four to midnight."

"That must be a busy time."

"We're slammed most nights, especially on the weekends."

"Then why do you keep a table open for Officer O'Reilly?"

Miss O'Brien blushed and fussed with her hair. Frank leaned over to O'Reilly. O'Reilly pulled away and shook his head in answer to whatever Frank had asked.

The DA raised his voice. "Do you want me to repeat the question?"

"No. Officer O'Reilly is a good customer and has little time for a dinner break. It's not uncommon for the Slippery Eel to give all officers special treatment."

The DA faced the jury. "I understand—special treatment," he said. He took his time asking his next question.

"Did you ever meet Mrs. O'Reilly?"

"Yes, once."

"How long ago was that?"

"Two, maybe three, years."

"How is it that you remember Bridget?"

"She made a scene."

"Explain."

"She was in the restaurant for less than ten minutes when she got up and yelled at Officer O'Reilly and rushed out, knocking into several customers."

"What did she yell?"

"That she deserved better."

"Did Officer O'Reilly say why she left?"

"Only that his wife had a higher opinion of herself than she should."

"Wouldn't you say, based on that experience and other interactions you've had with Officer O'Reilly over the years, that he and his wife didn't have a very good relationship?"

Frank jumped to his feet. "I object. The prosecutor is leading the witness and making an inappropriate innuendo."

"Objection sustained," the judge said with a tap of his gavel. "That question will be stricken from the record. District Attorney Peterson, you know better, and if you try something like that again, I will hold you in contempt."

"I have no further questions for the witness," the DA said and returned to his table.

Frank addressed the DA's insinuation that O'Reilly was unfaithful right off the bat, shocking the witness, but also the jury.

"Miss O'Brien, have you ever slept with Officer O'Reilly?"

All thirteen jurors leaned forward as O'Brien gripped the railing in front of her and glared at Frank.

"Miss O'Brien, I'm sorry for asking such a blunt question, but the DA has implied that you have a special relationship with Officer O'Reilly. Please answer the question."

"No, I have not."

"Have you ever gone out with Officer O'Reilly?"

"No."

"Has he ever asked you on a date?"

"No."

"Later on in this trial will the DA be able to prove that you are lying?"

"No, he will not because Officer O'Reilly is just another customer and nothing more."

"Thank you, Miss O'Brien."

* * * * *

Mr. Quinlan, one of O'Reilly's neighbors who lived in the building across the street from his, had provided the DA with an affidavit prior to the trial that stated he saw O'Reilly enter his building before the shots were fired. We all knew his testimony would be pivotal to the DA's case and so did the DA.

Once on the witness stand, the DA asked Quinlan to recall every painstaking detail of his pre-dawn experience, down to the exact time he heard the first shot as he watched his wall clock tick off the seconds while boiling an egg. As expected, his testimony had a visible impact on the jury, many of whom took copious notes.

Frank had insisted that Jackie and I not interview Mr. Quinlan prior to the trial so as not to warn the DA of his approach. Instead, he had assigned Martha to do a thorough investigation into his background. As usual, Martha took the initiative to go beyond what was expected and had hired a private investigator from another agency to befriend the man at his local speakeasy and to get him to talk about the upcoming trial.

The investigator had picked up an interesting tidbit that Frank honed in on.

"Mr. Quinlan, do you know the penalty for lying under oath?" Frank asked.

"Doesn't everyone? But that don't apply to me."

The judge leaned toward the witness. "Why is that?"

"I don't believe in the Bible."

The judge shook his head but told Frank to continue.

"I'm afraid, Mr. Quinlan, your beliefs are between you and your maker. On the other hand, when you swear 'to tell the truth and nothing but the truth'—it is also between you and the judicial system. Given your lack of understanding, I just want to make sure you're aware that the penalty for perjury, especially in a murder trial, can be significant prison time."

The DA objected violently. "The defense hasn't presented evidence that my witness has given false testimony. He's intimidating the witness, and committing slander to boot."

The judge fired back at the DA. "I disagree. It is your responsibility to make sure your witnesses understands the concept of perjury."

"Mr. Quinlan?" the judge asked. "Do you wish to alter any part of your testimony?"

The witness looked past Frank to the DA and back to

the judge. "Before you answer," Frank said, pulling some items from an envelope. "Mr. Quinlan, you stated that you didn't see Lieutenant O'Reilly's car abandoned in the street below your window. However, if I showed you a photograph of Officer O'Reilly's police car, taken on the night of the murders, parked in the street with its door swung open—wouldn't that suggest you might be mistaken as to when Officer O'Reilly arrived home?"

"Well, I don't know. It—"

"And if I pointed out that Officer O'Reilly arrested you three times for being drunken and disorderly in the last two years, wouldn't that suggest you just might hold a grudge against him?"

Mr. Quinlan looked at the judge. "Your Honor, I was drinking that night and was hung over, so I could have been mistaken."

The judge tapped his gavel. "Mr. Quinlan, I'm going to do you a favor and not ask where you get your booze. You may step down. The jury will disregard Mr. Quinlan's testimony. This court is recessed for one hour. Mr. District Attorney, I would like to see you in my chambers. Now!"

* * * * *

The judge's dressing-down didn't seem to affect the DA's confidence as he called his next witness.

"Mr. McKenzie, please tell the court what you do for a living."

"I'm a watchman and retired police officer."

"I can see why you were so quick to respond to the gunshots on the floor of your apartment building."

Frank objected. "How long it took for Lieutenant

O'Reilly's neighbors to react to the gun shots has not been established."

The DA conceded his error and moved on.

"As a watchman, you must be conscious of time. I say this because I assume you have to make your rounds in a timely manner."

"That's correct. I vary my routine but keep on the move and clock in at various locations."

"Tell us in your own words what happened on the night of the murders."

"My wife and I were awakened by a shrill scream, and then we heard rapid gunfire. It took me a few minutes to calm my wife down before I peered into the hallway."

"Let me stop you there. Can you be more precise? How long before you entered the hallway?"

"No more than five minutes."

"Thank you. Please continue."

"I knocked on the doors of three of my neighbors and asked them to join me. We went to O'Reilly's apartment and entered as quietly as possible."

The DA interrupted again. "How did you get into the apartment?"

"The door was ajar. That's how I knew the shots came from his apartment."

"Tell us what happened next."

"The place was dark except for the bedroom directly off the parlor. The scene was horrific. The back wall looked as though it was oozing blood. O'Reilly sat on the bed in a pool of blood with his head down. He didn't even react when we entered. In his hand, he held a gun."

At that point there wasn't a sound in the courtroom other than the witness describing how he had taken the gun from

O'Reilly and how they made sure he didn't leave until the police arrived.

"Did Officer O'Reilly resist in any way?"

"No, it was as if he was in shock at what he had done."

Frank objected. "The witness is assuming the defendant is guilty."

"Did he say anything?" the DA asked.

"Just that he couldn't stop the bleeding. He then looked toward the window and said 'It was too late.'"

"Too late to get away?" the DA inquired.

"Objection!"

"Sustained."

In the end, the testimony was devastating. Five minutes. Not enough time for O'Reilly to hear the shots as he drove up to the building, get out of his car, open the front door while fumbling with his keys, run up four double flights of stairs, enter his apartment, and react to the horrible scene. One could only conclude that O'Reilly was in the apartment when the shots were fired.

When Mr. McKenzie finished, the clerk adjourned the session for the weekend.

Chapter 43

Castellano stopped Luigi on the way out of the courtroom and asked if he had two rooms for rent. He felt it prudent to oversee union business daily, so he needed to move back into the neighborhood. This certainly made Luigi happy, but I wasn't sure how Ma would take the news now that she'd have two more mouths to feed. But the thought of having Angela living in the building seemed to make her happy. Pop did his share by working all day Saturday to add a two-foot section to the dining table.

I expected the trial to be the main topic that weekend, but I think everyone realized that Frank needed to get away from the details, if not for his sanity, then for his digestion. And Castellano had other things he wanted to discuss.

"Big Ben is sensing an opportunity."

"What's he up to now?" Luigi asked.

"Vigliotti mentioned that Big Ben demanded to know why Carmine wasn't at the council meeting last week."

Luigi looked unconcerned. "Is that it?"

"He's gaining support from the other bosses to consolidate the waterfront under him."

"You'd think he'd get tired of trying," Luigi said.

"This time it's different. They sense Carmine is weak, especially after what happened to Toby. When they find out Carmine is dead and not out recruiting, it'll be a done deal."

Castellano's news didn't surprise me, but it increased the urgency in my mind to find Carmine's replacement, and to find a way to deal with Big Ben once and for all. Castellano was no longer up to the role, and we all knew it, including him. I'd been mulling over a possible solution, but a few critical details were missing, so I wasn't ready to share it yet. Still, we couldn't just ignore the rumors and Big Ben's influence in the syndicate.

"I suggest you tell Vigliotti you'll attend the next meeting and that you'll be bringing along a proposal," I said to Castellano. I went back to eating my pasta.

"What? You're not gonna tell us what you have in mind?"

"I haven't worked out all the details. But I'll tell you this, how the waterfront is managed will change drastically with the unions. I don't think Big Ben understands that fact."

"I'm not sure I do yet," Castellano said.

"I promise, Mr. Castellano, when I'm ready, I'll share everything. Hopefully, at that time we can all agree on how to settle with Big Ben."

Castellano was wise enough not to push the issue in such a large group, and so was Jackie. She changed the subject by asking about the brothel Carmine had ordered built.

"I noticed that construction has stopped. Is that temporary?"

"I shut it down. Carmine didn't consult me, so the project never had my approval. I fought for years to keep the filth from the docks out of our streets, and I'm not going to stop now."

Luigi didn't look up from his plate as he commented. "I don't see the harm in having one brothel."

Ma swatted the back of his head. "You can walk a few

blocks over when you feel the need. Besides, the exercise would do you good—get your blood pumping."

When everyone stopped laughing, Castellano turned serious again. "It's difficult to stop at one of anything. I'm thinking of hiring an architect to build a recreation center for the kids instead. During the winter there's nothing for them to do except find ways to get into trouble."

"I know the perfect guy for the job," Martha said. "I'll have him contact you at the union office in the next few days."

I knew she was thinking about Dom. I wasn't sure I wanted him back in our lives, but Martha had just given me an idea for solving one of my problems. I'd been wrestling with how to convince Big Ben to go along with anything I might suggest. Dom certainly had the skills necessary to grab someone's attention.

Chapter 44

Monday morning Mr. McKenzie, the retired cop, was back on the stand looking eager to joust with Frank. Frank ignored the witness at first while he spoke briefly with the court recorder. He then moseyed toward the witness stand with his hands in his pockets. Looking at the jury, he asked his first question.

"Mr. McKenzie, you must be a brave man."

"Nah, just following my training. Police officers don't run away from danger, even in retirement."

"Your wife hasn't gotten much credit, but she must be an exceptional woman."

"She is, but what does that have to do with my testimony?"

"I think most women would not want to be left alone after being jolted out of bed at five in the morning by gunshots. It must have sounded as if they came from within your apartment."

"She was a little upset."

Frank pointed an accusing finger at the witness, his voice rising.

"Yet you left her alone. Alone, knowing that in all likelihood someone had been murdered on your floor. I understand that you have been trained to deal with life-threatening situations, but what about your wife? Are you telling us that she calmly watched you get dressed and leave her to fend for herself?"

"I made sure she was safe."

"How?"

"After we got dressed, I led her into the bathroom, and she laid down in the bathtub in case there was more shooting."

"She didn't try to get you to stay with her?"

"There was some of that."

"Some of that—would you say ten seconds?"

McKenzie hesitated. "More like a few minutes."

Frank walked back to his table and picked up a piece of paper.

"Over the weekend I tried to make a timeline of events, but obviously I didn't have all the details. So, let's recreate those frightening moments.

"You and your wife were awakened out of a deep sleep by a series of gunshots in the dead of night.

"You immediately jumped out of bed, unlocked your front door, and peered into the hallway.

"By the time you came back into your bedroom, your wife was already dressed. You threw on some clothes.

"You then took your wife into the bathroom and had her lie down in the bathtub for her safety.

"You bravely went into the hallway, without any protection, and organized your neighbors to investigate.

"That is what you've said, right?"

"Yeah, that's how I remember it."

"But that's not exactly how it happened on that morning, is it? Stop me when I get it wrong.

"You both woke, startled, confused, not sure what happened. Your wife clung to you. You tried to calm her down and told her to stay put.

"You went into your parlor and listened at the apartment door. For how long, Mr. McKenzie—a minute, two minutes?

"Did you slowly unbolt the locks so as not to make a

noise? Did you look out and then quietly close and relock your door?

"You went back into the bedroom. Your wife was clutching the covers to her in near panic."

The DA objected, but the judge overruled, and Frank continued.

"You went to her, got her calmed down, and you both got dressed.

"She tried to prevent you from leaving her alone. You convinced her that she would be safe in the bathtub. She pleaded for you to stay with her.

"You're a brave man, Mr. McKenzie, but did you leave your apartment without a weapon? Do you have an illegal gun that you had to retrieve? Or did you take the time to grab a knife from the kitchen?"

Before the witness could answer, Frank shouted a different question.

"Mr. McKenzie! How long have you been on the witness stand this morning?"

"What?"

"You heard me. How long?"

"Ten, maybe twelve minutes."

Frank turned to the court reporter. "How long has Mr. McKenzie been testifying?"

"Twenty-two and a half minutes," she replied.

Frank faced the jury.

"Five minutes now becomes ten to eleven. Maybe even more time passed before he entered that hallway."

"Testifying is stressful," Mr. McKenzie shouted at Frank.

Frank turned aggressively.

"I agree! You were under a lot of pressure on the

morning of the murders, and so were your neighbors. Did they eagerly join you or did you have to coax them out of their apartments? How long did it take, Mr. McKenzie? Another fifteen to twenty minutes? Or longer?

"No more questions, Your Honor."

Frank returned to his table, but the witness didn't budge.

"You're dismissed, Mr. McKenzie," the judge said. He nodded for the DA to proceed.

* * * * *

Josephine Covina was the next witness for the prosecution. The DA handed her photographs of the crime scene to the jury foreman who passed them along as Josephine described what she had witnessed. Her testimony corroborated parts of Mr. McKenzie's. Every juror now knew without a doubt that O'Reilly was caught with the murder weapon in his hand. Pictures don't exaggerate.

Unbeknownst to the DA, he had opened his own personal Pandora's Box when he turned the witness over to Frank for cross-examination.

Frank stood midway between the witness stand and the DA's table and smiled at the DA. "Miss Corvina, did you take more pictures on the night in question than the ones in the possession of the District Attorney's office?"

"Yes, many more."

The DA's reaction was instantaneous. He turned to the assistant DA and then twisted around to look at his investigative team. They conferred for a few seconds in an awkward jangle, and then the DA faced the judge.

"I object, Your Honor. My office confiscated all the

photographs from the *Daily News* editor that were taken by Miss Corvina."

"Miss Corvina, do you wish to clarify your response?" the judge asked.

"Normally the paper develops their reporter's film and photographic plates, but I have my own lab. I gave my editor only the pictures I thought would go along with my front page cover story."

"Objection! The Defense has withheld evidence."

"Mr. Galvano, do you wish to respond to the DA's accusation before I rule on his objection?"

Frank replied quickly, "With your permission, Judge, I'll let the witness answer for me."

"Proceed."

"Miss Corvina, how many times did someone from the DA's office interview you?"

"Three."

"Please elaborate."

"One of the prosecutor's investigators interviewed most of the residents in my building. He only asked me one question—did I see anyone enter the building where the murders took place before or after the shooting?"

"What was your response?"

"That Officer O'Reilly entered after the shots were fired and that I saw someone exit the alley next to the building."

"Did the investigator follow up on your response?"

"Yes, and I told him exactly what I told your investigators."

"When was your next encounter with the DA's office?"

"Soon after the paper with my photographs of the murder scene hit the newsstands."

"What was the focus of that interview?"

"It took place in my editor's office. I was called in to confirm that I took the pictures and to inform me that I would be called as a witness for the prosecution."

"Miss Corvina, why didn't you mention to the first investigator that you took pictures?"

"I didn't want my material confiscated, and he never asked. As I said, once I mentioned that Officer O'Reilly was innocent, he lost interest."

"Tell us about the third interview."

"The DA called me to his office to confirm that I took the pictures."

"Is that all? He could have done that on the phone."

"He wanted to know more about the person I saw who came out of the alley. I told him that I was too far away to see who it was."

"Did the DA ask you about your statement concerning O'Reilly?"

"He tried to convince me that I was mistaken. He said that he had witnesses that contradicted my statement."

Frank backed away from the witness and looked up at the judge.

"Your Honor, I believe the DA and his associates had every opportunity to gather the information I'm about to ask the witness, but they chose not to pursue questioning that would have weakened their case against my client."

The judge taped his gavel. "Objection overruled. You may continue, Mr. Galvano."

Frank removed a picture from the folder and handed it to Miss Corvina.

"Is this one of the pictures you took at the crime scene?"

"Yes."

"Why did you take such a picture?"

"When the police arrived, they asked me to leave. On the way out of the apartment this particular item looked out of place."

"Please describe to the jury the essence of the picture."

"It shows a very expensive overcoat hanging on a coat rack by the apartment door."

Frank took his time to remove another photo from the folder and handed it to the witness.

"Please describe what you see in this official crime scene photograph."

She compared both side-by-side.

"It's basically the same picture except it shows a different overcoat—an inexpensive one."

"Look more closely, especially at the bottom of the coat."

"Oh, I see what you mean. It appears that the less expensive coat is covering up the one in my picture."

"And now, this one," Frank said, as he handed her another photo. "This was taken a day later and is also an official police photograph."

Miss Covina examined all three carefully.

"The expensive coat has been removed," she declared.

Frank submitted the folder with all three pictures as evidence, and then he turned to the jury.

"These pictures raise interesting questions. Who did the fancy coat belong to? Not the victim. He lived on the same floor and wouldn't bring a coat. Not Lieutenant O'Reilly, too expensive. Why was it removed? Who removed the coat?"

Frank pointed at the DA.

"I'm sure the District Attorney will hunt down the

answers. To help, we will provide him with prints of the remaining pictures that Miss Corvina took on that night. I'm sure he'll find them interesting on a professional level."

The DA and Frank stared at each other, as an awkward silence spread across the courtroom. Frank broke the intensity and approached the bench.

"Your Honor, I have a few more questions for Miss Corvina. Questions the DA neglected to ask."

"I object, Your Honor. This is my witness."

"I agree, but it's hard to tell at this point. I would like to hear what else the witness has to say. You will get a chance to reexamine."

"Miss Corvina, I'm sure everyone is wondering how you got on the scene before the police," Frank said.

"I live across the street. I was sitting at my typewriter in my bathrobe when I heard the shots."

"How did you react?"

"I went to my window first and then onto the fire escape to get a better look."

"Tell the court what you saw."

"I noticed a police car in the middle of the street and Officer O'Reilly entering the building."

"Let me stop you there. You heard the shots, and then noticed Lieutenant O'Reilly entering his building?"

"That's correct."

"Then what happened?"

"I went back inside and grabbed my camera equipment by the parlor window. That's when I noticed a man coming out of the alleyway."

"Let me stop you again. Please repeat that statement."

"A man came out of the alleyway next to O'Reilly's building."

"Did you get a picture?"

"No, by the time I got back out onto the fire escape, he was down the street and had hailed a cab."

"Was there anything unusual about this person, other than running out of a dark alleyway late at night?"

Miss Corvina looked at the jury. "He wore a hat, but no overcoat."

There was a strange sound, as if the air had been sucked out of the courtroom.

"No more questions, Your Honor."

The DA went straight to the witness stand, attacking his own witness.

"Miss Corvina, didn't Officer O'Reilly come to your rescue less than a year ago to prevent you from being gang raped?"

"He did."

"And didn't he sustain injuries in that incident?"

"He did."

"Don't you feel obligated to him?"

"I do. But if you're implying that I would lie on this witness stand—you're mistaken. I understand the penalty for perjury, but more importantly, I *do* believe in the Bible."

The DA shook his head. He dismissed Miss Corvina. After a moment, he called his next witness, and then several more. By the end of the day, he had rested his case against O'Reilly built on three hard facts: O'Reilly left his shift early on the night of the murder—implying that he knew he would find his wife in bed with another man; O'Reilly was caught minutes after the shootings with the murder weapon in hand; and finally, no one in the building heard or saw

O'Reilly enter the building or race up four flights of stairs after the shots were fired.

All three were difficult obstacles that Frank had to overcome during his defense.

Chapter 45

"Given the evidence we presented so far, the DA has to know we suspect he's the murderer," Frank said, cutting into his steak. "What we have to do now is convince him we can prove he's guilty."

"How will that help? You already told us you wouldn't use the evidence even if you had it."

"He doesn't know that, Joey. That's how wars are won. You make the enemy believe one thing while you do something different."

"Okay, let's say he suspects you have the goods on him," Jackie said. "What will he do then?"

"We'll have to wait and see. But I'm betting he won't take the risk of being accused in open court. So keep digging. There is a point at which he'll back off—we just need to find it."

"I know what you're thinking, but I doubt you can bluff the DA into dropping the charges against O'Reilly," Martha said to Frank.

"You'd be surprised what guilt can do to a person. It's an ugly beast to carry around, and most of us think everyone can see it, so we do our best to cover it up."

Maria, the owner of our favorite restaurant, came over to check on the food and to ask about the trial.

"I hear the DA doesn't have much."

Frank stopped chewing. "I'm afraid at this point he has enough."

I thought Maria was going to slap Frank across the head. Instead she gave him a brutal dressing-down.

"For an accomplished lip you sound more like a weak sister with a gimp. You need to get a wiggle on and put the screws to the DA."

When she had said her piece, she yelled across the restaurant for a plate of oysters to be delivered to our table and left to greet some locals as they entered the restaurant.

"What was that all about?" I asked.

"You tell me," Frank said.

Martha caught on before the rest of us, and downed the first oyster. "Frank, she's telling you that you sound more like a Daisy—a loser—than a successful criminal lawyer. Down some oysters, get some juice back in your veins, and stick it to the DA. At least that's what I think she meant."

Frank asked Martha to pass the oysters.

* * * * *

Frank called Molly Ferguson as his first witness and opened with a benign question. "Miss Ferguson, tell the jury what your relationship was with Lieutenant O'Reilly and his now-deceased wife."

"I've known O'Reilly since he was a small child. I took care of him and other kids in the neighborhood from time to time. We remained friends over the years."

"What about his wife, Bridget?"

"O'Reilly would bring her to the diner where I work when they were dating. Over the years, I became a confidant."

"Did she tell you recently that she was cheating on her husband?"

"She did."

The DA leapt to his feet, but when everyone stared at him, he sat back down. Frank continued.

"How did she describe the man she was seeing behind her husband's back?"

"Her sugar daddy. A man in a position of authority."

"That doesn't sound like the person who was murdered with her."

"No, it doesn't."

"So, you're suggesting that Bridget had more than one lover."

"Looks that way to me."

"So this other lover could have discovered her in bed with her neighbor and committed the murders."

"Objection, the defense is leading the witness."

"Sustained."

Frank continued. "Did you tell O'Reilly that his wife was unfaithful?"

"No."

"Why not?"

"It was not my place to betray a confidence or get involved in their marital difficulties."

"Your witness," Frank said to the DA.

The DA raised his hands in disbelief. "I'm not sure where to begin. I could easily discredit this witness. She was forced out of her neighborhood for being a chippy, a women of loose morals, not the type of witness you'd typically believe. But I'm not sure I want to go into those details. She just gave you another reason for Officer O'Reilly to kill his wife. Isn't that right, Miss Ferguson?"

"You could say that, or the jury might realize that I also said her other lover was a man in a position of authority. A person who was maybe seen leaving the scene of the crime without his overcoat in the dead of winter. Someone in a position to retrieve his expensive overcoat during the crime scene investigation. Someone, not unlike yourself, who could afford such a coat."

"Miss Ferguson, this jury isn't going to be swayed by such rubbish. A drunk stumbling out of an alley, hailing a cab, and a missing overcoat cannot wipe out the fact that Officer O'Reilly was caught sitting on the bed with the murder weapon in his hand moments after the shots were fired."

The DA looked up at the judge. "Your Honor, I have no more questions for this witness."

Frank didn't let the DA's offhand dismissal of the defense he was building deter him from his strategy. Frank called the cab driver to the stand. He confirmed Josephine Corvina's story, saying he had picked up a man with a hat, but no coat, and dropped him off in front of a vacant lot. He said when he'd turned around to ask his passenger if the lot was the correct location, the man covered his face with his arm and quickly left the cab, tossing a sawbuck at the driver.

Recognizing the DA's comments may have done some damage to his defense, Frank asked the cabbie one last question.

"Was your customer drunk?"

"No."

"How can you be so sure?"

"There was no smell of alcohol and he had his wits about him."

The DA tried to shake the cabbie's story, but the cab driver had a record that listed the time and location, which Frank had put into evidence.

Mrs. Flanagan, Frank's next witness, also corroborated

the testimony of Miss Covina and stated emphatically that O'Reilly had arrived after the shots were fired. Frank then took her questioning in a different direction.

"Mrs. Flanagan, your husband and O'Reilly's father were partners on the force. Would you please describe for the jury how O'Reilly's father died?"

The DA objected on the basis that the question was irrelevant and immaterial to the proceedings. Frank argued differently.

"Your Honor, the murder weapon belonged to Lieutenant O'Reilly's father and the same weapon was, in a sense, responsible for his father's death. If allowed to continue, I will show the relevance."

"Objection overruled. You may answer the question, Mrs. Flanagan."

"My husband and O'Reilly's father had agreed to meet at one of the piers. They had heard that a Mafia execution was going to go down. My husband arrived late and found his partner shot five times in the chest and once in the head. He never forgave himself."

"My understanding is that there was another wound," Frank stated.

"That's correct. The gun in question was shot out of O'Reilly's father's hand, leaving him defenseless."

Frank walked over to the evidence table.

"Is this the gun that your husband picked up and later gave to O'Reilly?"

She turned the gun over several times, looking bewildered.

"What's wrong, Mrs. Flanagan? Is that the weapon that belonged to O'Reilly's father?"

"Yes and no. There was a deep groove cut into the side

of the gun where the bullet struck. This only has a groove in the wooden grip."

"You're sure?'"

"Of course I'm sure. On the day my husband turned the gun over to O'Reilly, my husband showed me where the bullet had struck. I'll never forget the look on his face as he ran his finger over the rough edges and admitted to me that he had stopped for a drink and lost track of time. He took that guilt to his grave. You don't need to take my word. There are photographs. At the time, the execution of a police officer was front page news. I remember clearly that a life-size image of the gun appeared on the second page of the *Daily News*. I have a copy of the paper in my apartment."

I grabbed Martha's notepad and scribbled a short note for Sadie to give Frank. He took notice and walked over to his table.

Having read the note he addressed the judge. "Your Honor, it's getting close to lunch time and the witness just made a remarkable statement that was unexpected. May I suggest we take a recess to give both the prosecution and the defense teams a chance to think about the implications?"

The DA objected, but the judge called a recess in spite of his protest. Frank offered his hand to Mrs. Flanagan to help her exit the witness stand and walked her back to her seat, as I had hoped.

* * * * *

Frank did as I had asked in the note and passed me the key to Mrs. Flanagan's apartment as we shook hands. Jackie got up to leave the courthouse with me, but I thought it best that she stay behind so the DA wouldn't suspect we were up to something. I knew exactly where to find the old newspaper Mrs. Flanagan had mentioned. It would be in the small breakfront in the parlor under the pictures of her husband.

When I returned, I placed a satchel on Frank's table containing the newspaper.

"Frank, we can finally prove that the DA is the murderer. His gun is in the court lockup. You can ask for it to be presented as evidence. The barrel assembly from his gun must have a groove cut into it. We know the DA switched the barrel assemblies because of the results from the ballistics tests."

"And what if it doesn't? You don't think the DA noticed the groove later and replaced the assembly or got a new gun? My next witness will present enough evidence to get a hung jury. If we accuse the DA and fail, we will lose all credibility and O'Reilly will fry."

"Frank—"

"Batista, this is my decision. Deal with the DA any way you want, but do it after the trial—and don't tell me about it."

* * * * *

Frank handed the judge a copy of the paper that Mrs. Flanagan had referenced.

The DA objected vigorously.

"Your Honor, this is all nonsense. There is no evidence to suggest that that barrel assembly was switched on the night of the murder. It could have happened at any time."

Frank silenced the courtroom with one comment.

"After the DA finishes with my witness, I will present such evidence."

The DA returned to his table and looked toward the jury. "I have no questions for Mrs. Flanagan. The witness has already stated that she has sufficient motive to lie for the defense. She admitted that her husband was somewhat responsible for the death of O'Reilly's father, leaving him to stop a Mafia hit on his own for the sake of a drink. How can we trust any part of her testimony?"

The judge pounded his gavel and stood red-faced.

"That's the second time you insulted a witness. You will apologize for that comment or I will hold you in contempt."

The DA did as he was told. Not just once, but twice, with more sincerity the second time to satisfy the judge.

During the lunch recess, with the judge's permission, Frank had set up a table in front of the jury box and placed two semiautomatic 1911 Colt .45 handguns in plain view. One was the murder weapon labeled with the letter A, which was taped on the grip and also on the barrel. The other gun was labeled similarly, but with the letter B.

Frank called the lead detective on the case to the witness stand.

"Officer Jenkins, how long have you been working homicide?"

"A little over ten years."

"And before that?"

"I was a weapons instructor."

"I understand you spent several days at O'Reilly's apartment with your team of forensic experts gathering evidence. Is that correct?"

"Yes sir."

"Can you tell us if any shell casings were recovered from the crime scene?"

"There were no shell casings left behind."

"Were they tossed out the window, or in the trash bin?"

"We even looked in the trap of the toilet. I'm telling you, the shell casings had been removed from the crime scene."

"Who removed them?"

"We don't know."

"In your considerable experience, tell us why a murderer would remove the shell casings."

"The firing pin leaves an identifiable strike mark on the casing."

"In other words, you can tie the shell casing to the gun that fired the bullet."

"That's correct."

"Since the murder weapon was left behind, why would someone take the time to gather up the casings? They must have scattered all over the room—possibly under the bed or even behind the radiator."

"That remains a mystery, sir."

"I think we can clear that up with a little demonstration. Please take a seat at the table in front of the jury box. The guns I held up are on the table."

Once the reporters got their pictures, the courtroom settled down, and all eyes were on Frank and Officer Jenkins.

"Officer Jenkins, I asked you to bring some blank .45 bullets for this demonstration. Do you have them?"

"Yes."

"Did security confirm they are blanks?"

"They did."

"Please slowly show the jury how a clip is loaded with bullets."

Jenkins held the clip in his left hand, picked up a bullet with two fingers, and used his thumb to push and slide the bullet into the clip. He repeated this several times.

Frank stopped him. "Officer Jenkins, did you leave a fingerprint on the shell casing of each of those bullets you just loaded?"

"Most definitely."

Frank picked up the gun that was labeled B and showed the jury once again where the letters were placed. He then gave that gun to Officer Jenkins, who loaded in the clip and placed the gun into his shoulder holster.

"Gentlemen of the jury, do not be alarmed. Officer Jenkins is going to fire the blanks into the insulated box on the floor by the table, and then he is going to disassemble the guns and switch barrel assemblies."

The scene was dramatic—deafening noise and shell casings bouncing in all directions as they hit the tile floor. In less than seventy seconds after firing, Officer Jenkins disassembled and then reassembled both guns and stood before the jury with a gun with the clip in his holster.

Frank held up the gun labeled A on the grip, which represented the gun found at the crime scene, and showed that the barrel was now labeled B. As further proof that the barrel assemblies had indeed been switched, the gun he held up had no clip loaded.

"Officer Jenkins, this make-believe crime scene would show that the bullets were fired from the gun I'm holding and the same is true of the shell casings. Is that correct?"

"Yes."

"Why is that?"

"The firing pin is part of the barrel assembly, and as I previously mentioned, it leaves a marking on the shell casings."

"Yet my gun doesn't have a clip. The gun in your holster fired the blank bullets. If you just killed someone, and then switched barrel assemblies to frame another person, what would you now do?"

"Pick up the shell casings because my fingerprints are on them, and then get the hell out."

"Does this demonstration convince you that the barrel assembly on O'Reilly's father's gun was switched on the night of the murders?"

"It sure does. There's no other explanation for the missing shell casings."

Frank walked over to the DA. "Your witness."

"I have no questions for this witness," he said in a whisper. He then turned to look at the back of the courtroom and saw me standing by the doors. Any thought of him getting to his gun without creating a scene surely vanished from his mind.

Frank approached the bench.

"Your Honor, I rest my case. I contend that a murderer, a wealthy, influential person with easy access to a crime scene committed these murders. That person likely has the authority to carry a gun and is walking around with the proof that will put him away for life or worse."

The DA got Frank's message that we suspected he was the murderer. He approached the bench and stood alongside Frank.

"Your Honor, I request a closed-door session between the three of us given these new insights. The defense has presented persuasive arguments that another person could have committed these murders."

The judge ordered a recess and went into his chambers along with Frank and the DA.

* * * * *

The judge made the following announcement to the jury:

"Due to the compelling circumstantial evidence presented by the defense that another person may have been present on the night of the murders and the sworn statements of eye witnesses that Officer O'Reilly arrived after shots were fired, the District Attorney's office has decided to drop all charges against Lieutenant O'Reilly and to reopen the investigation. The state appreciates your time and commitment to public service. This trial is now adjourned."

O'Reilly was freed by the sound of the judge's gavel and was quickly surrounded by friends and neighbors.

The DA vanished from the courtroom, no doubt to retrieve his gun from the court lockdown area.

Chapter 46

Ma and Pop offered their place to celebrate the outcome of the trial, but O'Reilly wisely opted for La Cucina restaurant. The turnout was the largest the neighborhood had ever seen, even larger than some of the wakes the old-timers fondly reminisced about when they ran out of gossip. Everyone wanted to be a part of neighborhood folklore—and it didn't stop with the locals. The influx of O'Reilly's friends from surrounding precincts was endless—to the point that Luigi had to tap other speakeasies for booze to keep up with the demand.

At the end of the night, nearly everyone staggered out of the restaurant holding onto someone else, but none had drunk more than O'Reilly. As he'd made the rounds throughout the evening, each group had offered up a toast in his honor and made sure his shot glass was full.

As the party broke up, a group of us congregated at a long table with O'Reilly at the head. It was amazing to see how quickly he sobered up. Throughout the night, he had tried to probe for details of our investigation, but each time he'd been pulled away by some well-wisher. Now that the crowds were gone, he demanded answers. We walked him through the logic behind the defense Frank had presented during his trial, but in the end, one question hung in the air. O'Reilly picked up a bottle of whiskey and came over to me. He poured me a shot then set the bottle down so hard I thought it was going to shatter. I looked up and saw pure hatred in his bloodshot eyes. It didn't matter that his marriage wasn't perfect. He wanted revenge.

"It was the DA," I said, and threw back my drink. When I lowered the glass, O'Reilly was gone.

* * * * *

George dropped in the next day.

He nodded toward Jackie. "Tell your dame to take a powder. I have something I want to talk over with you."

Jackie planted a shiv in his chair as he was about to plop down. Instinctively, George reached for his rod.

"I wouldn't do that if I were you," I said, pointing toward the butcher knife Jackie was ready to let loose.

"Jackie's my fiancée and partner, and you've already given her reason to hate your guts," I said, touching my side. "I suggest you refrain from giving her more."

Jackie retrieved her knife on her way out.

"Sorry, miss. I didn't mean to offend," George said. "I'm new in town and don't know all the ropes yet."

"I suggest you do your homework if you want to survive," Jackie said. She slammed the office door shut.

"That's one tough bitch you got there."

"I'll ignore that remark. What's on your mind?"

"Your pal, O'Reilly."

"What about him?"

"Last night at the restaurant, I couldn't help but notice that this O'Reilly guy—he's not thinking straight. He's gonna get himself in another jam."

"How does that concern you?"

"Normally it wouldn't. But I saw how highly he's

regarded, and not just locally— Castellano, as well as Vigliotti, spent considerable time with him, so that makes him someone I need to know. And given my line of work, it wouldn't hurt to have a homicide detective indebted to me."

"What are you saying?"

George got up to leave. "I'll take care of the DA."

"If going after the DA is risky for O'Reilly, what about you?"

"Killing people is my profession, and I'm good at it. You have to know when to seize an unexpected opportunity, and it helps if you're emotionally detached. It might take a while, but I'll get it done, one way or another. Be sure to tell O'Reilly."

"I'll do that. But first, some advice, show a little respect for the dames around here. They all have their special talents—including my ma, and it's not just cooking."

George smiled for the first time since I'd known him.

"I'll remember that."

So far Capone had been right about George—loyal and deadly. Typical traits for a Mafia wiseguy. I decided to give my uncle Torrio a call, though, to find out what Capone had meant when he also said George was unpredictable.

My uncle didn't answer the call and neither did Capone.

* * * * *

You never know who you'll find when you enter my folks' apartment, and tonight was no exception. I was more surprised to see Dom than I was to find George eagerly helping Ma set the table. I had suspected George was a quick learner.

Dom knelt at a coffee table in the parlor with Martha at his side. He was furiously sketching a drawing on a large sheet of paper as Castellano described what he had in mind for the youth center. Luigi walked by mumbling under his breath. "I still think a brothel would add more character to the neighborhood."

I put my arm around his shoulder and offered him the drink I had just poured for myself.

"Uncle, if its change you want, it's coming, and my guess is you'll be in the middle of it."

"What makes you say that?"

"It's in your nature to take charge, and it's what the neighborhood needs."

"I wish you would stop talking in riddles and get to the point. You think too much, you know that?"

"Sometimes a little thought can go a long way especially when Big Ben's shadow still lurks along the waterfront."

Martha interrupted before Luigi could come up with a smart-aleck comment or probe deeper into what I was saying.

"Isn't that the guy who shot you in the side?" she asked me, pointing to George.

"That happened before we were formally introduced."

"Hmm," she said, fluffing her hair and heading for the kitchen. I grabbed her around the waist and pulled her in close. "Don't get too interested."

"Why? He seems nice enough."

"He's not."

"Let me be the judge of that," she said, pushing me away.

Jackie put a bowl of spaghetti on the table and came over to me.

"What was that all about?"

"I think I just made a big mistake with Martha."

"How's that?"

"I should've kept my mouth shut. Some women can't resist forbidden fruit," I said, as we watched Martha take a seat next to George.

"Neither can some men," Jackie said, looking up at me, and then leading the way to the table.

The meal was delicious and the grub just kept coming. I always found it amazing how so much food could come from such a small space. As a kid, I thought my mother was a witch who could conjure up whatever meals she wanted, especially desserts. And tonight was no exception. Pop shut out the lights, and Ma walked in with a flaming rum pound cake. You could hear the anticipation as everyone cleared a spot for their dessert plate.

It was a Friday night, and with O'Reilly's trial behind us and less urgent matters on our minds, we went back to tradition and congregated in the parlor after devouring the cake.

O'Reilly was working the evening shift and dropped in to have a few words with George. I had given him George's message that he would take care of the DA, and O'Reilly was more than a little interested. It was unlike him not to greet everyone personally, but that's exactly what he did. He and George sat in a corner with a bottle of whiskey, and when they were done talking, O'Reilly wished us a good evening and left to finish his shift.

George wedged between Jackie and me as we looked down at the sketch Dom had made for Castellano. Dom pointed to the spot where the cornerstone would be installed with an inscribed dedication.

"I'd make that bigger," George said to Dom, and he then walked away to join Martha and Sadie.

"What was that all about?" Dom asked. "Who does he think he is, an amateur architect?"

"No, but I'm sure he's had experience working with concrete. I'd do what he suggests. Did Castellano give you the job?" I asked.

"I'll have a professional drawing for him in two weeks."

"What about the Colonel? Does he still have his claws in you?"

"Sorry pal, I should have told you. Thanks to you, I got my discharge papers, picked up my stash, and I'm living large."

"Good to hear. Now I need a favor. I imagine you're gonna have to do some blasting to build that recreation center?"

"Some."

"Buy extra explosives. I might need you to take on that challenge I promised you a while back."

"The pier? I'm ready anytime."

"Did you ever figure out how to get it to collapse in on itself?"

"Won't know for sure until I light the fuse. How soon will you need the job done?"

"Be patient. I'll be in touch and give you plenty of time to prepare."

I walked away thinking how life tends to move us in a positive direction if we just pay attention to what's happening around us and put all the pieces together. I was starting to see how to stabilize the neighborhood in a way that might give Jackie and me the chance to settle down and run a normal business.

Chapter 47

Castellano had hit the mother lode when he charged a fee to join his union. To create a sense of urgency, he raised the cost at the beginning of each week, and he justified the increases to the longshoremen by announcing that he wanted to reward those who'd had the courage to be among the first to join the union by giving them a discount.

Not surprisingly, it took longer and longer for his office staff to approve applicants, causing many to pay the rising fees. As time passed, rumors spread that eventually only union members would be hired to work the docks. Once that rumor took hold, there was a mad frenzy to sign up, causing long lines to form outside the union office.

Fights frequently broke out as some of the men tried to cut in line to join their friends, but that wasn't much of a concern since fighting was a common pastime on the docks. What got Castellano's attention was that his foremen were behind schedule unloading the cargo ships. To remedy the situation he implemented a lottery system, which eliminated the need for the longshoremen to wait in line. Twenty-five members were added to the union register each and every day, including weekends.

George proved to be invaluable during the formative stage of the union. If anyone objected to how Castellano was running things, they had an "industrial accident." Nothing serious, but bad enough to keep them out of work for a few days and to send a clear message that Castellano wasn't going to take any guff from the longshoremen.

George had taken my advice not to try to convince Castellano to establish loansharking, prostitution, or other Mafia enterprises, and he focused on learning the internal workings of a successful union instead. He selected the shift foremen and hired the accountants and collection agents. At the same time, he rebuilt Castellano's internal organization by hiring experienced hit men—mostly Sicilians—and letting go of anyone with strong ties to Toby Tobias, his predecessor. George knew from his experience in Chicago that it was important to make it clear to the ethnic groups surrounding our neighborhood that Castellano could protect his territory.

Everything was running smoothly until the Communist Party members insisted on a stronger role in recruitment and active participation in local ward politics. Castellano's first instinct was to have George take care of them before they gained too much support from the members. There was an election coming up, and Castellano was counting on his candidates to replace the two men Hawk had originally brought in from the Communist Party. Castellano had placed them in leadership positions to begin with to give the impression the Mafia was treating them as equal partners. He now felt it was time to end that charade.

Hawk had a less violent suggestion: one, no doubt, supported by the government.

Luigi, Castellano, Hawk, and I came to an agreement on his idea late one night after Luigi closed up his speakeasy.

Hawk insisted that the way to eliminate the Communist threat was by bringing it out of the shadows. "People didn't come to this country to be held down. They want opportunities for themselves and their families. Let the Party give their speeches. The people will see through them."

"I don't know if that's wise," I said. "It seems to me the Communist message can be compelling. Why else are people joining their movement?"

"We're finding that the more radical their speeches become, the less support they're getting. A greater share in the wealth of the country is one thing, but when they start preaching armed insurrection, seizure of private property, and government control of the industrial complex—the common folks start backing away."

"Hawk, let me make this clear," Castellano said. "If my men don't win the upcoming election for officers, your Commie pals will be floating down river."

"I understand, and I agree that it's time to get them out," Hawk said. "What I'm suggesting is that we let the Communist Party start a new union along the docks and give them complete control. Once they're in the open, they won't be able to stop themselves from spewing their garbage."

"What do you have in mind?" I asked.

"Let them unionize the security workers along the docks. There aren't many people employed in that area compared to the number of longshoremen in Castellano's union. And if this new union becomes a problem, you can shut them down and replace every security guard without much trouble."

Castellano agreed, but with one condition.

"You can tell your government pals their little game is over if the election doesn't go my way."

"I don't think you or Vigliotti want the feds snooping around your empires. Just make sure you win the vote. Stuff the ballot box, pay off the folks in charge of counting—do whatever it takes," Hawk advised.

"That'll take money and a lot of it," Luigi said.

Hawk finished his beer and got up to leave. "That's not a problem. The feds have a printing press."

That got Luigi's attention, and he volunteered to run the election for Castellano.

It was settled. The Communists would lose their positions in Castellano's union through a "fair" vote, and then he would suggest they unionize the security force along the piers to appease them.

Everyone walked away from the meeting satisfied, especially Luigi. We all knew he'd find a way to siphon off some of that federal money.

* * * * *

The next day Luigi and I were discussing how to ensure stability in the neighborhood as the Mafia integrated unions into the waterfront operations. With Carmine gone and Castellano concentrating all his energy on union issues, there wasn't anyone to resolve day-to-day problems that were usually taken care of by Castellano. There were always conflicts between neighbors or business owners that needed resolution and financial emergencies that could devastate a family if arrangements weren't made.

I had about convinced Luigi that he should step up and fill the gap when Martha, Jackie, and Frank barged into my office. Frank slapped a copy of the *Daily News* on my desk.

"He's taking out every witness we put on the stand," Frank said, pounding the front page.

At first it was hard to believe what I was seeing. There were two pictures side by side, one of a body lying in a street among a tangled mess of smashed cars and the other of a burning building. The headline said it all: "Is the Coatless Man Taking Out Witnesses?"

"When did this happen?" I asked, skimming the article. It recapped O'Reilly's trial and the details of the witnesses' testimonies.

"The guy in the street is the cab driver. He got his a day after the trial. At the time it didn't even make the papers. Josephine Corvina's apartment exploded last night. A supposed gas leak. One of her colleagues at the paper put the two deaths together—too much of a coincidence," Jackie said.

Luigi looked over my shoulder as we talked, and then he suddenly bolted for the door yelling, "That son of a bitch. We need to get to Molly!"

I ran after him and turned him around.

"Get Frank and Sadie to a safe place. They're also prime targets for the DA. We'll get Molly."

"Out of my way," Luigi shouted.

"Uncle, the DA is using professionals and may have more than one team taking out witnesses. Trust me on this. I won't let anything happen to Molly."

Jackie tossed me my shoulder holster, told Luigi to stay put, and headed downstairs. We were at the diner in less than ten minutes.

* * * * *

The street in front of the diner looked deserted, so I felt confident that nothing had happened yet. I entered first with my gun held low at my side so as not to cause a panic. There were two old-timers sitting at the counter talking with Molly and one couple seated at a table near the back.

I sat in a booth facing the entrance and told Jackie to get Molly ready to leave. But Molly wasn't about to walk off the job.

"I'm the only waitress for the next half hour. I can't leave."

Jackie tried to explain, but Molly wouldn't listen. I grabbed a copy of the *Daily News* off one of the tables and tossed it onto the counter. Just then two men came into the diner.

Jackie pushed Molly aside and swiped a cleaver from the back counter. I was about to raise my rod when one of the men shouted to Molly they would have their usual.

"What in the world is wrong with you two?" Molly said, taking the cleaver from Jackie.

"Take off your apron and come with us—now," Jackie ordered.

"I told you I can't—"

Jackie tapped the pictures on the front page. "The cab driver's dead and so is the reporter. You're next."

Molly yelled back to the cook. "Hey Charlie, you're on your own. I gotta leave." She tossed her apron over the counter and stood next to me.

Jackie grabbed two carving knives from behind the counter and walked past us to the exit. "I don't have my knife harness on," she said.

I left the diner first and opened the car doors. The girls hopped in. As the engine turned over, a car screeched to a stop behind us. Two men popped out and raised their Tommy guns.

I swerved into traffic, darted across the street, and entered a pier warehouse, dodging crates and longshoremen as they dove for cover. The car followed with one of the men firing from the side window. We took several hits. We wouldn't stand a chance unless I could find a place where we could get the hell out of the car.

I headed at full speed down the pier toward a massive stack of crates the work crew had just off-loaded from a large steamer. I slammed on the brakes and swerved behind the crates for cover. I pulled Jackie out across the driver's side. Molly was already out of the car. I opened fire as the car pursuing us whizzed by, stopping twenty feet further down the pier. Jackie held onto Molly and pulled her around to the other side of the crates as I continued firing. While I reloaded, the two men ducked out of their car and moved apart to catch us in a crossfire.

I crouched just in time as several bullets slammed into the crate where I had been standing. I was outgunned, and Jackie couldn't use her knives without exposing herself. The bullets came closer as the gunmen moved nearer to the edges of the pier.

I was reloading again when I heard a shrill whistle coming from behind us. I turned and saw a foreman waving me toward the girls. I didn't know what he had in mind, but I did as he signaled. He let out a yell, which was followed by a loud crash. The concrete floor shook under our feet, knocking Molly down. It took me a few seconds to realize what had just happened. Now the foreman was waving me forward. I ran into the open and fired at the remaining gunman, who stood stunned. His partner was crushed under a full pallet of heavy machinery that the crane operator had dropped at the foreman's direction.

One of my bullets hit its mark, but my victim was able to swing his gun in my direction before he fell to one knee. I was out of clips and reaching frantically for my ankle holster when one of Jackie's knives sliced open his forearm. I then finished him off with two shots to the head. Jackie went back to help Molly. She was unhurt but shaking uncontrollably as she struggled to her feet.

I recognized the foreman who had saved our lives as a guy from my neighborhood. He waved as we drove back down the pier into traffic. We took Molly to Luigi's speakeasy and got her settled in one of the back rooms. Jackie stayed with her while I relieved Luigi at our apartment building. A short time later, Jackie joined me in Frank's office.

We had to find a way to put an end to this madness.

Chapter 48

When Jackie and I had left to find Molly, Martha had gone looking for O'Reilly. It stood to reason that the DA would go after him just for his own peace of mind. He knew O'Reilly was a tough cop and would seek revenge once he found out the truth. I wouldn't put anything past the DA, including paying a crooked cop to take out O'Reilly as a way to catch him off guard. I hoped it wasn't too late.

We had returned to Frank's office just a few minutes ahead of Martha and O'Reilly.

"By the look of your car, I'd say the DA is still playing rough," O'Reilly said, looking out the office window. "Your pop is moving your jalopy around back. I'll have it hauled off to a junkyard tonight."

"Jalopy! That's a new car."

"Not any more. It has so many bullet holes you're lucky it still runs. What happened?"

Jackie answered, "I'm sure Martha told you about the cab driver and the reporter who testified at your trial. Fortunately, we got to Molly minutes before two torpedoes arrived at the diner."

"That settles it. I'm taking that bastard out tonight," O'Reilly said. He headed for the door.

"Hold on," I shouted. "That's just what he wants. You'll be dead before you get within ten feet of him. He'd be an idiot not to protect himself around the clock."

"You got a better idea?"

"Let George handle the DA. They won't be watching for him."

"He hasn't done a damn thing yet."

I reminded O'Reilly that George had said it would take time. "What we need to do is find a way to get the DA to back off and let George do what he does best."

"The DA's not about to stop," Jackie said.

"He'll stop if we do what we should've done in the first place—throw suspicion on him for the murders." I went over to Sadie. "Do you have the original prints that Josephine Corvina took at the crime scene?"

"They're in the safe."

"Jackie, I say we use your contacts at the paper. Give them the pictures of the two coats and the ones that show the DA entering with the cheap coat and leaving with the more expensive one."

Jackie smiled. "A dramatic headline would pull him back into his hole and buy George the time he needs—'Is the DA our Mystery Killer?'"

"That'll do it," I said. "Have them follow up a day or two later by asking the public if anyone had seen the DA with Bridget. A picture of Bridget and the DA in his expensive coat—side by side—should be effective."

"Why the hell didn't you accuse him during the trial?" O'Reilly shouted at Frank.

"It's all circumstantial—we had no proof. We tried to find a motel owner who would testify that he recognized them, but didn't have any luck."

"What about his gun? That would've been enough to hang him," O'Reilly said.

"Sure, I could have made a big scene of accusing the DA

of a double murder, and then had security get his gun out of lockup to prove it."

"Why didn't you?"

"I already went through this with Joey. If the DA had already gotten rid of the gun barrel assembly or the gun itself, you'd be sitting on death row cursing me for my stupidity."

Jackie got on the horn with the editor of the *Daily News,* and Sadie put together a package of the pictures I'd mentioned.

The next day, the paper couldn't print enough copies to keep up with the demand. The DA was deluged with questions from every reporter in the city. He argued that he owned both types of coats and was so disturbed by what O'Reilly had done that he simply grabbed the wrong coat on the way out of the apartment.

At a news conference he announced bringing a lawsuit against the *Daily News*, which put him in the spotlight even more. We had bought ourselves some time.

Frank wanted to report the attack on Molly to put more pressure on the DA but both O'Reilly and I thought that would be unwise and difficult to prove. Evidence of violence on the waterfront is dealt with swiftly by the Mafia. The last thing they want are cops poking around the piers and stumbling upon illegal cargo. As it turned out the shift foreman had removed the evidence within minutes of us leaving the scene. The car driven by our attackers had been taken to a scrap yard, and the bodies weighed down and dumped into the bay. Work continued as if nothing unusual had happened on the pier.

It was now up to George to deal with the DA, and to be honest, I didn't blame him for taking his time. My only concern at this point was controlling O'Reilly, which was never easy.

Chapter 49

In less than a week after the *Daily News* ran its first article on the DA, three different motel owners came forward and swore that the DA and Bridget had been frequent customers. Every newspaper in the city picked up the story and had pictures of cheap motels plastered on their front pages, pressuring the mayor to take action. He had no choice but to suspend the DA until a full investigation could be completed.

The DA's suspension wasn't enough to appease O'Reilly, who was growing weary of waiting for George to follow through. Concerned that O'Reilly would take matters into his own hands, I had called a meeting to give George a chance to explain what the hell was taking him so long to off the DA.

O'Reilly didn't even give George or Castellano a chance to take a seat before he went straight for the jugular.

"Those two witnesses put their lives at risk to save mine. They'd be alive today if I had taken the DA out when I wanted to."

"That's true, and it's also true you'd be rotting in jail for murder," George said in his defense. "I've had someone keeping track of the DA's routine, and I was ready to make a move, but that's all changed since his suspension."

O'Reilly got out of his chair and stood over George. "Are you telling us you have to start over?"

"Will you relax? I said I'd take care of him and I will. Actually, all that's been goin' on is working to our advantage. Now, when the DA disappears, there'll be no investigation. Everyone will assume he's guilty and went on the lam."

"It better happen soon." O'Reilly brushed past Vigliotti as the mob boss entered the office.

I half expected O'Reilly to return to hear what Vigliotti had to say, since it was rare for Vigliotti to venture outside the protective confines of Little Italy. No doubt O'Reilly assumed Vigliotti would clam up with a cop in the room.

Vigliotti got right to the point.

"You've got a problem, Joey, a big one. A huge contract has been put on your head and every hit man from here to the west coast is converging on New York. I've stationed men still loyal to me around the neighborhood."

"Still loyal? What the hell is goin' on?" Castellano asked, as he greeted Vigliotti.

"Big Ben has been gaining support from the other bosses to take over the syndicate. They don't like this union business we've been pushing, and most agree that the waterfront should be consolidated."

"Why is he going after Joey?" Jackie asked.

Vigliotti removed his coat and hat. "Joey practically destroyed his organization. It's more symbolic. He gets rid of Joey and he gets his full respect back—then those still loyal to me might go over to his side."

I ordered Jackie and Martha to get everyone out of town. "I don't want anyone left in this building or Luigi's place."

"What about you?" Jackie asked, not showing any emotion.

"I'm going to take care of Big Ben."

"That won't stop a thing," Vigliotti said. "He didn't put

out the contract. He didn't have to. All he had to do was finger you for blowing up his home on Long Island."

I'd forgotten all about that threat. I'd violated the sanctity of the money bags' private island. They had sworn they'd find who attacked one of their own, and now, thanks to Big Ben, they knew.

"Why now?" Martha asked. "That all happened months ago."

"Understand this," Vigliotti said, "In my world, revenge is relentless. I should have known better than to take my eye off Big Ben. I've been so focused on establishing unions throughout the city that I didn't take the rumors about him seriously. But when I heard that he had ratted out Joey—after I had ordered a truce between them—I knew Ben was making a move on my authority."

Castellano hadn't said much, and neither had George. Castellano, I knew, was looking for a solution, but not George. He was looking for an opportunity to move up in the ranks. No doubt trying to decide if he should side with Big Ben or help Vigliotti.

"Do you know who put out the hit?" Castellano asked.

Vigliotti handed him a slip of paper. Castellano looked at it and shook his head. He gave it to me.

"Joey, this guy is known as the Baron and he has loads of dough. He lives in the most expensive mansion on the shoreline. Your only chance is to get to this guy tonight and have him call off the dogs. He's as crooked as they come, with Jersey connections, and he'll be well protected. The chances of even getting into his estate are slim."

"I know how to get to him. Now clear the buildings," I said. "I don't want anyone getting hurt."

Jackie moved to my side and gave Martha instructions.

"Get everyone to Staten Island and ask Lieutenant Sullivan for protection. He's a friend of O'Reilly's. I'm going with Joey."

Jackie looked at me. "We'll get out of this together or not at all."

"Count me in too," George said. He'd evidently decided to back Vigliotti. At least I hoped so.

There was no sense in trying to talk Jackie out of coming along, and I had to admit that both of them would increase my chances of getting to the Baron. Now all I needed was the Colonel's cooperation, and a hell of a lot of luck.

Chapter 50

Though I was facing certain death if I didn't get the Colonel's support, it was difficult not to crack a smile when he entered Castellano's union office. The Colonel had tried to look the part of a longshoreman, but had missed the mark. He wore the right clothes, but they were spotless.

"Batista, you better have a damn good reason for dragging my ass down here out of uniform."

"I didn't have an option, Colonel. The waterfront is the only place that wouldn't draw attention to someone meeting with two Mafia bosses. But we're getting ahead of ourselves. Let me make introductions. Colonel Benton, I'd like you to meet Mr. Vigliotti and Mr. Castellano. They run things in this part of the city."

The Colonel didn't look impressed and took charge of the conversation as soon as we sat around a small table.

"Gentlemen, my man Hawk has been giving me regular updates on your union activities. I appreciate your help in getting rid of this Commie scourge that threatens our democracy. Having said that, why the hell am I here?"

Vigliotti and Castellano had made it clear to me they wanted to say as little as possible to the Colonel. After all, he did work for the government, and the day might come when they could get dragged into court.

"Sorry Colonel, but I lied to get you to attend this meeting. It has nothing to do with the unions. A contract has been placed on my head. If I don't get it lifted by tonight, I'll be dead in the morning."

"Why the hell should that concern me? Didn't you last leave my office waving your discharge papers in my face?"

I knew the Colonel too well to take his remarks seriously. He had figured out that we were about to drag him into something big and was laying the foundation for negotiation. Just in case, though, I gave him a damn good reason.

"If I'm gone, your union deal is off—not only here, but also in Chicago."

Vigliotti and Castellano nodded their agreement.

"Batista, I expected better from you—a deal is a deal. Now that I know what type of people I'm involved with, what do you want from me?"

"Full amphibian night infiltration gear for five, a fast boat, and an appropriate raft to get us ashore undetected."

"Given the organization involved in this mission," the Colonel said, glancing over at Vigliotti and Castellano, "I have questions that need answers."

I knew what the Colonel wanted to know.

"Possibly a large number of casualties and dramatic headlines. But you needn't worry. We intend to leave behind strong evidence that ties everything to gangland violence. There'll be no link back to you."

"Anyone but you, Batista, I'd tell to go to hell. When do you need the gear?"

"We leave at dusk. That gives you three hours to get the boat and everything else to the end of Pier 17. One more thing, I want Hawk to be part of this operation."

"That's impossible. I can't risk losing him. His current assignment is too critical."

"Colonel, if Hawk doesn't join Joey, there is no assignment," Vigliotti said.

The Colonel had never liked ultimatums, so I wasn't sure how he'd react. When finally he asked if we had a stash of booze, I knew we had him. Castellano placed a bottle of high-quality whiskey on the table. After we had all taken a shot, the Colonel set his terms.

"I'll get everything you asked for except the boat. I'd have to go to the Coast Guard to commandeer such a craft, and that's not gonna happen. Besides, you don't need a fast boat. You want an invisible one. Something that won't draw attention. I'm sure you have access to whatever you need."

The Colonel grabbed the bottle and refilled everyone's glass, and then continued.

"I have one condition. I want your word that no military gear will be left behind. That means you bring your dead back on board."

Once I agreed, he downed his shot of whiskey and headed for the door.

"Gentlemen, I have work to do. I was never here, and this conversation never took place. Good hunting."

He turned as he was about to exit. "Joey, I do hope you make it back in one piece."

Chapter 51

Jackie's knife harness wasn't suitable for what I had in mind. She would have to wear it on the outside of her night bodysuit, which would be impractical. A sliver of moonlight reflecting off one of her assortment of butcher knives could get us all killed.

She needed to learn how to use the army's black military-style throwing knives, which were shorter and lighter than what she was used to.

We practiced in the hallway outside our office as Pop stitched together two belts with slits to hold twenty-two knives. At most, she had a little more than an hour to get ready. We paced off three distances from a back wall: ten, twenty, and thirty feet. I handed her the three knives I had brought home from the war and was about to give her instructions when she let one fly. She was deadly accurate at the shorter distances but missed the mark one out of five times at thirty feet. I was confident that with more practice she'd have been perfect, but we had to head to Pier 17 to meet the others.

The Colonel delivered as promised. Hawk and Dom were unloading crates from an unmarked boat as Jackie and I drove into the pier warehouse. Luigi and Pop were helping George move the crates onto a smaller fishing vessel. Fishing boats were a common site on the Hudson and wouldn't draw much attention.

Luigi was first to open a crate and whistled low and long when he saw the contents. He picked up a mini-submachine gun with the loving care you'd show a newborn. I snatched it away and placed it back in the box.

"We have to keep the gunfire to a minimum, if at all," I said. "The mansions along the shoreline are heavily patrolled by local law enforcement. A blast from one of those would draw them like flies, and the last thing we need is a slew of dead cops."

Luigi waved Pop over, and they picked up the crate and walked it down the gangplank.

"What are you doing now?" I shouted.

"Hell, if you're not gonna use the damn things, I'm taking them home. I can get a darn good price," Luigi said.

"The Colonel's gonna want everything back. You can't just take that stuff."

"Don't worry," Pop shouted. "Just tell him the Coast Guard was approaching so you had to toss everything overboard. What's he gonna do? Report you for stealing gear that he commandeered for a Mafia hit job?"

Knowing Dom I'm sure he was eyeing any leftover gear to line his own pockets, so I wasn't surprised to see him trying to block Luigi and Pop from getting back on board the boat as we opened the rest of the crates.

The Colonel had outdone himself. We had plenty of knives, a couple of grappling hooks, explosives—which I was confident Dom could make use of for a different job that I had in mind for him—five unmarked semiautomatic handguns with holsters, a utility belt for rappelling, rope, several twelve-inch hunting knives with sheaths, an assortment of weapons with which to quietly strangle someone, and, of course, a night bodysuit for each of us.

The sun had been down for two hours and darkness had settled over the bay except for the lights along the shoreline reflecting off the water. Thankfully, storm clouds had moved in and blanketed the sky, blocking any moonlight.

Dom, George, and Hawk picked out their suits and started to strip. I grabbed the remaining two suits and led Jackie into the wheelhouse. The captain discreetly left the cabin.

"Get naked," I said, as I tossed my clothes aside.

"Joey, this is no place—" she said, smiling.

"Jackie, get serious. These suits are designed to cling to your skin. Any clothes you leave on will clump and limit your mobility."

"What's this metal thing?" she said, pointing to the crotch.

"That's for protection. They don't make these suits for women, but there are ways to adjust the fit. Put the suit on and I'll do the best I can. Pop's knife belt should make it tighter around the middle. Most men don't have a twenty-two inch waist."

Hawk came into the wheelhouse, handed us the rest of our gear and called the captain back to start the engine. The captain worked for Vigliotti and knew where to drop us off. He asked no questions, although, he couldn't take his eyes off Jackie. I couldn't blame him. With her waist wrapped with over twenty throwing knives, a hunting knife strapped to her thigh, and a shoulder holster—she looked like one deadly broad.

There was only one last item to get Jackie ready. I covered her hands in a black paste and reached for her face. She pulled back. "What is that?" she asked.

"You don't want to know. Obviously we need to cover our skin, but this stuff also changes our scent. There might be guard dogs prowling the grounds."

Pop and Luigi came back on board. They hugged Jackie and me and wished us luck. Luigi looked around.

"You gonna need any of this stuff left in the crates?"

Dom threw up his hands. "Just take what you want, but leave the explosives."

"First tell me if Vigliotti is still willing to help," I said to Luigi.

"He's headed for Long Island now and will be at the gatehouse of the estate, ten-thirty sharp. He doesn't think he'll have any trouble getting onto the grounds. He's disguised as the chauffeur and has a guy in the back seat that could be Big Ben's double. Once the sentries get the okay from the main house to allow who they think is Big Ben to enter the grounds, Vigliotti's men in a second car will take care of the sentries. They'll be left alive so they can finger Big Ben."

"Vigliotti's taking a hell of a chance," I said.

Luigi pulled me aside. "If Big Ben takes over the syndicate, Vigliotti and his family will be wiped out. He's motivated. Good luck, kid."

Chapter 52

I had estimated it would take fifteen to twenty minutes to clear the grounds surrounding the Baron's mansion of security guards. The plan was to enter the house with Vigliotti, eliminate any threat inside, and have a little chat with my new antagonist.

We intentionally continued up the bay, past the mansion to get a look at the back of the house. There was a fifty-foot sailboat moored to a dock, and the light was on in the lower level. That threat became our first order of business. We had to prevent anyone on the boat from sounding an alarm.

The mansion had three floors, and all the windows in back were dark except for one, which had a faint glow. We suspected the light was coming from the main part of the house through a door that was ajar. There were two small servant cottages to the left of the house. They were also occupied.

It was fortunate that we had left early. I hadn't anticipated having to deal with occupants of a yacht and two outbuildings. I called the team together and ordered the captain to head back to the drop-off point. I laid out a plan.

"This is more complicated than I expected."

"Isn't it always," Dom said.

"That's true. Here's what we're gonna do. Dom, when we get the inflatable to within twenty feet of the sailboat, I want you to go over the side and deal with whoever's in the boat. If its innocents, use minimum force."

"And if they're not so innocent, then what?"

"We need to move quickly—take them out. Hawk and George, when we get ashore, you handle the cottages. If you can, avoid any of the security personnel until the cottages are neutralized. Do whatever it takes to stop anyone from warning others, but remember, if they're domestic help, I don't want them injured. When you're done, clear the grounds leading to the house, but stay away from the gatehouse at the entrance to the estate."

"That doesn't make sense," George said. "The men manning the entry gate have a clear view of the grounds. They might notice something is wrong. I'd rather take them out after we finish with the servant quarters and then work our way toward the house."

"Vigliotti and his men will neutralize them. We want the guards at the gate to believe Big Ben is the one visiting the Baron. They will be left alive so they can later testify to that fact."

"What are you and Jackie gonna be doing? Taking a siesta?" George asked with a bit of a smile.

"We'll work the grounds around the house. The roof is gabled at a steep angle, so there's probably no one up there keeping watch. When we all see Vigliotti's car coming up the drive, we'll gather on either side of the front of the house and enter when he does."

The captain dropped anchor.

"Any questions?"

"What happens when we're inside the house?" Jackie asked.

"I'll politely ask the Baron to call off his hit."

"And if he doesn't cooperate?"

"Then I eliminate the source of money—no Baron, no money. No money, no reason for anyone to risk taking me down."

"One more thing," I said. "Look for chances to implicate Big Ben."

"How the hell are we supposed to do that?" George asked.

"It doesn't need to be complicated. Mention his name when you're in the cottages. Maybe one of you reminds the other that Big Ben said not to harm the help. That should do it."

George shook his head. "Why go through all this trouble to frame Big Ben? If he's a threat to Vigliotti, just shoot the bastard."

"Vigliotti is trying to avoid a split in his organization. He needs the other bosses to think Big Ben is out of control, so they'll think twice about backing him. If he just kills Big Ben outright, he'll have dissention—remember what happened in Detroit. Bodies lined the streets and few bosses and their families made it through that rift alive."

George mumbled something and left to load his gear in the raft. I glanced at Jackie to see if she heard him.

"He said this is not how Capone does business."

* * * * *

We pushed the inflatable away from the hull and took our time paddling toward the sailboat, making as little noise as possible. Once Dom was overboard and had reached the dock, we moved in closer and tethered to one of the end pilings. Dom had agreed to wait for us if he felt there were more than two people on board the sailboat. Since he was nowhere in sight, we swam the short distance to the shoreline at the back of the mansion.

Hawk and George went off in the direction of the cottages. Jackie and I were about to begin our search for security guards when Dom came crouching toward us down the dock. As we watched him approach, he suddenly flattened out on the planks. We instinctively pulled back into the shadows. A flashlight beam appeared from the side of the house and moved closer to the water's edge. Before I could pull her back, Jackie had stepped away from the house and, as the guy rounded the corner, she hit him with three shivs—one in the throat and two in the chest. If she hadn't hit his heart, she'd come damn close. He fell forward without a sound.

I stood behind her with my rod drawn in case the guards traveled in pairs. Jackie looked surprised when she saw my gun.

"Next time wait in the shadows until we know how many we're dealing with."

Jackie nodded and leaned back against the house. I had no doubt she would not make that mistake again.

Dom joined us and was about to say something when a cigarette butt landed at his feet. There was someone on the roof. It was dumb luck that he hadn't noticed us coming ashore. We had to figure out how to get in the house unnoticed and find a way onto the roof.

I turned to get Dom's opinion when I saw him scaling a drain pipe. I got to him before he was out of reach and tugged him down, much to his annoyance. I pointed at the clouds, which were moving fast. The moon would light that side of the house in less than a minute. We moved to the other corner of the house and found a similar downspout.

Dom was on the roof in a matter of seconds. It didn't take him long to return. The front of his night suit was dripping blood.

"He didn't go easily. I damn near fell off the roof."

We were behind schedule. Vigliotti was about to arrive, and we hadn't yet cleared the grounds. The lights went out in the last cottage, indicating that Hawk and George were now clearing the grounds on the left side of the driveway. Jackie made her way along the side of the house to get a look at the front porch. The news wasn't good.

"There are two guards stationed by the front door, and it doesn't look like they leave their post to make rounds."

That would create a problem for Vigliotti when he drove up to the house. If we tried to take them down now, though, the scuffle would warn others. I made the tough decision to leave Jackie behind with instructions to deal with both guards when Vigliotti arrived, using his car as cover. Dom and I continued our search for more security to the right of the driveway.

* * * * *

Dom and I dispatched three more goons and headed back to join Jackie. George was approaching the main house from the opposite side of the driveway and didn't sense that a security guard had stepped out from behind some bushes as he passed. I was about to risk a warning when the person crumbled to the ground.

Jackie had taken up a position by one of the cottages so she could duck in behind Vigliotti's car when it arrived. She noticed that George was about to be killed. I don't know how she hit her mark from that distance.

Hawk came out of the brush near George, wiping his knife on his leg. It turns out that some of the guards did travel in pairs.

Hawk and George joined Dom and I as we watched Jackie run alongside Vigliotti's car.

When the car came to a stop, the two men on the porch moved to the top of the steps and raised their weapons. As the back car door opened, Jackie rose from behind the car and planted two knives in each of the guards. I was starting to wonder why the rest of us had come along.

* * * * *

Dom went into the mansion first. Once the butler was knocked out cold, he and Hawk searched the house, while the rest of us paid the Baron a visit. He was relaxing in the reading room with a drink waiting for Big Ben who had been announced by the gatehouse guards. He bumped into the liquor table as he went to stand and spilled a bottle of whiskey.

"He's not Big Ben! How did you get past my security?" the Baron shouted, still trying to stand.

George had moved behind the Baron's chair and pulled him back into his seat.

Vigliotti took the lead. "Getting in here was not difficult," he said, pulling forward the Big Ben look-alike. "You should train your guards to be more observant, the ones that are still alive, that is."

Dom and Hawk entered the room with a terrified middle-aged woman struggling between them.

Vigliotti removed his chauffeur cap and tried to calm the woman. "Scarlet, take a seat next to your husband. We're conducting some business that impacts the both of you." He then turned his attention back to the Baron.

"Baron, your first mistake was teaming up with Big Ben to gain control over my organization. You should have known better. Our joint enterprises have enriched us both over the years. Your second mistake was going after Batista—he's a deadly man. He has taken on the best and has always walked away unscathed."

Vigliotti pointed to a wall phone. "Baron, call your contacts in Jersey and tell them you and Big Ben have called off the hit on Batista."

"It's too late."

"It's never too late. Batista will have to deal with a few stragglers that don't get the message, but that shouldn't be a problem."

The Baron made the call, cursing into the mouthpiece to get his point across. He then took his seat next to his wife.

"I did my best, but whatever happens, happens."

Vigliotti looked up from the Baron and nodded to George, who then shot both the Baron and his wife in the back of the head. Jackie turned away from the gruesome sight and looked up at me.

"There was no other option." I said. "You do realize she knew what the Baron did for a living."

Vigliotti ignored Jackie's reaction. "Joey, I don't think you need worry any longer. Once what happened here tonight hits the morning papers, there isn't a hit man anywhere in the country that will come near you."

Vigliotti stopped at the front door and gave George an order. "Give me twenty minutes, then torch this joint."

He then turned to me. "Castellano tells me that you have some ideas for how to run the docks with the unions in the mix. Times are changing and we need new thinking. I'm looking forward to the details. While you're at it, Batista, if you could also find a way to put Big Ben back in his place—I'd be indebted."

Luigi had been right. Vigliotti was using me to save himself. Before he left, he acknowledged George, "Nice work," he said. "I hear you used to work for Capone."

George nodded.

"Come and talk to me," Vigliotti said, casting a look at Castellano that warned him not to interfere. It wouldn't be long before George was working directly for Vigliotti, which was fine with me. He had already outgrown our little neighborhood. If he stayed around much longer, we would eventually clash. As far as I was concerned, he just needed to take care of the DA before moving on.

Chapter 53

The Colonel wasn't happy with the headlines and intense scrutiny the slaughter at the Baron's estate received from state and local authorities. The Baron was a respected philanthropist, which had given him cover for his illegal activities. The Colonel knew there would be heat, but he expected the story to die down sooner than it did. He became especially nervous after two teenagers, who had been gagged and tied up while they sat inside a moored sailboat, testified that their attacker came out of the bay dripping wet, wearing a tight, black, tactical outfit. The implication was that the assailants had military training, which was backed up by the fact that a large security force was taken out without firing a shot.

The Colonel stopped pestering me when the story quickly broke that Big Ben Napoli was implicated by the gate security guards and the servants. It also helped that I assured the Colonel that none of the equipment he had supplied was left behind.

Big Ben was dragged in for questioning, but soon released. He had attended a special event honoring the mayor on the night of the attack and several influential people testified that he was present past midnight. This discredited the testimony of the security guards, who swore Ben himself was on the grounds, and shifted the investigation away from Big Ben toward the Baron's business dealings and possible rivals who would benefit from his death. One reporter speculated that mercenaries had been hired, which would explain the tactics used during the attack. Within a few days, the Baron's demise faded into the archives of sensational stories that caught people's attention on a daily basis.

I asked my folks and the others not to return to the city for at least a week, just to make sure some wiseguy didn't show up to make a name for himself and follow through on the Baron's contract. As it turned out, the quiet time gave Jackie and me a chance to talk about our future and reassure each other the life we really wanted was still possible. Seeing the sudden callous murder of the Baron and his wife had been the last straw for Jackie. She had seen and caused enough death. It didn't matter that her actions had always been in self-defense or aimed at saving others. She wanted out.

There was a brief moment that reaffirmed how much I wanted to start over with Jackie by my side.

"Joey, what did Vigliotti mean when he said you have a plan for how he should run things in the future?" Jackie asked.

"It's complicated, and I haven't worked out all the details yet, but if it works, you and I have a chance to live a more normal life. We'll be reduced to snooping around windows trying to catch women cheating on their husbands, finding lost dogs, and if we're lucky, landing an occasional murder investigation."

"Can you tell me about it?"

"Not yet. I don't want to get your hopes up. But how do you feel about Staten Island?"

"What?"

"I'm thinking that might be a good place to start over.

It's growing and seems like a nice place to someday raise a family."

Jackie teared up. She sat on my lap and rested her head against my shoulder.

"I would like that. To be normal, to raise my kids the way they should be—so they will always know they're loved and will never be abandoned."

I held her tight and she fell asleep in my arms.

We had a wonderful few days. No clients, no interruptions, and more importantly, no violence.

* * * * *

I had my meeting with Vigliotti, Castellano, and my uncle Luigi. They had lots of questions about my ideas for merging the unions with the day-to-day legal and illegal activities along the waterfront. In the end, we all agreed on a course of action for the waterfront and for maintaining the independence of our neighborhood from Little Italy. I would make my proposal at the next council meeting. We expected Big Ben to object, but Vigliotti would deal with him—with a little help from me.

It turned out I wasn't the only one focused on solving our neighborhood problems. George kept his promise to O'Reilly. On the night before the concrete cornerstone for Castellano's Youth Center was scheduled to be poured, the DA disappeared. His car was found abandoned at one of the piers. The speculation in the papers was that he escaped the country on one of the Canadian smuggling boats that provided booze to the city's hundreds of illegal speakeasies.

I never told Jackie that Luigi, O'Reilly, and I played a key role in the DA's demise. George had laid out his plan over a few beers one night at Luigi's joint.

"The DA's desperate. He's suspended and expecting to be arrested any day for murder. I took advantage of that fact and had one of my men strike up a conversation with him at his favorite watering hole. After a few drinks, he offered to help the DA get out of the country. We'll take him tonight when he goes to meet my contact. If you want in, be at Dom's construction site at midnight."

O'Reilly dropped a shot of whiskey in his beer. "Oh, I'll be there."

"Anyone else?"

"I have a few scores to settle with the bastard. Count me in," I said.

Luigi volunteered to keep watch.

* * * * *

A car rolled into the construction site ten minutes past midnight. Dom closed the gate and secured it with a massive chain and lock.

The DA was pulled out of the back seat with his hands tied together in front and a gag in his mouth secured with a strap around his head. His eyes bulged when he saw O'Reilly standing on a platform next to a cement mixing barrel that I was churning. He now knew his fate.

George and his men brought the DA up to the platform, tied his legs together, and lowered him in a standing position into the cornerstone form that measured four-foot by four-foot by eight-foot high. George reached down into the form and cut the rope binding the DA's hands before he hit bottom. I know for sure that George wasn't the only one who wanted to hear the DA beg for his life. The DA groped for his gag and worked it loose as Dom dumped the first load of cement. It splashed on the DA's head and reached past his knees.

"O'Reilly, I swear I didn't do it!"

George brought over a second cement barrel that his men had been mixing; a third was in the works.

It was my turn.

"You've been a pain in my ass since I returned from the army. But this is for having Jackie kidnapped and for the slaughter of those street kids," I said, taking my time dumping the load.

He wiped the crud from his eyes as he stood in chest deep cement and pleaded for us to stop. "I have a lot of dough stashed. You can have it all. You'll never see me again. I just want out of the country. You can't do this, I'm the District Attorney."

We let him sit, or should I say stand—to think about his transgressions—while the final mixing barrel churned. When everything was ready, we all left except for O'Reilly.

He wanted some time alone with the DA.

* * * * *

Jackie and I both thought the inscription on the youth center cornerstone was not as formal as on city buildings, but it was appropriate: *If you live life with a healthy body, an open mind and a warm heart, you will move mountains. If you live a lazy life, with a closed mind and a heart of stone, you will become a cold, immovable object.*

"If you ask me, those in City Hall would be better off if they saw this inscription each day they came to work," I stated.

Jackie put her arm around mine and we turned to head

back to the office. "I don't think it would make much of a difference. Time tends to corrupt all politicians—no matter how noble their intentions."

* * * * *

In the week prior to Vigliotti's planned syndicate meeting, where everyone expected a showdown between him and Big Ben, two of the minor bosses, who had aligned themselves with Ben, were assassinated in public, along with their bodyguards and some members of their families. To send an even stronger message, Vigliotti invited Al Capone to the meeting to prove that he had the backing of the Chicago mob.

Vigliotti and Capone entered the meeting room after everyone else had taken their normal positions around the table. As I waited in the antechamber, I could hear the rumblings of surprise at the appearance of Capone. Many of the bosses personally knew him from his days as a brutal member of the Five Points Gang.

Vigliotti normally sat alone at the head of the table, but for this meeting, there were three chairs. Capone sat to his left, leaving the chair on his right empty.

Big Ben wasn't one to back down. Even though I wasn't yet in the room, I heard his chair scrape along the floor as he stood.

"You expecting another guest?" he asked Vigliotti in his booming voice. "Or are you symbolically expressing sympathy for the colleagues we lost this past week?"

"Lack of judgment isn't a trait deserving of sympathy. I hope for the sake of *your* personal health, and that of your family, you will take your seat and listen to what I have to say."

"You're threatening me? Without the money my organization generates, you wouldn't have the resources to run this part of the city."

Vigliotti's anger was evident in his tone. "That's the only reason you're alive today, but remember this—you're not irreplaceable. Neither was the Baron and, unfortunately for him, he paid the ultimate price for your treachery."

"This is getting us nowhere," Big Ben shouted. "I demand a council vote. You're no longer fit to run this organization."

"You will get your vote when this meeting is over. I will abide by the outcome—and so will you. Now, take your seat and keep that big trap of yours shut if you want to walk out of here alive."

Big Ben's face turned a deep shade of red when Vigliotti called me into the meeting room to sit in the empty chair at the head of the table. I half expected Big Ben to keel over from a heart attack before I had a chance to utter a sound. He no doubt had heard I wasn't dead, but I'm sure this was the last place he expected me to show up.

Castellano stood to address the council.

"You'll notice that once again my son Carmine is not present. The rumors of his death are true. Needless to say it was a most difficult decision, but a necessary one for the good of the syndicate and my neighborhood. I have been working with Batista and Vigliotti to come up with a means to manage my territory in the most profitable way possible in conjunction with my union. Batista is here to make that proposal."

Big Ben couldn't control himself any longer. "This is outrageous. I will not listen to an outsider telling us how to run our business."

Vigliotti pulled a gun from under his jacket behind his back and placed it on the table. "Ben, I'm not gonna say this again. Take your damn seat and keep your mouth shut. You'll get your chance to respond to Batista, and then we'll take the vote."

It was my turn to speak.

"Ben, I'm not your enemy. I don't want your territory or to be a part of anything this syndicate does. What I want is peace for my neighborhood. If you don't give me that, then, and only then, do you need to fear me.

"The waterfront is changing. Unions are forming, not only here but in Chicago and across the country. There's money to be made, which is why Vigliotti and Johnny Torrio, along with Al Capone, are leading this effort.

"Ben, you think you control your section of the waterfront, but you don't and never have. All you do is load and unload cargo, and then move it to various destinations. Some legal, some illegal. For years Carmine was really in control. He ran the shipping company that made all the arrangements for the cargo, negotiated fees, planned the sequence of events, decided which docks to use for the various types of merchandise. Take a moment and think about that.

"Going forward, the unions will control the labor on the waterfront. The only thing left is distribution.

"So, Big Ben, if you're following me, the waterfront has been consolidated all along—*under Castellano*. We are proposing that we move that responsibility to you."

Big Ben leaned back in his chair with a huge grin. But his grin wouldn't last long.

"But, we want your son, Sam, to take over Carmine's shipping company, not you. This will give your family complete control over the volume and type of illegal cargo flowing into the city and its distribution.

"The union for the entire waterfront will be run by Castellano. My uncle Luigi will manage our neighborhood, and each merchant will contribute to the syndicate for protection."

I answered a few questions and then took my seat. It was Big Ben's turn.

"Interesting, but not enough. Sam is the wrong person. My oldest son should be in charge of the shipping company. This union crap is nothing more than bullshit. I will not give up control of my longshoremen. They work for me."

Sirens suddenly blared in the near distance, from police and fire trucks responding to a small explosion Dom had set to clear the docks of workers. I had told Vigliotti that this would be his signal to put Big Ben in his place.

"Ben, everyone knows that your two oldest sons are drunken bums whose brains are in their pants," Vigliotti said. "You yourself haven't demonstrated you can manage your own organization—not when Batista, one man, can disrupt everything you do. Unions are going forward, with or without your cooperation."

"My territory is as safe as ever. If Batista or anyone else tries to move in, they'll wish they never—"

Several windows shattered as a blast shook the building. A second explosion followed.

Most everyone shouted at once. "What the hell was that?"

Vigliotti made his final statement. "That, gentlemen, is proof that Big Ben is not someone you want to follow. Two of his warehouse piers just collapsed into the bay."

The meeting was essentially over. There was no need for

a vote. Vigliotti had achieved unanimous support for moving forward with unions throughout the city, and Big Ben's son, Sam, would control the shipping company.

Big Ben had no choice but to agree to the terms I laid out. I was confident that Sam would do a good job, which in the end, would appease Big Ben.

At least, that's what I hoped.

Chapter 54

As the new neighborhood boss, Luigi realized not everyone would want to meet with him at his speakeasy, especially the elderly women in our neighborhood, so he set up shop in Castellano's old office behind the pizza joint for a few hours every week.

To help Luigi, Molly quit her job at the diner and took over the day-to-day running of the speakeasy. The neighborhood was willing to forget her past now that she had stood up to the DA and testified in O'Reilly's behalf. Even Ma was willing to forgive and forget and invited her to join us for dinners whenever she and Luigi could find the time.

Luigi was a natural for his new role since he had been the de facto leader of the business community for years. He had already convinced the businesses to pay protection money to the syndicate in response to Carmine's past demands, but he also promised to hold a percentage in reserve for neighbors who fell on hard times. He was so successful in meeting the needs of the underprivileged that some of the local churches donated to his neighborhood fund as a way to reach out to the community. It helped that Luigi wasn't an official Mafia member.

Castellano's handpicked candidates won all the union elections for officers, which came as no surprise to me since I'd seen Luigi hauling a couple of election ballot boxes out of his car to the back of the union meeting hall where the election had taken place.

Hawk appeared to be right about letting the Communist Party take over a few of the smaller unions to compensate for their election defeat. It didn't take long for their anti-democratic rhetoric and revolutionary speeches to infuriate members. Many of the workers along the waterfront had come to America to get away from such talk. It wouldn't be long before those Party officials were also voted out of office or worse yet, disappeared—without the need for the Mafia to get involved. To say that the Colonel was ecstatic about how his plan was unfolding would be an understatement.

As for Dom, he supervised the construction of the youth center until the Colonel recruited him to start up a demolition unit with its own research facility. He didn't hesitate to re-enlist.

There was no doubt in Jackie's mind or mine that Big Ben would cause trouble in the future, but for now, he was keeping a low profile, partly because his son Sam was proving to be an effective executive and had quickly increased revenue by allowing importers to bid for the piers with the most modern loading equipment and for the more powerful tugboats.

The neighborhood had come back to life with the end of hostilities along the waterfront. People felt safer sitting on their stoops to share gossip or heading out in the evening to enjoy the local entertainment.

As for me, it was the first time since returning home from the army and opening my detective agency that no one was trying to bump me off.

Both Jackie and I felt the time had come to break ties with the neighborhood and move on.

All that remained was to pick a date for our wedding. Ma took over from there. She made up the list of invited guests that included relatives I didn't know I had, and she didn't stop there. Current and past neighbors all made the list. She generously gave us twenty-five slots for other people *we* might want to invite. I expected Jackie to be upset, but she wasn't.

"Your ma knows I was an orphan. I can only think of a handful of people to invite anyway, a few nuns from the orphanage who helped me when I first moved to town, and maybe a couple of people from the *Daily News*."

"The only additions I have are the Colonel, Dom, and Hawk."

As I wrote their names on the list, Castellano dropped in unexpectedly.

"I hear you guys are moving to the Island. Can't say I blame you."

"We intend to restart our business as one that's less inclined to attract trouble," Jackie said.

"Like me?"

Jackie gave him a hug and kissed him on the cheek. "It's not you. It's this city."

Castellano pulled an envelope out of his inside pocket and placed it in her hand.

"I have some property on the Island—in a good neighborhood—no Mafia types. It's yours, a nice place, not too large. There will also be something extra for you at the wedding. Don't be surprised if I take all the dances, though."

Jackie opened the envelope and stepped back. I went to her and put my arm around her waist.

"Mr. Castellano, you're too generous," I said.

"Nonsense—not after all you've done for this neighborhood—for me."

Castellano left as quietly as he came. When he was gone, Jackie embraced me.

"Is this happening? Are we really gonna leave? What about your family, your friends? This is where you grew up."

"Which is why I have to go. If I don't, nothing will change, and my luck will run out. They say a cat has nine lives. I don't know how many I have, but I'm certain I've used up most of them."

"What about your family?"

"Staten Island isn't that far away, but I will miss Ma's cooking."

"Oh, don't worry about that. I'm no ace in the kitchen, but I've been watching your ma lately, and it doesn't look so hard. I've noticed there's a lot of chopping involved in cooking. Garlic, spices, onions. I think I could get used to that. As you know, I'm pretty handy with a knife," Jackie laughed. "The rest is simple—a pinch here and a pinch there."

"I suspect it's a little more complicated than that."

We had just gone back to finishing our list of names when Martha burst through the door, out of breath.

"I got a great lead on who killed Gino's family!"

"How?" Jackie asked.

"Rosalie! Sam was telling her about his family and mentioned that he vaguely remembers a couple of uncles on his mother's side who had suddenly dropped out of his life when he was just a tyke."

I reached for her notes when Jackie pushed my hand away. "We don't want to tangle with Big Ben again, not over something that happened twenty years ago," she said, waving Castellano's envelope at me as a reminder of what we'd decided.

"Jackie's right," I said to Martha. "Give the information to O'Reilly. He'll follow up and let us know if he needs help."

Martha was about to object when Jackie asked a pointed question. "Martha, have you made up your mind if you're coming with us when we move to the Island?"

"I've checked out a few other agencies and received offers from most, but I'm thinking the Island might be a place to latch onto a more stable man. In this town, all I've found so far is a murderer, a coward, a crooked lawyer, and a pyromaniac."

I was glad to hear that Martha had decided to stay with us. She would seek out some challenging cases that would ensure we maintained all our skills. On the way out of the office, Martha gave me a wink and slipped her notes about Gino into the pocket of my overcoat hanging on the coat rack. If Jackie noticed, she didn't say anything.

George showed up just as Martha was leaving. He caught her by the arm and brought her with him into the room.

"Vigliotti wants to see you. I have a car waiting downstairs," he said to me.

"What the hell is goin' on now?" I asked, annoyed at his tone.

"The Jersey mob is upset about what happened to the Baron. Vigliotti convinced them to have a sit-down before taking action. He wants you there."

George then turned to Martha. "Are we still on for tonight?"

"Dinner will be waiting."

When they left the office, Jackie sighed and slipped Castellano's envelope in the top drawer of her desk.

"Who are we kidding? She'll never change, and neither will we. Why don't you hand me the notes she slipped into your coat pocket. I'll work on Gino's case. We owe him that."

"What about our wedding?"

"Ma will kill us if we back out now. The wedding will go on, but you can tell Castellano he can hold onto his house. You turned out okay living in the city, so I guess our kids can too."

I knew if I didn't appease the notorious Jersey mob, I was a dead man, but in that moment, I felt like one lucky guy.